Froderick
Gay Son of Dracula

Cali Kitsu

Winnipeg, Canada

Table of Contents

FRODERICK
GAY SON OF DRACULA

Chapter 1
Oh My Fangs

"I vant to suck your blood," I say into my mirror before school. Ugh gross…I really don't. Being the seventeen-year-old son of the legendary Count Dracula, though, that's what people expect me to say. But if you really want to know, there's only one thing I'm interested in, and that's keeping my very secret obsession with guys a secret. "Yes, Dad, I'm gay," I say in my dreams.

In my dream, my most far away unrealistic dream, he hugs me and supports me. Hell, maybe he even takes me out to a bar afterward. But in reality, my dad would say it was Wolfie's fault for sure. Wolfie is my best friend; his dad, the Wolfman, is far more accepting than mine. If Wolfie came out today, I have no doubt that his dad would hold an honorary parade and rename a street to mark the day…shoot; he may even rename the family salon for him. His dad is all about acceptance. It's why his parents aren't together anymore. Still, Wolfie hasn't come out yet either, so me and my bestie stay locked in our metaphorical closets as we start our junior year of high school, but at least we have each other. I mean, it's not like either of us is going to come out any time soon.

It's almost time for school. What an effing chore school is. I hate it. I grab my favorite cloak from my closet. It's black, of course, so boring, but Wolfman spiced it up for me over the weekend. He sewed a sparkling red ruby in place of the black clasp that secures the cape around my neck. It looks fabulous. It gives it that nice dramatic contrast. The cape is shiny black, and the material doesn't wrinkle easily. It's plain and has no personality, but this gorgeous oval ruby that secures it makes all the difference to me. It feels like, for once, there's a little bit of me on display. I proudly button my red ruby clasp around my neck and make sure my cape isn't wrinkled. Then I tie my long black hair into a bun on top, nice and tight. My skin looks a bit tanner than normal from being at the beach over the weekend. It's funny that people always assume vampires are pale-skinned; we aren't. Well, at least I'm not; my father is Greek, and my mother is Italian, so the second I hit the sun, my golden tan pops right out. "You got this!" I tell myself in the mirror before I head downstairs. My green eyes know that I'm far from in the clear, though. I've gotta go downstairs past Dad, who is probably going to yell about something the second he sees me. But, still, you know, I am good-looking, much better looking than my father, of course, whose receding hairline is on full display.

"Good morning, Frode," my dad says while looking up from his morning paper. Yes, my father still reads the newspaper. "I'm keeping the paper business alive," he says whenever I tease him. Yeah, right, keeping the paper business alive; more like turning every beautiful woman he sees into a vampire, then reading about his exploits the next day. Ugh, such a show-off. "Did you see the article this morning?" he asks me.

He hasn't noticed the ruby yet, that's good. I debate my answer for a moment. I don't really want him to notice the ruby, especially when I'm running late, but if I seem too interested in his stupid article, he'll not only know I'm hiding something, but he'll definitely give me a lookover and notice the ruby.

"Nope, I haven't, but there's a hot new girl that just moved in; hopefully, she's gonna be in my class. I was hanging around outside her place until early this morning." That should do it. He should be happy with that. Those words disgusted me as I spoke them.

"Oh?" he says as he folds his paper and looks up at me.

Shit, I really didn't want him to look up. I grab my smoothie and spin around to face the door quickly. My cape gives a nice exaggerative flourish. Ugh, if only I were on the runway, that spin was perfect.

"Yeah, she's new this year. Her mom is half-mermaid, half-vampire," I say.

He picks his paper back up. "Absolutely not. No son of mine is going to bite a mermie, purebloods only for you."

He's such a jerk, and I want to put him in his place, but he won't listen anyway, and I'm gonna be late for my first day of school.

"Right, pureblood, got it, pops," I say on my way out before he can argue.

It's a bright sunny day, nice and warm. I'm so glad vampires aren't affected by sunlight like they are in books and movies. Flying would be almost impossible if that were true. We do hate garlic, though, not because it can hurt us, of course, but because it makes blood taste icky, and if there's one thing I hate, it's anything icky. Oooh! I just flew past a vibrant red cardinal; it was stunning. I think he sang a little tune as I went by, or maybe he noticed the red ruby and was giving it a whistle. Haha, that's funny, a bird with a personality...maybe he's a closeted bird, like me, we could be friends...what the hell am I thinking today?

"Yo, Froderick, we're gonna be late. Better pick up the pace!" my buddy Robert says to me on my left. Robert is a vampire, too, pureblood, delicious. He's flying at the same pace as me. I wish it were because he liked me, but he's just a friend. There's no way he's gay, too.

"Yo, Robbie boy, sup?" I replied. Oh my fangs, I just said sup? I hate this version of me. I must sound like an idiot.

"Nothing much. Read about your dad last night. He's next level, bro. Biting five chicks in one night, man, his fangs must be sore! Dude is legendary!" he says.

This must have been what the old sack of blood was talking about this morning. So effing embarrassing. But Robert thinks it's cool, so I'll play along. Besides, it's not like I can come out and say what I really think.

"Yeah, he is definitely something. Not really my style, though," I say. Gosh, I wish he'd pick up on my disinterest…or notice anything…or care.

We both begin our descent and land smoothly in front of the school. Robert is looking me over, as his gorgeous blue eyes pause on my ruby.

Holy fangs, he's getting closer, very close, very…his hand is touching the ruby!! I'm trying not to squeal!!

"This is gorgeous," he says. His eyes meet mine for just a moment. I can feel my cheeks warming, and I know they're redder than O-positive blood right now.

I want to bite his neck, and he's so close that I could do it. But what would happen if I did?

"I've never seen any other clasp aside from black on your capes, Frode. This ruby is a really nice touch."

OMF, he's noticed my clasps? What is happening? His smell is intoxicating, like freshly made cake or brownies, just pure hot sugar. My dad may be a dick, but he's right about purebloods; they really do give off an erotic scent. Oh no, oh no, something is happening.

Shit, my pants are way too tight, and Robert is way too close. Damn it! I gotta get out of here!

"Um, hellloooo? Frody? What the hell are you doing?" Kat says.

Kat is my best girl friend; she's a pureblood, too. She's every straight male vampire's dream. Huge boobs (gross), tiny waist (blech), and a perfectly round ass (I'm kind of jealous of that). Her hair is long and brown and her skin is smooth and soft. She stands at about five-three and weighs somewhere around one-fifteen, if I had to guess. She's perfect for tossing around, or fun size. That's what she always says, anyway.

Robert is still holding onto the ruby as we both look over at her.

"Hello, Kat, Robert was just checking something out," I said.

What the? Oh my, his face is getting closer, my pants….no, no, no.

"Checking something out indeed," he whispers in my ear. He releases the ruby, smiles at me, and turns to face Kat.

Whaaat?! Did he mean to whisper that in the way I thought he did? No way. But the guy in my pants is giving me a hell of a time right now. What a personality my guy down below has. Robert whispers in my ear and shwing…near full mast at 8:00 am. I just have to stare at Kat for a bit and hold my breath. That'll get him down.

"Sup, Kat, new school year, you ready?" he says to her.

Kat thinks Robert is hot; they'll probably be banging by lunchtime. Robert is tall, six-one, about two inches taller than me. His hair is dirty blond, and his skin is lightly tanned from all the outside activities he does. He doesn't wear a cape; most vampires don't, just me. I'm meant to stand out because of my dad, the man, the myth, the legend—the insufferable bag of blood whose face is staring at us as we walk toward the school entrance.

To make being the son of Dracula even more difficult, my dad is also the ruler of the school. Basically, he's the face of the school, the reason it exists, the one everyone strives to be like. He's the perfect picture of a vampire. Normally, he isn't here, but with it being a new school year, here he is in all his proud glory, standing on the stone steps high above the rest of us, greeting the students and faculty. His cape is long and just barely misses the ground. His collar is open, and so is his top button. There are just a few offensive black hairs that can be seen peeking out from between the top buttons. He's such an effing show-off. Should a school ruler really be allowed to show off that tiny bit of chest hair? Ugh, no. Not if you ask me, but if you ask the fawning teachers, that would be a different story. Students are flocking to him as we walk up the steps. Robert to my left and Kat beside Robert. Where the hell is Wolfie? He always helps me deal with these uncomfortable situations. I look around and don't see him anywhere, but he's usually late, so it's not to be unexpected. It is the first day of school, though.

Oh wow, a breeze from the left just brushed past my face, tantalizing; it was the smell of Robert. Woah, that is going to be hard to deal with. I just got the blood from earlier to stop rushing below, and now this smell again.

"Velcome, velcome," my father is saying to a group of giggling girls. My left nostril, along with the left side of my lip, rises in agitation. Really? Velcome? He doesn't talk like that. He's such an effing cliché. He loves it, vamps falling all over him.

He breaks character for a moment and approaches the three of us. "Hello, Kat, you are looking lovely today," my dad says. Kat loves the attention, and she loves my dad. All women do; I can't understand why. They all dream of the day that he bites them. It's so stupid.

Our uniforms are highly inappropriate if you ask me. Regardless of gender, you can wear either a black and red plaid skirt with a black button-down shirt or black and red plaid pants with a black button-down. I'm pretty sure ninety percent of the skirt-wearing population have had their skirts altered, though. The skirts are so short that if a strong breeze blew by, you'd be flooded with either panties or bare asses. It's ridiculous. Then again, I'm much more interested in the pants-wearing crowd for the most part. I haven't seen any guys wearing skirts yet, but I think I might like it. Kat is wearing thigh-high black stockings along with her dress shoes, and she's giving my dad a playfully-inappropriate twirl. "Good morning, Mr. Drac," she says.

My left nostril and my lip are moving up again in disgust. "Kat, gross, that's my dad."

My dad isn't paying attention to her. "Good morning, Robert. How is your mother?" he asks.

Robert thinks my dad is the coolest. I have no idea why. The dream of most vampires is to be bitten by my dad. That goes for all vampires, regardless of gender. It's so damn weird. Sex is secondary to being bitten. I can't understand that…holy, sweet mother. If this breeze doesn't stop, I'm going to die. Never mind what I just said; at this point, with Robert next to me and his scent wafting through the air, I'm definitely feeling the need to bite, but that other urge is pretty strong, too. Man, he would taste so good. I haven't bitten anyone yet, but I'd take a piece of Robert's neck as my first.

My father's fingers snap in front of my face. "Frode, straighten up. I've adjusted your schedule; they had you in a bunch of classes with only boy vampires. Thankfully, I was there to fix it. Gotta get that first bite out of the way sooner rather than later."

Are you fucking kidding me? Did he really just say that? In front of Robert? So damn embarrassing; not only that, but he moved my schedule?

"Dad, why did you do that? What criteria did you use to decide if they were boys or girls? We've talked about this before." I hate his ignorance.

"I looked carefully at their names. I know it's a boy when I see a boy's name," he says proudly.

My mouth is wide open as I look around and really hope no one heard that. My dad's attitude toward gender is so embarrassing. I have some leeway here to mouth off a bit because he's standing in front of the school. Besides, what's he gonna do? If he laid a hand on me, my mother would destroy him. He's no match for her. "Dad, you are not very smart. I have told you, and the principal has told you at least a hundred times, not to judge vamps based on their names, their ID's, or their looks. How many times? How many times do we have to go over it?"

Ms. Tansy, the principal, cuts in and pulls my dad aside before he can answer. She didn't hear what I was saying, but it was good timing for him. I'm sure he was more grateful than I was at that moment. I don't often get the opportunity to lay into him. When one appears before me, I sink my fangs into it.

"Yoooooowwww!!!" a raucous howl from the right side came in loud and crisp. There he is, right on time; it's Wolfie. My savior, my very best...what the fuck? I can't believe what I'm seeing.

Kat just ran over to Wolfie and jumped in his arms. He's carrying her back up the stairs with his face in her chest. They're both giggling as they head my way.

Robert elbows me. "That looks like fun," he whispers while looking at Wolfie and Kat.

"What the fangs is happening?" I ask the two of them as Wolfie grips Kat's behind. The bell rings loudly before they can answer. It's time for morning assembly. On any other day, we would only have an assembly if there were an emergency or special event, but with it being a new school year, we always have one to start the first day off.

Wolfie places Kat down, and the two are holding hands, walking in front of me. They're both acting like they didn't hear my question, pretending this behavior is normal. Well, this behavior is normal, just not for them, not for my gay best friend and my other best friend. Just as I start to open my mouth to try and get some answers, Leslie pushes in between Robert and me. Leslie's skirt is even shorter than Kat's, which is saying something. "Hey, baby," she says to me as she kisses my cheek.

Fangs, I want to throw up when she kisses my cheek. I'm not going to dance around this. Leslie is my RP…my release partner. I'm not going to say girlfriend because I will never have a girlfriend. Not interested, but normal releases; yeah, I'm okay with that. Besides, the vampire I imagine, when we're doing things, is standing right next to her. With any luck, his scent will rub off on her, which will make free period easier and definitely more enjoyable.

Leslie is probably prettier than Kat, and she's definitely more popular. She has long, wavy brown hair and big brown, doe-like eyes. Her body is no better or worse than Kat's. It's all the same. She's the captain of the cheerleading squad, really smart, and pretty funny. I don't entirely hate her company. I'm just not interested in biting her, which is what she's really after. There's no way I'm marking a girl, though. It's just not happening. She knows that, but she chooses to continue this pretend game. As far as vampire families go, hers is ranked number two. The house of Marnkov is led by her mother, Darna, who was, of course, one of my father's first bites. Her mother really feels like she's special because of that, in contrast to my mother, who couldn't care less that she'd been bitten by and had a baby with my father.

"Don't call me baby," I say as I pull back from her.

She smiles and then gives me a little pout, one that I assume she thinks is sexy. It isn't.

Robert appears to be observing closely. He's probably interested in Leslie. What did he say to me earlier? He said something; I can't remember what, though. I'm too distracted by Leslie's scent. It's entirely different. It smells like watermelon, and it's far too sweet for me. Well, now free period is gonna be a problem.

The auditorium is large enough to hold the entire student population. It's decorated with pictures of famous vampire families. Of course, my father's picture, which is larger than the others, hangs proudly in the center of the room.

Kat and Wolfie head down the row to the left, and I push past Leslie and Robert to sit next to Wolfie. There's no way I'm not getting an explanation for this. We're in about the eighth row back from the stage. Leslie pushes past Robert to claim the seat beside me.

"Oh, I was hoping to sit next to Froderick." I hear Robert say.

Leslie is giving Robert a pinch on his chin. "Aww, you want to sit next to my guy? That's so cute! Like little boy besties!"

She touched Robert's chin. Oh man, I gotta get ahold of her hand. Wait, she actually moved aside for him to sit next to me? I can't believe what I'm seeing!

Robert just sat down next to me. He's smiling, and his face is getting strangely close to mine. "Oh, fangs...the smell." His mouth is right beside my face!

"Do you really like Leslie?" he whispers in my ear.

What the hell do I say? What the eff do I do? If he likes her, he can have her. Why is he whispering with his hot, sugary scent all in my ear?

Before I can answer, Wolfie is whispering in my left ear, "RP's, just for show, for both of us."

Okay, so I have pureblood delectableness on my right, the sugary-sweet scent of Robert, and my best friend on the left, who smells like a mix between mustard and, wait, he just smells like mustard.

"What the hell did you eat this morning? You smell like mustard!" I say to Wolfie.

"Dad made a breakfast casserole for the first day of school. You always say I smell like pickles and bacon, and now, today, it's mustard. You smell the weirdest shit, Frode."

I'm still a bit confused by what Wolfie said a few seconds ago, and honestly, I don't really want to explain to Robert that Leslie is just my RP. It would bother me if he knew that. RP's are pretty normal here, though; no less normal than biting someone. Sinking your fangs in is an act of marking, a territorial type of claim, and since teenagers are nothing if not territorial, it happens all the time. Not for me, though. I'm saving that bite.

Anyway, Robert already knows, thanks to my dad, that I haven't bitten anyone, which is already abnormal, especially for the son of Dracula. If he knew I really didn't like Leslie, he may start to suspect my secret. I don't want that. I'm just going to ignore his question. If he's that interested in her, he can talk to her about it. We're friends, but I'm not interested in helping him get laid or lining up a bite for him. Obviously, him biting me would be a different story, but that's not gonna happen.

"Okay, wait, you guys are actually having sex, or it's just for show? I don't understand," I say to Wolfie.

"Both," he replies.

"You had sex with Kat?" Oops, I may have screamed that a bit louder than intended. All eyes nearby have turned to face us. Damn it, now I've given away my position and, in the process, leaked a secret, or not secret, about my two besties.

"Hi, Frode!" Kressa says from the row in front of me. She turns all the way around in her seat.

Kressa is the half-mermaid, half-vampire girl we met at the beach over the weekend. She is a really nice girl. Of course, I wasn't actually around her house like I told my dad I was earlier; that was just a distraction.

"Oh fangs…" My dad is standing in front of Kressa. She doesn't even realize it.

"Excuse me, miss," my dad says to her. Students are clamoring and whispering excitedly because my dad is standing so close by. "I don't believe we've been properly introduced. I am Count Dracula, and you are?"

"Hello! Of course, I know who you are! Everyone talks about you! You're so famous! Even among mermies, you're famous! Is it true you can tell anything about someone once you bite them? Like, do you have the power to read their mind? And control them? I've always wondered. I'm only half-vampire, so I'm not sure how it works. I've never bitten anyone either or been bitten. At my school before this, it was all mermaid lessons, so now it's vampire lessons."

Now, my father loves to look cool, but he also hates unnecessary conversation, and in a conversation with a seventeen-year-old, he's definitely not going to answer her. He's going to just walk away.

"Ohhh, you're the one," he says. "Frode, is this the girl whose house you said you were outside of all night?"

Why am I alive? What is my purpose? I honestly have no idea. I can't believe he just said that. Oh shit…

Leslie is standing up from her seat. "Who the hell are you even?" she says to Kressa.

"Yeah, who the hell are you that Froderick was outside of your house?" Robert asks.

I have no idea why he cares, but it doesn't matter right now. I need to step in and save Kressa before Leslie jumps on her. "I was not outside her house; that was someone else," I say.

"Who?" Leslie and Robert ask simultaneously.

What the hell is happening? I don't even know who to respond to right now.

"That strapping young vamp behind you is my son. I'm not sure if you knew that." My dad says to Kressa.

She did not know that because I choose not to tell anyone that. When Wolfie and I met her at the beach, our band, Fangs Come First, was doing a free gig. So, no, I was definitely not introducing myself as Dracula's son.

"I had no idea! Wow! Vampire royalty!" she says.

Thankfully, Ms. Tansy, the Principal, just walked up to the stage podium. My dad left quickly to join her on stage.

Leslie sits back down, and Robert removes his hand from my armrest. Wait, when did that get there, by the way? Was his hand there the whole time?

"Good morning, and welcome to another year at Fangula High. It is wonderful to see all of your smiling faces and fangs this morning!" Ms. Tansy says. "Now, many of you know this is the first year that we've accepted transfer students, and I hope you'll all be very velcoming"—she looks at my dad—"to them!"

My dad is clapping. He thinks Ms. Tansy is hilarious. Don't even bother wondering if he's bitten her; the answer is yes, of course, he has.

Ms. Tansy just gave him a flirtatious smile. I don't even know which of them is more inappropriate.

"Ahem," Ms. Tansy clears her throat. "Now, among the many

transfers, there is one in particular I'd like to introduce: Caleb Cheval. Can you come up here, please?"

There is a lot of whispering from behind me. I'm not turning around, though. I don't want to sound like a jerk, but the more vamps that know where I am, the worse this assembly will be for me. Everyone will want to talk about how great my dad is afterward and probably gossip about that stupid…HOLY SHIT!

Whistles and howls fill the room as a handsome blond-haired vampire walks on stage. He's wearing a cape, it's black, his clasp is purple…Wait? It's effing purple? I look down briefly at my own ruby and then back up. This guy is gorgeous. Who the hell is he? What did she say his name was?

Ms. Tansy is rubbing his back, and he's smiling. His mouth may be the most fangtastic mouth I've ever seen. His lips are full and almost pink, he has very light blue eyes, and his skin is just perfection. Oh wow. His shaggy blond hair is gorgeous.

"This is Caleb Cheval," Ms. Tansy says. "Caleb has transferred from another school following a family move. We are happy to have him, and I expect that all of you will show him what a fabulous place our school is. Do you have anything to say, Caleb?"

Damn, he just licked his lips. This guy is seriously fire up there. I'm getting a little heated.

"Hello, I'm Caleb," he says. Everyone is clapping, along with some whoops and hollers. Wolfie is one of the loudest whistlers in here right now, and Kat seems to find that entertaining.

My dad is walking up beside him. He smiles brightly at Caleb and takes the microphone from him.

"Frode?" my dad says while looking in my direction.

Oh my fangs, what the eff? I'm holding my forehead and trying to slink down in my seat. But I better not do that. Who knows what he'll say if I don't acknowledge him? I begrudgingly stand up and acknowledge him, in a voice full of agitation, "Yes…father?"

Caleb is tilting his head and looking at me.

"Frode, come up here. I want you to meet Caleb before anyone else does." My dad says.

Caleb is staring at me pretty hard as I walk past Wolfie, Kat, and the rest of the row. He's definitely interested in who I am.

Okay, what is happening? Caleb is walking toward me as I step onto the stage. He extends his hand and reaches for mine. Do I let him hold my hand? What? No. I wave politely and smile at him. He is devastatingly handsome, and he smells like freshly baked Italian bread with a touch of cotton candy. Oh my…I'm not gonna make it through this. He looks a bit perturbed that I didn't hold his hand; maybe I'm imagining it, though.

"Caleb, this is my son, Frode. He is the number one vamp in the school. Since you were number one in your school, you'll have a lot in common, I'm sure. I've arranged your classes to be in sync with Frode's," my dad says.

Caleb is eyeing my ruby; he's rubbing his purple jeweled clasp. I'm turning slightly so my dad doesn't see the ruby on my clasp, which is currently sparkling from the stage lights. Caleb's clasp is actually a purple crystal bat upon closer inspection. It's beautiful, very nice. This makes sense; he's vampire royalty, too. That's why he's wearing a cape. You can only be considered number one at any vampire school if you're born of a noble house. He's giving me a strangely seductive look. If we weren't on stage right now, I'd actually guard my neck. Well, on second thought, maybe I wouldn't.

As we stand beside one another, the air feels different. It's hot, very hot. I swear there is actual heat coming off this guy.

"Thank you, Mr. Dracula. I think Frode and I are going to get along more than fine," Caleb says with a wink.

What the hell was that wink? How does he know we'll get along? Ah, yes, I'm sure he's heard all about how nice I am. Eyeroll. He's probably already planning to use me for social status, too. Not that he'd need that, not with that face. He looks like he's fresh from a commercial about first bites. I could imagine that…him there with some trampy vamp pushing bite spray as a product. Some vampires believe in bite spray and the effect it has on others. I don't know if it's because I'm gay or because of my pureblood, but that shit has never worked on me. I can say that the only vampire I've considered biting is Robert, and I doubt that any spray would entice me to do that any quicker. Still, the lockers of other vamps will be lined with cans of bite spray, same as always.

"Now, Frode," Ms. Tansy says. "I want you to take some time this morning to show Caleb around. Your teachers already know that you'll be giving him a tour for most of the day. It's fine to take all the time you need. We want Caleb to feel welcome here. You two can go on ahead. The rest of the assembly doesn't pertain to either of you."

What the hell? Now I'm supposed to show him around the school? Okay, he just grabbed my hand. We're holding hands as we walk off the stage toward the exit. I'm not sure if I'm uncomfortable or turned on. This guy is something fierce. Who would hold someone's hand like this?

"Hey, you can let go of my hand," I say as we exit the auditorium into the bright sunlight.

He's squeezing my hand tighter. "Do you dislike holding my hand?" he asks as he turns his body toward mine.

What the fangs am I supposed to say? I don't know how I feel. He's hot, though. I mean, I guess I'm okay with it, but, no, I can't hold hands with a guy. Everyone will know I'm gay then. I can't do that. I have to stay safe inside my—

His face is directly in front of mine. You'd be hard-pressed to fit a piece of paper in between us. OH MY FANGS!! My back is against the wall! What is happening? I'm screaming inside. My guy below is too far gone; he's not gonna go down for the rest of my life after this.

"You're very close," I say while staring into his pale blue eyes.

"I can't help it. You smell like cotton candy and Italian bread, and I can't help but wonder if you're feeling what I'm feeling," he says.

I swallow hard. How does he think I smell exactly the same as he does? I've never asked anyone what they think I smell like, but it was just a little bit freaky to have him describe my scent that way. Can he read my mind? That's not possible. What am I supposed to do right now? How do I get out of this? Do I even want to get out of this?

With my voice full of false self-righteousness, I say, "You know who I am, and yet you are so bold as to pin me against a wall like this?" Why did I say that? What am I getting at? He's obviously into guys, but is it okay that I let him know that I am, too? If his bottom half gets any closer, I won't need to tell him anything; my guy downstairs will take care of that.

He's chuckling, and it's kind of a deviant open-mouth laugh. I like it, and it's pulling me in. His fangs are exquisite, and I can see how sparkly they are as he tilts his head back. That neck of his, it's clean and clear, delectable. He's never been bitten on it. I'm sure of that. You can tell when someone has; the scars heal, but they never go away.

"What did I say that was funny?" I ask him.

His mouth is pulled to the side, and if eyes could have sex or bite, he'd have taken me fifty times over during this brief yet strangely sensual conversation. His mouth is near my ear, and our warm cheeks are pressed together on the left side; his hand is on the right side of my waist, barely squeezing me.

"I think it's funny because I can feel your heat. I know that you can feel mine." He's inhaling my scent, face next to my ear. "Your neck is magnificent," he says.

I have to stop this before someone comes out. "What heat? What are you talking about? I have to be nice to you because my dad said I did. You heard him." I say as I place my hands on his chest. Oh, my, that's very firm, very firm. He's noticed the interest in my eyes, I'm sure of it.

"That's not what you want to do. You can place your hands lower," Caleb says.

"Are you some kind of a pervert? Who does this to someone? What is your problem?" I ask. I have no idea why I'm pushing him away. He's right. I do want to place my hands lower, but for now, they are secure on both sides of his chest.

Fangs! His gorgeous fangs and that deviant open-mouth laugh again. "You don't want me?" he asks, tilting his head.

"FRODE!" Robert screams from down the hall.

"Frody!" Leslie shouts, following beside him.

Wow, Caleb really doesn't care. I'm still pinned against the brick wall here. I slowly turn my head and give a half-smile. Caleb's face is still beside mine; this must look quite scandalous.

"You need to move," I whisper to Caleb.

"Why should I?" Caleb asks loudly while looking over, unimpressed, at Robert and Leslie.

"Sup, I'm Robert. Why are you...? What are you doing to Frode?" he asks Caleb with a look of confusion.

"Yeah, and I'm Leslie, but I'm sure you already know who I am. Why are you pushing my boyfriend against a wall, dude?"

"Boyfriend?" Caleb says, looking at my face.

"Not boyfriend," I say while shaking my head. Damn it, why did I correct her? I said I didn't want Robert to know! AAAAHHHH!!!

My scream is so loud inside my head right now. A thousand screeching bats can't compare to the cacophony of cries inside my mind. I am an idiot, an absolute idiot.

"Okay, Frody's not my boyfriend," Leslie says. "But he's my RP, and you need to back up. What, does he, like, owe you money or something?" she asks.

Robert is staring over; his face is hard to read. It looks like he's disappointed for some reason. But what is he disappointed about? Gosh, just take Leslie already. Her scent is really pungent right now.

"You smell like a disgusting watermelon candy," Caleb says to Leslie.

Her mouth is wide open, and she's staring at him in shock.

"What's an RP?" Caleb asks me innocently.

"It's, you know, a vampire that you, you know…do stuff with," I say. He's not understanding what I'm saying, though. He's looking at Leslie, and now he's back to staring at me. You know, I'm strong enough to push him off, and for some reason, I'm still here against this hard wall; in between his arms.

His mouth is next to my ear. "That's not possible," he whispers.

"We have sex, do you understand, Callum?" Leslie says, with attitude.

"His name is Caleb," I say. Whyyy do I keep correcting things? Someone should just sew my mouth shut.

"Frode lets you have sex with him?" Caleb turns his head and asks Leslie. Now he's looking at me. "Like friends with benefits?" he asks me.

"What the hell are friends with benefits?" I ask.

"Friends who only have sex, with no interest in a relationship. You would sleep with this vampire, but you would never bite them. Like that," Caleb explains.

My eyes are wide. "Oh yes, exactly. We call them RP's, release partners."

"How crude," he says while looking me over.

I shrug my shoulders. "Sometimes you just need a release."

"He's done with you," Caleb says to Leslie.

"Whaaat?!" I scream.

"Shush, you're not interested in her. You're interested in me," Caleb whispers in a voice only I can hear.

"I'd like to hear that from Frody, not from you, Callum," she says.

"It's Caleb. Damn it, Leslie, get his name right," I say. Aaand I've corrected her unnecessarily, again. I have no idea why I keep doing that. He doesn't need me to tell anyone what his name is. She is being quite annoying, though.

Speaking of feeling annoyed. Robert appears to be either very irritated or confused. He starts to walk away and says, "I'm going over to building E. That was the bell for the first class. I'll see you later, Frode. I guess."

Caleb is making a gesture with his hand at Leslie. "Shoo, Shoo, go away. Frode gave you his answer," Caleb says to her.

She's looking at me, eyebrows raised, waiting to see if I correct him. I'm not going to because now I'm actually pretty interested to see what happens next, and she doesn't look all that upset. She's not going to give up no matter what she says anyway.

"Fine. You'll be back. You know we belong together, Frody. Whatever this fake number one is after, he'll move on once he gets it," Leslie says.

I don't know why, but I just instinctively covered Caleb's mouth with my hand. I'm sure he was going to say something that would've exposed the fact that I'm gay. It was almost like I could sense it. But now, his warm, full lips are pressed against the inside of my palm. They're really soft. I wonder how many vamps have felt them.

Honestly, you would think that his behavior already alluded to his own sexuality, but that's not true. Like I said, being bitten by my dad is the dream of all vampires. As Dracula's son, I'm the next closest thing to the original. No one would think Caleb was gay, just for pushing me up against a wall. I'm ninety-nine percent sure he's at least interested in me, though. Now, whether that's because he likes me or just wants to bite me, I have no idea. He's definitely turned on, though. He wasn't kidding about the heat earlier; our bodies are calling to one another.

Leslie just stomped away. And what could be worse at this time? Nothing? Wrong.

"Frode, Caleb? Everything okay over here?" my dad asks while walking over.

Caleb pulls my hand off his mouth, and he's looking at the inside of it. "Yes, Mr. Dracula, I think Frode had a tiny splinter. I was trying to get it out for him," he says.

My dad is straightening his own collar. "Well, he can certainly go see Ms. Plurf in the nurse's office. No need to suck it out for him," my dad says.

"Nope, he got it out," I say while showing him my palm. "Alright, Dad, I'm gonna keep showing Caleb around."

Caleb has finally backed up, and I exhale. Wow, I don't even know where I am right now. It's only time for first class, and I'm already so flustered. This is going to be one hell of a school year.

Chapter 2
Frode the Birgin

Most vamps have gone to class, there are a few stragglers around, but it's mostly newbies who are lost. No one is skipping class yet, since it's the first day of school. "Are you always like this?" I ask Caleb, as we walk down the now empty halls.

"Can I hold your hand now?" he asks, while reaching for my hand.

"What? No. Did you hear what I asked you? Is there something wrong with you? You can be honest with me. Are you actually here because you attacked someone or something?" I ask him.

He's looking at me confused, it's as if he has no idea what I'm talking about, but he's smiling.

"Hand?" he asks again, reaching once more toward my side.

"Okay, stop, stop walking," I say, with a hand on my forehead. I have to get a handle on what is going on here.

Oh shit, he's very close again and I'm back against the brick wall, with his body close to mine.

"Back up! I can't be seen doing these things! Did you not see my dad here earlier? Where the hell did you come from, that you think it's okay to act the way you're acting? I don't even know anything about you! You've pinned me against the wall twice, dumped my RP for me, and you keep trying to hold my hand. What the hell is your deal?" I say, almost breathless.

A long sigh escapes his full lips, he's looking side to side. "Bite me," he says.

"Whaaat?!" I scream.

That deviant, open-mouth laugh, again, he's even tilting his head back this time. Probably on purpose to show off his neck.

"We're purebloods of the highest caliber," he says. "If you bite me, they'll be no secrets between us. You'll know everything instantly. I can bite you, too, if you'll let me," he says, with his strong hand on my neck.

Okay a few things here, I do want to bite him, and I would definitely let him bite me. He smells better than anything I've ever smelled in my life. He is hotter than anything I've ever seen in my life, and he is seriously just pulling me in. But I can't bite someone I don't even know; I need to save that bite. You only get one first bite, and I want it to be special. I don't want to use it on someone that I don't even know. What he said about us knowing each other's secrets instantly is true, of course. That's what happens when a noble pureblood bites someone. Once we bite, we can see everything that's ever happened to that vampire, and we can also read their thoughts. The connection is broken once any bond is severed, though. The reading their thoughts thing is exclusive to nobles, which is lucky for all the teenagers that run around biting just anyone. It must be crazy loud in my dad's head; with all the women he's bitten. I've never talked to him about it, but it seems like it would be chaos inside his mind.

Anyway, back to Caleb, I don't know what to do, but this whole time he's been rubbing the back of his hand against my neck, softly.

"I can't bite you…and you can't bite me," I say, my voice lacking conviction and oozing self-doubt.

What the…? Okay, his arms are crossed and he's pouting, actually pouting at me.

"Why not?" he asks.

Where do I even start with him? "What do you mean why not? I just told you. I don't even know you. I haven't…bitten anyone before. I can't bite you just because you ask me to. I just met you. Where are you from that this behavior is normal?"

He's still pouting, he actually looks hurt. What the hell is his deal?

"I'm relieved that you haven't bitten anyone," he says. "What with that second-tier girl thing that was hanging around you earlier, and that other guy that was obviously interested in you. Thank fangs you didn't bite either of them. They're both beneath you."

"What is this mood shift with you? I don't even know how to respond to what you just said. Come on, I need to show you around. I can't believe another teacher hasn't walked by yet. You're gonna get me in trouble," I say, as I turn toward the left.

"Why won't you hold my hand?" he asks.

How do I answer him? I won't hold his hand for a multitude of reasons, but he doesn't seem to care about any of the things I've said to him, so why should I bother answering?

"Hold my hand, then I'll look at the school with you," he says.

"I can't," I say, weakly.

"I want to, though. Don't you care about what I want?" he asks.

This guy is either very spoiled or… No, I think he's just very spoiled. "Are you, like, an only child or something? Is that what's going on? Or the youngest in a large family? Why should I care about your feelings?" I ask.

Okay, that looked like it hurt him. His pout is back.

"Bite me and you'll know everything or hold my hand and I'll tell you everything while we walk. Those are your options," he says.

"Is there harassment where you come from? You can't be serious, giving me those choices. Listen, Caleb, I will admit that I'm feeling…something, but I can't just hold your hand or bite you. What are you after? You just want me to bite you because I'm Dracula's son? I don't understand. Every time I ask you a question, you tell me to bite you, I'm not gonna do that today. So just tell me what you want so we can get on with the tour. The school is so damn big, and we've only made it down one hallway," I say.

"Okay, on with the tour," he says. "You said you're not gonna bite me *today*, which means you *will* bite me at some point. That's good enough. No, I don't want you to bite me because you're Dracula's son. I don't care about that… Well, I care that you're a pureblood, but that's not what I'm after. What I'm after is you. Your scent is the first one to make me go crazy like this. I have an older and a younger brother, making me the middle child. I am not spoiled by any means; I assume that's why you asked me that. I like the way you look and the way you smell, what else is there? I like the way you talk, too. I want to bite you, I want you to bite me, but I can wait. If…"

See he was doing pretty good until he just said that and spun on his heel.

"If what?" I ask. Yes, I'm completely terrified of what he's going to say.

"If you promise to only go out with me. No more friends with benefits, or whatever the hell disgusting term you used earlier," he says.

"Sure, where do you want to go?" I ask.

His brow is furrowed and he's close again, his hands are on my cheeks, his touch is so warm.

"I'll go wherever you want," he says. "But do you understand that I'm not asking you to go somewhere, not like a place? I'm asking you to go out with me, Frode."

Now I'm confused. "We're already outside, so where do you want to go?" I ask, as he still holds my face.

He's tilting his head at me. "What do you call it here when vampires are together? They have sex and do other things, they hold hands, and they don't do those things with anyone else. It's only two vampires going out. Do you call that something different?" he asks.

"A relationship? A couple? Is that what you're saying when you're asking me to go out with you? Like be your boyfriend?" I ask. He can't mean that, surely. How could he mean that?

He's nodding his head. Okay, he did mean that. Whaaat?! Aaaah, screeching bats in my head again! How the hell am I supposed to deal with this?

"I can't do that," I say, looking into those damn pale blue eyes, with his lips so close I can almost taste them.

"Why not? Can you just tell me why not? I know you like me; you're attracted to me. Our scents are already one and the same, you can't say you don't realize that. So, why not, then? Don't tell me you like that other guy from earlier?" he asks.

"It's not because of anyone except my father, really. My dad doesn't know that I'm…" I can't finish my sentence. What if vamps don't say *gay* where he's from? He may not even know what I mean. Then I'll have to go into extreme detail, fangs, I can see that trainwreck of an explanation already. Every freaking thing I say comes out wrong. I have to just see if he picks up on it.

He asks, "Your dad doesn't know that you're a birgin?"

"No. I'm not a virgin, we've been over this," I say. I guess he really just doesn't listen. Honestly, I'm okay with someone who doesn't really listen if that's the case. I have so many damn conversations in my head that I'm not sure most of the time if I even have any words left for anyone else.

"You are a birgin, you told me so. What are you saying, Frode?"

I pull his hands off of my cheeks, yes, they've been there the whole time and my cheeks are very warm. I nearly kiss them as I remove them, but I won't because I am seriously confused here. I ask, "Wait, are you saying virgin or birgin? I feel like you're saying virgin, but with a B in the beginning."

"I'm saying birgin, someone who has never bitten or been bitten, not a virgin, why would I say virgin?" he asks.

"What the fuck is that term?" I ask, as I cover my mouth. Didn't mean to say that out loud.

He's laughing at me now. That damn deviant laugh, it's too sexy. I'm gonna do it. I'm gonna bite him, right now. No, no, no. I can't. Damn it. Somebody help me!

"Listen, Caleb, here's the thing, my dad knows that I'm a birgin, stupid as that term is."

"No less stupid, than release partner," he says.

"Yes, well, I can't argue with that. They're both stupid terms, okay? I didn't come up with them. Probably some vampire housewife somewhere writing novels in her bedroom, decided to come up with those terms. I don't effing know, Caleb. The point is my dad doesn't know that I am gay. Now, before you ask what gay is, because you have no idea, it means that I like guys, not girls. I am not interested in girls. I have never been, and I will never be interested in a girl. My dad will absolutely lose his fangs if he finds out, so I can't date you, or go out with you, because of that. That's really all that's to it," I say, with a shrug.

Caleb's hands are on his hips and his brow is tightly knit. "Why should this have anything to do with your father? I'm not trying to go out with him. By the way, gay means the same thing where I'm from. I'm gay, so I am definitely familiar with the term, but I appreciate the over explanation," he says with a smile.

"It has to do with my father, well, because he's my father and I live with him, but also as you can see, he's at school a lot. My father is not like other vampire parents, he's not as understanding when it comes to sexuality, or gender. If you're a boy, you're a boy and you like girls, girls are girls and they like boys, that's as far as his tiny blood-sucking mind can take him. Trust me, my mother is a, forget it. That's a conversation for another day, anyway, suffice to say, my mother would be thrilled to find out I was dating you, my father would not. So, what can I do, Caleb? I can't go out with you."

He's looking left to right now, like he's checking for something. I don't know what, though.

"Frode, do you like me? Do you like what you see? Do you like my scent?" he asks.

"Well, yes, but…my father."

Oh shit…

Our lips are pressed together, oh my fangs! This feels fangtastic, holy shit. Who cares about anything else? Our tongues meet only for a moment. I've never tasted anything so sweet. The taste is extraordinary.

"Mmm…now, what were you saying?" he asks, as he pulls back.

"Here," I say, as I hold my hand out.

"You're gonna go out with me? Or are you just letting me hold your hand?" he asks, while licking his damn cotton candy lips.

I can barely fucking breathe, and he wants me to define this? "Together, yes, me and you but not in front of my dad. How about that?" I ask.

He's holding my hand now. "I'll take it," he says.

As we walk a few steps further I can't help but wonder what the hell just happened. I just agreed to date this guy after I only met him like two hours ago, and I'm willing to be in a relationship with him? Who does something like this? I give my dad a hard time for biting women based on looks, but I'm doing the same thing, aren't I? No, no this is not the same. This is something else. Caleb is the first guy I've ever kissed and, boy, if I had any doubts about being gay, which I didn't, they would have all been erased in those fangtastic thirty seconds. It was the best feeling I've ever had.

Shit, wait, I said we wouldn't show off our relationship in front of my dad, but I didn't say anything about the whole school. Should I try and convince him to only hold hands when no one else is around? No, I can't do that. I mean, his face is just too perfect, and he looks happy, proud even.

What a weird kind of satisfaction that I feel right now. It's really making me forget everything else. Wait, what are we doing? Why aren't we in class? Oh shit, I'm supposed to be showing him around. Haha…this is kind of funny, you know? My dad put me in a bunch of classes with girls to get me my first bite, then added Caleb, who is now my boyfriend, into all the classes with me. Hahaha…what a clown, he has no idea…

"Alright, so our classes will be in this hall to the left," I say. "We're considered juniors, since we have one more year after this, and juniors are only in this hall."

Caleb is swinging our hands lightly, as we walk past the hallway. "What about the cafeteria and library, where are those?" he asks.

"I'll show you both; the cafeteria is this way," I say, as we go around the corner to the right.

Shit, it's Ms. Tansy. Caleb is squeezing my hand, there is no way he's letting go. Okay, this is fine. I just decided to come out in front of everyone except for my dad… Wait… What the hell am I doing? I can't do this! Our fingers are interlocked, and suddenly I feel a little less afraid, as he squeezes my hand three times, then smiles at me.

"Oh, hello, boys!" Ms. Tansy says.

Caleb is on my right side holding my hand tightly. I'm turning slightly toward him, hoping my cape stops Ms. Tansy from noticing our hands. Listen, I said I felt a *little less afraid*, I didn't say completely unafraid. She's been bitten by my dad; I have no idea if their connection has been severed or not. If she sees something, he may very well be able to see it, too. I don't really understand how it works, since I've never personally experienced it.

"Hello, Principal Tansy," Caleb says, with a charming smile.

"Yeah, um, hello, Ms. Tansy," I say, avoiding eye contact.

"I'm so happy to see you boys are getting along. I knew you two would make a smart match for your first day, Caleb! Now, Froderick, your father is going to try and take all the credit, but don't believe him. It was my idea to put you two together," she says.

"Oh, I don't think he's going to want to take credit for this," I say.

"You two boys look stellar together, the girls will be climbing the walls soon! Probably some boys, too," she says, with a wink our way.

Ms. Tansy tries, she really does, but she's hopeless when it comes to gender identities. I find that most adults are, honestly. We've had many talks about it, and each time she understands as the conversation ends. Now, here we are, back to just boys and girls again. Maybe my dad *can* control vampires, now that I think about it.

"Yes, well, I'd better take Caleb and finish up this tour," I say. "We haven't gotten very far, and I'd like to go to some of my classes today. Bye, Ms. Tansy." Caleb and I both turn away, before she can stop us.

Caleb is smiling brightly, fangs and all. "How was that?" he asks me.

"Be more specific. How was what?"

"How did it feel to hold my hand in front of someone else? Your pulse was erratic, and your hand was trembling until I squeezed it, then it felt like you relaxed a bit. Did you understand what I said when I squeezed your hand?" he asks.

Understand what he said… He didn't say anything. He just squeezed my hand three times. What the hell is he talking about? I don't think he said anything. "Well, your squeezes definitely relaxed me a bit, that much is true, but I was still pretty scared. She's close with my dad, so I don't want her saying anything to him."

"So, you didn't understand what those three squeezes meant?" he asks.

I'm tilting my head at him as we walk down the hallway. "No, I thought it was just comforting. Was there a meaning behind the squeezes?"

"I'm with you, those three words; I said them with three squeezes to comfort you."

I really don't know what to make of him. I should probably mention that as a pureblood, my insight is usually pretty good, which is also the reason I chose to be in a relationship with him so quickly…okay, well, that and the feeling of his lips against mine…but mostly it was my insight. Either way, I didn't peg him for the type to say something so sweet.

"Thanks," I say, and give him a little smile.

"Well, I could feel how nervous you were. Your temperature dropped a few degrees, as soon as she walked over. I wanted you to remember that you weren't alone, but I didn't want to whisper it in your ear. I'm going to hold your hand through this, I want you to know that. It will be different for you than it was for me. I didn't have a problem coming out to my mom, she accepted it right away. My dad is not really involved with me and my brothers. He and my mom don't really get along, so I'm not sure what he knows and what he doesn't. I don't really care, though," he says.

I'm always interested in what separates couples personally.

Maybe that's a very un-guy like thing for me to say, but I can't help myself. While I do love gossip, it's more from an educational standpoint. I think of it as a guide of what *not* to do; once I hear why a marriage fell apart. When I get married, I want it to be forever, the same as my first bite, I'd like those to be the same vampire. I don't know how vamps can bite one another so easily, either. Just holding Caleb's hand like this, feels like enough for me right now. What more is there to claim, once you're holding someone's hand publicly?

"I was definitely nervous, Caleb. I've never held anyone else's hand in public. Before you ask, no, I never held Leslie's hand, either. But the squeeze words were sweet. I'll remember that for next time. So, does your dad live with you?"

"Sometimes he does, sometimes he doesn't. He just comes and goes. I'm not sure if that's the way my mom likes it, or if that's how he likes it; maybe it's both. I spend most of my time in my room, reading," he says.

"Here is the cafeteria," I say, pointing to the large glass doors. Inside the large brightly lit room, many cafeteria employees are rushing around, trying to get ready for their first lunch rush of the day.

"What time is lunch?" he asks.

"We have lunch at 12:00, what time do you normally have lunch?"

"That's the same as it was at my old school, 12:00 for lunch, then dismissal was at 2:00. Is the library nearby? Will they let me check out books even though I'm a new student?"

He can't be serious with that question, right? I mean, he definitely realizes that his welcome was special just for him, because of his status, right? Wait, why am I asking myself this?

"Are you serious, Caleb? Of course, they'll let you check books out. They'll even let us have the library to ourselves if I ask them. If you asked, it would probably be the same. Why would you not be able to check a book out on your first day? Seems like a ridiculous question."

He's stopped walking and is looking around again. Uh oh, last time this happened was when he kissed me. I don't think I can handle that again right now. I'm gonna back up just a few steps.

"Why are you backing up? I was going to say that if they'll let us have the library to ourselves, we should do that. Why are you stepping back like that?" he asks, while dropping his right eyebrow.

"Why would we need the library to ourselves? There's not gonna be anyone there anyway. Everyone else is in class." I take his hand in mine again.

His eyebrows are raised, he appears to be trying to decide what to say. He has a sort of devilish, mischievous grin on his face. He's thinking of sex in the library, I'm sure of it.

"Well, I can think of several reasons why we would need the library to ourselves, but in this instance, I wanted to be alone, for you. I would like to look at the books while holding hands, and I want you to be comfortable. Libraries are safe havens for me. I love losing myself in a good book, but I'll feel bad if I think you're uncomfortable," he says.

"I'll be okay. There won't be anyone there. It will be fine," I say. "You'll have to check out the library at my place, it's huge. I bet you'll love it." I give his hand a squeeze.

"Could I see it, though? Would your dad let me come over?" he asks, eyes wide.

"Another ridiculous question, Caleb. You're a complex character, you know that? Of course, he'll let you come over. He won't have any idea that we are together, so why would he have a problem with it? He'll be thrilled to have you in the house, trust me. I just have to make sure you aren't there when my mom stops by. She's got a real nose for…I can't even say it. I just need to be sure we aren't there if she comes over. No more questions about my mom. Please. If you like me as much as it seems, just don't bring her up again."

He's pouting a bit as he swings our hands in between us. "I do really like you, but I kinda want to ask about her even more now," he says.

"Shh! This is the library, there's no talking in the library," I say, as I open the door.

We enter the library holding hands. The two-story room is lined with black and gold bookcases, each case has eight rows of books on it, and they are separated by gold and black pillars with ornate crests. Each crest holds the number range of the books that are in that particular section. A small librarian that I don't recognize is sitting behind the counter. Her gray hair is tied in a bun atop her head, and there is a bright red pencil sticking through the bun. She looks miserable for the first day of school. I wonder why? Normally, employees everywhere look miserable in general, but this vampire, right now…I have no idea why she's upset. The nameplate across from her says *Ms. Beagle.* I kind of want to talk to her to see what's going on. I hate seeing anyone upset, but Caleb's eyes are quickly scanning the room, and I can feel his pulse racing. He really does love books; I can feel it.

I whisper, "Alright, which books do you want to look at?"

"I like almost everything…I don't know where to start," he whispers.

"Well, you have to start somewhere. What's your favorite genre?"

"I like historical books, but I also like romance, and comedy, and manga and comics, oh, and lately I've really gotten into some"—he looks left to right and he's cupping my ear now— "erotic fiction."

"Whaaat?!" I accidentally scream in a high-pitched voice. Oh my fangs, what have I gotten myself into? What does that even mean, erotic fiction? Just, like, sex books? I want to ask him, but Ms. Beagle from behind the counter is tapping the *No talking in the library* sign that hangs from the counter. I give her a nod and silently mouth, "Sorry."

Caleb's brow is squished together and he's tilting his head at me. Now he's pulling me toward Ms. Beagle. Oh my fangs, he's not gonna—

"Hello, I am Caleb Cheval, I'm a transfer student. How are you today, Ms. Beagle?" he asks, with a smile bright enough to blind someone.

"Good morning, I've heard a lot about you, Caleb. Your family's reputation precedes you. It is a great honor to have you here, and with Froderick, the son of our beloved Count Dracula, too."

I give her a nervous smile. If there's one thing I've learned about Caleb, it's that he's unpredictable and I'm a little afraid of what he's going to ask her.

"Well, yes, I'm thrilled to have Frode showing me around today. I'm quite a lucky guy. Ms. Beagle, let me ask you, and please don't perceive me impertinent, but do you have any erotic fiction here?"

OH MY FANGS! He asked her! He literally asked her! And she…wait, she doesn't care?

"What kind are you looking for? Mind you this is a high school, so what we do have, is a very small selection and barely made it past the censors, so don't get your hopes up."

"Well, one's taste in erotica is best left between that vampire and their partner, or just for themselves, wouldn't you say, Ms. Beagle? How about you just tell me where I might find the section, and I can peruse them with Frode?"

Great. Now she's looking at the two of us. Yes, we are holding hands, but she can't see that from behind the counter. "You don't mean to say that…" she says, her voice trailing off, before she finishes.

I jump into the conversation, to try and stop her from any further questioning. "He doesn't mean to say anything. He's just trying to explain something to me, and we need a book like that to clear something up. I am a very visual vampire; I need to see something before I understand it."

Caleb is sucking his lips in, trying not to say something. His mouth is near my ear now. "Do you think you made the situation better by saying that?" he whispers.

"Yes, well, section 545 on the second floor is where you'll find the books you're asking about," she says.

"Thank you, Ms. Beagle," I say.

I pull Caleb's hand to the left, toward the stairs in the back of the library. "Caleb, I am going to smack you. I'm serious."

He's pulling his head back again, like he's done nothing wrong. "Why would you smack me? Like in a kinky way?" he asks.

I can't describe my face honestly, it's like if you saw a pink gorilla flying overhead, then that gorilla landed in front of you, and asked if you ordered a pizza. The way you'd look at that. Does that make sense? No, probably not. Either way, my face is all squished up, as I try and really understand if he's serious.

"You can't say things like that to teachers. I told you I don't want my dad to find out about us. Don't you think she's going to tell everyone that we were in here asking about erotic fiction together?"

"Well, first, I'm sorry, but, also, *I* was asking, *you* inserted yourself into the conversation and made it that much worse. Otherwise, she would have just said that *I* was looking for it, but now she knows that I want to show *you* something in an erotic fiction book, so that *you* understand it. You became a willing participant at that point. I can't take the blame for that."

Well, he isn't wrong. I did make it worse, like I always do.

"Fine, but please try to remember that this is really new for me and I'm not fully comfortable with it. I don't feel like that's too much to ask," I say, as we begin walking up the stairs.

He's giving me that confused look again. "What are you talking about? You're not comfortable with erotic fiction? They probably don't even have anything good. Don't worry too much about it. We can fly over to a bookstore in my old town after school if you want. They have a ton of good books there."

I feel rather insane right now. One second, he's smart and charming and the next, he's dumb and charming. "No, not erotic fiction, even though I am uncomfortable with it. I'm talking about us." I raise our clasped hands.

He just squeezed my hand three times and smiled at me, with his eyebrows raised. Back to just charming again. I'm getting emotional whiplash, and we've only been together for a few hours. I wonder if all relationships are like this. Maybe it's so intense because we're both purebloods. I have no idea, since I have nothing to compare it to. One thing I do know is that I have definitely lost my mind. I can't imagine there is another vampire in the whole world that is as ridiculous as I am.

Caleb quickly finds the section where the erotic fiction books are. I'm not gonna ask any questions, because, to be honest, the part of me that is interested in what's in those books is outweighed heavily by the fear of what's in them. I mean, is it just pornography? Like, with words? I read a lot of science fiction and fantasy, there's not a lot of sex in those. Occasionally, there are some relationships that may take things into a bedroom or backseat of a car, but nothing erotic. All of this talk about it is getting me a little nervous though.

I have no idea what he's done and who he's done it with. I mean, I also don't know what he expects to do with me.

"I don't expect you to do anything," Caleb whispers to me, while flipping through a book.

What? Why is he saying that to me? I didn't say anything out loud, did I? Maybe I was making a face? I've been told my face is louder than my voice sometimes, so that is entirely possible.

"Why did you say that to me, Caleb? I'm just standing here."

He's not looking up from his book. "Just had a feeling that you were worried, I guess," he says.

This is weird, right? I mean, he seems like he can hear my inner thoughts sometimes. I also feel like there are times when I can predict what he's going to do. Then again, I can't really, though. I mean I would have stopped more than ninety percent of the things he's done so far if that was the case. I'm sure I'm just imagining it. I kind of want to go to class, but I also kind of don't. A new school year is lame and all but it's also fun sometimes. I do hate school but part of me craves the feeling of walking into class holding Caleb's hand. I feel like it will be really freeing… Then again, maybe it won't. Never mind, I'm terrified, I can't do it. Okay, Caleb is holding the book open with his right hand, and he just squeezed my hand three times with his left. He can definitely read my thoughts…how is this possible?

"You're panicking, I can feel your pulse. Your body temperature is all over the place right now," he says to me. "What are you freaking out about? If the book makes you that nervous, I don't have to borrow it. It's not that great anyway. I think it's a story about two male love interests, but I can't tell where it goes and how far their relationship is gonna get, by what I've read. We can leave if you want." He closes the book and is looking at me softly now.

"I'm nervous, Caleb. I was just imagining walking into class holding hands with you. It's a weird feeling. I've never felt so nervous about anything. I'm not worried about vampires judging me, I mean, I'm the number one vamp in the school, so there's no chance of that. Honestly, other vamps may pretend they're gay after they see the two of us." I'm smiling at him; he looks like he doubts what I said.

He's shaking his head. "Why would anyone do that? You are delicious and yes, you're number one, but why would anyone do that?"

I have to set him straight and this is embarrassing but sometimes you gotta tell the truth. Even if it makes you sound like an idiot. "One time, I had two different socks on, one was gray, and the other was black, it was a total accident, and you couldn't see it under my uniform pants, but in gym that day, with my gym uniform shorts on, everyone saw the socks. For the next two weeks, vamps were wearing two different colored socks. It was the most ridiculous thing. So, yes, there is an actual chance that vamps will pretend they are gay."

Tssss…he's doing a silent version of that sexy, open-mouth deviant laugh. Fangs, I want to bite him.

"Frode, don't think of it like that. You really think too much about other vampires, you know that? Do you see me doing that? No. Who cares about other vampires? Anyway, why not think of it in a different way. Think for a moment that because you're so popular that someone else who is like you might be struggling to come out, too, and maybe seeing us together will give them courage? Or at least comfort them? I personally can't relate to these things. Where I'm from, most vamps are not straight, lots of other things going on, lots of other relationships, but it's more out of the norm to be straight than anything else. Just the way it is, so this is all very weird to me. But I've read a lot of books where the main character is in a situation like you are. In one of my favorite books, the main character's dad has a lot of expectations for him, so he hides his true…oh my fangs. No…"

Caleb is covering his mouth, and his eyes are wide. He looks like he just had some kind of realization that he isn't happy with. Oh shit, what if I scared him? Now he's probably gonna dump me. I haven't even been dating him for a day yet, and I'm gonna get dumped by my first boyfriend. Way to go Frode.

"What's wrong, Caleb?"

He's shaking his head at me. Now he's pulling me into his arms. "I think I pushed you into this. I just remembered a story exactly like this. I think I forced you to be in a relationship with me and come out to everyone, and I don't want that." He's rubbing my back while holding me.

"Are you breaking up with me?" I ask. Fangs, please don't say yes.

"Never. I will never break up with you. What I am saying, though, is that if you want me to back off, in front of others until you're ready, then I want to do that. I'll be fine if we can just be together in private. I won't like it as much, but I don't want to be the guy in the story that everyone hates. I'm not that guy, Frode."

"Okay, this is not a story, well it's our story, yes, but it's reality, not fiction. I don't care who sees us as what. Also, you are *that* guy, I mean you pushed me up against a wall like three times and kissed me before you even knew how I felt, so calm down with the good guy speech. I like your aggressive behavior, honestly. If you had approached this from a different way, like a softer way, I probably wouldn't have responded to it. I like the fact that you care about my feelings, and what you just said was very sweet. I hope you always care for me that way. But, seriously, I'm seventeen and I'm gonna do this. You were right about what you said earlier, why should I pretend for other vampires? Obviously, that doesn't apply to my dad, but for everyone else; it's fine, really." I just kissed his cheek; it was so warm. I kind of want to screech right now. I've never felt this way before. Is it okay that I'm doing this? Really?

Caleb is smiling at me. "See, you were fine, and I could feel it, but your pulse is all over the place again. Don't force yourself to do something you aren't ready to do. I mean it. I don't want you to," he says softly.

I want to feel his lips, I want to show him that I'm not afraid. Can I do it, though? If he's the stronger one, which I think he is, can I kiss him when I want to? Wait, what the fuck is that line of thinking? I'm not weak and neither is he. We're both strong, and I'll kiss him whenever I want. He may be stronger than me physically, but then again, maybe he isn't. Who cares? I'm gonna do it.

I'm pressing my lips against his now, mmm…cotton effing candy sweetness…his tongue is warm and soft. I want to take his entire mouth in mine, but I don't know if he even likes the way this feels. Never mind that, he definitely likes it, our bottom halves are pressed together, and our parts are pressed tightly against one another. I kiss him deeper against the bookcase. This feels so amazing…I'm in complete control and I like it. Oh shit, he just flipped me and now my back is against the bookcase and my hands are pinned over my head. He's hungry…he's kissing me like he's starving…I've never craved blood like in movies, but he is craving something right now. Holy shit…I am so fucking turned on. I want to touch more of him, but my hands are pinned over my head. I think he's going to run my mouth dry; he's sucking my mouth so intensely.

"MMMPHH!" I pull my mouth back from him, as I hear footsteps approaching. I'm panting and he's finally let go of my hands. I'm pulling my cloak around my body tightly. I have no idea who is coming, but my pants are really strained right now, thanks to my guy down below.

It's Ms. Beagle. "Ah, you found the section. Good. Did you find anything you like?" she asks Caleb.

Caleb looks no better than I do right now, his face is flushed and there is a little bit of sweat on his brow.

She's looking at both of us closely now. She doesn't really have the right to say anything to me, honestly. What kind of a person would say anything?

"What were you two doing? I was certain I heard panting and other such noises when I came upstairs," she says, arms crossed, as she continues looking us over.

Okay, I hate to do this, but I don't have a choice. I'm playing the dad card. Shit, I can't talk, no words are coming out. Caleb really did suck my mouth dry! It's like there's no saliva in it. I'm giving him a helpless sort of look right now.

His eyes are wide and he's pointing at his throat. I'm shrugging at him, while Ms. Beagle is still staring at us. What does she hope to do here? Does she want to yell at us? I don't understand this woman.

Caleb is clearing his throat and giving me a look. Oh, I get it, he really can't talk either. I didn't suck him dry, too, did I? He's nodding at me... See! See! I knew it! It's like he can read my mind. I ask myself a question and somehow, he answers it? That's no coincidence.

Ms. Beagle is looking around and now she's pulling a book from the shelf. She's holding the book toward Caleb. "Here, this is a beautiful coming of age story. It gets a little spicy, but I think you two will be able to handle it. In the meantime, I don't really care who your parents are, the library is not a place for panting, or whatever you two were doing. Use your free period and go in the locker rooms, like the other vamps. Don't do that stuff in the library. Next time, I'll call your father myself," she says, while looking at me.

I've got some wetness back in my mouth and I'm not used to being threatened. "Excuse me. I'm sorry, but I don't know who you're talking to right now. You couldn't be talking to me like that. I'll call my father myself. I don't need you to do it. And just what are you going to tell my father? That you think you heard panting? That we were looking at erotic fiction? My dad will throw you out of this place. Give me a break. We weren't doing anything," I say.

Caleb is clearing his throat. "Ahem, yes, and my mother certainly wouldn't take too kindly to what you are saying either. Are you saying there is something wrong with two teenage boys looking at books of this nature together? Or are you saying that because you heard panting, we were doing something we shouldn't have been doing? Also, what do you think we were doing anyway? The shelves are very high, and we were having some difficulty reaching the top shelf. Frode said I couldn't fly inside, so we were hoisting one another to try and reach. What do you think you heard aside from that?"

"There are cameras all around you," she says, while pointing up toward one. "I could see everything from the screen down below."

My face couldn't be any redder, I'm sure of it.

"I want to see the footage!" Caleb demands.

I don't think he's kidding either, his arms are crossed and he's almost challenging her, with his facial expression. I can't believe she saw that. Oh my fangs. I knew it, I am truly the stupidest vamp alive.

I don't like where this is going. I really don't like to be a jerk, but I was embarrassed and afraid earlier when I said those things to her. I'll be in so much trouble if she really does call my dad and tell him what she saw. Besides the fact that I feel bad, I really can't afford to have this vamp call my father. I have to jump in. Caleb is obviously super dramatic, and he's not going to stop anytime soon, if I don't get this under control.

I say softly, "Ms. Beagle, I apologize...ahem..." Damn it, my mouth is still pretty dry. "Ms. Beagle, we both apologize. We won't do these things in the library again. I noticed earlier that you seemed upset when we came in. Is there perhaps something that I can fix for you? Since my father is the ruler of the school, if there is something you are unhappy with, I'd be happy to talk to him about it."

There we go. That was good. I think. Although Caleb doesn't think it was good. He's shaking his head disapprovingly at me. Fangs, he is a handful.

Ms. Beagle is considering my proposal, as she looks around. It seems like she wants to be sure no one is listening.

She's a bit closer than I'm comfortable with at this point, she's making Caleb uncomfortable, too, he's tucked against my side, while she is whispering near my face. Oh bats, she's really close.

"Listen," she whispers. "My niece wanted to come to this school, but my sister was told that it's a vampire only school. My niece is half vampire, half mermaid and she was denied admission. Now this morning I saw a kid, who I'm pretty sure was a werewolf, or at least partly, holding hands with another vampire, she was a pureblood. So, obviously, they allow half vamps in the school. I'm mad about it. It's not right."

I already know she's talking about Leslie and Wolfie. You see, until two years ago, the school was only for purebloods, then they decided that if you were in some part vampire, you could attend, provided your family can afford tuition that is.

"Ms. Beagle," I say. "You are talking about my best friend, Wolfie, I'm certain of it. He is part werewolf and part vampire. His mom was a pureblood, but after she got with his dad…never mind, not the point. We also have a new girl here, she is half mermaid and half vampire, so I'm not sure what happened with your niece. Maybe there was a misunderstanding? Have you talked to Ms. Tansy about it?"

She is shaking her head at me, while Caleb is looking at the book she gave him earlier. He seems to like it, there's a small smile on his face.

"I haven't talked to anyone about it," she says. "I just got this job, and I don't want to make any enemies."

Caleb scoffs at her and closes the book in his hand. "Well, if you don't want to make any enemies, threatening to call the parents of the two highest ranking vampires in the school, is probably not your best bet," he says.

He's cocky. I really like that. It's a turn on for me, I can't deny that. I meant what I said to him earlier, I like the aggressive side of him. The cocky side, I might like that even more. His right eyebrow kind of moves in accordance with his mood, too, it's fangtastic.

She's rolling her eyes at him, and she just pulled the pencil out of her bun. Oh my, now she's pointing it at us. "Listen, I caught you two tangled up here on camera. Now, I know where you're from, Caleb, everything is really easy, but something tells me, here in this boring town, with your traditionalist father, Froderick, that he would not be happy to see that footage of you two kissing. So don't try to play the big vampire cards with me. I'm still the adult here."

Okay, obviously she's right. But I can't let this vampire hold this over my head all year. That would not be good. Wait, what if she doesn't even have a recording of us? "Show me the footage and I'll find out why your niece didn't get into the school. I'll do it right now." Oops, apparently Caleb doesn't like that I said that. He's covering my mouth.

"Shush, Frode," he says to me. Now he's looking at Ms. Beagle. "No, we won't. You delete the footage while we watch, then we'll go see the principal and discuss your niece, and if that doesn't work, he'll call his dad. But we aren't doing any of that, until the footage is erased. I'm not going to be held by my fangs by a librarian all year and neither is Frode."

This is an intense standoff. I've never been in the middle of a negotiation like this. It's kind of exciting and terrifying at the same time. What a day so far. Definitely the most exciting first day of school I've ever had.

Chapter 3
He Kissed Me First

The standoff ended with Ms. Beagle showing us the very scandalous footage and Caleb erasing it. Ms. Beagle was unsure how to do so herself. I can't believe another person besides the two of us saw that. Still, though, it seemed like such a shame to erase the make-out session. Well, not the first part with me in the lead, I think I looked clumsy, and I was okay with erasing that, but when Caleb pinned me against the bookcase, it looked just as hot as it felt. He is stronger than me, by the way, but I don't really care. I'm not really into stereotypes, but even though I've constantly fought against them, that brainwashing still creeps in every once in a while. I'll have to be sure I don't slip into any unhealthy thinking again, going forward. Hahaha…that's funny. Me control my thoughts… Yeah, right. I can't control my thoughts, it's impossible.

Caleb apparently is very good with computers. While he was erasing the footage, he told me he does a lot of coding for games and websites. I do some coding, too, but being able to hack into the school's security system and erase footage was a bit too advanced for me. The school he went to must have been a really good one, or he's just naturally gifted. His mouth seems naturally gifted; I can say that much. Or maybe he's had a lot of practice… No, that's unhealthy thinking. Stop it, Frode. See, I can control my thoughts. Easy as that.

We're heading to Ms. Tansy's office on behalf of Ms. Beagle now. I can't believe I have to do this, but I do hate injustice, so if she feels like her niece was treated unfairly, I really do want to help if I can. I can't hold Caleb's hand once we get inside. He just gave me the three squeezes, telling me he's with me, but I still have to let go of his warm comforting hand. "Is it okay if we don't hold hands in front of Ms. Tansy?" I ask.

He's tilting his head at me. "Of course, I already told you to go at your own pace. I'll need a kiss after we're done with her, though. Whichever part of me you choose to kiss is fine." He's raising his eyebrows at me, while he holds the door open.

Our two capes make everyone pause as we enter the room. All eyes of the office staff are on us. I'm used to it, though, and Caleb doesn't seem to mind either. Now, if we were holding hands, that would have really made them stare. I really do hate that I had to let go of his hand. But Ms. Tansy is a special case, I'll have to try and see how much control my dad has over her before I feel comfortable enough to hold hands in front of her.

Ms. Tansy is already expecting us, thanks to the call I gave her from the library. Ms. Beagle didn't trust that we were going to follow through with our end of the deal, so while Caleb deleted the footage, I called Ms. Tansy as she watched. What a sight it was, that librarian was quite stubborn. I'll try to avoid the library for the rest of the year. With my new book-loving boyfriend that may not be so easy, though.

"Hello again, boys, have a seat," Ms. Tansy says as we enter the office. "Also, if you would close the door behind you, please, Caleb."

Caleb and I are sitting across from Ms. Tansy. He wants to pull his chair closer to mine, I can feel it. I'm giving him a look right now.

He seems to understand that I'm telling him not to move his chair, as he holds his palms out toward me, with a smirk. What a weird connection we have.

The round French guest chairs in Ms. Tansy's office are black, with gold beaded detailing and vibrant red cushions; I like sitting in them, they're very comfortable. Most of the school is red, black and gold, her office décor is no different. I will say, though, her office is one of the fanciest decorated ones in the school. Second only to my dad's, but his is just gaudy. While Ms. Tansy's office has the most beautiful window I've ever seen. It takes up the entire right-side wall. The black framed window is arched, and made up of sixteen smaller windows, each separated by black. Barely covering the sides of it are long, floor length, gorgeous, blood red drapes, with gold tassels tied around them. The light that comes in from the side is refreshing. I'm sure some vamps who come in here when they are in trouble want to fly right out of it, but it doesn't open.

Ms. Tansy is sitting in a black, high-back leather chair, and she's sort of moving her chair side-to-side while she looks at us. She isn't really spinning; it looks like both she and her chair are in deep thought as she stares at us. Haha that's funny, a chair deep in thought. Where do I come up with this stuff? Caleb is looking at me weirdly. I really need to find out if he can hear my thoughts. Because with that look, right now, it seems like he can.

"Alright, boys," Ms. Tansy says, "what should we talk about first?"

"Well, Caleb and I were wondering why Ms. Beagle's niece wasn't given admission into the school. We started accepting transfers two years ago, why didn't she get in? Ms. Beagle is very upset about it," I say.

She's looking the two of us over before she answers. "I am used to you coming in here in defense of people Froderick, I really am, and I normally find it rather endearing, but not today, not on the first day of school. Especially not with Caleb here, when we're trying to make a good impression. Wait, when did you add that ruby clasp to your cape?" she asks me.

OH SHIT, I forgot about the ruby. Alright, time to switch topics for a moment.

I rub my ruby and look over at Caleb as I reply, "Ms. Tansy, can I ask you a personal question?"

Caleb's eyebrows are raised, he thinks I'm going to come out to her, here and now, but there's no way I'm doing that.

Ms. Tansy's face is bright now. "Of course, Froderick, ask away. I love personal questions." She's smiling very giddily at me, and I can hear her high heels tapping the floor in excitement beneath her desk.

"Well, Ms. Tansy, it's about my father. I'm sure he's told you that I've never bitten anyone."

"Thank fangs," Caleb just mumbled.

I really will smack him before the day is over. I'm sure of it.

I start again, "Anyway, Ms. Tansy, how much can my dad see of what you see? Can he read your mind, or your thoughts? Can he actually see through your eyes?"

She's looking at the large window, there is a small black vampire bat perched on the outside of the windowsill, it definitely wasn't there before. She's gesturing for the bat to go away as she stands and closes the red drapes. The lights in the room dim automatically, as the room darkens.

She's coming back around to sit at her desk again, while shaking her head. "Your father and I never had a deep connection. I have no idea what he can see or hear. I don't think he can see what I see, though. And for your father, there's only been one person who was able to hear his thoughts, and that person is your mother."

Caleb is looking at me now. "Your mom can hear your dad's thoughts? Now I really want to meet her," he says with a grin.

"Caleb, I told you not to bring my mother up!" Oops, I yelled that a bit louder than I meant to.

Ms. Tansy is clapping, she obviously found that little exchange hilarious. "Oh, Caleb, you should meet Alessandra, she's fabulous. She's the role model for so many, she's especially popular with a certain population."

"DON'T!" I yell. I soften my tone and start again, "Ms. Tansy, Caleb doesn't need to know any more about my mother. We want to talk to you about Ms. Beagle."

She rolls her eyes at me. Why is she doing that? I know I'm ridiculous, but what teenager wants their boyfriend to know about their mother? I can't imagine many that do.

"You're asking me about your father because you have something you want to share with me, right? Well, I've already confirmed that he can't hear you, so go ahead. I know the Ms. Beagle thing isn't the only reason you're here," she says.

I'm tilting my head and sucking my lips in as I look at Caleb. He's getting ready to say something stupid; I can feel it again.

I'm shaking my head no at him and he's nodding at me. What the hell is this?

"Can you boys read each other's thoughts?" Ms. Tansy asks.

"No," we both say.

Her arms are crossed and she's flipping a red crystal pen in between her fingers now. "Hmm…well, I've seen the two of you walking around all morning, you know?"

My eyes are wide, as Caleb smiles at me. Come on, what the hell does she mean? I know she saw us earlier, why does she need to say it like that?

She's waiting for a response to her, almost accusation, but I can't find the right words.

"About Ms. Beagle's niece," I say.

She's tapping the pen against the desk but looking into my eyes. "About the footage that was erased in the library," she says.

"What footage?" Caleb asks, raising his chin.

I can't breathe. I actually can't breathe. My mind is racing. I gotta get out of here.

Caleb is scooting his chair close to mine. He's holding my hand now. Screw it, I'm just gonna let him. His touch is so comforting. Oh my fangs, she knows, she effing knows. What am I gonna do? I have to get out of here.

"Your pulse, dear," Caleb says to me.

My mouth is open. "Don't call me dear!" I shout. I am definitely gonna smack him.

My head just drops, as he squeezes my hand sweetly, three times. *I'm with you.* Ugh, I can't be mad at him.

Ms. Tansy is flaring her nostrils and shaking her head. "Are we going to keep pretending here? The footage from the library of you two slamming each other around. You know very well what I'm talking about, Caleb.

She turns her face toward me. She's never been mad at me before. Normally, when we debate, I have the upper hand, but right now in this situation, I definitely don't.

"Frode, I had no idea that you would be so brave as to stroll the halls while holding hands. Not to mention you pinning sweet Caleb here against the bookcase," she says with a giggle.

Caleb thinks that's funny. I'm not as amused. I yell, "Are you kidding me? If you've been watching all morning, then you should have seen all the things he did to me! Don't give me that *sweet Caleb* garbage! *Sweet Caleb* has nearly bitten me fifty times already! While I'm just trying not to freak out about everything! But he's got that deviant laugh and perfect face and he's very…I don't know what I'm even allowed to say. Fangs, okay, he's perfect and I want to hold his hand. I want to be his boyfriend, so yes, I kissed him, but he kissed me first and did a bunch of other things to me!"

"Your pulse is rather calm for someone who is screaming, do you realize that?" Caleb asks me.

Ms. Tansy is more than amused; she's giving us a big open-mouth smile. "Listen, let's get down to business now. You came here to ask about the librarian's niece, it's more complicated than her just being half-mermaid. Your father was the one who stopped her from getting in. So, if you really care, you'll have to ask him for more details. In this case, I really can't say anything else. But as your principal, I can tell you, if you bring this up to him, you'd better be ready to argue. I'm not talking about the arguments that you and I have, Frode. I'm talking about the kind that your parents have. You know what I'm talking about."

"So interested," Caleb mumbles, while he shakes his head.

I sigh loudly at both Ms. Tansy and Caleb. "Yes, I understand but let me ask you, is it worth it? You've argued with me plenty of times before and I nearly always win. Can I win? Or should I just tell Ms. Beagle that I can't do anything."

Caleb is shaking his head at me. "We told Ms. Beagle that if Ms. Tansy couldn't help, then we'd go to your dad. We told her we would, so we have to do it," he says. "I'll be with you, so it will be fine, maybe he won't yell at you."

Ms. Tansy and I both know there's no chance that my dad won't yell at me. Caleb has no idea how unreasonable the old bag of blood can be. He really doesn't. Others think my dad is like a really chill vamp, but in reality, that couldn't be further from the truth.

"Oh, Caleb," Ms. Tansy says. "You have no idea what his father is like. When he makes his mind up, he hardly ever changes it, and as for the yelling, that will definitely happen."

Ms. Tansy's desk phone is ringing. She answers, "Yes, I still have

Froderick and Caleb in here with me. Is this urgent?" Her eyes are wide, and she's straightening her long black sleeves while she listens to whomever is talking. "She's here now?" she asks as she stands up from her desk. "Fine, I'll be finished in another two minutes, tell her to hold onto her waist cincher while she waits. No, wait don't say that to her, really. I'll be done in two minutes. Get her some coffee or something. Thank you."

Ms. Tansy is rubbing her temples; her bright red nail polish is really eye catching. "What did you two do to Leslie Marnkov? Her mother is here saying you two made her upset. Fangs help me, I can't deal with this woman. I really wish your mother had taken a job here, Frode. I've never seen a woman like Darna Marnkov, who feels so special just because she was bitten by your father. We're all special, okay, but for fangs sake, somehow, she gets elevated above the rest of the houses because she was one of the first. Vampire royalists are so stupid." She's covering her mouth now.

Caleb stands up, and I stand up, too.

"Ms. Tansy, Frode was sort of in a disgusting entanglement with her, I simply told her to get lost," Caleb says.

Ms. Tansy knows the things that go on in the school, she's not out of touch like my father. "I thought you two were RP's," she says to me.

My face is all squished up again. "Ick! Ms. Tansy don't say that to me. Yes, we were that, but Caleb cut that off no more than fifteen minutes after we met. I'm sure you have the footage. I wouldn't show her mom that, though, *sweet little Caleb* had me pinned against a wall when he did it."

Tsss, Caleb's doing the open-mouth deviant laugh. Yeah…it's so sexy. I'm gonna have him do that when I bite him eventually. It's a perfect angle and there's nothing better as far as I can tell. My guy downstairs agrees, even with this uncomfortable situation we're in.

"Alright. Listen, Frode, you, too, Caleb, it's great that you two are together. I think it's really cute, and I know that your mother will, too, Frode, but still, you should be careful. As much as vamps crave to be bitten by you, Frode, and I'm sure by you, too, Caleb, if Drac sees you two holding hands or kissing, I don't know what will happen. Since we don't allow phones in school, gossip or him seeing you will be the two things you should watch out for. Of course, with the gossip, you could probably just cover it up. You shouldn't have dumped Leslie, though, not just because her mother is a horrible crone, but because it was a good cover. Anyway, just be careful of your surroundings, or just tell your father the truth… No, don't do that. Definitely don't do that. Keep this hidden for now. Sorry, I should be more reassuring but, no, I work with your father and, no, you should not. My suggestion would be that when you're ready, you bring your mother into it. She'll put him in his place. I'd like to see that. When you do it, if it's not too much trouble, could I be there? I really do love watching your mom tear into him. He always gets this stupid look on his face around her. It's fangtastic. I love her. Alright, now get out of here, it's lunch time in five minutes, and I have to deal with this absolute nightmare that's waiting for me outside."

Chapter 4
That's One Way to Come Out

We're both waving goodbye as we leave her office. We aren't holding hands yet. I want to wait until I pass Leslie's mother. There she is in all her false glory, standing beside the wall. Her black hair looks like she has a bat living in it. Why did she even decide on such a hairstyle? It's straight out of an old Victorian novel, and her gray dress is ridiculous. Ms. Tansy wasn't kidding, Ms. Marnkov probably *is* wearing a waist cincher under the tacky, frilly thing. I'm not going to say anything to her, she actually doesn't have the right to speak to me. I quickly grab Caleb's hand instinctively; I sensed that he was about to say something as we approached her. She's avoiding eye contact as we walk by.

"She smells disgusting, just like her daughter," Caleb whispers, as we reach the door.

Well, she may have perceived my pulling Caleb, as us holding hands, I don't really care. My father hates her anyway. He won't believe whatever she says.

"Such a ridiculous woman," I say.

"Why was she dressed like that?" Caleb asks. "And really how did you do anything with her daughter? They both smell disgusting.

I almost vomited as we got near her. The thought of her touching you makes me sick."

That's kind of funny. I guess he has no idea that I feel the same. But I'm certainly not going to explain that I always pictured another guy, while Leslie and I were doing things. Wait, wait, back up…earlier Caleb said something about Robert. I know he did. What the fangs did he say? That's right, he said something about Robert liking me, didn't he? I didn't even react to it when he said it. I probably shouldn't bring that up either, though. Robert is as straight as they come. I guess Caleb isn't a very good judge of people's sexuality.

He's giving me a look right now. I want to ask him if he can read my mind, but I'm honestly afraid that he'll say yes.

"Your pulse, Frode," he says. "Don't tell me you're thinking about that disgusting watermelon vamp, are you?"

I'm looking side to side; the lunch bell hasn't sounded yet, so the hallways are clear. I push him against the brick wall, with one hand on his chest "You said I needed to kiss you, since I let go of your hand earlier, right?"

He nods at me. "Yes, I did. I also said that you could—"

My mouth is pressed tightly against his, he tastes unbelievable. I want to do this forever. The way our tongues move around is spectacular. This is only our third kiss, and it feels perfect, like our mouths were made for each other. He's holding my face and going in deeper with his tongue, this is…

Damn it, the bell is ringing. I pull back and lick my lips. Caleb's not having that, he pulls me in tightly, and holds me close. I can't catch my breath, and our bodies are pressed firmly, very firmly, against one another, as the sound of vamps leaving their classrooms floods the outdoor walkway.

I whisper, "Let's go eat lunch." His pale blue eyes and full lips are going to be the death of me. I really made a good bun in my hair this morning, it's still nice and tight atop my head; in contrast, Caleb's hair is a bit messy from our kiss, well the last two kisses that is. I quite like running my fingers through his hair, it's nice and soft.

"Fine, let's go eat lunch," he says, with a bit of a pout.

I'm holding his hand and we're walking toward the cafeteria, which is on the opposite end of the school. We're surrounded by vamps on all sides now. They're all rushing to get to the cafeteria, not paying too much attention to us. This feels…really good. I feel really good, really happy, really free. Is this feeling just from holding his hand, or maybe it was the kiss? I don't know, either way, there's nothing that could make me—OH SHIT.

"Lunch time!" I hear my father saying, right down the hall. I just let go of Caleb's hand. Damn it, why is my dad still here? Shouldn't he be lining up his bites for tonight? I need to talk to him about the Ms. Beagle thing anyway, but I really didn't want to let go of Caleb's hand yet. Also, I should probably save that discussion for home, based on what Ms. Tansy said.

"Ah, boys!" My father shouts as he sees us. "Just who I was looking for! I'm going to have lunch with you today!"

Oh my fangs, what could be worse? Never mind, I better not ask myself that, there are several things that could be worse, and this is bad enough as it is. He really thinks we'll be happy about this. He's grinning ear to ear, fangs on full display and all.

"Mind your pulse," Caleb says to me.

"We aren't holding hands anymore. How do you know what my pulse is doing?" I ask him.

"Frode, I've been with you for most of the day, and I know you're freaking out right now. I'm thinking your dad can probably sense how fast your blood is pumping, based on what I've read about him. You and Ms. Tansy make him sound kind of stupid, but I don't think that's the case. Before we reach him, let me ask you, how many times since you've been in high school, has he eaten lunch with you?"

"First and foremost, he is stupid, and you'll see that soon. But as far as eating lunch with me…never. This will be a first."

Caleb nods slowly while raising his eyebrows at me. "He may suspect or know that we are together already, or maybe he just wants to get to know me."

"Probably wants to bite your mom," I say.

"She wouldn't let him," Caleb says, with a smile.

"Boys, come, I vant to hear all about the tour, the cafeteria, the library, all of it. Tell me everything. This vamp has been bored most of the day. I need some guy-time with two cool dudes," my dad says.

I want to correct all of what he just said, but he mentioned the library, did he mean that the way I took it? No, he couldn't know. We erased the footage, only Ms. Tansy would have seen it. I'm certain.

We enter the cafeteria with my dad in front of the two of us, our three black capes catch the wind from the open door. All vamps are staring over at us now. Who wouldn't be? My dad never comes in here, plus most people haven't gotten a good look at Caleb, and he is definitely worth looking at. Wait, that kind of pisses me off. I don't want people looking at him. He's mine. I quickly switch places with him, he's walking beside the wall now, and I'm on the right side beside the other students. If I said I was staring down my fellow vamps, I wouldn't be lying. I feel almost possessive, what a strange feeling. If I were holding his hand, I'd feel better.

"Frody!" Kat screams from the right. Of course, Wolfie is right behind her, holding her waist. I completely forgot about this situation with them. How dare they not tell me! They owe me an explanation. What kind of best friends go off and become RP's for show, or not show, without telling their other best friend? Who would do that? Who gets into any type of relationship without running it by their bestie?

Oh…I would. I would do that. Well, I did do that. If anything, what I've done may be a greater betrayal of friendship. But I haven't had the opportunity to tell them yet, and I would have if my dad weren't here. I'll tell them once he leaves, though. Of course, they'll have to explain themselves first.

"Hey, Kat, Wolfie, how were your classes?" I ask.

Wolfie hangs his arm around Kat's neck, and they walk beside me.

Wolfie is looking to the left at Caleb, as we bypass the lunch line. Man, I love being a noble in the cafeteria, I'll be biting into my favorite pizza in a matter of minutes, and it won't be cold. I can already taste the cheesy goodness. I also love that Kat and Wolfie have latched on to me at this moment. My dad seems irritated, though, he isn't irritated with Kat, I'm sure it's because of Wolfie.

"Do I just tell the person at the end here, what I want?" Caleb asks, while my dad chats up the employee with the large black chef hat.

"Well, they already have your preferences, so they'll have a tray ready for you. Your mom would have filled out the paperwork when she signed you up for school. If your tray has something you don't like on it, you just have to say so, they'll replace it with whatever you want," I explain.

"It's nice that we don't have to wait in line. By the way who are those two next to you?" he asks.

"They're my best friends. I'll introduce you when we sit down," I say.

Caleb is pouting now.

"Oh Caleb, don't pout at me, I had a life before I met you. You can't be serious with that face," I say.

My father is looking over at us now, and he's gesturing for us to move faster. Man, he's so impatient. We grab our trays, mine has pizza, and Caleb's has a burger. I guess he must like burgers better than pizza. Never mind, he doesn't look pleased at all.

"What's wrong? Is there something you don't like?" I ask him.

"I want pizza, too. Pizza is my favorite and yours looks so cheesy. This looks okay, but I would never choose a burger over pizza."

My dad overheard that, he's snapping his fingers at the chef with the black hat and pointing at Caleb's tray. My dad is explaining that Caleb wants pizza, the poor chef looks incredibly flustered. He is making Caleb a new tray, with a fresh piece of pizza, fruit and yogurt. It's cute that Caleb likes yogurt. I don't know why I think that, but the idea of him sucking yogurt off a spoon just seems cute. Wolfie and Kat have their trays, and now Caleb does, too.

We're walking toward the small circular table that is reserved for nobility. Kat and Wolfie are joining us, and my dad doesn't look too pleased with that. I don't really care what he thinks. I normally sit here with Wolfie and Kat anyway. Caleb looks a bit annoyed as Kat sits happily on my right side. Wolfie is sitting on her right and Caleb is on my left. Caleb is scooting his chair right next to mine, what is he thinking?

"What is that on your neck Frode?" Kat asks.

I reflexively cover my neck; I have no idea why. My dad is very interested, though, he's staring over at me.

"What are you talking about Kat? There's nothing on my neck," I say.

Caleb is eating his pizza and looking at my neck. Fangs, he better not touch me. He looks like he's going to.

"I'm talking about the ruby on your cape. When did you get that?" she asks.

Wolfie's eyes are wide looking at me. "Oh that! My dad sewed that on for Frode over the weekend, after our concert on Saturday!" Wolfie says proudly, as he shovels a mountain of spaghetti into his mouth. He's such a disgusting eater.

Damn it, how did I forget about the ruby? My dad is going to flip out on me. And is my best friend an actual moron? Wolfie knows that my dad hates his dad. Why the hell would he even mention that? Fangs, he also mentioned our band, which my dad hates even more than he hates Wolfman. I'm not even going to say anything. I'll just make everything worse.

My dad isn't eating his food, he's just staring over. His eyes are dark and cold, as he looks at the ruby.

"I like the ruby," Caleb says. "I have this purple bat because I want to stand out even more than I already do. It's just an extra touch, so that people know I'm from a noble house."

My dad likes that. He's nodding and smiling. "Well, yes, that is a good idea, Caleb. But both clasps are a bit feminine if you ask me," my father says.

"Dad! How many times do we have to talk about these things? There is no such thing as feminine or masculine, things just exist, and we see them as we want. If I have a damn red ruby around my neck, does that make me gay?"

What the fuck did I just say?

Wait, I'm okay, my dad thinks that was funny.

"No, Frode, I would never think that you were gay because you have a ruby sewn on your cape. What do you take me for?" my dad asks, still somewhat smiling.

I wish I was brave enough to say that I am gay, and tell him that Caleb is my boyfriend, but I definitely can't do that.

"What if he was?" Caleb asks. "Is that a strange thing here, for people to be gay?"

I can't believe Caleb just asked that. My dad is gonna lose it. He can't have a rational conversation about this. He just can't.

My dad is taking his cape off, he's laying it across his lap. Why the hell is he doing that?

"Sorry, the collar on this cape is quite tight," my dad says. "I'll need to have it adjusted. But to answer your questions, Caleb, for the first part, that is impossible; Frode already has a girlfriend. As for the second part, it isn't strange to other people, but I do find it somewhat strange, yes. But if you want me to give you the answer as the ruler of the school, I will say, I have no problem with it. I accept all vamps, just as they are. Does that clear things up? Why are you asking me this anyway? Rather ridiculous lunch conversation," he says.

He absolutely does not accept all vamps, he's full of it. Bullshit.

Caleb is obviously annoyed, as are Wolfie and I. Three gay vamps at the table, and my dad who feels that everyone should just accept his ignorant way of thinking, while Kat appears to be deep in thought, quietly eating her pizza.

Caleb's right eyebrow drops down and he's not eating anymore. He looks at my dad and says, "Frode doesn't have a girl—"

Leslie is holding hands with Robert and they're standing next to the table. I have no idea what is going on. Has this really only been one day? How is so much happening? Anyway, I don't really care, Robert's scent isn't even hitting me anymore. All I can smell is Leslie's watermelon scent. It really is awful.

Leslie is leaning her head against Robert's shoulder. "Hello, Mr. Dracula, Kat, Wolfie, Frody, and, ugh, Callum," she says.

She's so annoying. "How many times does someone have to tell you their name? His name is Caleb. I told you like two or three times this morning," I say to Leslie.

My dad is pointing at Leslie and Robert. "Why are you two

holding hands? I thought you were Froderick's girlfriend, Leslie," my dad says.

"She was not my girlfriend," I say.

My dad is confused, and he looks angry as he says, "Yes, she most certainly was."

"See, even your dad knew I was your girlfriend," Leslie says. "Anyway, doesn't matter. I'm with Robert now, and our free period is after lunch, so we're gonna go. Bye, Frody."

Caleb whispers in my ear, "That guy with her is gay. Is that a normal thing here, for gay guys to just hook up with girls as a cover, or something?"

"What does 'hook up with' mean?" I ask.

Caleb whispers in my ear while covering the space in between our faces, "Hooking up, like having sex, it's the same thing. I think your friend next to you is gay, too, maybe both of them if I'm not mistaken. The girl I'm not sure about, but definitely the guy is. Did you already know that?"

I'm gonna kiss him if I don't get his face away from mine. I almost just did it. But now I've remembered that my dad is sitting across from us, and he looks really mad.

"What happened with Leslie, Froderick? I need an explanation. You two have always been together," my dad says.

"I don't know why you thought that, Mr. Drac," Wolfie says. "They only started doing stuff with each other at the end of last year, there was maybe a few times before that, but they were never together. I feel like you knew this, though. You never called Leslie his girlfriend before, I'm at your place all the time. I would have told you they weren't together."

"Me, too," Kat says. "I didn't think you thought they were a couple, Mr. Drac. I assumed you knew that it was just a...thing. Leslie always wanted more, but Frody was never about that with her."

My dad twists his neck side to side. He's annoyed and confused. "You didn't even bite her, Froderick. What were you even doing with her? Don't tell me you were just having sex with her." He shakes his head a bit in disbelief. "She's still from the number two family, you two couldn't have been doing just that. That wouldn't have been smart for her."

"I don't mean to get in between you two," Caleb says. "But why wouldn't that have been smart for her? If anything, it wasn't smart for him. She's the same as every other trampy little vamp that comes around. I can't stand it when families that aren't noble are given higher status for stupid reasons. You're noble or you aren't. Who cares if you bit her mother? I understand who you are, and I mean no disrespect, but why should her family have been elevated because of that? Leslie is disgusting and she smells horrible, she's beneath Frode, and I saw her mother, she's beneath you, too."

"When did you see Darna?" my father asks.

"She was in Ms. Tansy's office, just a few minutes ago," I say.

"Frode, we'll talk more about this later," my father says, as he gets up from his seat. He's putting on his cape and staring down at Caleb and me.

He's walking quickly out of the cafeteria. I'm not sure what he's in such a rush over. I don't care, though, he's gone. That's all that matters.

Oh boy, Caleb is holding my face. "Mmm," a moan just escaped my lips briefly; Caleb is kissing me really hard right now. Damn…he tastes so good. I'm holding his face, too; my eyes are closed, and it feels like there is no one else around. Just us two in this moment, this hot effing moment. It's so quiet, all I can hear are our desperate breaths, and the sound of our mouths together.

The bell is ringing…the bell is…WAIT! I'm in the cafeteria! I pull back and open my eyes. Everyone, every single vampire in the cafeteria is staring. OH MY FANGS.

"Well, that's one way to come out," Wolfie says, followed by a round of applause.

"Wolfie, Kat, this is Caleb, my boyfriend," I say, while I drop my head on Caleb's shoulder. Better late than never, when it comes to an introduction.

"Boyfriend?" Kat says. "I had no idea you two even knew each other before this morning. When did you decide this? What happened on your tour? I'm so confused."

"I'm Wolfie, this is Kat, we're your boyfriend's best friends. We're kind of in a situation together but it's a bit more complicated than RP's. It's not important right now."

My head is still on Caleb's shoulder and he's lightly running his fingertips over my back. My eyes are closed. I want to pretend no one else exists. I liked it earlier when we were kissing, and it was quiet. It was just us. I want to imagine that again.

"That's fine, I try not to get too involved in things that don't concern me anyway. Whatever you have going on is your business," Caleb says.

"Hello, Frody?" Kat says. "You didn't answer me."

My eyes are still closed as I reply, "Go away, Kat, you'll be late for class."

"Nice try," she says, "It's our free period. We aren't going anywhere. So, start talking you little wimp."

I lift my head and turn to look at her. She knew that would get my head off his shoulder. "What did you just call me? Why would you say that? And why should I explain anything? You two didn't bother to explain whatever this thing is, that you have going on. I like Caleb and he likes me. What's next?" I ask.

Kat rolls her eyes at me. "Okay fine," she says. "We just did it and it felt good for both of us over the weekend. I mean, obviously we don't want to be in a real relationship, because Wolfie is not into me that way. I'm kind of questioning some things myself, but while we both try and decide what we want, there's no harm in us having fun together. Wait, when did Leslie and Robert get together? I was picking up on a weird vibe from him this morning."

Wolfie adds, "Yeah and he didn't even say anything the whole time that Leslie was blabbing to your dad just now, Frode. I don't know what you two are smelling by the way. I think she smells good. Not as good as Kat, but I like Leslie's scent. It's always been the same."

I'm sitting comfortably in my chair again and holding Caleb's hand. I really am confused by Robert's behavior, now that I think about it. I haven't given it much thought, but I guess he was acting weird this morning. Anyway, what's there to think about? He's with Leslie and that's fine with me. I'm not interested in him anymore, but why did he just ignore me? We're friends. Maybe he doesn't like the fact that Leslie and I were doing stuff together. That's funny if that's the case, since I was imagining him all those times. Caleb is right, what the hell was I thinking doing that with her?

"Let me ask you something, Wolfie," Caleb says. "Do you agree that the guy that was with the watermelon vamp is gay, too?"

Wolfie is sipping from the straw in his milk carton. Fangs…milk and spaghetti is just disgusting. I can't even look at him.

"Robert? No, I don't think so. He's never seemed gay to me. What makes you think that?" Wolfie asks Caleb.

Caleb is shaking his head, and his right eyebrow is down. "Just a feeling," he says. "Seemed like he was very interested in Frode this morning, and just now I noticed he kept looking at the two of us. It doesn't matter either way."

Kat says, "Well, of course, he was looking at the two of you.

You're both gorgeous, I mean absolutely fangsquisite, truly. The whole school just saw the two of you kissing, too. I won't be surprised if there are a ton of vamps that come out this week. Remember the socks, Frode?"

Kat is giggling, along with Wolfie.

"Of course, I remember. I told Caleb about it earlier."

I just noticed that Caleb isn't eating his yogurt, I really wanted to see that, too. I wonder if he didn't like it. No, he didn't even try it. His spoon is still inside the wrapping.

He's picking up his spoon and opening the packaging. "Do you want my yogurt?" he asks, as he holds the spoon toward me.

I lightly push the spoon away. "No, I already ate mine. Why don't you eat it? Besides, why are you asking me that, out of nowhere?"

Caleb is swirling the pink yogurt around. "Not out of nowhere. You were staring at the yogurt like you wanted it. Are you sure? If not, I'm gonna eat it. I actually forgot it was there," he says.

I let go of his hand and pat him on the back. I wish I had my phone so I could record this. I bet it's gonna look so cute when he eats it. Anything he does with those full lips, makes me feel things. I'm eagerly awaiting that first bite…the first bite of the yogurt that is. Well, I'm more than eager for a bite of Caleb, too.

It's happening…he's scooping the yogurt onto the black plastic spoon. "Are you sure you don't want it?" he asks right as the bite almost reaches his mouth.

"NO, EAT IT, CALEB!" I shout. Extreme overreaction, yes, but I really want to see him eat that bite.

"Damn, Frode!" Kat says.

"Yeah, calm down, Frode," Wolfie adds.

Caleb is studying my face. I swear he knows what I want. He knows I want to see him eat that yogurt. When Kat and Wolfie leave,

I'm gonna ask him about the mind reading thing. No, I can't, because if he says yes, I don't know what I'll do.

Oh boy, Caleb's mouth is beside my ear. "Do you have a food fetish?" he whispers to me. Before I can answer he whispers, "What I mean is, will watching me eat this yogurt, make you think dirty things?"

I let out a long slow breath. I cup my hand over his ear and whisper, "Maybe. I just want to watch you eat it for some reason."

I hold a finger up to Caleb and say, "Wait. Don't do it yet."

I turn to Kat and Wolfie, who are actually making out beside us. I'm gonna try to get rid of them in the nicest way possible, by making them think leaving is their idea. "Ahem, are you two gonna hit the locker room before free period is over? You only have about twenty minutes left now."

They break apart and look at each other. "Do you want to?" Kat asks Wolfie.

Wolfie is already standing and reaching for her hand. "Alright, later you two," he says. "We're not having practice tonight, right, Frode?"

I'm gesturing wildly toward the door, "No, no, just go, I'll talk to you both later."

They're hurrying toward the exit; they can't keep their hands off each other.

"I'm gonna eat it now," Caleb says, as he holds the spoon near his mouth. His mouth is slightly open, and I can see just the tip of his tongue.

OH MY FANGS! He did it, he took a bite… It was hot. Damn, I want to be that spoon right now.

"So, you liked that, right?" he asks, already knowing the answer.

I can feel how warm my cheeks are. Should I be embarrassed to admit that I liked it? I mean he can already tell I did. Oh fangs, he's taking another bite. Tsss…I can't watch anymore.

"You didn't answer me with words, but I can see that you liked it," he says, moving his gaze purposefully to my lap. "Do you want to go somewhere to take care of that? I can do it for you. You said that free period is when these things happen. So maybe we should do it, too," he says, while placing his hand on my thigh, ever so close to my guy.

I'm shaking my head no at him, as I cover his hand with mine, and move it away. "No, we can't do that, Caleb. I really want to learn more about you before we do. I really know so little and besides, I've never done that with a guy before…I can't do that in a locker room or behind a bench or something."

Damn it, he looks disappointed, but at least he doesn't look angry. I want to do it, but I can't really imagine that happening in the locker room. I don't think it's crazy for me to ask questions before we do that anyway.

"Your pulse is crazy right now. I'm actually worried about you. Do you freak out like this all the time? Or is this just because I'm here?" he asks.

"Caleb, you just brought up sex, so of course I'm freaking out. Maybe it's not a big deal to you, but it's a big deal to me. Doing it with you would be a big deal to me. Not like any other time."

Caleb's brow is tightly pulled together, as he stares at me. "I wasn't talking about having sex. I was talking about just using hands. I wouldn't suggest our first time be at school. What do you take me for?"

The cafeteria workers are cleaning up the tables around us, they're too polite to tell us to leave. I feel bad staying here any longer. I stand and extend my hand to Caleb. "Come on, let's go. Do you want to go to our last class? Or do you want to walk around a bit more?"

Caleb has my hand held tightly in his, and we're headed for the cafeteria exit. "Let's walk around a bit more, you can show me the gym and whatever else is left of the school. Gym is the last class anyway, right?" he asks.

"Right," I say. "The gym teacher is a real pain in the neck, too. Especially if you're late. Of course, no one is usually late for gym, since the locker room is attached. Free period is right before gym, no matter which grade you are in. Different times, yes, but same set up for each grade."

"Don't you think biting each other would be easier than going over everything that we want to learn about each other?" he asks.

I stop walking and reply, "Where did that come from? I thought we were talking about gym. How did we get back to talking about biting each other, again?"

"Sorry, I was just thinking about it. There's a lot of stuff that I don't think I want to hear you say. Like who your first crush was, how you realized you were gay…I could think of a lot of things. I want to know them, but I don't want to hear you say them. I feel very jealous when I think about any of that. I can't explain it. But I think if I heard you say that you had a crush on a guy, I would probably want to punch them. I'm sure I sound crazy, but thinking of that conversation makes me think biting each other would be easier. I mean, do you want to hear me talk about all of those things? Wouldn't biting each other be easier on you, too?"

He's making some good points here, plus I do want to bite him. Of course, I don't want to hear about those things, but what can I do? They happened before we were together, and isn't the point of being with someone to accept everything and move forward? Or is that wrong? I don't know. I'm definitely the wrong person to decide this for us.

"It does make sense," I finally say, as we start walking again. "I'm not looking forward to hearing you say those things either but whatever happened was before we knew each other. How can either of us be mad about anything that happened in the past?"

Chapter 5
My Father the Idiot

It's already 4:00 pm. I can't believe we've been standing inside my bedroom shouting at each other for the past twenty minutes. Caleb is just so passionate, but then again, I am too. I'm not really angry over anything, but I don't know when this sharing our history session is going to be over. I really can't take much more. Maybe I should just bite him, then this will all be over. Why is sharing these things with him so hard?

"HOW Frode? HOW? How could you let her do those things to you, if you weren't even attracted to her?" Caleb screams, animatedly, while still stuck on my history with Leslie.

My head is leaning back, and my hands are on my hips as I stand across from Caleb beside my bedroom window. "I don't know, I just did. I'm not gonna apologize if that's what you're hoping. I didn't even know you. If anyone deserves an apology, it's…well, no one because she was lucky that I did those things with her. My guy downstairs is probably the one that deserves an apology!"

Yeah, that's right. I didn't do anything wrong. Wait a minute…I'm not done.

"What about you, Caleb? Do you think it's easier for me to think that there were other guys that touched you and did things to you?

Fangs, you said you were thankful I was a birgin, thank fangs that you are, with as many things as you've done!"

Caleb is rolling his head in circles and stretching his arms out. He's really bothered. I can't understand why he thinks that what I've done is worse.

"I didn't care about any of those vampires, of course I didn't bite them! Just because I did things because I was curious doesn't mean I had feelings for them! There wasn't ever a real relationship with anyone. I, for damn sure, never had a friends with benefits thing going on. They were just one-time things. Not a constant partner that I used whenever I felt like it, while also picturing some guy in their place!"

"Oooooh! I am gonna smack you! What was I supposed to do? Just come home and deal with it myself every day? Fuck, I'm the son of Dracula. People expect things of me, I also needed to cover up the fact that I was gay, Caleb!"

Caleb's hands are on his hips. I don't think he liked that last remark. "Why do you do that? Sometimes you say 'fuck' and sometimes you say 'fangs' or 'fang' in its place. Does one mean you're angrier than the other? I want to be sure I understand, so I know how to answer you in these situations," he says.

"YES! Caleb. If I say 'fuck' or 'fucking,' then I am very mad, or shocked, or just flustered. I try hard to use other words in their place, but sometimes they just slip out."

The deviant open-mouth laugh, ahhh...I've been waiting for that. I beckon him with my finger and he's already holding me close.

"I'm sorry," I whisper.

"Don't be sorry, Frode. I overreacted. But to be fair, I told you that I would."

He's pressing his mouth against mine. Mmmm...cotton candy kisses, he tastes so good. Shit, no wait. "Mmmph," I moan, as I push

Caleb back a step. "Wait, I hear my dad downstairs. He'll hear us. We can't kiss like this right now."

Caleb's mouth is in front of mine, his scent is more than wicked, it's drawing me back into his mouth. "We can be quiet," he says softly.

He's kissing me again, while I swallow all that cotton candy heat down, as we move our tongues thirstily around inside one another's mouths. His hands are all over me, and mine are in his hair. I want to pull it; I want to grip it but that probably shouldn't be done. I really should read a book about this. Oh, a book! I need to show him the library when we stop. Shit what's a library…I feel dizzy.

Caleb just stopped kissing me. "Breathe, you forgot to breathe, Frode. You need to breathe through your nose when we kiss like that," he says, while rubbing my back.

I think I almost fainted. My cheeks are really hot, but that's nothing compared to my guy down below. He's never felt like this, despite the fact that I almost just fainted.

"Froderick!" my father yells from downstairs.

"Oh fangs, Caleb. My dad is already calling for me. Probably wants to pick up from where we left off at lunch. You can fly out the window if you want. I won't blame you. Actually, on second thought, you probably really should just go. I couldn't get a read on how he felt about you earlier."

Caleb is shaking his head at me, while reaching for the doorknob. "Nah, I can do it. I'm not going anywhere. Whatever he says, can't be any worse than everything we just told each other. One more kiss, though, just on the cheek."

"With pleasure," I say, then give him a quick kiss. Thankfully, my guy down below has retreated for the time being. "I'm sorry that we can't hold hands, but just remember that in front of him, we're just friends. Really, you kind of pushed it with him earlier. If he wasn't such an idiot, he would've picked up on everything you were saying."

"What makes you think he didn't figure it out afterward?" Caleb asks.

Caleb is following me downstairs into the kitchen now. "Because he's not that smart," I whisper.

My dad's back is to us, as we enter the kitchen. "Froderick… and…Caleb. I recognize that scent from earlier," my dad says, not turning around to greet us.

"Yes, it's me. Hello, Mr. Dracula," Caleb says, as we sit at the kitchen table across from my father.

What are those papers that my dad is looking at? There must be fifty pages spread in front of him.

"What are you working on, Dad? Did you need help with something?" I ask.

"Oh, it's a big mess. We have a girl whose parents tried to get her in on a transfer scholarship, which you know I hate, but I was willing to do it. Anyway, the parents are lying about something, I just can't figure out what it is. I rejected her application and now the parents are threatening to file a lawsuit. I've never heard of something so ridiculous. It's my school, who should be able to decide who is allowed in, if not me? It doesn't even make sense. Same as a store, right? If I go to a store and the cashier doesn't want to let me buy things, what can I do?"

"Uh, tell the manager," I say.

My dad hates to be wrong. "That is not the same thing!" he says. "That was a bad example, what if I was at the store and the employees locked the door on me as I approached? Hmm?"

I'm nodding at him, while sucking my lips in. I'm so embarrassed of his lack of intelligence. "Again, tell the manager," I say.

"No, Frode. What about if the store manager—"

Caleb interrupts him, "I think the example you're going for, would be more like if the store owner refused to let you in the store. You're saying it's your school, and you have the right to decide who is allowed in. Same with the store owner, in your eyes, he can choose who he likes and who he doesn't. Is that right?"

"Thank you, Caleb," my father says. "Your test scores and records from your previous school were outstanding, I knew you were worthy of our school as soon as I saw them. I'm very glad to see that you and Frode have gotten so close already. He always has friends over, but normally I'm not a fan of them hanging around here. Wait, you're not in Frode's band, are you? I really hope not. It's so noisy and half their songs don't make any sense. Everything is about feelings. Blech."

Caleb is looking at me like he really wants to say something, but he turns to my father instead. "No, I'm not in his band. I don't know much about it. I do think that what you said before that is kind of wrong, though. I'm happy you think I'm intelligent, but I disagree with the point you made. Not about the band, I have no idea what they sing about yet. I mean about the school and the store owner. That was just…wrong."

Oh shit…I'm tilting my head back and staring at the ceiling fan. I like his cocky attitude and his upfront way of speaking, but, fangs, I told him to take it easy with the old man.

"Is that right?" My dad says. "Well, explain to me how I'm wrong. Tell me in a way that makes me understand, don't be all long winded about it like Frode. Sometimes I let him win arguments just so he stops talking. If you do that, I'll just keep arguing. There's no mercy rule when it comes to someone else's kid. Go ahead, explain away." He folds his arms and looks at Caleb.

This is going to be hideous.

"Well, first of all, vampires all deserve to be treated fairly. With the hierarchy, we can't treat everyone the same, and there is a part of me that agrees with that, partly because of my upbringing, but also because there are a lot of very sick, depraved vampires that just want to cause trouble, and they don't belong around vampires like Froderick, or myself, or really anyone, so in those instances, the hierarchy works and it is necessary—"

"You're already boring me," my dad says. "Get to the point quicker. I'm Count Dracula, I don't care about depraved vampires, or whatever the hell you're talking about."

"Okay, well, if you don't want someone treating Frode badly just because he's your son, or just because, I don't know, he has very long hair, then you need to stop doing the same thing to other people. How about that?" Caleb says.

"Why would anyone treat Frode badly, just because he's my son? The hair, I understand, it's far too long, but to treat him badly because he's my son… Why would anyone have a problem with that?"

"That's not the point, the point is that someone *could* do that, which is what you're doing every time you write someone off because you don't like, or understand, something about them."

"Those are not the same things," my dad says. "I think that vampires need to follow the laws that were placed before us by my ancestors, anything else is irrelevant. Besides, if someone treated Froderick badly, his mother would destroy them, before I ever heard about it. She's very protective of him."

Caleb is touching my foot with his under the table. He looks really cute right now, all flustered from arguing with my dad. He starts in again, while he still touches my foot. "Do you understand that a lot of people feel that way about their own kids? The same way that you say Frode's mom feels about protecting him, is the same way that other people feel about their own vamps. The same girl that you don't want to let into the school, is someone's Frode."

My dad doesn't seem like he knows what to make of what Caleb just said. He looks so confused, even though it was a pretty basic argument. It was good but not mind blowing, but then again, it's entirely possible that he'd never thought of it that way. He's such an elitist that I don't think he's ever considered that someone would treat me bad for any reason.

My father is pulling a few of the papers together as he replies, "Listen, I can't get into details, but the parents lied, and I don't reward lying. Plain and simple. Forget about what I think of the family and their secrets. If you lie, you have to suffer the consequences."

My turn. "But, Dad, maybe they lied because they knew what you would think of them? Take the queer vamps at the school—"

"Do you have to use that word?" My father asks.

"Yes, Dad, there's nothing wrong with the word, shut up and listen. The queer vamps at school, all know how you feel about them. They'll never be recognized by you or accepted by you. Do you think that's right? What if someone thought you were an insufferable bag of old B-negative blood, who only bites women because he's so old that he can't get a woman any other way? Would you like that? What if that same person who thought that, also wrote your entire way of living off, and said that you were just a confused old vampire who needs therapy? Would you agree with them? Would you be able to change who you are? That's how all the queer vamps in school that are too ashamed to let you see who they really are feel. I know that much for a fact."

"I stopped listening probably five seconds after you started talking, Frode. How dare you compare me to some B-negative trash, like a commoner. This is why I can't talk to you. You're just like your mother; you love to argue, when you can't even make a decent point."

"Oh my fangs! Are you serious? I did make a good point, you just stopped listening. I'm not going to argue in front of Caleb. Mom taught me better than that," I say.

That will shut him up. He hates it when I make it sound like I like my mom better than him.

"Of course, of course, your mother, your perfect mother. The only woman who wants nothing to do with me, that you think is so fangtastic. I don't care if you say she taught you things. Why should I care? I'm Count Dracula and she's just a… Forget it, I can't even bring myself to say it. Especially not in front of Caleb. It's too embarrassing for me."

"Say it, please. She's a what? Frode won't tell me anything about his mother," Caleb says to my dad.

"Caleb, shut up." I say as I kick him lightly under the table.

My dad is tilting his head and leaning back in his chair, while looking at the two of us. He's rubbing his neck, but to be more specific, he's rubbing the spot where my mom bit him. She's the only one to ever do that, that's how I know what he's rubbing. Also, whenever he gets upset about my mom, his posture drops, and he just falls apart. Then he normally goes on a biting frenzy. The poor vampire housewives are gonna get it tonight. I should call the news and warn them. Never mind, they wouldn't listen to me anyway. I've called before, they laughed at me. It was when I was younger, I didn't really understand that my dad was supposed to bite as many women as he could, well, not that he's supposed to, but that it's accepted. I didn't understand that it was accepted, so I called the news and told them he was going on a biting spree. The news person that answered the phone laughed at me. And you know what? I saw the footage, there were actually vampire housewives standing at the end of their driveways, holding signs that said, *Bite me.* The banner on the bottom of the screen said something like *Panicked son of Count Dracula warns that Dad is hungry tonight.*

My dad sighs, then says, "I'm not going to talk about Alessandra, Caleb. You shouldn't either. That woman has ears everywhere. If she hears you, she'll be at your house—actually, she would never go to your house, but she will be more than interested to know that you and her precious Frode are friends. I will warn you, though, you should stay away from her. Frode is right to keep details about his mother from you, it's far too embarrassing to discuss. Just like that ridiculous Wolfman, the two of them, they are quite a pair."

"Dad, don't make it sound like Mom is dating Wolfman, they're just best friends. Mom would really smack you for that. Anyway, what did you call us down here for?"

"I don't even know anymore," my dad says.

"Okay, well, I guess there isn't really any more for us to talk about," I say while I stand up from the table. I give Caleb a nod and he stands, too.

"Yes, go ahead and leave me…just like your mother," my father says in a pitiful voice.

He's just trying to get me to comfort him, but I'm not gonna do that. He's the adult, and, honestly, my mom is better off without him, as crazy as she is. Whenever they're together, they're either fighting or…ugh, forget it, but, yes, they're fighting or doing the opposite, but fighting is far more common with the two of them.

Caleb is buying my father's pitiful act. He's looking at me like we should stay. Ah, there we go, here comes Alexandra. Alexandra is my dad's cat. Her gorgeous black fur is blocked by the ridiculous red vampire cape that my dad had specially made for her. My mom's name is Alessandra, the cat's name is Alexandra, he got the cat as soon as my mother left him. Obviously, the cat was meant to be a sort-of replacement for my mother. Sometimes he calls it the wrong name and I pretend not to notice. What can you even say when someone does something like that? Like I'm going to correct him; no chance of that happening. Besides, he'd just say I was imagining it.

"Alright, dad, I'm going to show Caleb the library. Bye, Alexandra," I say while I quickly rub under her chin. She loves it when I pet her.

"Don't talk to her, you traitor," my father says to me, as he pulls Alexandra back.

Caleb and I walk down the long halls side by side. I know he wants to hold hands and I do, too, but I can't do that. My dad is insanely fast, and he could be behind us like in a second. It's far too risky. Although, I'm certain he's still sitting at the table pouting with his cat.

"This place is huge," Caleb says. "I don't know what I was expecting but I wasn't expecting anything this big."

"That's funny. My dad complains about how small it is, but he won't leave this place. He has enough money to do it, but he won't."

I shouldn't have said that because now I'm gonna have to explain why not.

"Why won't he move out? Or just add onto the mansion?" Caleb asks.

"Stop eyeing my hand," I whisper. "Listen, he won't move out because he bought this house for my mom. Now, stop, before you get to feeling all bad for him. Don't. Remember that he is a disgusting sexist vampire. My mother was right to leave him. No, I will not say anything else about it. Just leave it at that. Library is in here," I say, walking into the room with Caleb beside me.

If he brings my mother up one more time, I am going to smack him. It's bad enough that he's already curious, but why does she keep coming up in conversation? I never talk about her this much.

Caleb's face is bright looking around the library. Our library is rather extraordinary, though. The two floors are covered wall-to-wall in books and the red carpeting on the spiral iron staircase is a really nice complement to the gigantic black chandelier in the center of the room.

"Is there a system for the books?" Caleb asks.

I shake my head at him. "No, they're just all here. My dad knows where everything is, but I'm sure he doesn't have any erotic fiction. So just stop that line of thinking." Wait, Caleb is getting closer to me, too close. I push him back slightly. Damn it, his chest is too hot, I move my hands down to his waist, oh my fangs, that's worse! It's worse! I cannot, absolutely cannot let this—"mmm…." Caleb's lips are pressing lightly on mine near the back of the library. "No," I say as I painstakingly push him off.

What is wrong with him? Maybe he doesn't like me at all. Maybe he really just wants to have sex with me. I've heard of these things before. Hot new vampire comes into town and finds the unattainable mate, sleeps with them, then dumps them after they've gotten their bite. That shit is not happening. I'll put a stop to that right now. Caleb is giving me a look like he knows what I'm thinking again.

"What?" I ask. "Why are you looking at me like that? I can't believe you just did that. What if my dad had come in? Fangs, Caleb. And also, what? You're looking at me like I'm ridiculous, what is it?" I ask, stepping back a few steps.

"You were thinking something ridiculous, so I looked at you like you were ridiculous," he says.

"How do you know what I was thinking?" I ask with my arms crossed.

"I don't have to know *exactly* what you were thinking. I could just tell it was ridiculous. Your face was having a conversation all by itself," Caleb says looking at the shelves. "Who cleans in here? I've already touched around twenty books and not a single one was dusty." He wipes his finger down the spine of an all-red book, that I immediately recognize.

Oh Fangs! "Not that book!" I grab the book from his hands and hold it behind my back.

Damn it, how am I going to get rid of this? I shouldn't have drawn attention to it. I don't know if he saw the author's name.

Caleb drops his right eyebrow and leans in. "Did that say what I think it said?" he whispers.

My mouth turns down in reply, I back up a few steps and tighten my grip on this horrible piece of literature. "I have no idea what you think you saw, but if you bring my mother up, I am going to—back up, Caleb!"

Shit, he's grabbing for the book. I am a fangtastic soccer player, there is no way his feet can move faster than mine. "You will never get this book!" I scream and run down the stairs.

He is very fast, holy hell! What am I doing? The floor is smooth and my foot slips just a little, fangs, I lost a step. "Alright, alright, stop, Caleb!" I yell while holding the book behind my back at the bottom of the stairs. "Caleb, listen, I really need to tell you something," I say.

"You're a terrible person," Caleb says.

My mouth drops open. "What? Why would you—"

Caleb isn't out of breath at all, he's studying my face. "You were going to say something that sounded serious and then run away. I know you were, that's why I said you were a terrible person. Just let me see the book."

I point the book at his face, we're only a foot or so apart. "Can you read my thoughts? Answer the question, just tell me the truth." I say.

"I can't explain it, sometimes I feel like I can hear or see a little bit of what you're thinking or feeling. What about you? It seems like you can, then again, maybe you can't. You really would have to be better at controlling your thoughts if you were hearing mine. I assume at least."

Okay, so there we go, he *can* hear my thoughts sometimes. Well, isn't that the best news I've had all day? I swear, the perfect vampire finds me, gets dropped in my lap and somehow, he can kind of hear and feel my thoughts. This relationship is doomed. I should just end it now.

"I just told you I can kind of hear your thoughts. You're not really considering that, right?" Caleb asks.

"Tell me exactly what you heard or felt," I say with my eyebrows drawn together. The red book is behind my back now, tight in my hands.

"That time, I didn't hear anything. I could just feel that you were thinking that we would separate. I don't know if you were thinking of dumping me, or me dumping you. That's what I felt."

"How is this possible, Caleb? We need to ask my dad, as much as I don't want to talk to him, especially since he's pouting. He's probably the only one that will know the answer, which is quite terrifying, because as I've said before, he's an idiot. Come on, you walk in front of me. I'm putting this book back. Don't you dare try to grab it when I do."

Caleb walks in front of me like I asked him to. I'm so freaking annoyed right now about so many things. I don't even know which one of my many problems to freak out about. Oh my fangs! How can I have a normal conversation with myself now? What am I supposed to do about that?

Once Caleb is a few feet ahead, I stick this red piece of

embarrassing trash safely back on the shelf where it belongs. Technically, it belongs in a dumpster, but I can't do that.

I sigh as we exit the library. "Well, my dad is probably in his bedroom pouting now. He's gotta save all his energy for his rampage tonight, and after his little display at the table, I have no doubt that we'll find him in his room."

Caleb grabs my hand; he's giving me a very mischievous smile. I think I can just let him hold my hand this time. My dad is definitely, most definitely in his roo—

Caleb and I drop our hands to our sides. My dad is staring straight at us. Luckily, he's holding Alexandra, so I'm sure he didn't notice. That was way too close, though.

"Dad, I need to talk to you, before you go in your room."

Caleb and I stand across from him in the hallway with our arms at our sides. Caleb actually looks nervous for once. I wonder why. I wish I could hold his hand, but I can't, so forget it. He just looked over at me and gave me a smile. Right, I'm sure he knew what I was thinking.

My father looks up from Alexandra. "What do you want? You want to talk, go ask your mother, she's the one you like best."

Does my dad really think I'm going to beg him to talk to me? I'm definitely not. "Fine, I'll call mom. Let's go, Caleb." Caleb and I take one step past my father. I'm giving Caleb a very knowing smirk. Three, two, one…

"Stop, stop, don't call your mother," my father says. He places the cat down. "But you should apologize to me. You are very heartless; just like her sometimes. What were you even bullying me for?"

Is he fucking for real? He really thinks he did nothing wrong. How many different groups of people did he offend while we were at the table, and at lunch, and before school? Or every day? I mean, there is no end to the doltish phrases that come out of his mouth.

Yet here he stands in front of me, his seventeen-year-old gay son, that's being forced to hide his sexuality, while standing in my home, next to my boyfriend—and he wants me to apologize? That's not happening.

"Dad, I can't even begin to tell you how many things you've done today that would be considered bullying. I literally just tried to come up with a list in my head and there were so many asinine things that I can't even choose one."

Caleb nods in agreement.

"Look," I say, pointing at Caleb, while speaking to my dad. "Caleb and I can sort of read each other's minds, and we can feel each other's thoughts."

"That's impossible. Two male vampires can do no such thing," he says.

Worthless bloodsucker, he's back to genders and not listening again. "Son of a bat!" I scream. "Dad, obviously we are two male vampires standing in front of you. We are telling you that this is happening, we *can* feel each other's thoughts and, on a level, read them, too. Do you have any idea how it's possible? The question is, *how* is this happening? Not, *is* this happening?"

"I have only heard of two noble purebloods reading each other's minds once they have bitten one another. I have never heard of any other instance. Now, I know you two didn't bite each other, so I truly have no idea. But I will say that I feel bad for Caleb. If he can read your mind, that's gonna be pretty rough for him as your friend. You're always freaking out about something. Oh, and hells help him when you have band practice. Caleb, do yourself a favor and don't go near Frode at that time. If he invites you to a concert, just spare yourself and don't go. It sounds bad enough on the outside, I can't imagine how awful it sounds on the inside." My father grabs the handle to his bedroom and opens the door.

Caleb is covering his smile, I guess he thought that was funny.

"Do you think Mom would know anything about it?" I ask before my father steps inside his room.

"No, she would not, and do not mention Caleb's name around her. I'm warning you," he says in a very serious tone. He walks in his room and closes the door.

Alexandra paws at the door, my father opens it just enough for her to squeeze inside, then closes it behind her. The cape is just so ridiculous on the cat. I've never seen a cape on a cat before, maybe that's why I think it's so ridicu—

Wait, why was he so serious about me not bringing Caleb up to my mother? It's not like he knows we're dating. I mean, I would never bring Caleb around my mother. I definitely would not, not by choice anyway. If she shows up, or we run into her, then honestly, I'll just try and convince Caleb to fly away or something. But now I'm very curious as to why my dad would say that.

Caleb and I are walking toward my bedroom, which is on the opposite side of the mansion.

"Do you know why your dad said that?" Caleb asks. "I know you told me not to ask about your mom, but there was something weird about his tone when he said not to mention my name around her. He doesn't know we're a couple, I'm sure of that much. Still, I didn't like that."

I grab Caleb's hand and we interlock our fingers. I'm not afraid of my dad coming out, now. He definitely won't. I squeeze Caleb's hand three times and smile at him.

"You know, I actually like you," I say to Caleb, while our hands sway.

Oh yeah…Caleb's head tilts back and I can see those gorgeous fangs, he's doing that open-mouth deviant laugh, again. I want to kiss him right now, but I'm not going to, and I better not think about it, or else he's gonna read my thoughts, and do it. But, mmm, I love watching his mouth open like this. Does this make me a pervert? Or is this normal to get turned on by your boyfriend's mouth?

Caleb is almost blushing; he tilts his head while looking at me. "Well, I should hope so. I really like you, too. I thought we went over this already. Are you saying you, just now, realized that you like me? Come on, you've liked me all day. You liked me as soon as you saw me." He raises his eyebrows twice with a smile.

I pull my hand away and shove him lightly. "I didn't know what to think when I saw you, honestly. But what I meant was that I feel something more for you, than just a small amount of like. But it's too soon to call it anything. I'm not really sure of what it is. You're my first boyfriend, so I'm sure its normal that I'd feel a strong connection with you."

Caleb shakes his head and grabs my hand. "No, that's not true. There is something stronger here. For some reason I think your mom may be the one that we need to ask. Now before you scream 'Whaaat' or yell or threaten to smack me, just hear me out. Your dad does not know we are together, why would he say not to bring my name up to your mom? Seems strange. If it's a mom thing, we could ask my mom, though. She's a noble pureblood, too. Maybe she might know. Do you want to do that? We could go to my place. No one will bother us there, like I said, my mom already knows I'm gay. She'll be thrilled to see that I'm going out with you."

Chapter 6
Frode and His Fruit

I pull my phone from my pocket to check the time. Oh fangs, I have so many missed calls and texts. My phone was on silent and I didn't even realize it. When I got home, I just slid it into my pants and didn't check the volume. I hold a finger up to Caleb, who is walking over to look at my phone. I send a quick reply to the first text, just as Caleb reaches my side. "Hey! You can't just look at someone's phone without asking, Caleb!" I pull my phone back from his gaze.

"You're not someone, you're my boyfriend. Also, as previously discussed, I can basically hear your thoughts. You've already read one text, and I can tell you, it was not pretty to listen to. I have no idea who that was from, but it was like chaos a few seconds ago inside your head. So, would you prefer I stand back and enjoy the show, or read along?"

My head falls forward and I let out a sigh. I hold my phone against my chest and point at him. "Fine. Read while we walk. But don't you even think about getting mad about whatever you see."

"I won't. How ridiculous of a vampire do you think I am? How could I get mad over texts or phone calls? Start with the last one, though. That was a lot of noise inside your head. What was that about?"

I scroll back, open the message, and hold the screen in between us while we walk.

Robert: Hey 2:05pm

Robert: Can u talk? 2:30pm

Robert: I want to talk about Leslie 2:45pm

Robert: And Caleb 3:30pm

Robert: Can u text me when u get this? I'm going a lil crazy. lol. 4:30pm

Frode: Hey sry my phone was on silent. I'm busy rn. I'll text u later 6:05pm

Oh fangs, Caleb is mad. He said he wasn't going to get mad, but he is mad. He's really mad. I'm not reading any more texts in front of him. Forget it. What is he mad about, though? Am I really stupid? I don't understand. Maybe he's mad that I texted Robert? No. That would be dumb. It's not like I said anything wrong. I open the door to my room and Caleb follows behind me.

"I'm gonna go," he says, barely meeting my eyes, then looks down at the floor. "Seems like you want to talk to Robert, and that's fine. I just don't want to be here when you do that."

"Caleb, I don't need to talk to Robert. He asked me to call or text him, so I did. I don't need to talk to him about any of the things he mentioned."

My phone is no longer on silent mode, a high-pitched scream accompanies an incoming text. I forgot I changed my notification sound to that. What am I supposed to do right now? I haven't been on my phone all afternoon. As soon as I texted Robert, my status changed to show I was active, so I have no idea who is texting me. But I still have more than thirty other texts to go through. I'm not looking at it now; not with him pouting like this.

"He is going to ask you out. I promise you, Frode. I want to be chill about this, but I...you told me that he was the one that you, you know imagined, and I can't get that out of my head. I want to be mature, but I just don't feel like I can be in the room when that guy asks you out. I'm not mad, I don't have anything to be mad about. I just don't like it. It's okay, I should go home anyway."

Caleb's cheeks are flushed. He looks heartbroken for some reason. I told him that I didn't feel that way about Robert anymore. I don't know what to say to make him feel better. What does he even need from me and WHY does he keep thinking that Robert is gay? I don't effing understand that. Now I'm getting mad, and I have no idea why.

"Sit, please," I say gesturing to my bed.

Caleb sits down and looks up at me. His pale blue eyes are full of anguish, they're desperate, it's like all of the light in them is gone. But why?

I take his hands in mine softly. "What is the matter? Why do you look like this? I don't like Robert anymore. I told you; he stood near us in the cafeteria, and I didn't even register his scent. I am all in on you. I even told you that I really liked you a few minutes ago. Do you know how many guys I've said those words to?"

"I know, but—"

His warm hands are shaking in mine. I softly kiss the top of each hand. "I have told one guy that I liked him, in my whole life. The guy who claimed me as his own five minutes after meeting me, this morning. The same guy that pinned me against a wall, even though I was strong enough to push him off. The guy that I'm looking at right now, who is looking rather pitiful for no reason at all. I only like you. I only want you, Caleb. I don't even have to call him, or text him, if you don't want me to. I couldn't care less."

Caleb kisses the top of my hands. "No. It's okay if you call him, he's your friend. You said you've been friends for a long time.

Admittedly, I am jealous of your friends, which is a strange feeling for me."

Caleb's face is more than confused right now. I can feel the conflict within him. It must be really intense, especially since I can feel it this strongly. It feels like he wants to squeeze me and sink his fangs in, and at the same time it feels like he's only softly holding my hand. Two very different types of affection are battling inside of him.

I sit beside him on the bed and stare into his eyes. "You are so torn right now. I can feel it. You don't have to be," I say.

I am just now realizing that we are on my bed together. Sex happens in bed. Yep, I just now came to that realization. I should really stand up because otherwise Caleb is gonna—

Caleb turns his body toward mine. His eyes are hungry now. I think that I shouldn't have thought about the fact that we are on my bed together, or about sex. Aaaaahh, I'm all freaking confused. People can't just go around reading or feeling each other's thoughts. This isn't fair!

I hold my right hand up toward him and move a bit to the left. "Now, Caleb we need to finish this discussion. Just because you heard what I was thinking doesn't mean I am going to do anything about it. I've already done more than I've done in my lifetime with you today."

Caleb tilts his head at me, and his right eyebrow drops. "What are you talking about? You've done so much more with other people. We've kissed, that's it. We haven't done anything else. I'm not asking for more either, but if you're gonna imagine it, then allow me the honor of actually doing it. Don't just imagine it. That hardly seems fair."

"What I meant was that as far as guys go, this is the furthest I've gone, and whether I just thought about something more is not up for discussion, because that is not happening. Now every time I've said I wouldn't do something today, I've done it, but this is not one of those times. So don't look at me like that. I'm serious. I still have a lot of texts I haven't read; I don't want to feel like I'm doing something wrong by talking to my friends, Caleb. But I also can kind of understand how it must feel for you to be here without any friends."

Caleb's mouth drops open. He looks really offended.

Holy bats, this guy is even more dramatic than me! What did I say that was wrong? I can't…I'm really trying to remember.

"What did I say that was wrong, Caleb? Why is your mouth open?" I shrug my shoulders.

"You said I had no friends. I have a lot of friends. That was actually very mean of you to say."

The left side of my lip and my left nostril are moving up in annoyance. "That is not what I meant. Why would I be mean to you? You're not serious. I can tell you aren't. Really, I just meant that I don't want to make you uncomfortable by reading texts. It's unrealistic to think there aren't unread texts from people that are actually flirting with me, though. I haven't seen who texted me yet, but try and remember that today was only the first day of school, and I am very popular. That didn't change just because I didn't go to class and we became a couple."

Caleb crosses his arms and lays the top half of his body down on my bed. "Frode, are you saying there are worse texts than what we just read? That was an obvious lead up to a proposition. Do you get more than that from girls? I know you don't get them from guys, because you said no one else besides Wolfie and Kat know that you're gay."

This is hilarious. Hilarious and terrifying. I know that I am not the only high school vampire that gets dirty pictures and texts sent to him. I know that I'm not, and there is nothing he could say that will make me think otherwise.

I blow air from my mouth. "Girls send me pictures and texts that I don't ask for. Don't try and act like they don't do it to you, too, Caleb. I will absolutely not believe you if you say they don't."

Caleb stands up, he runs one hand down his face and the other is on his hip. "They don't, Frode. Absolutely not. Why would any girl have my phone number? Why would anyone at all have my phone number? You're the son of Dracula, and you just give anyone your phone number? I have never gotten a text from anyone that I didn't want to get a text from. I would show you if I had my phone, but I don't have it, since we're not allowed to bring them to school. Seriously, though, if you really think I'm lying, I don't even know what to say to convince you."

I lie flat on my bed, since Caleb is standing up. This is exhausting. I pull my phone out of my pocket and pass it to him. "Here, just go through the texts. There is nothing I want to see anyway. I'm a little mad at you, though. I don't just give anyone my phone number, but I have a lot of friends. Just let me know if there is anything I need to see, and delete the rest, or just delete them all."

Caleb is shaking his head at me. "No, that's not what I want. I'm not trying to take over your life. I'm just confused, because I don't get those kinds of texts. You absolutely can text other people. Not guys, though, and girls shouldn't be sending you inappropriate things, but friends are fine. Guy friends are fine, too, but I'm not okay with Robert. Not gonna lie about that. You need to tell him we are together, unless you want to go out with him. Before you say that he isn't gay, I think you should just call him or text him. Let's just get it over with. I can stay or leave, whichever you prefer, but I can't sit around like this. We've been talking about it for thirty-five minutes."

"I'm not going to call him. Who calls someone on the phone? That would be so effing weird. I'll text him. You sit."

Caleb cups my face in his hands. He's looking at me softly. "I like you. I like you a lot and whatever he says is okay. Don't be nervous."

Caleb presses our lips together. His tongue lightly meets mine. "Mmm," a moan escapes my mouth. He tastes so delicious. Caleb's thumbs and forefingers are rubbing both of my earlobes. Holy shit…this is so hot. Our kiss is heavy now, it's thirsty. I feel impatient, ravenous…I'm fucking hungry and I'm gonna bite him.

"AAAHH" My scream ringtone shocks me back into reality. We break apart and we're both panting. Holy bats, I almost just bit him. Thank fangs for this ringtone. Caleb's lips are parted as he pants, looking me over like a starved animal. I can see his tongue inside his mouth. Oh my fangs. My guy down below may seriously revolt against me when I finally decide to let him have his way, because right now, he is ready and there is only one thing he wants, which he's not getting.

I look at my phone, it's a text from Robert. Why the hell is he texting me again? This is crazy. I don't even want to talk to him. I want to have sex with Caleb right now. I really do. But even stronger than the urge for sex, is the need to bite. I've never felt a feeling so strong. How do I quell this? What do I do? Maybe when Caleb leaves, I'll grab a peach or something from downstairs, or an apple. I need to bite, and I think Caleb feels the same. His lips are sucked in, and his breaths are silent, but his chest is moving rapidly.

"Text that guy, Frode. DO it, or I'm gonna bite you!" Caleb is covering his mouth; he looks like he's in excruciating pain. I can relate, this does feel painful, and my willpower is not that strong. But why does he want me to text Robert right now? That's the last thing I want to do.

"Frode, stop overthinking. Text him, so we both can get out of this sanguineous state." His right hand is cupped tightly over his mouth.

"Okay, Okay, Okay," I stammer.

Frode: Hey Wdyn?

Robert: Can you talk?

Frode: That's why I'm texting you.

Caleb's pupils are dilated, there is barely any pale blue coloring to be seen, as he looks at me while standing beside the bed. His breaths are still heavy and he's still covering his mouth.

Robert: I meant talk on the phone.

Frode: That would be weird

Robert: lol why?

Frode: I never talk on the phone. Who does that?

Robert: Are u alone?

Okay, now I'm sucking my lips in. Damn it, my lips taste like Caleb. My whole mouth does. Fangs help me. I lean my head back in frustration.

Frode: Why?

Robert: Who is with you? Wolfie or Kat? Both?

Frode: Why does it matter? I haven't eaten dinner yet, and I need to shower. I thought you wanted to talk but you're just asking me questions about nothing.

Robert: I don't really like Leslie.

Frode: Ok

Why the hell should I care? Why did this require a conversation? Also, if he doesn't like her, why is dating her?

Robert: I've been thinking a lot.

Frode: Ok

Robert: About stuff. Please don't tell anyone what I'm about to say though.

Frode: Uh…don't say anything that you don't want to.

Caleb can see I'm uncomfortable, and not sexually uncomfortable, but not in a state of bloodlust either. I'm uncomfortable because I don't like the way Robert sounds right now. No one should ever tell me a secret. That's like common knowledge among my friends. I cannot keep a secret; they always end up coming out.

Robert: I think I figured something out.

I stand from my bed and pass Caleb the phone. I don't know what Robert's gonna say next, but I don't want to deal with it.

Caleb is looking over the texts. His eyebrows are raised, and his pupils look normal again, yet somehow his eyes look cold as he reads the texts.

"I'm going to deal with this. Is that what you want, Frode? I assume its fine since you handed me the phone."

I sigh and reply, "Yes, go ahead. I have no idea where he's going with this, but I don't want to deal with it."

I really don't want to deal with it. If that makes me a bad friend, that's fine. All I know is that right now, I only care about Caleb's feelings. If Robert talking to me makes him uncomfortable, I don't want that. Also, I really am not that interested in whatever he wants to tell me. It's not like he isn't popular, too, he has a lot of other people he can talk to.

Frode: Robert, this is Caleb. Frode and I are going out.

Robert: Oh, ok. Hi Caleb. Where r u guys going?

Caleb chuckles as he shows me the screen. "Why does going out mean something different here? That's so weird," he says.

I shrug my shoulders. "Just tell him I'm your boyfriend. I'm quite certain he heard about the kiss in the cafeteria."

Caleb: Frode is my boyfriend.

Several minutes have passed since Caleb sent the text and Robert hasn't texted anything back.

"His status shows unavailable now. Here's your phone back," he says while handing me my phone.

"Thank you, Caleb. That was strangely uncomfortable for me. What was he even gonna say? He's dating Leslie, why would he need to tell me something that I shouldn't tell anyone else? Anyway, I'm glad that's over. I guess he figured that he didn't need to."

Caleb is standing next to me, while I scroll through my texts. I cringe and close my eyes while I press the delete button. "I really do not find the female body attractive at all," I say.

Caleb's eyes are wide in shock. "I can not believe that some trampy vamp actually sent you that. Disgusting. What did she hope to gain by doing that? Were you supposed to want to hook up with her? You should change your phone number or block vamps like that."

I nod at him while I scroll through more texts. "Oh fangs, well, that bites. The venue for our gig next weekend got taken by some other band. Wolfie is pissed."

"Will you be able to find another place to play?"

"Oh, I don't know. It happens a lot. I never tell people that I'm Dracula's son, so at new venues, they tend to treat us badly until someone inevitably recognizes me, then everything is different. It's ridiculous, really. Then I have to beg whoever the person is, not to say anything, which is always a headache. Anyway, it will be fine. Wolfie wanted that spot because it was a new one that we hadn't been to yet, it's outside of town. They said we could use it the following weekend. It's cool."

"I really can't wait to hear you sing, Frode. What type of music do you guys play?"

My eyes quickly scan the entirety of my room. How the fangs did he know that I was the vocalist? I didn't even tell him that. "How did you know I was the lead singer?" I ask.

"That's easy. You're always the center of attention, you told me so yourself. Even though you say you hate being the center of attention, I can't see you being in the background of the band. I also don't see any instruments anywhere, or sign of any instruments. Not to mention, every time you scream 'Whaaat' it sounds almost like heavy metal. Seems like you've practiced screaming."

"Well, you aren't wrong. We are a progressive metal band. I have practiced screaming a lot. We have some softer stuff, too, but I have to be in the mood for that. It's not too hard for me to get in the mood normally, though. Having to keep my feelings locked away for so long; most days I either wanted to scream or just cry. I don't know why I should have to even continue pretending in front of my dad, but I just do. Anyway, it's not really relatable to you, since you're already out and your parents are fine with it.

"It is, though. Not for me personally, but do you remember when we were talking earlier, and I said you reminded me of a character in one of my favorite books?"

"Yes, I remember, then you freaked out and made me think you were going to break up with me."

"I need to bring you that book, so you can read it. Are you done reading texts? I should probably head out soon. My mom is probably dying to know about how my first day of school went."

"Oh, your mom, no, my mom! Well, what should we do about my mom? Should I just ask her, or should you ask your mom? Or should we just each ask our own moms?"

Caleb's head tilts back and his gorgeous clean neck in on full display, along with that deviant open-mouth laugh. Fuck...those fangs he has. So perfect.

"I really like it when you ask me five questions at once. It's a very fun thing that you do. I find it to be most adorable," Caleb says. "I can ask my mom and, yes, maybe you should ask your mom. Although, I'll probably wait until tomorrow. Oh no...I forgot tomorrow after school I have a physical at the stupid doctor. I was supposed to have it before the first day of school, but my mom couldn't get me in until tomorrow. Damn it, I won't be able to see you right after school then."

My left eyebrow drops down and I tilt my head at him. "We are in all of the same classes. We'll be together all day tomorrow. You probably forgot about that since we didn't make it to a single class today."

Caleb squeezes me tight in an embrace. He smells so good. I love his scent. I'm not trying to be a pervert here, but I really feel like our bottom halves are joined together by a magnet. A magnet that may also be in my hand, because my right hand really wants to reach down there right now. No, no, I can't do that. I'm too afraid to kiss him right now. My face is tucked tightly in the side of his neck. This is even more dangerous than kissing him. He rubs the left side of my neck softly. The heat I feel between us is insane. I really have to ask my mom about this chemical reaction that the two of us have going on. I'll try and meet up with her after school tomorrow.

"AAAHH" my scream ringtone sounds. I kiss Caleb very quickly on his full wet lips and pull my phone out of my pocket. I drop my head forward, seeing that it's my mom calling. "It's my mom. I really don't want to talk to her right now, but she's probably just calling to see how my first day of school went. You can go out the window or I can walk you back downstairs."

Caleb gestures toward the window. I open the latch, and swing the double windows open for him to leave through. A strong wind blows in, and Caleb's hair is kind of being blown around slightly. Sweet hell, it looks like he's in a damn commercial. My phone stops ringing.

Caleb is standing near the window and holds my hand. "Today was the best day of school, or any other day…just the best day that I've ever had," he says.

I smile bigger than I feel like I ever have before. "Me, too. I'm really happy that my idiot father paired us up. Thank fangs for that. Who knows what would have happened if he hadn't done that."

Caleb pulls me back into an embrace. "I still would have found you today. It was meant to be. My blood knew as soon as I saw you. It was almost like it was searching for you. I felt it as I passed by your row, but I was too nervous to look over. I had no idea what I was feeling, but now that I recall it, there was something strong even then…and I couldn't even see you. Why do you think I tried to hold your hand when you came on stage. I almost ran over to you. It was like my body moved on its own, it felt your presence, and it needed to be near you. I needed you. It was the craziest thing that's ever happened to me. So, we definitely can't give your father credit for this." Caleb kisses my forehead and continues squeezing me.

I can't find any words to say. Nothing I could ever say will sound as good as what he just said to me. "I really like you, Caleb. I'm happy that you held my hand," I say.

"I'll always hold your hand."

"Call me when you get home, or, actually, text me if talking on the phone is too strange." What did I just say? Call me? Where did that come from? I don't care. If I can hear his voice, I'd rather do that.

Caleb's hands are on my shoulders, we're about the same height, so our eyes meet perfectly.

"I don't know your phone number, Frode." Caleb lets out a big laugh.

Damn, that laugh is sexy. too. It's not the deviant one, it's a really happy, beautiful laugh.

I tell Caleb my phone number, there's no need to write it down. I've seen how good his memory is several times today. I'm sure he'll remember it.

He recites it back to me, then squeezes me one more time. "It's really hard for me to leave you. But I know I need to. I'll call you when I get home."

I put my hands behind my back and give Caleb one more quick kiss on the lips. "Fly safe, don't rush home," I say. Fangs, he was flying so fast on the way here, that I almost couldn't keep up. I don't want him to get hurt on his way home.

"I'll fly safe, just because you told me to." He gives me a wink then leaves through the window.

I close the window and sit on my bed. Oh no, his cape is here. I rub the purple jeweled bat. It really is quite beautiful. I gather the cape in my arms and hold it tightly. It smells just like him. What a crazy, amazing day, I just had. I started the day off thinking I would stay locked in my metaphorical closet, and here I am dating a guy. It's still a bit frightening to think about what may happen if my dad finds out.

But, holding Caleb's cape like this, it feels like Caleb is the strongest form of armor that I can imagine. Just holding this and smelling Caleb's scent makes me feel so strong. Shit, I forgot I have to call my mother back.

"Froderick," my dad's voice calls from outside the door, along with a knock.

Ugh, bats. "Yes, Father?"

"Your mother wants you to call her. She said she only saw you online for a few minutes earlier, and then you didn't answer your phone. In her mind, that means you're in the middle of some type of torrid love affair, or off committing some form of indecency. That woman and her imagination," he says, while walking away from my door.

I have to call her, or else she'll just show up here in the middle of the night. I'm starving, though. I need something to eat. I dial my mom's phone number and start walking downstairs.

My mom answers on the first ring, "Frody, my baby. How was your first day of school? Meet any cute new friends?"

"Hello, Mother. You always ask me about boys. Just because you're boy crazy, doesn't mean that I am."

I mean, I am, though, well more specifically I'm crazy about one boy, but she doesn't need to know that.

"How was your first day? Your father sounded miserable. Did something happen with him?" she asks.

"Something always happens with him, but he's just mad because I... Actually, I don't even remember what he's upset about, but I wanted to talk to you about something important."

"Oh, of course, honey, you know I always have time for my little vampster."

A loud howl comes through the phone. That's Wolfman, no doubt about it.

"Frody, honey, mommy's gotta go play with some boys now. Wolfster and I are hitting a few bars tonight," she says.

"Is that Frode?" Wolfman asks.

"Yes, why?" my mother says.

"Tell him that I have that new conditioning treatment for his hair. He can come grab it after school tomorrow," Wolfman says.

"Oh, that's perfect, Wolfster, because my appointment with you is at 2:30. So you give Frode the treatment and we can all sit around and talk about boys, and whatever the hell is pulling on Drac's fangs. Ugh, you should've heard him when I called. He was like whining and pitiful. Him and that replacement cat. So pathetic."

"Mom, I'm still here. Are you asking me to go to the salon tomorrow, or did you just decide that I would do that?"

"Yes, of course it's up to you, but you said you wanted to talk, and Wolf has your hair treatment for you, so we might as well do everything together. It makes sense Frody. It will be fun. Now I really have to go. I'll meet you at the salon after school. Kisses."

I open the fridge which I hadn't done during that brief, bossy exchange. Donut peaches! I love donut peaches; they are so juicy. Yes, I want a donut peach and…what else do I want. I'm looking through the shelves, and I can't find anything else that looks good. Well, I'll just have a peach for now and then see what I want after I finish it. I pull the clear plastic container of four peaches out of the fridge. I hate it when my dad puts them in there. They're always juicy but I like them better at room temperature.

I open the lid on the container and stare at the peaches. You know, donut peaches look rather obscene if I do say so, at least the ones I'm looking at right now do. Fangs, it looks like this damn thing should be wearing underwear! I pull the ripest one out and begrudgingly put the container back in the fridge.

There are a few bananas on the counter. I think I'll have a banana, too. They're a bit greener than I like, but I'm really hungry, and I do love the way donut peaches and bananas taste. Oh my, this is so funny. I have the banana next to the donut peach on the counter. It looks kind of like…hahaha. I'm so happy no one is here. I just held the banana end against the donut peach. What's wrong with me that I find this hilarious? I really do, though. I kind of want to post it. No, no, I can't post it. I'll get yelled at. Well, probably not yelled at, but maybe.

OH MY FANGS. I have a boyfriend. I just remembered. How am I gonna do what the banana just did to the sweet donut peach with Caleb? Wait. Am I the donut peach or the banana? Holy shit. I hadn't even considered which position or how… How do I even ask such a question? Thank fangs Caleb isn't here, or he'd know what I was thinking. I'm rinsing the donut peach under the running water in the kitchen sink. It's so soft and delicate, and I rammed that damn banana right into it just messing around. Oh, no. I can't be the donut peach. Who decides these things? Is there a way for me to determine? Is there a book that tells me if I'm the top or the bottom? Can I be both? Can we switch or is it exclusive? Is one always the banana? Oh my fangs. I really should have thought about this. I always imagined things in a sort of ambiguous way when I pictured them. I never pictured myself on top or bottom. I was just imagining pleasure, but now I'm just not sure which I would prefer.

I cannot have this conversation with Caleb. I absolutely cannot. Wait! I got it. I'll tell him that I have to bite him first, before we ever have sex. Then I'll be able to see if when he did it before, he was on the top or bottom. I hate thinking about this. It feels so stupid to try and define a role like this, but I mean I have to think about it. Who's going to decide, if not me? Well, Caleb, I guess, but what if we both want to do the same thing?

I sink my fangs cleanly into the juicy donut peach. Juice runs down my chin and onto my wrist. Man, that's good.

You know, I've never touched another guy's D. Maybe I should start with that. Maybe once I have a feel for it, I can figure out what I want to do with it. Oh shit…I'm already thinking about what I want to do with it, while holding this banana in my hand. I peel the banana. I wonder how much of this I can fit inside my mouth. I mean no one's here, it's not like I'm doing anything wrong. I'm just really curious how much I can actually get inside there. I look left to right while holding the banana. *Cough, Cough.* Holy shit, not far at all. What the hell? Why is my gag reflex so strong? Is there like another technique? Oh my fangs. Forget it. *Cough Cough.* That actually hurt. I put it in way too deep. Well, it felt like I did, but the bite marks I put on the banana as a marker say otherwise. The bite marks indicate that I will not be good at that, so I shouldn't even try. Damn it. I don't really need to think about this. It's stupid. We don't need to do it anytime soon anyway. Besides, the new plan is to bite Caleb first, sex will come second.

My phone is ringing, well, screeching. Fangs, I need to change my ringtone. That scream is too much. It's a number I don't recognize. Oh wait, it's probably Caleb.

I answer the phone, "Hello?"

Caleb's voice sounds even better on the phone. "Hey…"

I feel so happy right now, just from hearing his voice. I'm smiling so wide. "That was fast, Caleb. You told me you were going to fly slow. Did you eat? I just had some, ahem, fruit."

"I did fly slow; our houses aren't actually that far away from one another. As far as the eating goes, yes, I ate."

"That's good," I say as I walk upstairs toward my room. "I'm going to the salon with my mom after school tomorrow, at the same time as your doctor's appointment. So, we'll both busy"

"Well, I talked to my mom, as soon as I got home. Really quick, though, because she was going out somewhere. I didn't get to ask her about what's happening to us. Will you be at the salon for a long time? Or can we meet up after? I'm sure my mom will want to meet you. Maybe after we're both finished with what we're doing, we can hang at my place."

"I'm not having sex with you yet!" I shout.

"What? Why did you say that? I didn't mention sex."

Well, no, he didn't, that's true. But after the peach and the banana, I needed to make it clear.

"Sorry, there was…I did something stupid. I'm sure that's no surprise to you, but I don't want to talk about it. It was dumb. Sorry for yelling. I just think that I'd rather bite you before we do that. That meaning sex. Bite before sex, is what I'm saying."

I hear only silence. Caleb hasn't said anything.

"Caleb? Are you there?"

"Yeah, I'm here. I'm a little shocked to hear you say that, though. I'm not upset or opposed to that idea, just surprised. I was trying to see if the feelings connection worked from this distance, but I don't think it does. So, I guess we need to be near each other. I know it worked when I passed by your row in the auditorium today and that was quite a distance between us, maybe twenty feet apart? I guess if we're miles apart, it doesn't work. Damn. I would really love to know what the stupid thing was that you did. Must have been very dumb to make you yell like that."

He's so sassy. It's not just me, Caleb is really full of just…sass. I can't think of another word for it.

"Let's not talk about it," I say. "Yes, I'd like to see your house tomorrow, after we're both finished with everything."

Chapter 7
The Need to Bite

The sun is shining brightly through the dark curtains in my bedroom. Even though my curtains are black, they still allow light through, because of the gauze-like fabric. I'm really tired. I stayed on the phone with Caleb until around 4:00 am and now it's 7:30 am. I barely got any sleep. We talked about so many different things. It was really nice. I've never even talked to Wolfie for that long at one time. Even though we were on the phone all night, I'm still really looking forward to seeing Caleb. Ugh, but I'm not looking forward to going to gym today. My hair is really getting so long and whenever the teacher makes us run, my bun always falls out. That draws all kinds of attention from vampires. I stand and look in the mirror and see that it's reaching past my waistline now. My hair is so thick, but today it feels really dry. Normally, it's silky and soft; that's why Wolfman is gonna do the conditioning treatment for me. I guess he's gonna give me a bottle of whatever he uses, too. Originally, I thought I was just bringing the hair product home, but I guess he's gonna condition it for me. I don't mind, though; I love it when he does my hair. It's so comforting. He always gives me a scalp massage, too.

Oh wait, it's Tuesday! Tuesdays are non-physical days in gym. I dress myself quickly and gather my hair in my hand, then tie it tightly in a bun on top. You know, what? Eff it. I'm gonna do something different today. I walk into my bathroom in search of a spool of ribbon, that was from my Halloween costume last year. Wolfie, Kat, and I, along with a few others, dressed up as a band of pirates. I used the ribbon around my pirate bandana, but I had a lot of leftover material. I know it's in this random drawer.

My random bathroom drawer holds all kinds of mysterious things. I always play a game with myself when I reach in. Like what will I pull out? Will it be something useful, or will I die? Okay, I probably won't die, but I have cut myself before. The drawer is packed so full of stuff that I usually just shuffle things around blindly until I find what I'm looking for. There it is! The white spool still holds several yards of bright-red, satin ribbon material on it.

I really want to just tie my hair up in a high ponytail today. Ugh, but with it feeling so dry, I don't want to chance that anyone touches it, and thinks that's what my hair normally feels like. Fangs, that would be so humiliating. I am going to do something different, though. I snip a very long piece of ribbon using the scissors that were in the random drawer. I'm pulling my bun a little farther forward. Alright, I can do this. I like the ribbon, and I think it will look really good alongside my cape, especially with my sparkling ruby clasp. I tie the ribbon around the bun and leave two long strands of the red ribbon hanging down on each side. I stare at my reflection in the mirror; Fangs, I look good.

I'm not bringing Caleb's cape with me, as I head out of my bedroom. He said he'd grab it the next time he comes over. He actually thought it was funny that I was worried about him leaving it here. I mean, it was kind of dumb of me to worry about that. He's nobility, of course he has a closet full of capes. I have at least thirty, Caleb said he has around the same number. Even though I have so many capes, I'm sticking with the one I wore yesterday. I should find

some more gems to have Wolfman sew on for me. Now that my dad has seen the ruby, and Caleb convinced him that it was a way for us to stand out, he isn't going to care about the gems. I kind of want to push it, though, and get a pink one. I do love getting him all flustered. Such a pain in the fangs, he is.

My dad isn't in the kitchen today, like he normally is at breakfast time. He must have been out late last night. I'm still very curious as to why he told me not to bring up Caleb's name to my mom. I'm definitely going to do that when I see her after school. I open the fridge and I'm faced with a choice. I can grab a smoothie or have a donut peach and yogurt. I'm taking the smoothie, that's easier. I quickly peel the foil lid from the strawberry banana smoothie and chug it. I really do love smoothies, they're so delicious.

Alright, well I told Caleb that if I wasn't outside when he passed by to just head to school without me. Oh wow, it's very bright outside this morning. The sun is blinding me. Bats, I hate it when this happens. It is not easy to fly when you can't see.

I'm rubbing my closed eyes when a sultry, smooth voice whispers in my ear, "I really like that ribbon in your hair." I'm pulled into a warm embrace by my handsome boyfriend. My smile is out of control right now.

"How did the timing work out for you to be here? I told you not to wait," I say. I love the feeling of being in his arms like this. It is a bit early, though; I really shouldn't be getting worked up. I can't help it. He's too damn sexy, and his scent early in the morning like this, is just mouthwatering.

Caleb is looking left to right. I know this look; the same thing happened every time yesterday.

"Don't. Not in front of the house. I didn't see my dad before I walked outside, so I don't know where he is. He shouldn't be at school today, since he was there yesterday. Honestly, he could be watching us right now for all I know. Actually, no. He would've already run out here if he saw us holding each other like this. Still, let's wait for a kiss until we get a little distance in between us and the house."

Caleb rubs my back a few times and lets go of me. It's almost a cold sort of feeling that comes over me as we separate. It's so strange. He's right beside me, why does my body react like this? I'm actually cold, and it's the middle of summer. It's August, and too warm for me to feel cold.

Caleb and I head toward the school side by side. It's so nice flying together. It's pretty busy up here today. The sky around us is full of other vamps either on their way to school or work. Still, looking at Caleb beside me, I could almost forget that anyone else exists.

"Hey Frode, Caleb," Robert's voice says from my right side.

Damn it, why would he even come fly by us like this? He never did text me anything after Caleb texted him that I was his boyfriend. It's so awkward. Stuff like this always happens to me. One second, I'm flying high with my boyfriend, feeling free as a damn bat, and the next, I have Robert next to me, who is sure to annoy Caleb to death with his presence.

I give him a small, uncomfortable smile and say dryly, "Hi, Robert." With a greeting like that, anyone would know they weren't wanted.

Caleb hasn't said anything to him. He hasn't even looked his way once.

"Hey, sorry about not finishing our conversation last night," Robert says. "I dropped my phone on the floor in the kitchen and now it's not working. Did you guys end up going to wherever it was you were planning to?"

Whaaat?! No, no no. Does that mean he didn't get the text from Caleb that said he was my boyfriend? This is not happening right now. I just want to go to school with my hot boyfriend and then maybe kiss him later after I get my hair treatment. Is that so much to ask for? Just a normal day? I honestly don't even know anymore. How do I even ask Robert what part of the conversation he dropped his phone after? Do I just say, hey, did you get the text that says Caleb is my boyfriend? I don't effing know what to do here, but Robert is very close to my right side, and Caleb is not liking that.

We reach the school and land quickly. Caleb pulls me in tightly, we're standing a little bit away from the main entrance to the school. I can't see Robert's face, because Caleb's hand is holding the back of my head. My face is tucked into his neck. This is…this is…hot. This is fucking hot. Caleb's heart is pounding, and I can feel his pulse quickening. His skin feels very warm. This feels like a silent claim on me. My mouth opens on instinct, and my fangs lightly touch his neck. I can't see what Robert is doing, though, so for all I know he's already gone.

"He isn't gone," Caleb whispers.

I quickly close my mouth, what was I about to do? I was really about to bite him. I don't think that's ever happened to me before. The urge to taste him was so strong. If he hadn't said anything, I would have done it. Wait a minute—I whisper back, "Did you hear what I was thinking, like all of it?"

Caleb's hand still holds the back of my head. He softly kisses the side of my forehead.

"What the hell? Did you just kiss him, Caleb?" Robert asks.

Caleb sighs. It really feels like he is angry. I mean, I can tell he's angry, but I can also *feel* how angry he is. Any hope of me not thinking about sex is gone…everything he does turns me on. It's ridiculous.

"Robert, I told you last night that Frode was my boyfriend. Now,

I don't know if you really dropped your phone or not, but that doesn't really matter to me. What matters to me, is what you do next."

Holy hell! Come on, I can't take it. That was so hot. I try to lift my head and Caleb gently presses it back down, kissing the side of my forehead again. Oh shit it's happening again. My mouth opens on its own, and my fangs graze his skin. His scent is intoxicating, it's drawing me in like some kind of spell, and I want to bite him. I need to. I don't think I can wait any longer. Not with him pressing my face into his neck.

"I had no idea," Robert says. "I didn't know. I really didn't. People were talking about you guys being all over each other yesterday, but I didn't know you were a couple. I also didn't really believe what I heard, because I didn't think that Frode was…"

Spell broken. What the hell did he just say? I pull my head up quickly and ask, "You didn't think that Frode was what? Finish your sentence, Robert."

Caleb pulls my hand. Which is a good thing because for some reason I am really mad right now. What the hell? Robert's just standing here with one hand on his hip and the other covering his mouth.

"I didn't think you were gay," Robert says looking into my eyes.

"Okay, so, I am, and I'm with Caleb. What else do you need to talk about?" I ask. "Caleb is gay, too," I add.

Caleb is holding in the fact that he found that little addition of mine hilarious, but I can feel what he's feeling right now. He went from very angry to thinking that I am hilarious and maybe a bit of a trainwreck. Okay, I don't know *exactly* what he was thinking, but that's my best guess.

Robert's expression is somewhere between confused, sad, and angry. He says, "I, um, I understood that Caleb was gay when I saw him kiss you on the forehead and stare me down. I'm all caught up.

Doesn't really help my situation. I'll say that much. Oh well. Later." Robert shrugs and walks away.

Who the hell does he think he is? Looking at the two of us like we did something wrong and then walking away. What was with that "Oh well" he added on, too?

I exhale loudly and Caleb squeezes my hand three times, as we start walking toward the school entrance. A lot of vampires are looking over at us; most have stopped talking completely, as we reach the stone steps to the main doors.

Caleb and I walk inside, hands still tightly clasped. I'm really not worried about my dad being here. So, I think it's fine if we hold hands. My cape kind of blocks our hands anyway. Oh fangs. I can't catch a break.

Leslie stands directly in front of us, unmoving. "Good morning, have you two seen my boyfriend? You know, the vamp that's really hot. His name is… Oh, wait, I actually really like your hair ribbon today, Frody. Why haven't you worn one before?" she asks.

"Move, watermelon vamp," Caleb says.

Leslie places a hand on her hip and wags her finger side-to-side at us. "I will not move. You can't talk to me like this. My mom came here yesterday, and she told Ms. Tansy all about you two being mean to me and you know what? She said that you two have to be nice to me."

Caleb's right eyebrow is down, looking at her in doubt. "Oh, please," he says. "What even gives you the right to talk to the two of us? Frode has nothing to do with you anymore. Don't you know your place? Or has that tackily dressed mother of yours deluded your thoughts into thinking we're on equal footing?"

Daaamn.

Leslie is stunned. She isn't even moving. Her mouth is open and she's just staring at Caleb.

We really need to get to class, though.

In the nicest voice I can muster, I say, "Leslie, move out of the way. Ms. Tansy would never even dream of telling the two of us that we need to be nice to you. Give me a break. Also, we did see your mother yesterday, and even she knew she had no right to speak to us, and yet you're here blocking the way."

"This is funny," Caleb says.

"What's funny?" I ask.

He's whispering in my ear, "It's funny because both this disgusting watermelon vamp and her confused boyfriend are both trying to date you." But Caleb is not laughing, and he does not think it's funny. Caleb is mad. Like really mad. "Move, now," he says to Leslie.

Oh, look at that. She's moving to the side.

Caleb and I continue on toward our classroom which is just a few doors down. We enter holding hands and sit at two desks in the far back. We don't have assigned seating in our school. It's always just whoever gets here first, gets to sit where they want. I always prefer the back. I can't stand the feeling of someone behind me breathing down my neck. Well, I could stand the feeling of Caleb's breath on the back of my neck. Oh, what is wrong with me? How am I going to get through any classes with him beside me. He's in all of my classes! He's covering his smile right now, while looking over. Shit, I forgot he can read my thoughts…or feel them. Oh, hells help me if he felt what I just felt. I look at him and shake my head while I let out a sigh.

The teacher isn't here yet, other vampires are piling in through the door. I turn to face Caleb and notice his clasp is a red bat today. I didn't even see it on the way here.

"I really like that clasp. It's really nice. Now, we match." I instantly regret saying that. Why would I say that? Oh my fangs, I am so stupid.

Caleb tilts his head at me. "Why do you think I wore this cape?" he asks.

I shrug in response.

"Frode, I picked this one because you told me last night that the red ruby clasp cape is your favorite. I wanted to match."

I put my head in my hands on my desk. "That's very sweet."

The classroom smells horrible. I'm overwhelmed by the scent of cheap bite spray and perfume.

Caleb leans in close and whispers, "It's getting stronger."

You know? I'm almost afraid to ask what he's talking about, but since I'm me, I'm going to ask.

"What is getting stronger, Caleb?"

"The connection we have. I can hear your thoughts more clearly, and I feel what you're feeling a little more than yesterday, too. Is that the same for you?"

My eyebrows raise. I…is it even safe for me to think anymore? Oh my fangs, Caleb is laughing. It's not safe. I am no longer safe inside my own mind.

I'm trying to remain calm. "Yes, I do believe I am experiencing the same things. I would ask that you try very hard not to hear my thoughts, though. You feeling what I'm feeling doesn't bother me. But honestly, I don't feel safe inside my own head at this point, which is a problem for me, because I have a lot of conversations in there. Now, listen, you need to pay attention in class, because yesterday most teachers wouldn't have gone over many things, because it was the first day. So usually, people are still getting their schedules sorted and vamps are coming in and out. So, we didn't miss much, but today, they'll be going over everything that we'll be doing in each class."

The teacher walks in as all the seats are filled; with the exception of the seat in front of me. Oh my fangs. This is not real life. Rachel Bertoth raises her eyebrows at me, then sits in front of me, occupying the last remaining seat.

This is terrible. Just terrible. Rachel is the vampire that sent me the dirty pictures yesterday. Now, I didn't respond, so she has no idea if I've seen them or not, but either way, Caleb can hear my thoughts, so he knows exactly who she is now. I'm not even going to look over at him. I don't want to know what kind of a face he is making.

The teacher stands in front of the class. "Welcome to Biology. For the next three weeks, we will be working in pairs. Now, I have taken the liberty of pairing up Mr. Cheval and Mr. Dracula, so you little vamps don't have to fight over them," the teacher says.

Mr. Prinaldi is a very tall, thin vampire, with pale skin. He's probably only in his late thirties, but he's always stressed out. He's been my teacher for the last two years, and it's always the same with him. It's kind of a strange thing that my dad put in place at this school; teachers move up with the students each time the students finish a year in school. So, Mr. Prinaldi was my biology teacher in ninth grade and tenth grade, and he's my teacher again this year, and he will be again next year, too. Now, why would my father put such an asinine rule in place? Well, the answer is quite simple. My mother. He lashed out at everyone after my mother left and declared that all teachers had to stay with their original group of students through each grade. It was the craziest thing. Of course, no teacher would argue with him. Anyway, that's the story. It is kind of nice having the same teachers, though.

Rachel silently drops a folded piece of paper over her shoulder, onto my desk.

Caleb stands and grabs the paper before I can. He's walking toward the teacher with it. Rachel has no idea, because she didn't see

Caleb grab it. Caleb passes the paper to the teacher and points at Rachel while whispering.

He really is so hot. Every vamp in the class is staring at him. Why does that bother me? He's not even interested in anyone else. It doesn't make sense for me to be bothered. I wonder if any other vampires feel this way? My emotions are just all over the place when it comes to him.

The teacher opens the folded paper. Caleb is standing at his side, reading the note alongside him. Sweat can be seen through the teacher's thinning blond hair, under the bright classroom lights. Poor Mr. Prinaldi, he looks even more stressed out than normal.

"She needs to leave," Caleb says.

Mr. Prinaldi is nodding his head in agreement. "Rachel, gather your things and go to the office. This note that you put on Froderick's desk is unacceptable. I don't know why you would think it was okay to say things like this to him. Hurry up, now. I'll call Ms. Tansy and explain what happened."

Rachel stands and looks behind at me. "I can't believe you're not gonna stick up for me after you saw those pics I sent you. Wow," she says.

I avoid eye contact with her. "I didn't look at anything. Whatever you sent me was deleted as soon as I saw your name and the subject. I knew what was in there, I just chose not to look at them, because it doesn't interest me."

Rachel walks away, carrying her things, toward the door.

Caleb is really staring her down from the front of the classroom. He looks so cute in his uniform. I kind of wish he'd stand up there and teach the class or something. Ha ha. That's funny, imagining Caleb as a teacher.

If I remember later, I'm going to ask Wolfman if there's anything he can do to help Mr. Prinaldi out. Wolfman is pretty chill, he's always looking for new friends, plus he may be able to help with Mr. Prinaldi's thinning hair situation.

Caleb is walking back to his seat now. I'm shaking my head no at him as he approaches. He's thinking about kissing me, and he better not even try it. Actually, let's see how well he can read my mind. Caleb if you kiss me, I'm going to smack you. I will most definitely smack you.

Caleb sits in his seat with a wide grin. "I heard you. Don't smack me," he says.

I have no words for what just happened. No words and no thoughts.

The class ends shortly after everyone else separates into pairs. Caleb and I are headed toward the next class. As we step into the crowded hallway, a hand pulls at my cape and a voice says, "Stop walking, asshat!"

Ah, yes, it's Martin. Martin is a good friend of mine. He's been in a wheelchair since he was four years old. I've known him since we were around eight, he's a really cool vamp. Girls love him, too. He's quite a pervert, though, and he has a real dirty mouth. Of course, neither of those things bother me, but other guys tend to be jealous of all the attention he gets from girls.

"Hey, Martin," I say as we press our fists together.

"Who's the vamp beside you? This the guy I heard about yesterday?" he asks, looking at Caleb.

"Oh, this is my boyfriend Caleb Cheval, why? What did you hear?"

Yes, I just said boyfriend like it was nothing. I don't know how I did it, but it just came right out. It's amazing, I'm not even afraid of what anyone thinks. Caleb and I have been holding hands since before Martin approached us anyway, so it's not like he didn't already know. He came from behind us, though, so this could be a shock to him.

"What the finger snaps did you just say, bro?" Martin asks me.

"I said Caleb is my boyfriend. What the hell are finger snaps?"

Martin pulls his wheels back, then moves his chair directly in front of the two of us. Vamps are rushing around us to get to class.

"Oh, finger snaps is what I'm saying now, instead of the other word that I love so much. My girlfriend doesn't like me cursing. Unless it's when she's in my bed!" Martin is laughing loudly at his own comment. He stops laughing and starts again, "Seriously, I didn't know you were into guys, Frode."

Caleb speaks up, "Hi, I'm Caleb Cheval, sorry for not introducing myself earlier. I've met a lot of very strange vamps, all who seem to be obsessed with Frode, so I was just trying to get a read on you."

Martin's eyebrows are pulled down, along with his mouth. "You were trying to see if I liked Frode? Nah, man. I'm into biscuits of the frontal kind. I'm not into guys."

Caleb looks disgusted. "Everyone here speaks so crudely. It's really beyond my understanding. Come on, Frode, we're going to be late."

Caleb turns toward Martin and says, "It was…I met you. I met you and now I know you."

"Alright, later, Martin," I say, as Caleb pulls me away by the hand.

We enter the classroom and most of the seats have already been taken. Oh boy, Caleb is not going to like this. I can fix it, though; Kat is sitting in the back row, and she'll move if I ask her to.

We walk toward Kat, and I say, "Hey, Kat, can I sit here? There aren't any other open seats beside each other and I really want to sit by Caleb."

Kat is shaking her head no, and tilting her head toward the left where Kressa is sitting. She's giving me the craziest eyes right now, too.

Caleb seems to understand. He pulls my hand. "That's what I thought," he whispers.

The teacher isn't inside the classroom yet. Caleb is carrying a desk over toward the empty one beside Kat. He places it down then goes back for the chair. I sit in the seat next to Kat, and Caleb sits at his newly placed desk beside me. I have no idea how he thinks the teacher won't mind this. The rows were all neatly organized and even. He just made a complete mess of the pattern back here.

All the girls in class are giggling at the two of us. I think enough people have seen us now to know we're together.

What…what is happening? Kressa is walking over. Her long blonde hair now has pink on the ends. It wasn't like that yesterday. It looks cool, though. She stands in front of Caleb and me, and leans down. She whispers, "Frode, I had no idea you liked guys. I just heard about this. First, you don't tell me you're Dracula's son and then you don't tell me you're into guys. That's super lame. I'm bi, so you're in good company. I like both, we could've spent so much time over the weekend talking about guys, you know? But speaking of my taste in vamps—is Kat actually straight? Because she is definitely my type. She's perfect, but I've seen her all over Wolfie a few times. Seems like it's not real, though." She covers her mouth. "I'm sorry, I shouldn't have said that about her. I shouldn't have asked either. Don't say anything, okay? Sorry, bye." She hurries back to her desk just as the teacher walks in.

This teacher is one of my favorites, but not because she's nice. Most vamps hate her because she's quite strict. I don't really mind it, though. She treats us all the same, regardless of who we are. So, she definitely isn't going to let Caleb leave his desk beside mine.

Ms. Phlip is a much older woman, with short gray hair. My dad told me that she was a private security officer before she became a teacher, which explains her no-nonsense temperament.

"You really think she's going to challenge me?" Caleb asks me.

I nod silently in reply.

Caleb raises his hand. Ms. Phlip acknowledges him, "Yes, Caleb Cheval, welcome. I'm Ms. Phlip. How can I help you, now that you've already made a mess of my desks back there?"

Caleb is so charming, and he isn't fazed at all. He's smiling brightly at her. "I apologize, I really am not yet acclimated, and I feel comfortable sitting next to Frode. Since there were no desks open beside him, I moved one. I didn't think it would be a problem. I don't want to make myself an inconvenience, and Frode has been so helpful that I've been relying on his guidance since yesterday."

Ms. Phlip beckons him with her finger. "Mr. Cheval, do you have any idea how many vamps in this school want to sit beside Frode? Come up here, I'll show you."

She walks around to the chair behind her desk and shows him her computer screen. Caleb's eyes are wide, looking at whatever she's showing him.

"Yes," she says. "All, except two students in this class, you would've been the third, have asked to sit beside Frode. I have all kinds of messages in here from parents, vamps, sisters, best friends. Everyone wants to be friends with him. If I let you move your desk like that today, what's to stop anyone else from asking me to do the same tomorrow?"

I stand and walk to the front of the class beside Ms. Phlip. "Ms. Phlip, I'm your favorite, we both know that. Please let Caleb sit by me. I don't want to sit by anyone else, and my dad asked me to keep a close eye on him. I'm sure my dad would consider it a favor as well. Do you like my ribbon by the way? I haven't gotten that many compliments on it. I'm rather shocked by that," I say, tightening the ribbon.

Ms. Phlip whispers, "Maybe no one has complimented you on it, because your boyfriend is burning holes through them with his eyes." She raises her chin at Caleb, who is indeed staring down the rest of the vampires in the classroom.

"Ms. Phlip, who said Caleb is my boyfriend?"

"Oh, Froderick. Teachers talk, dear. That little display you two put on in the lunchroom yesterday had vampires climbing the walls. Not to mention, Darna Marnkov coming into the school screaming about the two of you and, then, the cafeteria incident, set the whole thing up rather nicely. Now, as you know, you are my favorite, so I can ask you this plainly; what the hell are you thinking kissing him in school? Aren't you afraid of your father finding out? Surely you know how he responds when he doesn't understand something? He's completely irrational, then he just goes from teacher to teacher looking for a sympathetic ear. If that fails, he just puts a rule in place that makes him feel better about whatever the situation is. Don't get me started on his time traveler's theory. He's always going on about it in the staff lounge. It's ridiculous."

"Of course, I'm afraid, but also what am I supposed to—"

I stop speaking to Ms. Phlip and tug at Caleb's cape. "Hey, stop staring everyone down," I say. Caleb grabs my hand and holds it. That didn't work, now he's just staring at everyone while he holds my hand. With my right hand I rub my temples with my thumb and index finger.

"Ms. Phlip, yes, I am scared but I've hid this for so long and I really like Caleb. I should be allowed to be myself. If I can't be myself in my own home, shouldn't I at least be able to be myself at school?"

Caleb squeezes my hand three times and smiles softly at me,

momentarily breaking his intense stare-down with the rest of the class.

Ms. Phlip sees Caleb and I exchange a soft glance and says, "Okay, fine, leave the desk where it is, it's alright. Both of you go back to your seats. You have my permission to move the desk beside Frode whenever there isn't an open seat. You have to put it back in its correct place after class. That's the deal."

We thank her and walk toward our desks. Caleb is quite proud of himself, even though I was the reason we won this round. Ms. Phlip turns her back to the class and writes on the large white dry erase board on the front wall of the classroom.

Caleb quickly kisses my cheek. "Thank you. You did win this round for us."

Kat tosses a folded piece of paper on my desk. I open it and immediately read it:

Hey, what was Kressa saying to you earlier? She's not into you or Wolfie is she? Did she say anything like that?

I quickly write back:

No. She does not like Wolfie or me.

I fold the note and toss it onto Kat's desk.

Kat seems happy now. She folds the note and sticks it inside her bag.

Ms. Phlip reads the remaining items on the syllabus one at a time. This is so boring. Thankfully, the greatest sound in the world can be heard. It's the sound of the bell. Thank fangs, I thought I was gonna die if I had to listen to any more of this.

Caleb grabs the desk and lifts it, while I grab the chair he moved and follow behind. We place the desk and chair down, then leave for the next class.

"Let's walk fast," Caleb says while pulling my hand. "Which door is it? I want to get there early this time."

We're the first ones inside and we choose the two seats in the back right corner. This is a lab, though, so it's just one big desk with two chairs. Kind of great that I'm in here with Caleb, otherwise I would've gotten stuck with some other vamp. Normally, I hate desks like this but not right now. Caleb's chair is pulled right next to mine. It's really cozy back here, too. The air vent overhead blows strongly in this corner, which is good. It keeps all of the weird smells away from me.

Caleb takes his cape off, he places it neatly across his lap. A slow stream of air leaves my mouth, looking at him. The top button of his shirt is open, and his neck is on full display beside me. He's tilting his head side to side.

"What's wrong with your neck?" I ask.

He raises the left side of his mouth into a half smirk and whispers, "After this class is lunch, then it's free period, right? Locker room time, if I'm not mistaken. I'm just stretching my neck out. The sooner I do it, the better I can be in there."

What the eff did he just whisper? He didn't whisper that. Maybe our thoughts are getting mixed up now. Yeah, I bet that's what it is. Since we can hear each other's thoughts, I probably just imagined that he said that.

Caleb and I are still the only ones in the classroom. Caleb grabs my face and looks into my eyes. "You didn't imagine that. I said what you heard. Should I stop stretching my neck?" he asks then softly presses our lips together momentarily.

"No. Stretch it out," I say.

I said that, I really did, but I can't look at him. If I look at him, I'm not going to be able to wait until we… Oh fangs, his hand is on my thigh. I shake my head, and place my hand firmly atop his, stopping it from creeping up any further.

"Hey," Caleb whispers. "Let me just move my hand closer. I won't do anything. I promise."

I squeeze his hand, while looking ahead, avoiding eye contact. Caleb's hand is moving closer toward the inside of my thigh. I have to trust him, he said he wouldn't do anything. The problem here isn't him, the problem is me. I want him, very badly.

"Shh, your thoughts are so vulgar. I'm not going to move any closer. I promised you, didn't I? Now, you need to stop thinking those things," he says.

Holy bats, is there a thing where vampires in couples get turned on when their partner tells them what to do? Because if there is, I have that thing, or I'm a fan of that, whatever it is. That was incredibly hot, him talking to me like that. Shit, I forgot he can hear my thoughts. I lean my head back and exhale.

Caleb's hand grips my thigh firmly. "Shhh, you're doing it again," he says.

Vampires are entering the class; the table in front of us and directly beside us are quickly claimed.

Oh no. Leslie just walked in with Robert. Caleb pulls his hand off my thigh and hangs his arm around my neck. I quickly kiss his cheek, bringing a big smile to his face.

Leslie and Robert sit at the desk that is one row up from ours to the right. Leslie is looking over her shoulder at us. Caleb's gaze hasn't left the two of them. Robert hasn't turned around once. I don't think he will either. Caleb was pretty serious this morning. Also, with Caleb being a noble, Robert would be in big trouble if they really did get into any kind of an argument. Robert was smart to walk away this morning.

The good news here is that our body temperatures cooled instantly when those two walked in. The class is loud with gossip of all kinds, since the teacher hasn't shown up yet.

The bad news, obviously, well, maybe not obviously, but the worst news by far, is that our connection is getting stronger with each moment. I really don't understand it. All I know is that I can feel how much Caleb hates both Leslie and Robert. I can hear the things that he's thinking. It's not pretty.

Caleb lightly pokes my cheek, drawing me out of my thoughts. "Hey, we already know I hate them. Where is the teacher? It's already almost lunch time. The class is over in fifteen minutes."

I playfully pinch his chin. "I don't know, but I was wondering if you thought the library might have some kind of a book on what's happening with us."

Caleb lightly kisses the inside of my hand before I can pull it back.

"I'm always down for a trip to the library, but that means we have to see Ms. Beagle which we should probably do anyway."

I stand from my seat and take Caleb's hand. "Come on, let's head to the cafeteria, then we'll go to the library. The teacher obviously isn't coming."

Caleb fastens his cape around his neck, and we leave the classroom together.

Chapter 8
Fancy Ass Nobles

Caleb looks side-to-side and lightly presses me against the brick wall. He whispers in my ear, "You said we were going to the library after the cafeteria. Does that mean we aren't going into the locker room? Because, if so, I'm going to need at least one kiss while no one else is out here."

Damn him, damn him and his cotton candy breath. It's like the taste of the cotton candy draws me in with its sweetness, then that damn fresh baked bread smell is just the final nail in the coffin.

"Kiss me, Caleb."

Caleb presses our mouths together fiercely. He tastes so good. I haven't tasted this since last night. The other kisses were too quick, but not this one, this one is hot, wet and fierce. His tongue is amazing. I want all of it.

Hearing the bell ring, we quickly break our kiss. Our mouths are apart, but our bodies are very close to one another. His hands are still firmly on my waist.

Caleb puffs his cheeks up with air, it's funny. He looks like a chipmunk with acorns in his mouth or something. I squeeze his cheeks quickly and a puff of air comes out. So cute. His face is adorable.

"Come on, let's go get lunch, then we can decide if we want the library or the locker room," I say holding his hand.

"I'm not even hungry. Are you hungry, Frode?"

I place a hand on my stomach. "No, I'm actually not hungry. Do you want to just go to the library?" I ask.

I'll be safe in the library from our urges. No one wants to deal with deleting footage again. I know I sure don't.

Caleb nods in agreement. We swing our clasped hands together while we walk toward the library. The halls are pretty empty, since everyone is at lunch right now. I really can't imagine a better feeling than this.

Caleb pulls the library door open, and we're greeted with the sight of Ms. Beagle's miserable face. I really did want to avoid her. I would have been more than happy to just send the info we got from my dad in an email. I didn't feel like seeing her today, honestly.

"Hello, Ms. Beagle," I say.

Caleb smiles and waves at her.

"Hello, you two. What did you find out about my niece?" she asks.

We stand in front of her on the other side of the tall desk.

"Well, Ms. Beagle, is there anything that you didn't tell us yesterday, that maybe you remembered after we left? Because it seems like you may have left some details out." I say.

Obviously, I'm bluffing here, because not even my dad knows what the family is supposedly hiding, he just said he *feels* like they are hiding something.

"No, certainly not," she says. "I told you everything. What did Ms. Tansy say? Or did you need to still speak with your father? How far did the investigation get?"

Caleb speaks up, "We spoke to Ms. Tansy, but she said the case is in Mr. Dracula's hands and she can't do anything about it. We still need to try and understand why Mr. Dracula didn't let it pass. Frode asked you that, because the whole thing seems rather strange, almost like there is a crucial detail that is missing. What you've said to us doesn't add up. Kressa is a new student here, she's half mermaid, he had no problem with her. Why would he reject an application due to your niece being a half mermie? That's a rhetorical question, he wouldn't do that. If he didn't want transfers, he would just say so. He has no need to just allow some in for show. He runs the entirety of the vampire world. How would this benefit him? There must be something that he didn't understand. He tends to get hung up on things that he can't understand. Wait, I think I might have thought of something."

My mouth is open. "No, you didn't! I thought of it, and you just heard it in my head! Don't steal my idea, Caleb! Ms. Beagle, before Caleb tries to take credit for something he heard inside my head, let me ask you, are your niece's parents still together?"

Ms. Beagle's eyes go wide, she looks at the papers on her desk. "I'm not going to answer that," she says.

I throw my hands up in frustration and question her, "Well, then why are you asking us to help you? How can you say one minute that you told us everything and the next say that you won't answer a simple question? That doesn't make sense."

Caleb is beside himself in frustration. He throws a hand up, then runs it down his face. He looks at me and shouts, "You stole what I was going to say. I thought of that and then you said it, Frode!"

"Whaaat?! I most certainly did not, Caleb! You heard it in my head and then you tried to say it, so I said it before you could say it!"

Caleb is shaking his head side to side. "No, no, sir. You heard it and stole it. You're like a little thought thief!" he says.

"Oooh, Caleb! Can you hear my thoughts right now? Because right now, I'm very angry."

Ms. Beagle says, "Sssshhh! Library, remember? Also, can you two hear each other's thoughts? You keep saying things that make it sound like you can."

"Yes," we both say.

"The other reason that Caleb and I are here, is so that we can see if you have a book that may explain why this is happening. We don't understand what's going on either. It doesn't make sense. We haven't even bitten one another yet."

"Did you just say yet?" she asks. "You're just kids, you can't be biting each other. Come on. We're all vampires, but save that bite for after marriage. I'm a realist, okay? I know what goes on in the locker room, but biting should not be one of those things."

I love it when adults say these things to me. My father has been begging me to bite someone for years. It's ridiculous.

Caleb is giving Ms. Beagle a very annoyed face. If he weren't a noble, that face would have gotten him into a lot of trouble by now.

"Ms. Beagle," Caleb says. "We didn't come here to hear your antiquated views. Are there any books here that cover topics on pureblood connections?"

"Well, I think there are a few," she says. "They are in section 547, upstairs, where you two were yesterday. Don't even think of doing that again, by the way. The cameras are on, and I'm going to sit right here and watch you both," she says.

"That's weird," Caleb says to her. "Why would you want to watch two teenagers making out? If you already know what we're going to do, shouldn't you just turn the camera off?"

I pull Caleb's hand away from Ms. Beagle's desk toward the stairs. "Come on, free period starts in fifteen minutes. Calm down," I whisper.

We walk upstairs holding hands, the section we're looking for is against the back wall. It would have been nice if she gave us a few book names to find. Caleb pulls me toward the shelves, scanning quickly. His eyes move very fast while searching.

"What are you even looking for? She gave us nothing to go on, besides a section," I say.

"Well, they are reference books so it's pretty easy to see what they're about on the spine. Here, this may be something," he says, pulling a black book from the shelf.

"*Pureblood Relations*, yeah that seems like it could have something useful. Let's check it out and we can read it at your house later." I say as Caleb reads the back cover.

"Yeah, let's do that," Caleb says grabbing my hand.

We walk downstairs back to Ms. Beagle who isn't at her desk. Caleb is so impatient right now. His head is moving all over the place, looking for her. He looks like one of those bobblehead vampires that people put inside their offices. "Ms. Beagle," he calls toward the open door behind the desk.

Ms. Beagle emerges, shrugging her shoulders at us. "What? Are you two done already?"

"Yes," I say. "We found a book. Is this one of the ones you were talking about?"

Ms. Beagle takes the book from Caleb's hand and looks it over, while scanning it with a handheld book scanner. "Yes, which one of you is checking it out? I need to assign it to one of you."

I raise my hand. "I'll take it, you can assign it to me."

She hands the book to me and whispers, "Listen, I really can't get into details about the thing with my niece. It's a very private family matter. I'm not sure my family would want me discussing such things. Do you think your father would agree to a private meeting with me? I'd like to make a sort of appeal if he would hear it. Although, I'm not quite sure where things stand as far as he's concerned. All I know is that the application was rejected and that it's under review, but I think the review has more to do with my sister-in-law saying that she's going to file a lawsuit against the school. Your father didn't seem too pleased about that and said he would review the application one more time."

I whisper to her, "I understand, Ms. Beagle, but my father hates lying. Just between you, me, and Caleb, he is convinced someone is lying about something on the application. My advice would be to try and meet with him yourself and tell him the truth. I think that's probably a good idea but if he thinks you're lying, he'll most likely fire you. Of course, I have no idea if he'll meet with you, but you're an employee, so I think he would if you ask him."

The bell is ringing, Caleb is pulling me toward the exit before I can even say another word to Ms. Beagle.

I whisper, "Hey, stop pulling me," while elbowing him playfully.

Caleb takes the book from me and smiles brightly as we step outside. "Free period. I've been waiting for this since last night," he says.

What the hell does that mean? Should I be afraid? Because, honestly, I don't know if I'm afraid or turned on... Feels like both. I mean, I'm gonna get to do things with Caleb in the locker room in just about two minutes. That makes me really hot just thinking about it but no, no, wait the donut peach... No, that's stupid we aren't going to get that far. I'm sure we'll just make out. Hopefully the whole class isn't in there, since it's still the beginning of the school year. Either way, the locker room is huge and it's not like people are right near each other.

"Why are you thinking about fruit?" Caleb asks.

Oh my fangs...I definitely can't even think about the real reason. I'm hungry, I'm hungry, I'm hungry. If I think the same thought over and over, maybe that's what Caleb will hear.

"I'm hungry, can't you hear my thoughts?" I ask.

Caleb drops his right eyebrow as we reach the closed locker room door.

I open the door and we walk inside. This is going to be quite a scene. I mean, we are the first two guy vampires that I know of that have come in the locker room during free period together. I've never seen it before. Oh, now I'm getting nervous. No, no, it's fine. Who cares? Everyone wants to make out with the both of us, anyway. It makes more sense that we'd want to make out with each other. It's pretty quiet as we enter, there doesn't seem to be many people inside. Everyone is generally quiet in here, but if anyone starts getting too loud, someone usually hits the speaker on the wall and turns the music on. That's killed the moods of many vampires, then again it just depends on the type of music that gets turned on.

Caleb points toward the wall controls, before we reach the interior changing rooms. "Can we put music on this? Or is this for something else?" he asks me.

"It's for music. A lot of the sports teams use it before and after games. We can use it."

Caleb presses several buttons finding a popular progressive rock band's channel. I actually love this band, too. Their music is insane, and the guitar playing is nothing if not impressively sexy. The lead guitarist is very cute, too, well actually he's hot, but not as hot as Caleb.

Caleb raises his eyebrows at me and pulls me toward the changing rooms. There are about thirty individual changing rooms inside the private area. Each has its own door and a small seat bench inside. Obviously, this wasn't made with teenagers making out in here in mind, it was made for athletes to have room to put their equipment on, and to be able to undress in private. Well, not just athletes, but everyone. Our locker room is also genderless. The old-style locker rooms are so strange. Who would feel comfortable changing in front of someone else? I definitely wouldn't. What a weird concept, too. Like just because you share the same gender at birth, you should be okay with being naked in front of someone else? That's dumb. I wouldn't be okay with it. I also wouldn't be okay with Caleb being naked in front of anyone else.

Caleb is leading us all the way down toward the last set of changing rooms. I can hear some heavy breathing and there are quite a few doors closed, which means they are occupied. No one saw us come in, so I feel a little more relaxed than I thought I would.

Caleb opens the last door on the left. "Is this one okay? Or is there…wait. No. Have you used this room before?" he asks me.

My mouth is open. I cannot believe he even asked me that. "No, I have not used this room. Why would you even—"

Caleb pulls me inside and throws the library book on the bench, then locks the door. He turns to me and aggressively grabs my face with both hands, pressing our mouths together. Mmm…cotton effing candy. His tongue is so hot and it's searching the entirety of my mouth. Where can I put my hands? What do I do with my hands? I want to…

Caleb briefly pulls back and pushes me against the wall of the room. He presses our mouths together again, grabbing my hands and placing them on his waist. He's unbuttoning my shirt. Oh my fangs… Shit… I pull his tucked shirt out of his pants and begin unbuttoning it. Our kiss is full of hunger and thirst, and our bodies are desperate to become one. My shirt buttons are open, and I quickly separate the last button on Caleb's, sliding his shirt off his strong shoulders, and gently pull my mouth back from his. He is less gentle with me; he grabs the top of my sleeves and pulls the shirt down my shoulders in one forceful move. Our chests are bare, and our mouths connect again. Caleb is coming at me hard right now. His right hand is on the lower part of my back and he's pressing our lower halves tightly together. I slide my hands up his back and pull him in closer. He's looking at me intensely, his pupils are dilated again. Oh shit. he's kissing me deeper; my head hits the wall. Caleb's hand moves quickly to where my head connected with the wall and holds the back of my head. His hand is moving up through my hair. My bun is definitely not going to survive this. Caleb's breaths are heavy and hot as he pulls his mouth back only slightly and whispers, "Can I take this out?"

Wait, what? Take what out, what is he asking me? Ah, screw it, he can take whatever he wants out. I nod and press our mouths back together. Caleb pulls the ribbon from my hair and tries to get my bun loose. I reach up top and take my hair tie out. My hair falls quickly down to my sides. Caleb backs up. His eyes are lost in lust, looking me over. He's never seen my hair down. I guess he likes it. He's nodding at me while he holds the ribbon in his hand. "Your hair is gorgeous, just like the rest of you," he whispers.

I avoid his gaze and turn my head slightly to the right. I tuck my hair behind my ear, exposing my neck. I know I shouldn't do this, but I want to feel his mouth on my neck. Caleb knows exactly what I want, he gently holds my face and presses his full wet lips softly against mine.

What the hell? Oh no…

"Come on let's go for a back room, then we don't have to be quiet," Leslie's voice says.

Caleb's eyes are wide as he pulls his lips back from mine. He inhales then says loudly, "Oh gross! Watermelon vamp, get out of here! No one wants to smell you right now!"

I assume she's with Robert, but I have no idea, whoever she's with hasn't said anything, and all I can smell is Caleb.

"Callum, what the hell are you doing in here? You are *not* in there with Frode, don't you tell me that you are!" she yells.

I let out an overexaggerated sigh. "Leslie, it is none of your business who *Caleb* is in here with. But whoever you're with, can you guys just please go to another section?"

"Go away!" Caleb shouts through the door.

His hands are on his hips, and I can finally take in the sight of his chest. It's perfect and I really want to put my mouth on it. Oh fangs, I was really about to let him bite me. It's kind of a good thing that Leslie came in, because I don't know what I was thinking. Imagine if he would've sunk his fangs into me and then Leslie's obnoxious voice interrupted our first bite. Oh, Caleb would've probably had her exiled. I think he may do that right now, honestly. He's yelling really loudly.

"Watermelon vamp! We are the two highest ranking vampires in this school. I don't care who you're with, if it's not Frode's father, then you have no right to be near us. I'm not asking you to leave; I'm telling you to. I assume you're with your boyfriend. It would be rather embarrassing for everyone involved, if you two hook up and start moaning, while saying my boyfriend's name. So, do yourselves a favor and go somewhere else."

"Oooh, I'm going to tell Ms. Tansy on you guys. I will not be treated this way! Come on, Robert." Leslie says, her voice trailing off as she stomps away loudly.

The sound of the bell ringing replaces Leslie's annoying voice.

Caleb's head drops forward, hearing the sound of the bell. He raises it slightly and our eyes meet. "I really wanted to do more, but I'm kind of glad we didn't. Man, I can't believe that smelly vamp came in here," he says.

I grab my shirt off the ground and quickly put it on, while Caleb does the same. Caleb is slowly buttoning my shirt for me. I don't know why, but there's something really sweet and intimate between us in this moment. I begin buttoning his shirt, too. We both reach the top buttons and Caleb gently holds my face, then kisses my forehead. I quite like kisses on the forehead. Not more than kisses on the mouth, but Caleb kissing my forehead makes me feel really safe and warm and wanted. It's an amazing feeling. I kiss his cheek, and button his top button. He grabs the book off the bench, and we head toward the door that leads to the gym, on the opposite side of the locker room. Today is Tuesday, which is a non-contact sports day. Basically, we'll be in the gym, but we'll be sitting around learning something, not doing any actual sports.

Caleb holds my hand, and we walk inside the open gym door. My face must be so flushed right now. Oh no, I just realized that my hair is down. Caleb of course realizes, too, probably because he heard my thoughts. He passes me my red ribbon from inside his pocket. I quickly gather my hair and tie it into a floppy bun on top. My mom calls it my housewife bun. It's always funny when she says it. I tie the ribbon around the base of the bun and look to Caleb for confirmation that everything looks okay.

He nods. "Perfect," he says with a big smile.

"Oh, damn!" Martin yells from the opposite side of the room, upon seeing us. "Did you two just come out of the locker room together?"

The whole class is staring over at us, as we hold hands walking toward the group. "Shut up, Martin! Mind your business!" Wolfie yells.

Oh, good, Wolfie is in this class with us. We haven't seen him all day, I wasn't sure if he was here. Oh no….Leslie, Robert, Rachel, Kat, and Tessa are in this class, too. This is going to be uncomfortable for a number of reasons. I really question why my life is like this. Why do I have to go from being so unbelievably happy, or horny, to running smack into an effing problem? Really? It's terrible.

Leslie is whispering to Rachel, while Robert avoids looking at us. Everyone is sitting on the floor inside the gym.

Caleb shakes his head as we inch closer toward our classmates. "I am not sitting on the floor of a gymnasium, and neither are you," he says to me.

Martin who must have incredible hearing says, "Ha! You fancy ass nobles have to sit on the floor, while I get to sit on my throne right here above you suckers! Vampires say being in a wheelchair must suck, well, right now it doesn't. This shit is funny. Look at Caleb's face!"

Caleb is not amused. I find it funny, though. Martin's a pain in the fangs but he's a good guy. I whisper in Caleb's ear, "Hey, it's fine. You can sit on my cape."

Caleb's eyebrows raise and he covers his mouth. "How could you even suggest such a thing? If anything, you can sit on my cape. I would never sit on that cape, it's your favorite," he says.

I whisper again so Martin doesn't hear me, "Caleb, what part of your ass being on my cape do you think I would not like? Do you think I don't think about your ass? Sit your ass on my cape. Do it and see if I care." I raise my chin at him and unclasp my cape.

"Are you guys fighting?" Martin yells over.

"Shut up, Martin," Wolfie says.

The gym teacher enters from the right side of the room. Caleb pulls my hand toward them. Our teacher, Dahvi, is non-binary and they prefer we call them by their first name. Calling them by their first name feels informal, but that's what they like. I already told Caleb on the phone last night that Dahvi is no nonsense. They do not put up with any hierarchy crap. So, if Caleb thinks Dahvi is going to be nice, he's mistaken. Then again, he did have his way with Ms. Phlip earlier.

"Ah, Froderick and Caleb, nice to see you Froderick, and it's good to meet you Caleb," Dahvi says.

I smile. Dahvi is always wearing the best clothes, even when we're playing sports, they incorporate really gorgeous colors into their outfits. Teachers are supposed to only wear black, gray, or red, but Dahvi got special permission to add colors to their outfits. That took some joint convincing of my dad from myself and Ms. Tansy, but it worked out at the end of last year.

"Oh, Froderick, that ruby clasp is stunning! And Caleb the bat on yours is fangtastic!" Dahvi says.

"Thank you, the trouble Dahvi is that Caleb really doesn't want to sit on the floor. Now, I know how you feel when we nobles get all high and mighty so, it's fine if you tell him—"

Dahvi is pointing at us. "Are you two going out?" they ask us.

Caleb claps and smiles with his mouth open. "I am so happy that you know what going out means, Dahvi. You're the first vampire that has understood that, since I got here yesterday."

Dahvi raises their chin, "Well, that's because you came to a boring town, ruled by boring people, who are not allowed to think. Their tiny brains only think about being bitten by Dracula. I'm pretty sure Frode's father has told everyone to be as boring as possible, and that's probably how this all began. Such a drab vampire, no fun at all. One time, all the teachers went out for drinks, and do you know what he said to the group"—Dahvi looks around—"we were talking about nighttime relations, don't pretend that I shouldn't be talking about this either, because part of gym is also Health Education, which Dracula needs by the way. Anyway, this old timer says, 'A woman vampire is only to be taken in missionary style.' Who in the world would even say such a thing? Him, he said it, and he was very proud of himself. I tell you Frode, I've read your mother's work. I'm a big fan, I have no idea how someone so hot, with such a beautifully creative mind, ended up doing the horizontal nasty with him."

Both Caleb and I are silent. I truly don't know how to respond, and neither does Caleb. Hopefully, he didn't pick up on those hints Dahvi dropped about my mom, though. This is all so embarrassing.

"Dahvi, that was a terrible story. Thank you," I say.

Dahvi gestures over their shoulder. "Listen, go grab two chairs and bring them around from the back room. Your father will be mad if I make Caleb sit his hiney on this floor anyway. Oh, I can just imagine that conversation. Please, go get the chairs, I insist."

I can't believe it. Caleb even charmed Dahvi. Unbelievable.

"Wait," Dahvi says. "Boys, I'm happy to see you two out and about holding hands, and I can feel the heat off you two, but take it from a vampire who's been in a pair of similar shoes, there will be times when people reject you or try to make you feel bad about who you are, but don't you let them stomp out those fires you have. You keep 'em burning, but also pour some water on that shit if it gets too hot. Don't be hooking up in the locker room. Save that stuff for when you're home. It's better that way. Also, speaking of stomping your fires out, what are you doing as far as your dad is concerned? There's no way he's cool with this. Mr. Missionary, threw a fit over my purple nails one day, so I have some strong doubts that he is a fan of this relationship."

"He doesn't know," I say.

Dahvi sucks their teeth and says, "Tch, please, he has ears everywhere. Anyway, who cares. He can't throw Caleb out of this school, so I say tell him, but only if you're ready. If you aren't ready, then just be careful. This reminds me of one of my favorite books. I mean the dad was a military man and the son was an athlete, who was secretly performing as a drag queen. It's a beautiful story. Caleb why does your face look like that?"

Caleb's face lights up. "Dahvi, that is my favorite book. You're talking about *Drag Queens, Emo Teens & Big Dreams!*"

"OOOOOHHH! YES! YES!" Dahvi says, excitedly. Don't you love that one part—"

Caleb interrupts them, he says, "No spoilers, Dahvi. Frode hasn't read it yet."

Dahvi is looking at me like I smell bad. "What, do you live under a rock, Froderick? That book is amazing. I have an extra copy in my office if you want to borrow it. I was thinking of donating my office copy to the library, so all the vamps can check it out. But I don't like that new librarian, Ms. Beagle, she's a nasty little thing. But, you know, I volunteered in the library last year and I know how to add books to the system. I'm not asking for permission either. Nope. Anyone who reads this book will love it. I think it should be added to the required reading list. And your dad, Froderick…he definitely should read it. All I see him reading is the newspaper, though. Always looking at articles about himself or your mother. Anyway, forgiveness is easier to get than permission, that's my motto. I have a few other mottos, but you're not old enough for those yet. And this relationship between you two is between you two and not your dad, no matter what he says."

Caleb whispers to me, "I really want to talk to them about the book. If I have to hold this in, then you have to start reading it tonight, so we can talk about it. When we go to my house later, remind me to give you my copy before you leave. Deal?"

I nod in agreement.

The rest of the class doesn't even care that Dahvi has been here talking to us for this long. I have no idea what time it is, but I'm sure the class is almost over already.

"Alright, good talk. I'm proud of you, Froderick. I don't know you, Caleb, but you have good taste in books and your cape is dope, so I'm gonna say I'm proud of you, too."

"Thanks, Dahvi," I say.

"Yes, thank you," Caleb says.

Caleb passes me the book from the library as we walk to get chairs for ourselves. These are the parts of being a noble that I feel bad about, though. I mean, I like skipping in the lunch line and not getting in trouble for messing around, but who's to say anyone else wants to sit on the floor right now? Why should anyone have to sit on the floor if they don't want to? Caleb grabs two chairs. He's holding one in each hand, as we walk back toward our classmates.

Martin notices us walking back with the chairs and yells to the teacher, "Dahvi! You let Caleb have his way! Hell no! Come on Dahvi, you're stronger than that!"

"Oh, hold your tongue, you foul mouthed little cretin," Dahvi says.

We place our chairs behind the rest of the class and sit down.

"Alright, now yesterday was just chaos, all around, so, today, we get to sit and have a talk about the different things we'll be covering over the year."

Leslie stands up. "I am not going to be in two classes with Frode and *him*," she announces to Dahvi.

"Girl, sit yourself down," Dahvi says. "Don't come at me like that. If you have a problem, then go talk to Ms. Tansy about it. By the way, the boy's name is Caleb. Did you not know his name or was that just extra sass from you?"

"She knows his name," I say.

Caleb's posture is so much better than mine. It's almost as if he was raised with a ruler strapped to his back. He's sitting straight up, in this horribly small chair. I'm sort of slouching, but I try to match his posture now that I've noticed.

"I do know his name, but I don't care!" Leslie shouts in my direction.

Caleb did not like her talking to me like that. His right eyebrow drops, and he yells back, "Insolent watermelon vamp! Don't talk to Frode!" Caleb gestures with his finger, telling Leslie to turn around.

"Watermelon vamp? What does that mean? Is that a new term I haven't heard?" Dahvi asks.

Fangfully, the bell rings, ending this very strange day of school. Caleb grabs my free hand and I hold the library book with the other.

This sucks. I don't want to be away from Caleb. I want to just go to his house and make out. I don't even care about this library book right now. The way Caleb kisses me and can read my mind is actually quite spectacular. I mean, he knew exactly where I wanted his hands, and he also knew exactly what to do with his mouth. I'm sure that with whatever other things we do, he'll know what I want, and it will be mind-blowing, too. Ugh. I have to go see my mom now, though, and that is the opposite of sexy.

Caleb is flying with me toward my house. I didn't have time to stay and talk to Wolfie or Kat after class, because I need to get to the salon on time, but I want to grab my phone before heading over there. Plus, Caleb has his doctor's appointment, too.

"I think I'll be done before you," I say. "So, just text me when you're finished and then I can meet you at your house."

"I might be done before you," Caleb says looking over at me. "How about this? Whoever is done first, will text the other and then we'll figure out what time you're coming over. Because I'd really like to meet your mom, and if I get done first, I'm definitely going to stop by the salon."

"Caleb, don't! Okay, fine, I will text you, but don't come to the salon unless you text me first. Promise me."

We slowly land in front of my house. I wonder if my dad is

home. It was weird not seeing him before I left. I always see him at breakfast time. Hmm. Well, hopefully I don't see him right now, because I'm in a rush.

Caleb squeezes me tightly behind a large tree on the side of my house. The tree is near my window and the side we're on can't be seen from inside the house. I press my mouth quickly against his for just a quick tiny taste of cotton candy before we part. Caleb is not having any quick kiss, though; he's holding the back of my head with one hand and really coming after the inside of my mouth. His tongue is just wild, it's so…good. I don't even know what turns me on at this point, it happens so easily now. I'll just say Caleb turns me on. Anything he does to me, or around me, turns me on. I really need to pull back, though, because my mom is probably waiting at the salon already.

Caleb pulls his mouth back from mine, but our lips remain close. "I don't want to go," he says.

His breath brushes past my lips. I want to devour him. I forcefully pull his mouth back into mine, our kiss turns wild, it's so hot. Being outside feels almost dangerous, though, I mean my dad could come outside, or any number of vampires he knows could pass by. I force myself to pull back. Caleb pulls me into a tight embrace and kisses my forehead. His heart is beating so fast and so is mine.

"I really need to go meet my mom, and you're going to be late. Plus, I can't get a good grip on you with this library book in my hand," I say jokingly. I mean, it is true, though. I almost threw it on the ground at one point.

"Okay," Caleb says with a pout.

"Fly safe and text me when you're done," I say.

"I'll do both of those things," Caleb says giving me a big smile.

Chapter 9
Alessandra Slayer of Dracula

I head inside through the front door, carrying the book from the library. Ah, there he is, my dad is sitting at the dining room table. He looks terrible.

"Hey, Dad, didn't see you this morning before I left," I say quickly while walking past him toward the stairs.

I really can't get caught in conversation with him. I need to meet my mom, and If I get stuck here with him, I'll definitely be late.

"I didn't go to work today. I'm too exhausted. Last night was far too draining," he says.

I have no idea what he's talking about, and I'm not going to ask. "Okay, well, I'm meeting Mom at the salon, so I hope you feel better." I walk upstairs into my room and place the book on my dresser. Seeing Caleb's cape, I start to get heated remembering the locker room. Damn, that was really close. I mean I really was going to let him bite me earlier. I hold his cape to my face and breathe in his scent. This scent is really like a drug to me. It really puts me into such a frenzy, it's like I need all of it. I need all of Caleb. I want all of him. Okay, I have to stop. I really can't be getting all horny again right before I see my mother. She's already got a sense for these things.

I change my clothes into a normal pair of dark jeans and a black collared shirt. I brush through my hair quickly and tie it back into a bun. I'm not going to wear the ribbon, though. If my mom sees that, she'll definitely know something is up with me. She's probably going to figure it out. I'll just have to deny it. Alright, I'm all set.

I grab my phone to text her, so I can tell her I'm on my way. Wait, what the? There are like ten texts here from Robert. Ugh, I'm not even opening them. What is his deal? Maybe he really is gay, too; Caleb is probably right. Now that I think about it, with everything that's happened, it certainly seems like he is. He hasn't defended Leslie any of the times that Caleb and I were arguing with her. But I mean that's not really saying much. He wouldn't argue with a noble, even if it were me. He especially wouldn't argue with Caleb. Judging from their interactions today, it was more than obvious that Robert didn't want any part of Caleb's temper. Still, though, if he is gay, that should give him even more of a reason to back off of me. I'm never leaving Caleb and, truthfully, I don't know what I ever saw in Robert. He's not even my type. My type is Caleb. Oh fangs, I have to get out of here. My room smells like Caleb; probably from his cape being in here all day. I text my mom and tell her I'm on the way. I'm going out of the window; I'm not walking past my father who's probably just overexerted himself on housewives.

Walking into the salon, I see my mother whose hair is wrapped inside of many square foil packets. She has to get her roots done and she also has a ton of highlights that she gets touched up on a monthly basis. My mother's appearance is very important to her. The salon is closed today but Wolfman has it open for my mom and me. Since it's his business, he can do whatever he wants. Also, because my mom is famous, whenever she has to get her hair done, he closes the salon for the whole day. He and my mom are best friends, so they get the whole place to themselves to gossip about whatever they want.

"Vampster! There's my baby!" she says while extending her arms for a hug.

"No, Lessie, don't you try to hug him. You'll get his shirt all dirty. Don't you know anything?" Wolfman says to her.

"Hi, Frode! How was school?" Wolfman asks me while looking at my mom's foils.

"It was good. Normal, nothing too crazy. I barely saw Wolfie today. I was too busy with Ca—"

Oh shit. I almost just said it already. This is what Wolfman does to me. He's such a comforting presence. I have to shut up now.

Wolfman's face is squished together as he looks at me. "Too busy with Ca? What's Ca?" he asks.

"Oh, um, I don't know what I was going to say, but I just had a busy day." I smile at him from my seat.

"Uh huh… That's very interesting, don't you think so, too, Lessie?" he asks while tilting his chin down at my mother.

"I definitely do, but let me tell you about what Steven said today! It was hilarious, Wolfster. You would love him. He was complaining because Chris used the last of his shampoo, and he even added water to it so Steven wouldn't notice. Steven was furious. I was sitting there at the table just watching Steven fling things around. He was yelling, 'Should I add water to ketchup when we run out, how about adding water to milk, or better, what if I add water to your body wash? What kind of a husband does this to their partner?' It was so funny!"

Wolfman stops placing foils in my mom's hair and gives her a serious look. "Wait, Steven and Chris are married?" he asks.

"Of course, they're married," she says.

Wolfman's face is red, and his mouth is open. "You trollop! The role of your gay best friend has already been cast. How dare you try to talk to this, this…Steven character! Give me his phone number, this isn't happening." He pulls his phone from the back pocket of his light-colored ripped jeans.

My mom thinks this is hilarious. "Wolfster, don't call me a trollop, you know I can't take it when you talk dirty to me, especially when I haven't been bitten in so long!"

Wolfman is not amused like my mother is. "You think I'm joking?" he asks her. "I am not kidding, Alessandra; I will purposely use the wrong shade of brown on your roots! Don't you dare try to replace me!" he stomps his foot on the ground and gives her a no-nonsense look.

"Calm down, what, are your jeans too tight today? I would never replace you. Who would do my hair if I did?" She cheekily shows him her fangs.

"You're the worst best friend a wolf could have, Lessie. I would break up with you myself, but I don't want to become a villain in one of your damn books," he says.

Yes, that would be a problem for Wolfman. My mother is a romance author who mainly writes about male vampire couples. Occasionally, she slips some other genders and pairings in, but she's a very strong advocate for gay men. The way I understand it is that Wolfman met Wolfie's mother, who was a pureblood, they fell in love, got married, she gave birth to Wolfie, then he just woke up one day and told my mom that his entire life with Wolfie's mom had been a lie. So, he leaves Wolfie's mom, because he'd rather be alone than to continue living a lie. It was a bad situation. Wolfie's mom lost her pureblood status after giving birth to Wolfie, then she gets dumped by her husband, and somehow the person who felt the worst, apparently, was my mother. She said that she couldn't stand thinking that her best friend was pretending all these years. She felt so bad about it.

Of course, this caused a problem between my mother and father because my father is from the dark ages, obviously, and his bloodsucking mind could not understand Wolfman being gay, or leaving his wife. My mom and dad had a lot of fights about it. Anyway, my mom continued being Wolfman's best friend while being married to my dad. One day, Wolfman was really upset because he felt like there were no really nice love stories about gay male vampires or werewolves for him to read. So, my mother decided she was going to write one for him. She wrote her first novel, like, in a few weeks; it was a big novel, too. She approached a publisher who signed the book and then her career just took off. Shortly after the book was released, my father tried to read it, he was furious. They fought about a bunch of things that my mother wrote about. He couldn't understand how she felt, and that frustrated my mom. In the end, she chose to support her best friend, because she felt like she and my dad would never see eye to eye again.

Now she writes all kinds of stories, with a ton of things that a son never wants to hear his mother talk about. My mom is sought after by all kinds of vampires, but for me, as her son, it's just embarrassing. Anyway, she definitely would write Wolfman as a villain in her next book if their friendship ended. That's what she does, she's told me before. Someone makes her mad at a store or when she's signing books; they become her next villain. Wolfman is right to be afraid to break up with her. Although my mom would never leave him, their bond is stronger than the one my parents have.

My mother sighs then says, "I told you that Steven and Chris were married. Were you not listening to me earlier?"

"Okay, Lessie, that's enough about this *wonderful* Steven. I don't want to hear anymore. Just close your fangs for a minute. We're all done with foils, so just sit here and look ugly," he says.

He spins her chair, so she faces me. "Oh, good, now we can talk about boys. Are there any new vamps in school? I hope you're not still messing around with the daughter of that disgusting wannabe that your father sunk his fangs into," she says.

Wolfman pulls my bun out of my hair. He softly brushes my hair out. It feels so nice. I lean back a little in my chair, my head kind of falls into his hands. He massages the top of my head while I look up at him. "Oooh, who are we talking about? I didn't know you had a girlfriend, Frode."

My eyes are closed as I reply, "I don't have a girlfriend. I will nev—" Luckily, I stopped myself before I finished that sentence.

Wolfman stops massaging my head. "She caught that," he whispers to me.

What does he mean? What is he saying right now? Oh, no. I'm too afraid to look over there at my mother to see her expression. I thought I saved the word; I didn't think "never" came out. Maybe it did? Damn, I don't know. Well, if there's one parent that has to find out, I'd rather it be her, for obvious reasons, but I really didn't want to come out to her yet. I just wasn't ready to have this discussion with her. Then she's going to want to know all about Caleb and his family. She'll ask me really embarrassing questions about what we've done. It won't ever end. On the other hand, I could tell her, and she could talk to my dad about it for me, maybe soften him up to the idea. But, wait, I can't do that. My dad told me not to bring Caleb up in front of her. Aaahhh! Screeching bats in my head!

"Frody," my mother says. "Tell me, how are your classes this year? Same teachers of course, but how about the vampires? Any new friends?"

"Um, well. There is a new girl, she's half mermaid and half vampire. Her name is Kressa, she's really nice. Wolfie and I actually met her last weekend, but she's in a couple of my classes. She met

Dad yesterday at the morning assembly, she had no idea I was his son. That was pretty funny."

There we go, this is good. I'll use Kressa again. Man, if Kressa ever finds out that I used her as a cover I have no idea what she'll think of me. I don't know her well enough yet. Oh, I totally forgot what she said earlier until just now. I can't tell Kat, though, since she asked me not to, but I think Kat is into Kressa, too.

My mother says facetiously, "Yes…I'm very interested in hearing all about a half mermaid girl that you have zero interest in, Frode. Continue toying with me, dear."

Shit. What do I do?

Wolfman whispers close to my ear, "Give it up. She's going to eat you alive in a minute. Trust me."

I can't tell her yet, but I can ask about the other stuff to maybe distract her. My eyes are still closed. I can't look at her. I'm a terrible liar.

"Mom, I wanted to ask you about something that, um, a friend told me was happening to them," I say.

"Well, go on dear. Tell me about this *friend*."

"My friend said that he and this other pureblood vampire can hear each other's thoughts and feel what the other is feeling. It started out like a quiet kind of whisper that he could hear and kind of predict or make a guess as to what the other guy was thinking, but then it turned more into a definite strong connection and their thoughts are shared freely now. He told me it's not constant and even though it's gotten stronger since yesterday, he still can't hear everything, or feel everything, that the other guy is feeling. I told him it was weird, and we went to the library to find a book on it. We did find one, but I haven't read it yet. I'm just not sure what I should do, I mean the fact that he can read my mind is really frightening. So, my friend is just kind of freaking out. We asked Dad, but you know

Dad. He said that two male vampires couldn't have such a connection. He was no help. So, I don't know what to do for my friend."

"Hold on," my mom says. "First of all, you screwed up a lot of times during that conversation. There is no friend, and we are talking about you and some other guy. Which I am thrilled about. Shut up and don't interrupt me. I need to do something before I get into this with you."

Wolfman spins me around and begins washing my hair. He asks my mother, "Should I call that worthless ex-husband of yours? I haven't gotten to yell at him in a while. I'd be more than happy to take part in this discussion."

"Ah, you can leave him a voicemail," my mom says. "I'm going to kill him for this. Narrow-minded, selfish, bastard."

My eyes are closed but I can hear my mother calling my father on the phone. Wolfman called my dad her ex, but they never actually got divorced. They're just separated, but still kind of together.

"Put it on speaker, please. You owe me for stepping out with another man," Wolfman says.

I hear my father's voice answer, "Yes, how would you like to make me more miserable today? I feel awful, Alessandra. I'm not in the mood to fight. If you're calling to do the other thing, I could muster up the energy for that," he says.

"You, selfish, narrow-minded piece of pureblood, A-negative, garbage trash! How dare you say that to our son!"

"Say what to our son? I barely talked to him today. He ignored me and last night he and Cal…he and his friend were bullying me. It was ridiculous. Asking me all kinds of stupid questions like teenagers do. They told me that they could hear and feel the other's thoughts and feelings. It was ridiculous. He and his friend are both males. It's impossible."

I'm sitting up now, and Wolfman is combing the treatment through my hair.

"I just muted the phone," she says to me. "Now, you told your father you were dating this boy, or does he think you two are just friends? Truth."

I sigh. Wolfman rubs my shoulders a bit. He's really the nicest adult that I know.

"Well, he thinks that we are just friends…but we're not."

"Wolfster, check his neck," my mother says.

"I did that as soon as he sat down. It's clear. No marks, he hasn't been bitten."

I can hear my father's voice complaining, but a bit of product has seeped into my ears so I can't hear him clearly.

"Did you bite this guy?" she asks.

"No, but I'm gonna." I cover my mouth. What the hell is wrong with me? Where did that come from? It was like I was possessed, my mouth just moved on its own. Oh my fangs.

Wolfman claps his hands. "Yes! That is what we say to our mother, that is exactly how you say that you are really into this guy. Well done, Frode!"

My mom is nodding in understanding. Her face is impressed with that horrifying proclamation I made.

She unmutes the phone. "You son of a bitch! You told them that they couldn't hear each other's thoughts when they told you they could."

"Alessandra, you know I love it when you yell at me, but I really am tired. It's not like they bit one another, so how else could it happen? They probably just have similar ways of thinking. They thought they felt something and overreacted. They asked me and I dealt with it. It's fine."

"It is not fine!" my mother screams.

Wolfman calls out to my mother who is enraged, "Alessandra, your foils. Calm down. Well, no, keep yelling, but don't fling your head about, please."

"You fixed nothing. Frode is here with me right now getting his hair conditioned. He told me all about what you said. I think you are even more despicable today than I ever have before. I want you to know that. Honestly. I am so sick of this with you. I think Frode should just live with me. I know he would never, but, fangs, I really want him to. It's not healthy for him to be around you. You're really something else. I left you for this reason! Do you not remember this?"

"You left me because you said I was too interested in other women."

"Bullshit! Don't pretend you don't remember what happened. I have never been jealous of another female in my entire life. Give me a break. This is why I hate straight men. You don't listen. You're rude, you make everything about you, and you think that women should just fall at your damn feet. It's disgusting. You had better apologize to my son when he gets home. Now, I'm going to hang up before I really do come there and bite into your carotid artery. No, I did not mean that in a sexual way either. I will literally kill you if I see you right now. You are the worst vampire in the world."

"Were you thinking about sex with me for a moment there? I could tell you were. You're so naughty, Alessandra."

"Go die," she says to my father, and hangs up.

Wolfman has finished with my product and he's walking over to the small fridge behind the counter. My mother is staring at me. She hasn't said anything else. I'm not sure what she's feeling right now. Well, I know she's angry at my father, but I don't know if she's angry at me, too, or if she's just thinking. I can't really tell.

Wolfman is back with a glass of pink wine, which he passes to my mother. I don't know what kind of wine it is, but it's pretty.

"Thank you. I love you," she says to Wolfman.

"Ugh, I'm still not over the situation with Steven. But I love you, too," he says to her.

My mother drinks her wine while staring over at me. She places her glass down. "Alright, Frode. Try again. So, you and this pureblood are dating, since when? Give me the details. I need to try and figure out what's going on here. Can't believe you two even asked your father. You know he's an idiot. We talk about how stupid he is during the course of almost all of our conversations. Anyway, explain."

"We started dating yesterday like as soon as we met. There was a really weird connection between us. I can't explain it, but it was instantaneous—"

My mom interrupts me, "Was it a hot kind of connection, like full of want and desire? Or was it like a longing, like your souls were reaching for each other?"

"This is why I didn't come to you," I say.

"Honey, listen. I love a good boy-love story and I am over the blood moon with the fact that you are dating a boy, but right now, I'm asking as a mom. Well, not just as your mom, but also don't forget that I am the daughter of the highest-ranking vampires, across all bloodlines. I'm just trying to figure it out. If I understand the emotions; I can try to put it together. Answer the question."

"Fine. Well, I've experienced all of those feelings, but for me, I thought he was really hot. Hottest I'd ever seen. For Caleb, he said he knew as he passed by my row without ever seeing me. We were in the auditorium, and he said as he passed by that his blood was calling to me or something. I don't know. He tried to hold my hand as soon as he saw me, then five minutes later he was holding my hand for real and pushing me up against the brick wall."

"Holy shit! I like this guy!" Wolfman shouts. "Do you know his father? Is he available? What moves! He got you to hold his hand and pinned you against a wall within a matter of minutes?"

I nod my head. "Mmhmm, kissed me and got me to agree to be his boyfriend within maybe ten, fifteen minutes. It was crazy. But we spent the whole day together and it just felt really natural, really right. I kept thinking maybe I was only feeling this way because he's my first boyfriend, but throughout the day, the connection just got stronger. Last night, things got really intense and today they got even hotter. I almost let him bite me."

Whyyy? I did it again! I said too much!

My mom finishes off her wine and she's pulling the top of her shirt rapidly trying to cool herself.

"Okay, I cannot write about this. You are my son. I absolutely cannot write about this. Mom mode. Aside from the very heated moments, when you hear his thoughts, are you hearing his voice, or is it your voice saying what you perceive to be in his head?"

"No, it's Caleb's voice."

"I have never written a character named Caleb, sweet bats. This is hard, Frody. I want to be a good mom, but this is very difficult. I'm an artist and what you're telling me is so spectacular…okay, never mind, so Caleb. He is a pureblood, correct?"

"Yes, pureblood and noble," I say.

She tilts her head at me, she looks like she's figured something out and she doesn't look happy.

"Noble, you say? What other noble house is there aside from the house of Dracula in this town?"

"Um, mom, one other thing before I answer that."

"Lean your head back into the sink, Frode it's time to rinse," Wolfman says.

I lean my head back into the sink and say, "Dad said I shouldn't ever mention Caleb's name around you."

"Did he now? Well then, what family is Caleb from?"

"His name is Caleb Cheval."

Only the sound of the water running can be heard. My mother is silent. Shit. I really should have listened to my father.

Silence lingers. I feel really afraid for some reason. It's like all of the air has been sucked out of the room.

Wolfman breaks the silence. "You know, Frode, we really should give you just a small trim before you go. The ends could use it. I know how you love it this long, so I promise just to tap the ends."

"AAAHH!" my scream ringtone sounds loudly in my pocket That's probably Caleb. He knows where the salon is, if I don't answer it. He'll probably come here. Wolfman gives my hair a squeeze in the sink. I sit up and pull my phone out of my pocket. Fangs, I missed the call. My mother is staring at me silently. She doesn't look upset. I don't really know how to explain her expression, honestly. It's more like she's frozen or suspended in some sort of alternate reality. Like she's staring over but she's not even looking at me. I need to call Caleb and stop him from coming here.

I press his name in my contacts.

Caleb answers the phone, "Hey, I just got done with the doctor. Should I come meet you?"

"No, um. Wait, Caleb." I turn to Wolfman, "I'm gonna talk to him outside. I feel like you should deal with whatever is going on with my mom."

I walk outside with my head of wet hair wrapped in a black towel. Wolfman always wraps the towel so nice and tight. I really need to learn how to wrap like he does.

"Hey, Caleb, sorry, I'm back. So, a weird bunch of things just happened. But how was your appointment?"

Caleb is laughing. "Well, a weird bunch of things happened to me, too. The doctor was fine. My mom was watching when he inspected my neck. Made me only slightly thankful that we didn't bite each other today. Would have been awkward to talk about with my mom there."

"Yeah, well, my mom made Wolfman check my neck, since I told her that we're dating."

"Your mom? I really want to meet your mom. Let me come meet you, please?"

"No way, Caleb. We were having a really good conversation. She was all happy that I admitted that we were dating. I mean she caught me in a lie because I'm a terrible liar, but I did admit it once she pushed me for it. Okay, well, actually, Wolfman urged me to, and then I told her the truth."

"You are very cute. Can you hear my thoughts right now?"

"Mmm…no I don't think so. Can you hear mine?"

"Nope, I can't. Listen, Frode, the doctor's office is two minutes away from the salon. What if I just meet you outside? I'll just wave through the window. Come on. I don't want to be apart anymore. Please?"

I see through the salon storefront window that my mom appears to still be in the same position, but I can't see her face, so I'm not sure if she's talking or still staring silently.

I can't say no to Caleb, besides, I really want to see him, just as bad. "Okay, you can come, I say."

"I'll be there in two minutes," Caleb says.

I slide my phone back into my pocket. I forgot that I have to tell him that Robert sent me a bunch of texts that I didn't read. Damn it, he's gonna be so mad about that. Oh wow, he wasn't kidding about getting here in two minutes, there he is. Caleb is walking over toward me. I have never seen any clothed vampire look hotter than he does right now. I say clothed because shirtless Caleb is definitely hotter, I saw that today. He's wearing dark navy jeans, with a black long-sleeved henley shirt. Damn…my boyfriend is delicious. I can't wait to taste him. Caleb quickly pulls me into a tight, warm embrace.

"You smell like cotton candy," he whispers in my ear.

I giggle a little. "Do you like my hair wrap?" I ask, pulling back from the embrace.

"Hmm…it looks like you just got out of the shower, which is a very appealing image, so, yes, but those two are staring through the window at us right now," he says.

"I completely forgot where we were. Tell me, before I turn around. Is the woman with the long brown hair smiling?"

Caleb waves to my mom and Wolfman. "Yes, kind of, but she also looks like kind of mad or pained. I can't really explain it. It's the first time I'm seeing her face, so I don't know what it should look like. But you look a lot like your mother. She's very pretty."

"Okay, listen, let me catch you up quickly. She knows we are together, she yelled at my dad, she knows your family somehow, and she is an author of many gay love novels involving men. The end. Come on." I pull Caleb inside by the hand, before he can react.

I sigh as we walk inside. Holding Caleb's hand, I say, "Mom, Wolfman, this is my boyfriend, Caleb."

They exchange greetings while my mom looks Caleb over. Her face is exactly as Caleb said. She does almost look pained, but her smile is still there.

"Frode, sit, let's trim you up and get you boys on your way." Wolfman says.

I sit in the seat, while Caleb stands beside me.

"You're not going to cut his hair, are you?" Caleb asks.

Wolfman tilts his head while wagging a red comb in Caleb's direction. "Now, answer this, we heard you two got hot and heavy earlier. What I want to know is, was Frode's hair down or up? Look at me, Caleb, don't look at Frode. I'm curious about something," Wolfman says.

My mother is looking down at her phone. I think she's texting someone. I really want to know what she figured out, but she hasn't said a word to me yet.

Caleb answers Wolfman nervously, "Okay, well I don't know why Frode told you that, but his hair was up and then it was all down."

Wolfman gasps loudly. My mother drops her phone, eyes wide looking at Caleb, then at me.

She bends down and picks the phone up. Still, she hasn't said anything. This is so effing weird.

"You two are so dramatic, why did you gasp, and why did you drop your phone, Mom? Gosh, he said my hair was down, it's not like I was naked."

"You being naked in front of him would be less shocking," my mother says.

"Agreed, Wolfman says. "You never let your hair down. I try to get you to do it all the time. I've been telling you for years to leave it down. Now what? This little Casanova comes along, and you drop your hair down like a supermodel in a bite spray commercial?"

Caleb tilts his head back and his mouth slightly opens.

"NO!" I scream. "Caleb, no deviant open-mouth laugh, right now! Absolutely not. I told you my mother is a writer; she's probably over there right now writing down story ideas about the two of us. Don't give her any more material!"

"I am not writing down material. I'm texting someone. Don't ask who," my mother says.

Wolfman is trimming my ends now, so I can't react or move, no matter what happens, for the next few minutes.

"So, Caleb, can you explain the feelings you have for Frode?

More specifically explain if the feelings are just sexual or based on a soul level connection?" my mother asks.

Already I want to lift my head. Wolfman whispers, "Stay."

"Of course, I can explain them," Caleb says. "My soul has always been restless, my blood has never felt fire, my body has never experienced the bliss of another's mouth, my scent was alone, I was cold. I walked past Frode, my soul felt at peace, Frode walked toward me on the stage and my blood ran hot, I held his hand, and my body was light, our mouths pressed together, and our scents became one, I hold him in my arms, and I am warm."

Okay, that was so damn…hot…sweet…perfect. I don't even know what to say.

I can't see my mom's expression, but Wolfman has stopped cutting my hair momentarily.

"That was pretty deep for a seventeen-year-old, what, are you a poet?" Wolfman asks Caleb.

"No, I read a lot, though, and I just said the words that came to mind. I thought it probably sounded stupid as I said it, but I said it anyway."

"I liked that," my mother says. "That was real emotion. Very good. Sums it up for me. Frode, you mentioned a library book earlier. That isn't going to help you. Don't even bother with it."

I want to know what she's figured out. I should just ask her, but what if it's really bad? If she's telling me not to bother with the library book, she obviously knows the reason for the connection. I can hear Caleb's thoughts; he's telling me to just be patient.

Wolfman finishes trimming my hair. "Do you want me to blow dry it? Or you want to leave with it wet?" he asks.

"Can I vote?" Caleb asks.

I hold my hand out toward him. "Go ahead."

Caleb says, "I want him to dry it. I want to see it all down. Earlier it was only down for a few minutes."

Wolfman smiles at me in the mirror. "Let's dry it, buddy."

My mother and Caleb are discussing very boring things. She's asking him about his favorite color, favorite foods, favorite movies, books…it's all very boring stuff. Well, not that it's boring, I mean I learned that stuff last night when we talked all night, but it's boring because I'm really only interested in why she said that the book won't help. I'm kind of scared to hear what she says. I'll just call her later and ask, after I leave Caleb's.

Caleb is staring at my hair in the mirror. It feels really soft. I run my fingers through it as Wolfman turns the dryer off.

"Beautiful. Frode, you have the most fangtastic hair I've ever seen." Wolfman says.

Caleb is smiling brightly. I stand and hold his hand; he gives me a sweet kiss on the cheek.

I hug my mother with one arm. "Bye, Mom. I'll talk to you later. Let me know if you figure anything out," I say.

My mother smiles at me.

"It was nice meeting both of you," Caleb says as I pull him toward the door.

"Bye, boys!" Wolfman shouts.

Chapter 10
You Look Terrible

Caleb and I take off quickly, headed for Caleb's house. There are a lot of vampires flying around tonight. I don't know why there are so many out right now. Well, I guess most vampires are probably headed home from work since it's around 5:00 pm.

"My house isn't that much farther," Caleb says with a smile.

I'm kind of nervous. Now that I've come out to my mom, that just leaves my dad. I'm sure my mom won't tell him but there's always a chance she does. I mean she was really mad at him earlier. Also, I'm a little scared to meet Caleb's mom. I know he said it was fine but what if she doesn't like me? I still don't know what the deal is with Caleb's name and my mom, honestly, so I guess I have to just wait and see.

"Caleb, did you tell your mother that we are dating?"

"Yes, I told her as soon as I got home. She was thrilled."

"Okay, well maybe it isn't a thing between our families then. Surely, if it were, your mom would have given a reaction when you said my name. Which is what my mom did. She was really happy and then I said your last name and she froze."

"Well, I didn't tell my mother your last name. I just said I was dating a really perfect guy, named Froderick. She didn't ask for any other details. She was just happy. I know what you're thinking, and you may be right. Your mom seemed like she liked me, but she was also asking me really weird questions. Here's my house, let's land back here."

Our feet touch the ground and Caleb squeezes me, pulling my feet off the ground briefly.

He places me back down and holds my hand. His house looks as big as mine does, so I'm not sure why he was so surprised with the size of mine. We're walking on a gray stone pathway, lined with beautiful red rose bushes. This appears to be the back entrance.

"Yes, this is the back entrance, but my room is on this side, so if we come in this way, we can avoid seeing my brothers. Which will mean more time for other things. Once they know you're here, they'll bother us non-stop. I don't want that."

Caleb opens the large glass paneled door and walks inside with me, holding my hand.

"Caleb, honey, is that you?" a woman's voice asks.

"Yeah, mom, I'm back. Frode is here with me, too."

No sooner than Caleb finishes speaking, a woman with long blonde hair appears in front of us. Caleb looks just like her. This is definitely his mother. She looks familiar somehow, though. Almost like I've seen her before. But that's not possible.

"Mom, this is my boyfriend Frode Dracula," Caleb says.

"Dracula? Oh, okay. I did not know that he was from the house of Dracula. Well, you certainly do look a lot like your mother, or what I've seen of your mother, rather. I mean it's almost like a male clone, especially with that long thick hair you have. Wow. I mean, I don't know exactly what she looks like these days, but I bet that you look just like her because I've seen your father, that idio—never mind. You don't resemble the great Count Dracula, as far as I can tell. It makes sense that you would look like your beautiful mother, and not that stup—not Count Dracula," she says.

That was weird. She definitely knows my mom. Caleb is thinking the same thing. Well, it seems like she knows both my parents. She was going to call my dad stupid a couple of times. I'm sure of it.

"Alright, boys, I hate to leave but I have a…a meeting that just came up, and I need to go there now. It was nice to meet you, Frode."

"Yes, it was nice to meet you, too. I say with a smile."

Caleb pulls me toward a large spiral staircase. We walk up the stairs together, holding hands. Caleb's home is beautiful. The entire thing is decorated with pink and black, including the furniture and the walls. The dramatic contrast between the baby pink and black really works well together.

Caleb opens the door to his room. It's fabulous. Caleb's walls are a deep shade of red and his ceilings are really high and arched. His bed is much bigger than mine, too. All of the furniture is finely crafted. It's obvious that everything here was handmade. There is way too much detail for any of this to have been bought from a store.

"Okay, before I forget…" Caleb walks to the large black and red bookcase in the corner of the room. He pulls a book off the shelf and hands it to me. "Here is the book we were talking about. You have to start reading it tonight so we can talk about it."

"Yes, I will read it. I can't wait," I say. I'm looking at the back cover and reading it over. The book does look interesting and if Caleb likes it, I'll read it. Besides if it's a story about male love interests that my mom didn't write; I definitely want to read it.

Caleb softly takes the book from my hands and places it atop his dresser. "Now, we'll put this here and you'll bring it home later. But, for now, what would you rather do? See my collection of books, or lay down and hold each other? Those are the two things that I want to do most. If you have an equally appealing option, I'm happy to consider it," he says.

I pull my mouth to the side in thought. I don't really know what to do. I'm curious about the books, but I also just want to kiss Caleb. I put my hands on Caleb's face and press our lips together. Caleb smiles while allowing me to enter his mouth. Mmmm…this taste and this feeling…Caleb holds the sides of my face then slides his hands into my hair, he's almost gripping it but not quite. I want him to, though, I want him to squeeze me tighter. Caleb's hands tighten around two sections of my hair. Holy shit…I really like this. Caleb is walking toward his bed while our mouths are pressed together, he's guiding me backward forcefully. The back of my legs feel the bed and I lie down on the soft red comforter. Caleb quickly lies on top of me. This is the closest our bodies have been. There is no space in between us now. Our mouths are locked together, and our tongues move wildly. Caleb's hands aren't holding my hair anymore. He's reaching down in between us. He's reaching for the hardest part of my body. The part that is begging to be let loose. It's strained inside my jeans, and I can feel Caleb's pressed against mine. I want to touch his, too. Caleb's tongue is moving faster inside my mouth, we briefly separate our mouths and I pull his face back in, I press his mouth against my neck. He's gently kissing the softest part of my neck, his tongue is lightly rubbing against it. We are taught to guard this part of our neck, until we meet the person that we trust enough to bite us. I trust Caleb; I want him. I want him to fucking bite me and I want to devour him. Caleb's tongue is tracing my neckline, as his hand separates the button on my jeans…

"AAAHH!" the scream ringtone from my phone sounds. I ignore it. It rings again, "AAAHH!" Damn it! My life is so unfair! Every damn time. Caleb pulls my phone out of my pocket. It's my mom calling, I really don't want to answer it, but obviously she's not going to stop. It must be important.

I answer the phone. I'm panting, my guy below is still ready to go, and my neck is wet and smells like Caleb's scent. "Mom, what?" That's all I can get out in between my broken breaths.

"Frode, you wanted to know what I found out. I'm going to let you hear. Stop whatever you're doing that's got you out of breath. Get comfortable, you and Caleb put the phone on speaker. I'm meeting with an old friend. She's walking inside right now. Now, boys, don't say a word. Put yourselves on mute. I am in a bad mood, and this is the nicest way I can do this.

"Hello, Miranda, you look terrible," my mother says.

Caleb's eyes are wide. "Miranda is my mom's name," he says.

"Hello, Alessandra, I just met your son. He looks like a younger, better-looking version of you. What a shame that you aged so horribly. Nothing less than you deserve, of course. You horrible wench of a woman!"

"Oh my fangs! It's been fifteen years, Miranda!" my mother says.

"You didn't have to kill him, Alessandra! They could have lived happily ever after!"

My mother yells, "He died! What do you want me to do? I write what I see in my head! He died, there's nothing I can do about it if a character dies! If they die, they die!"

"You wrote the damn book! Of course, you can do something about it! What are you even saying? You write what you see? Don't you care about the characters or the readers? What about reader enjoyment? I hated that! Everyone hated that!" Miranda argues.

"How many questions are you asking me?" my mother asks. "You want an answer for each one? Fine…yes, I write what I see, almost like I'm watching a movie, yes, of course my brain develops the characters and everything but if I see someone die…then they die!

Do I care about reader enjoyment? Of course, I do, but not to the detriment of the story! He had an incurable disease, for fangs' sake, and he died in a car wreck! Would you have rather watched him die a slow agonizing death because of the illness? Do you think Vincent would have wanted that? Vincent wouldn't have been able to handle seeing Mario like that, and Mario wouldn't have been able to stand seeing Vincent suffer because of him! Fangs, use your brain, Miranda, unless all that hair dye you're using fried all your brain cells! I can't change the story, my characters are real to me! Do you know how hard I cried when Mario died? I needed therapy! I couldn't talk to Frode's idiot father about it, couldn't talk to you about it, I had no one! Just me and Vincent in my head mourning Mario. Then the book comes out and what is the first thing I see? A review from 'Number one vampire housewife' which I knew immediately was you…stupid username by the way."

"That's not my fault! All the good names were taken! It's hard to come up with a username!" Miranda yells.

"Oh, shut up, passwords are harder than usernames!" my mother yells. "So, the housewife, well, you left a scathing review of my book! My very first book! And what happens? That review becomes the talk of vampires everywhere! Took me a month to write again. It was awful."

"Are you saying you had a measly one-month drought in between writing?" Miranda asks.

"It was a whole month before I finished my next book."

Miranda asks, "Wait…you stopped writing, or it took you a month to write something else?"

"It took me a whole entire month to write a new book from beginning to end…I started working on something else right after I finished the first one, but I was so stressed out that it took me two months to get a meager 80,000 words out, Miranda!"

"I cried for longer than that over Mario's death! I cried for six months, Alessandra! What is wrong with you? Also, side note, it's really incredible that you write so quickly, doesn't show in your writing at all…or so I've been told."

"Alright, enough," my mother says. We need to talk about the boys…"

Oh my fangs, they know each other. Our moms know each other, forget about the stupid character thing—whatever that was about. I'm actually scared right now. What could they need to talk about? What if it's something that makes Caleb want to break up with me? Caleb squeezes my hand three times.

"I'm with you. I'm not going anywhere. We'll deal with whatever it is together."

Chapter 11
Grandpa Lugo

Okay, let's back up a few steps. Caleb was just about to bite me for the first time, and his hand was unbuttoning my pants. My mother calls—interrupting my almost-bite, and explains that we only need to listen in on her conversation with someone, who turned out to be Caleb's mother, through the phone. She promised that we would quickly find out the reason for the strange connection that Caleb and I share. Well, that was twenty minutes ago. After listening to our mothers settle their fifteen-year feud, the last words we heard were my mother saying, "We need to talk about the boys." Then the phone call ended.

Caleb and I have been sitting here trying to call our mothers, whose phones are either off or have possibly been thrown at one another. I have no idea, honestly. But this is quite literally the most ridiculous fanging thing to ever happen to me. The mood to be bitten is gone now, well, okay, it's not fully gone, I mean, Caleb is still sitting next to me on the bed and neither of us have fixed our clothing yet, but that's not important. What *is* important is that we were just about to find out why we can hear each other's thoughts and then the phone call ends? Who does this to a vampire? We've both texted and called them at least ten times each, with no reply. I have no idea where they were meeting, so I can't call the place and ask if they're still there and I already texted Wolfman, who has yet to reply.

Caleb's hand is resting on my leg. "I don't even know what to say, Frode. So, they were obviously close, then your mom kills a character off in a book, and then...the friendship between our mother's ended. How old were you when your mom wrote her first book?"

Damn, that mood is just hanging around, even when he's asking me something serious. Caleb just oozes sex appeal, it's like he doesn't even have to try. It's ridiculous, and I really do still want him to bite me, but I can't focus on that right now.

I place my hand atop Caleb's. "She wrote it when I was two years old. Caleb, listen, I don't know what to do here. What could the thing even be that they were talking about? I'm so frustrated right now. I really wanted to...you know, do *that* with you, and now we have this big mystery hanging over us. I mean, whatever it is, I guess my dad must know, though. He did warn me not to bring you up to my mother. Maybe we should ask him? No, no, forget I said that. He has never helped in any situation...ever. So, we can't ask him. What about your dad? I know you said he comes and goes; do you think he knows what this secret is? Could we try to talk to him?"

Caleb picks my hand up and brings it to his mouth. Holy hell, his eyes are hungry. The softest part of my hand, in between my thumb and pointer finger, is directly in front of his mouth. I can feel his warm, inviting breath as he teases me with a light bite using his fangs. Holy shit...my boyfriend is a damn bite teaser. I've heard of this before, I've just never personally experienced it. I'm not mad about it, but I am getting very turned on.

"What the hell did you do that for?" I ask while massaging the light bite spot with my other hand.

Caleb raises his eyebrows at me, his head tilts to the side as he stands up from the bed. He's looking at his reflection in his mirror and fixing his hair. "Sorry, I really want to bite you, too, and since I can't now, I just wanted a little taste. But as for the dads, no, we cannot ask my dad. I think that we should ask yours. We need to go to your place and get it out of him."

My head is starting to hurt. I hold my forehead in thought before answering Caleb. Words cannot express the utter disappointment I feel right now, truly. Which is worse for me, the fact that I can't get bitten right now, or that Caleb wants to talk to my dad?

"It's worse that you want to be bitten and I can't do it," Caleb answers aloud, after hearing my inner thoughts.

"I can't do this, Caleb. I can't have you inside my head. I can't. Our relationship will never last. You hear it in there, right? I-I…what the fangs am I supposed to do? I have to think. Vampires think, I mean it's not exclusive to me, that I think about things. I can't feel bad about this. You just have to try not to hear what I'm thinking."

Caleb's head leans back, and his eyes are wide, with his hands on his waist. He gives a small chuckle, then says, "Well, you liked it when I read your mind earlier. You wanted me to grip your hair and I did. Pretty nice to have a boyfriend, who can hear exactly what you want without you having to ask for it, isn't it?"

I sigh loudly. "Yes, for that stuff it's nice, but for everything else it's not nice. Okay, forget it," I say holding both hands outward. "My dad is incapable of helping. You've had like four different conversations with him, how can you possibly suggest that he could help us? I can hear your thoughts, too; you don't actually believe he can."

I'm lying, he does believe it and he's going to tell me why right now. And he's right, too.

Caleb gives me a big smile and motions toward his bedroom

door. "Yes, you've already figured it out. We're going to talk to him *because* he is an idiot. We are smarter than him and we can trick him into telling us what we want to know. Also, there is a chance that our moms are there. Small chance, but still, they could be. Grab the book that you're gonna start reading tonight off my dresser and let's go." He holds his hand out for me to hold while opening his door.

I grab the beautifully colored book off his dresser and hold his hand, adjusting my pants and shirt. I'm not used to being around other vampires with my hair down like this. It's nice and soft because of the treatment, though, so it's not even tangled from our make out session. Ugh, damn it, I can't think about that right now.

"Run!" Caleb yells, as he pulls my hand downstairs.

We're running quickly through the house toward the back door that we came in through earlier.

I can hear Caleb's brothers arguing, he doesn't want them to stop us. I kind of want to see them, though. I wonder if they look like Caleb. Wow, three Calebs…

"They don't look like me, don't even think about it," Caleb says as we leave the house.

We both reach a comfortable altitude as we fly toward my house to meet with my moron of a father. I really do hope my mom is there. I doubt it, though. Also, if she is there, there is a chance that she and my dad are…no, no that wouldn't happen to me.

"Your mom is not going to be having sex with your dad, gross. Come on. You said earlier she was threatening to kill him for what he did to us. Do you think she would just flip that quick? I only met her briefly, but she didn't strike me as the type to flip on something like that."

"Ha!" I say loudly looking at Caleb. "She threatens to kill him every time they are together. True that she seemed much madder this time than normal, but I have no idea. I've overheard them doing *things* together before and it was not pleasant. I'll never get over it."

"Don't think about it! Ugh, Frode! Now, I know what it sounds like, too!" Caleb shouts while tugging his ears.

The sun is beginning to set as we land in front of my house. The lights are on, but that doesn't really mean anything. My dad always forgets to turn the lights off, especially if he's having a pity party for himself. He was so whiny earlier, too, I mean he skipped work and everything today, then got yelled at by my mom because of Caleb and me. He is not going to be happy to see me and he will be even more annoyed that Caleb is here. Funny how things work, a day ago he loved Caleb, now after my mom yelling at him over the two of us, I can't imagine his opinion remains the same. I mean, also according to my dad, we bullied him yesterday, so, yeah, I think he's gonna be even more petulant than normal. I love that word, petulant. My mother uses it often when she describes my father. I gotta start using it more. It fits him.

Caleb is looking left to right; I know what he's going to do, but I beat him to it this time. I tuck the book under my arm, grab his face, and press our lips together quickly for a quick taste of cotton candy. Whooo…my boyfriend is hot.

"So is mine," Caleb says while licking his lips. "You know you just kissed me right in front of your house. I thought we weren't allowed to do that?"

"Oh, yeah," I say. "I forgot. My head is such a mess with everything, that I completely forgot about being careful. I'm sure my dad didn't see us."

Oh fangs. As we walk toward the front door, I can see the curtain in one of the top windows moving slightly. Oh no, if my dad saw that, I am dead. I am so dead.

Caleb looks really worried. "Somebody in that window just saw us kissing. What room is that?" Caleb asks.

"It's just a guest room. My dad wouldn't be in there. It was probably just the cat," I say.

Yeah, it's just the cat. For sure. Why would my dad be in that room? He never goes in there. We only use it when we have company, which is more often than you would think. I have so many aunts and uncles on both sides, cousins, vampires, who we consider family that really aren't. My mom wouldn't be in there either, it's definitely just the cat.

I open the front door with Caleb close behind me and I immediately freeze. I know that horrible scent. I grab Caleb's arm and turn back around. "NO, Caleb we have to—"

"Froderick, my little blood capsule!" a gruff voice calls out, before I can leave with Caleb.

My head drops in resignation. This is my life. It sucks. Every effing time I think things are okay, or I think they can't get worse, they always get worse. It's unbelievable.

My grandfather's bright round face and equally round belly greet me with a wide smile and open arms.

"Hello, Grandpa Lugo," I say while he hugs me tightly. Grandpa Lugo is my dad's father and he smells terrible. He lathers on this very strong bite spray, which doesn't help to cover the terrible scent of, well, I don't know what, but it smells like shit, literally. Not only does he smell terrible, but his personality is a bit much to deal with.

He's pinching my cheeks and pulling them outward so hard right now, as I try and separate from the smelly hug. Ugh, I am going to reek. Caleb is not going to want to touch me once this is over.

"Your hair has gotten so long! I never get to see it down," my grandfather says while lightly rubbing my hair. "Who is your friend?" he asks, extending his hand to Caleb.

My father is standing in front of us now and answers my grandfather's question, "Oh, that's Caleb." My father asks me with attitude, "Why is Caleb here again?"

My grandfather shakes Caleb's hand. "Hello, I'm Lugo. Yes, I know, I'm very famous, not as famous as my son, of course, but it's just because he's so handsome."

Caleb is beaming at my grandfather while his hand is being roughly shaken about. My grandfather is very rough by nature just due to his large physique. He's a gentle soul, he just doesn't realize how much stronger he is than most vamps, same goes for his smell, he has no idea how strong his scent is. There is literally no bite spray that could cover that up.

"It is very nice to meet you," Caleb says. "I've read many stories about you, as have most vampires, of course."

My grandfather gives Caleb a smile and pats my father on the shoulder. "Be a nice boy, Drac, this is your son's friend. You can't be mean to him just because Alessandra hurt your feelings."

"I am not being mean," my father says. "You have no idea what these two are like when they're together. Caleb seems intent on torturing me, just like Frode here. It's their fault Alessandra is so mad at me right now."

My father bends down to pick his cat up. He's talking to the cat now. "Not you, though, my perfect girl, Alexandra, you would never be mean to daddy. No, you wouldn't. Not like your brother and his friend."

The cat is purring so loud right now while my dad rubs his face next to hers.

"Grandpa, how long are you staying for?" I ask.

My grandfather walks toward the refrigerator and opens it. "Oooh! Donut peaches! You can't get these back at home! Don't mind if I do. Doctor says I need to eat healthier anyway and this is the perfect fruit to start with," he says as he pulls a peach from the container and closes the door.

I have a real problem listening to other vampires eat. The sound of their chewing just irks me. It makes my skin crawl. It's like even if someone's mouth is closed, I can still hear them chewing, or slurping, and this peach is going to be awful to my ears. Aaahh! My grandpa just bit right into the peach and didn't even wash it.

"This is delicious," he says while the juice drips down his chin.

Oh, fuck me. I completely forgot about the donut peach and the banana. What am I gonna do about that? What the hell was I going to do earlier if we got that far? Oh, that's right, I was going to let Caleb bite me fir—

Caleb's eyes and mouth are wide. I drop my head at the realization that Caleb now knows everything that I did with the peach and the banana.

Caleb whispers in my ear, "We can talk about that later. We need to talk to your dad. Don't forget why we're here."

"Shut up, Caleb! I know why we're here, don't whisper in my ear, now that you know about the damn banana!" I yell.

My grandfather is chewing with his mouth open and holds the half-eaten peach toward us. "What's happening with a banana? Is that some new joke for vamps?" he asks.

"Oh, who knows?" my father asks. "Frode is always overreacting and yelling. Probably a stupid song lyric from his band, don't waste your breath on them."

"It is not a song lyric, but Dad, we do need to talk to you. It's very important," I say.

My father is shaking his head no at me while he pets his cat in his arms. "No. You can call your mother. You got me in enough trouble with her. The both of you. Spouting that crazy nonsense and then telling your mother on me. You just wait, if she finds out that you and Caleb are friends—"

My grandfather rinses his hands in the sink and splashes a bit of water on his mouth. "Why can't Alessandra know they are friends?" my grandfather asks my dad.

"Because *this* is Caleb Cheval," my father says.

My grandfather's mouth couldn't be open any wider. "No! You're kidding, right?" my grandfather asks.

Before I can speak, Caleb tugs on the back of my shirt. I know he wants me to stay quiet. I can hear the beginning of a plan in his head, but he really thinks very fast. I can't quite follow it; I just know he wants me to be quiet.

"I am not kidding," my father says. "This is one Caleb Cheval, son of Miranda and, ugh, Andrew Cheval. Just moved into town. I paired him up with Frode at school yesterday and they've been running around causing all sorts of problems. Mostly for me."

Alright, so my dad doesn't know that Caleb has already met my mother, which means my mom didn't call him after the conversation that we lost the connection on. And he also has no idea that my mom met with Caleb's mom. But I can hear Caleb internally pleading with me to keep quiet, so I will.

My grandfather is scrutinizing Caleb's appearance, then says, "Well, now, you do look like your mother. I don't know why I didn't notice it before. Not at all like your father. How is your mother these days?"

"My mother is well. I didn't know that she was acquainted with so many from the house of Dracula," Caleb says.

That's cute. Caleb is trying hard not to lie. He should just lie, though, if he's good at it. I'm not good at it of course, so hells help us if they ask me.

"Of course your mother is well acquainted with us. She grew up with Alessandra, those two were best friends. Inseparable, if you ask me."

My father places his cat down and chides my grandfather. "Nobody asked you, so don't finish that thought. You've already said too much. Alessandra will have your head when she finds out you spoke of Miranda to Frode."

"Oh, alright. I'll be quiet," my grandfather says while he rubs my father's back. "Can't have my best boy being upset with me. Not when he's already had such a rough day."

My lip curls in agitation. My grandfather babies my father so much. Everyone thinks my father and grandfather are these two fiercely strong vampires, when in reality they are just an affectionate father and his spoiled adult son. "Okay, that's enough," I say. "Really. I can't take it anymore." I look softly at my grandfather. He loves me, but he definitely doesn't spoil me like he does my father. "Grandpa, Caleb and I have some kind of an unexplained connection. We can hear each other's thoughts and sometimes we feel the other's emotions. Have you ever heard of anything like this?"

My father rolls his eyes and throws his hand up. He opens the refrigerator and grabs two red bottled beers out. He passes one to my grandfather, then opens his own. The beer is so rancid smelling. It's a new vampire branded beer called "Bluhdy Goode." It smells anything but good, that's for sure.

My grandfather pops his bottle cap off and takes a big swig of beer. He looks at Caleb and I, then takes another drink before speaking. "Well, as far as the connection. I need some more information, that's not enough to go on. I saw you two out there hugging earlier when you landed. How long have you been this close? When did the connection start?" he asks.

Shit, he saw us. Well, he definitely didn't see the kiss because he would've said kiss, not hug.

My father's eyebrows are tightly pulled together. "Who was hugging?" he asks my grandfather. "Boys don't hug one another. Are you taking your vertigo medication like you're supposed to?"

"They were hugging, I saw them. What's wrong with two boys hugging anyway? I hug you and we're two guys," my grandfather says to my father.

My father takes a long sip of beer and sits down at the table. "I think it's time we had a talk," he says while motioning with his beer for Caleb and me to sit.

I sit down across the table from my father and place the book that Caleb loaned me on my lap while Caleb sits beside me. My grandfather takes a seat on the right side of the rectangular table.

My father twists his neck a bit. He looks very angry. He doesn't know about us, but he's not going to stand for me hugging Caleb. I really should just tell Caleb to leave. He's already had to listen to three of these conversations. I can hear Caleb's thoughts. He's trying hard to tell me he isn't going to leave no matter what I say.

My father places his beer bottle down. "We have a lot to talk about it seems. Now, you two said you felt the connection and I told you to drop it. You didn't listen. I told you that you were imagining it, and you went and told your mother. She is very mad at me now. Probably won't be coming here for a while. She also mentioned that she wants you to live with her. And why wouldn't she? You do love her best, right?"

My grandfather's bottom lip is sticking out. He actually feels bad for my father. He reaches across the table and rubs my father's hair-covered forearm. "No, no, my handsome boy. He doesn't love Alessandra more than he loves you. How could he? If he moved in with her, she'd try to force him to listen to her stories, or worse, she'd make him a character in one. Do you think Frode wants either of those things? Now, let's cheer up, okay? We need to listen to our

Frode to see what is going on. Can you do that? Can you listen to him and let him tell us what's happening? I can't help if I don't know what's happening."

My father is still pouting, but he's nodding at my grandfather. "Yes, I can do that. I can listen. So long as the two of them don't speak nonsense," my father says. "Wait, no, we need to clear up the hugging first. Were you two hugging in front of the house?" my father asks.

"Well, yeah, but friends hug each other. What more can I say?" I ask.

That is quite honestly the cleanest thing I can say. Otherwise, the terrible lies are going to start flying out.

"There," my grandfather says while patting my father's arm. "The boys were hugging because just like I told you, boys hug each other."

My father's gaze is a bit colder than normal looking at Caleb and me. "I don't think that it's normal for boys to hug each other. I've never seen you hug that delinquent Wolfie and he's here all the time. Why would you go around hugging Caleb for?" my father asks me while his eyes remain locked on Caleb.

"Dad, what is the big deal? I have so many other things going on. You know what—"

Caleb lightly nudges my foot under the table, stopping me from saying anything further. I wanted to threaten to just ask my mom, but I really do need this idiot's help. But, damn it, he won't focus, he's just stuck on the hug.

"Okay, I see what's going on," my grandfather says. "This Caleb definitely can hear his thoughts or at least he can predict what Frode is going to do. So, when did this start?" he asks me. My grandfather looks at my father, who is about to interject, and says, "No more nonsense about the hug, for now. There is something bigger going on."

I'm too afraid to look at Caleb, who has been uncharacteristically quiet during this conversation. Although, I'm sure with the massive number of ridiculous thoughts and worries he hears in my head, he probably can't even concentrate at this point.

Caleb is smiling brightly at me. "Mr. Lugo," Caleb says."We met each other yesterday and immediately there was a connection. It has gotten much stronger since then. I think I can hear everything inside Frode's head, and he seems to be able to hear my thoughts as well. The feelings connection is even stronger, although the two are connected, there is a distinct difference. If Frode is afraid, my body feels afraid as well. So, I'm not just feeling that he is afraid or upset, my body experiences the same sensations, like sweating, shaking, those kinds of things."

"What is Frode nervous about?" my grandfather asks.

Caleb doesn't hesitate and replies, "Well, right now he is uncomfortable because Mr. Dracula made him feel awkward about hugging me. He also is nervous because he is afraid of what is happening between us. Like Mr. Dracula told you, he said there is no logical reason for the connection and yet it exists, so that is making Frode feel very uneasy. He also doesn't like that I can hear everything he's thinking." Caleb gives me a big smile.

"Well, who would like that?" my grandfather asks with a chuckle.

My father stands and walks toward the refrigerator. He pulls another disgusting red beer out. "I would like that," he says. "Vampires in a relationship would like that. I had that with your mother before she left me. It made things easy. There was never a question of honesty because we could feel everything. But then that stupid Wolfman went and ruined everything," he says as he sits back down at the table and opens his beer.

"Dad, can you please for once, not make this about you? We really need some answers here," I say.

My grandfather shifts his attention to my father. "Alessandra will come back to you, son. You just need to give her space. But I can tell you a little secret. If you deal with this situation properly, in the way that Alessandra would want you to, I can guarantee you that she will be happy about it. She will not be happy if you don't listen. So, I need you to listen and not speak unless you can do it in a way that Alessandra would want you to. Because little Frode will definitely tell mommy everything that you did. We want Alessandra back, right?"

My father sips his beer and slouches in his chair. He is full-on pouting. "Yes…of course, I do. But this whole thing is stupid, Dad. Being a parent is so much work. Listen to them, they're whining about nothing, and all I want to do is tell them to leave. Why does being a parent mean I need to listen all the time?"

My grandfather shakes his head at my dad, and says, "Not helpful. What you just said was not helpful. I don't think you're thinking about this the right way. I just told you that Alessandra will be happy if you do a good job. So, what do you need to do?"

"I need to do a good job," my dad says reluctantly while rolling his eyes.

My grandfather's smile beams brightly at my father. "Yes, my sweet boy and you will. Now, tell the boys about their mothers," my grandfather says.

Thank fangs my grandfather is here. I don't even know where we would be in this conversation if he weren't here to keep my dad in line. Caleb is feeling pretty hopeful that we're going to get some answers here, but I'm not so sure. I mean, Caleb is probably smarter than me, so I should just try to align with his way of thinking. But, damn, we really need to just find out where our moms are. We shouldn't waste time here on my dad and my grandfather, whose stench is getting worse. That's it! My grandfather smells like a bottle gourd! Ugh, fangs it's disgusting. It smells like sulfur or just a toilet, I don't know, but I think the alcohol is making the smell even worse. I can barely keep a straight face.

Caleb is leaning close to my ear. He whispers, "What the hell is a bottle gourd? What are you thinking about right now?"

Wow, I almost just kissed him instinctively. His cotton candy scent is lingering near my nose. I playfully, and probably a little too roughly, push him back. But, hey, I gotta keep my cover up. We're just two guy vampires that are hanging out. He can't be whispering and turning me on right now, and I, for sure, can't let on in front of my father and grandfather that his scent drives me wild. Seriously though, I'm grateful because Caleb's scent really knocked out the disgusting smell of my grandfather.

My father has just been pouting this whole time. While my grandfather has been lightly patting his forearm like a child.

"Fine, I will say a few things," my father says. "Caleb, your mother and Alessandra were best friends, they grew up together. They were inseparable until I came into the picture. Of course, they remained close even after that, though. When you boys were small, don't ask me how old you were, but you would play together all the time. Then Frode's mother decided to begin a new career, she left me, and her friendship with your mother—and my marriage—ended. That's it. And it's Wolfman's fault. He could have just stayed married to his wife and everything would have been fine, but no, he decided to come out and make everything miserable for me. That's it. That's the story. The two haven't spoken since they ended their friendship. For the connection you two feel, I don't understand it and I don't want to. I think you're both just imagining what you're feeling. That's it. I can't give you anything else." He looks to my grandfather and says, "There. I did it. I helped. I'm going upstairs to watch TV with

Alexandra now." He stands up from the table and walks out of the kitchen.

My grandfather stands and walks behind him. He stops before leaving the kitchen and turns toward us. "Your dad is leaving some things out, but I would say that the relationship between your mothers was very close. I'm not sure exactly what happened between them, but as much as they dislike each other now, there was a time when they were inseparable. You shouldn't be here asking him for answers, you should be asking your mothers. The whole thing hurts your father too much. He would do anything to get your mother back. I'm sorry that you two are having a hard time, but whatever is going on between you two, I've never heard of it. Unless…unless you two aren't telling me everything?"

Oh no. I'm gonna screw up. I'm gonna say something stupid. I can't control myself. Shit, someone help me before I open my big fanging mouth.

Caleb stands and smiles at my grandfather. "No, we've told you everything," he says.

My grandfather gives us a nod. "Alright, well I'm going to go console your father. Like I said, you should reach out to your mothers. It was nice meeting you, Caleb. How is your father, by the way?"

"My father is fine. Are you acquainted with him as well?" Caleb asks while standing beside my chair.

My grandfather gives a hearty chuckle and taps the wall frame. "Yes, we are all well acquainted with your father," he says and leaves the room.

"Whaaat?! What the fuck was that?" I ask no one in particular while looking at the table. "How many things are going on here? I'm confused, Caleb. What does your dad have to do with anything?"

Caleb shrugs, then whispers, "No idea, but don't get distracted.

Remember, we still need to find out where our moms are. Let's try to call them again in your room."

I nod and stand up from my chair, grabbing the book Caleb loaned me off my lap. "That's a good idea. This whole freaking thing is driving me insane," I say.

I can hear Caleb's thoughts. He knows he is going to have to leave soon, and he doesn't want to. It can't be that late, yet. We still have some time before he has to go home.

Chapter 12
Take Your Hand Out of Your Shorts

As we enter my room, I notice the time is already 9:00 pm. Caleb closes the door behind us and grabs my face forcefully with both hands. He's walking me backward toward my bed while gripping my hair at just the right strength. Damn this squeeze is perfect, it's like not enough to hurt, but just enough to let me know that it could hurt if I wanted it to. His tongue is deep inside my mouth, as he guides me backward and lays on top of me. Our kiss is ravenous, I feel starved, and I can barely keep up with Caleb's mouth as he twists his tongue around.

He pulls back slightly, and whispers in between breaths, "I really want this." His hand is on the outside of my pants, where it was earlier. "I really want you," he says while his hand lightly teases the hardest part of my body. He's dragging the tips of his fingers down. Shit, I feel like I'm going to explode, and we haven't even done anything yet. I grab Caleb's face and bring it near my neck, lightly turning it to the side.

"Mmm…delicious," Caleb whispers while he continues teasing me. He's staring at my exposed neck, and I can tell he's reading my thoughts. All I want is for him to bite me. I can't take it anymore. I'm squeezing my toes in anticipation, and my damn hands have nowhere to go again. I grip the sides of my comforter. Caleb's soft tongue is on my neck and his scent is so enticing that if he doesn't hurry up and do it, I may bite him first. I'm starting to feel impatient, and I'm certain it's only been a few moments of Caleb kissing my neck, but damn it, I'm torn between wanting to be bitten and wanting to be ridden. Wow, that was a dirty thought. But I do, I want him to do it.

Caleb jumps off me quickly, hearing two knocks on my door, along with my grandfather's voice. "Frode, I think it's time for Caleb to head home. Your father says it's a school night and it's time to wrap it up," my grandfather calls through the door.

I'm panting and my neck is wet with Caleb's saliva. Mother fanger, I can't believe this.

"Yeah, okay, Grandpa," I say.

I didn't hear him approaching, but I can clearly hear his footsteps leaving the hallway.

"Do you think he heard us?" Caleb asks.

I can't form a thought. I can't think straight. Well, I'm not straight, so how could I think straight? Haha. Okay, seriously. I need to try and focus.

"I don't know, Caleb. I couldn't hear anything besides your breathing and heartbeats. Well, and my own thoughts."

Caleb is nodding with his hands on his waist. "Our kissing was pretty loud. I didn't hear him out there. He's a big guy, too. His footsteps were crazy loud when he just walked away. I think maybe he snuck over quietly to eavesdrop."

"I'll just tell him we were studying or reading," I say while I finally sit up. I grab a hair tie from my nightstand and tie my hair up in my housewife bun.

"You're so cute when you put your little housewife bun in," Caleb says. "I love that your mom calls it that."

"Shit, our moms! Caleb, we didn't even get to call them again."

Caleb takes my hands in his and smiles at me. "True, but think of it this way—they can see we tried to call them a bunch of times, we left voicemails and texts, they obviously don't want to be bothered. Besides, my mom will be home tonight, she never stays out. I'll try to stay awake and wait for her to come home, if not, I'll talk to her before school in the morning."

"I don't want you to go," I say, squeezing his hands.

"I know, me neither, but I can't stay, your grandpa just said I needed to leave. I hate to leave you if he heard us, though. I don't want you to deal with that on your own. Besides that, I really want to do what we were about to do, and if I stay any longer, I won't be able to stop myself."

I still haven't fully recovered from the shock of my grandfather knocking on the door. and I'm also really nervous. What if my grandfather heard us? I won't have Caleb here to help me, I'll have to deal with it all by myself. I feel kind of desperate for Caleb to stay right now.

I nod silently while looking down at Caleb's hands that are still holding mine. "Okay, fly safe and just let me know if you talk to your mom."

Caleb is lifting my chin with his hand. He presses his lips softly against mine. He pulls me into a tight squeeze while rubbing my back. "Don't be upset, Frode, and don't worry about your grandfather. Even though I know you're worried, I think it's going to be okay. Besides, even if he heard something, he couldn't have seen anything, so you can just deny it. There is another option, but I wouldn't recommend it."

I squeeze Caleb tighter and ask, "What's the other option?"

"We can't. Just forget it," he says and kisses my cheek.

Caleb is pulling back from the hug while I squeeze him back in after hearing his thoughts. "Do you think we would get caught?" I ask.

"I don't know. I mean, we shouldn't, you could possibly sneak out and I could definitely sneak you in for the night, but I think your grandpa is going to come back in a few minutes. I should just go. I can call you when I get home and we can talk again, like last night. I know you're a terrible liar, so if your grandpa comes back, just stay in bed and say you're tired. Just keep repeating that. If that doesn't work and you start to feel cornered, just tell your grandpa about what happened with our moms, that will distract him."

Caleb pulls back and gives me one more quick kiss. "Okay?" he asks.

I nod and say, "Okay."

Caleb leaves through the window and I instantly feel cold. Ugh, I hate this feeling. Alright, no time for feeling so sad about nothing. I head into my bathroom and brush my teeth. I'm not even hungry and I'm definitely not going into the kitchen right now. With any luck my grandpa will just leave me alone for the night. I know my dad won't bother me, not with my grandpa here babying him.

I remove my clothes and change into a pair of loose black athletic shorts. Walking past the mirror, I stop for a moment and stare at myself. I know it's not right to be obsessed with your own appearance, but I really do not hate the way I look. I am a damn good-looking vampire. Caleb thinks so, too, I hear it every time he looks at me. My chest and arms are all nice and toned. I don't have a six pack, but the definition is there, it's just not exaggerated. I pull the front of my shorts down a bit as I stare in the mirror. I'm trying to determine how much Caleb has seen. He didn't see this much tonight, but earlier at his house, I think my pants were unbuttoned and he could see like this much. This looks good. It's nice and my guy down below is impressive on his own, but I do keep things neat down here. I learned that I needed to do that a long time ago when Wolfie and I found some porny videos online. Those vamps had all different kinds of shapes and styles trimmed down below. There were even some that had removed all of the hair here, but for me looking like this, I think it's good. There's just the right amount of dark hair against my tan skin.

Dicks are funny, though, like they're sexy and hot, but like right now, he's not interested, well, because I'm looking at myself and also because I'm, you know, cooled off from earlier. But it's like just crazy how this one thing can do so much for someone else. Thank fangs I have a big one. Well, I think it's big, like I said I've never seen or touched another one in real life. I've seen them on TV and obviously online, but those pictures could all be fake for all I know.

I have myself firmly in my hand while I'm checking out my reflection. I just thought of Caleb's hand brushing against it. It was only on the outside of my jeans, but still, it drove me crazy. I wonder if that can happen. Could I finish just from that? That would be so embarrassing. I'm looking down and I'm really tempted here…but I shouldn't do anything. Even if I'm thinking about Caleb, it seems like, I don't know, I should wait until we actually do it first. Maybe I should ask him if that's okay? No, vampires don't ask their boyfriend that…right? What would it hurt anyway? He doesn't have to know. I'm all effing pent up right now and I haven't released in a while. My hand moves a bit while I struggle with what the right thing to do is.

"Frode, listen we need to—" my grandfather says while walking in my room without knocking.

Yes, my dick is in my hand. Yes, I was in between doing that and not doing that, right in front of my fucking mirror!

I scream, "Get out, Grandpa!" I'm quickly pulling my shorts up. I walk into my bathroom and stand over the sink with my head down.

How? How could this happen? Why the hell did he just walk in without knocking? As I see my reflection in the mirror, I am so embarrassed that I can't even look at myself. I don't even know what I'm going to say to my grandfather. I should have just gone home with Caleb. That would have been better than this.

I wash my hands and splash water on my face. Alright, I gotta deal with this, I guess. Actually, no. I'm just gonna get in bed. I don't owe anyone an apology or an explanation. If I'm standing in my own room, with my D in my hand, whose business is that? Yeah, that's right. I'm going to lie in bed and just wait for Caleb to call.

I lie in my bed and look at my phone. I still can't believe my mother hasn't called me. I try to call her again and get the same message saying that the phone number is temporarily unavailable. I really wonder what happened. I'm sure my mom is fine, though, I'm not worried about her being in danger; noble vampires are rarely in danger. Our senses are pretty good, and my mom is always well aware of her surroundings. Besides that, my mom would probably rip another vampire's head clean off if anyone dared to threaten her.

I don't hear my grandpa in the hallway. That's good. Hopefully, he just went to bed. It's late now, especially for him.

I changed Caleb's ringtone earlier, so he doesn't get the scream like everyone else has. It's a nice soothing chime sound now when he calls or texts. I place my phone on my bare chest, and I grab the book that Caleb loaned me off my nightstand. I really like the colors on the cover. My phone rings before I can open the book. I smile and place the book back on my nightstand. "Hey there," I say.

"Hey…" Caleb says.

"Is your mom home?" I ask.

"Nope, not home and her phone is still doing the same thing. Did your grandpa talk to you?"

I blow air into the phone, then say, "He came back in, but we didn't talk. Don't even ask what happened, it's too embarrassing. Just be happy that he hasn't come back in here."

"Frode, why do you always do embarrassing things whenever I leave? Next time, do the embarrassing thing when I'm there, so we can laugh together. It's no fun if you do something and then I have no idea what happened. Now, I have to wait until tomorrow and try and see if I can get you to think about it."

"Well, if you were here, I wouldn't have been doing what he saw me doing."

Oh shit…why did I say that? He definitely knows now; I couldn't have made that any clearer.

"Were you? No…you weren't doing what I think that sounded like…tell me you weren't," he says.

I can't tell if he's mad, shocked, or turned on. His tone is kind of indiscernible right now.

"I don't know what you're thinking I did, but if you're mad, then I didn't do whatever you're thinking, if you're shocked, I also didn't do what you're thinking," I say.

"I am neither of those things," Caleb says in a somewhat sultry tone.

"Oh yeah? Well, what are you then?" I ask while I slide my hand inside my shorts.

"Tch…don't start something that we can't finish right now. I'm not going to do this with you before we do it together," Caleb says.

I understand what he means, but I really want to do it. I've never had phone sex before, and I really want to try it. I honestly don't know how I'll fall asleep when I feel all constricted. I feel like all the blood in my body is rushing to one place, and I just want to release. Besides we *will* be doing it together. It will just be in our own rooms, but still, like, together.

"I'm not starting anything that we can't finish. I'm just curious what kind of a mood you're in. Besides, I don't know about you, but I can definitely finish."

My eyes widen. I can't believe I just said that. I am so stupid.

"Oh?" Caleb asks.

Time for me to double down, if this is what I want. "Yes. I can. I can definitely finish. But I don't know about you."

Caleb is silent. I have no idea if he's mad or not.

Caleb lets out a sigh. "I could finish, but I'm not going to do that, and neither are you," he says.

"My hand is already in my shorts. Sorry," I say.

"Frode! No, take it out. Take your hand out. It will be better to do it together."

I pull my hand out of my shorts and shake my head. "Caleb, do you know how many times I have turned him off without warning since meeting you? He's never going to forgive me if I don't let him at least have this. What am I supposed to do? I want you, and I can't have you. I wanted you like three times today and every time something interrupted us. Now, I can fix this with you on the phone, or I can fix this with you off the phone. This isn't a ridiculous thing I'm suggesting."

"Ugh! This *is* a ridiculous thing you're suggesting! Frode, it should be me doing it, not you. Isn't that what you want? Damn it, I really can't come back there right now. If your grandpa finds out I'm there, you'll be in trouble. Besides, what are you going to do if he comes back in and you're in the middle of doing that?"

"Caleb, he just caught me doing it. He's not coming back in here. There is no fanging way he is. But, no, you can't come back here. This is stupid. Honesty is dumb. I could've just done it and not said anything. What does it matter? I'll be thinking about you and imagining it's you. Come on, Caleb, you can do it, too. I really want to," I whine.

"Honesty is not dumb. And, if you did that and didn't tell me, I would have known tomorrow anyway. You literally think of a million things a minute, I guarantee that you would've—"

"You guarantee that I would've what?" I ask.

"Shh," Caleb says.

I put my hand back inside my shorts. This is ridiculous. Why should I have to listen to him?

Caleb whispers, "I hear my dad talking. I don't know who he's talking to, but he sounds mad. I think he may be talking to my mom."

I pull my hand back out. Eff it. I give up. If I can't get hard ever again after this, it's not my fault.

"Do you need to hang up?" I ask.

"Maybe," Caleb says. "If I want to hear him, I do. Not sure why he's here. It's kind of soon for him to be back. He just left a few days ago."

"Well, it's late anyway. I should go to bed. If you want to listen to him, then I'll just hang up."

"Do you think I'm stupid? I know exactly what you're going to do. Take your hand out of your damn shorts. I know you just put it back in there."

He isn't wrong. As he was talking, I'd put my hand in again.

"How the hell do you know what I'm doing? I thought we established that you can't hear my thoughts unless we're together."

"Take your hand out. Or I'm going to be really mad at you," Caleb says.

"Are you serious? Fine," I say while pulling my hand out. "Don't be mad at me. But really…how did you know?"

"Because, Frode, I literally keep putting my hand inside my sweatpants and taking it out. I've done it ten times, since we started this conversation. You definitely don't have as much willpower as I do, so of course you would go straight for it, the second you thought you were in the clear."

"Ha! Well, I feel better then. I won't do it, okay? Really, I promise. But tomorrow during free period, I'm going to need something. I don't think I'll be able to wait until after school."

"I don't think I'll be able to wait that long either. I'm gonna spy on my dad and then go to bed. Also, once more, honesty is not stupid, it's important, its especially important for vampires, who are terrible liars, that have boyfriends that can hear their thoughts."

Caleb is so hot when he kind of scolds me. There have to be other vampires that feel the same way when their boyfriend tells them what to do. I refuse to believe that I'm the only one that gets turned on by it. Damn it, no. I have to resist the urge to put my hand in my shorts.

"Alright. Good night. I'll see you in the morning, Caleb."

"Good night, Frode. See you in the morning."

I hang up the phone and place it on my nightstand. I turn on my side and close my eyes, falling asleep almost instantly.

"Good morning, Frode," my grandfather says.

I open my eyes to not only a terrible smell, but to the sight of my grandfather sitting next to me on my bed. Well, this is not the way anyone wants to be woken up after dreaming about their first bite with their boyfriend. Damn it, and his effing smell is gonna get all over my bed.

I rub my eyes awake and sit up. "Yeah, Good morning, Grandpa. Why are you in here right now? I need to get ready for school. It's already 7:00," I say, noticing my clock.

My grandfather looks uncomfortable. I'm sure that I do, too, because I sure as hell feel uncomfortable.

"You, uh, you got a text message there while you were sleeping," my grandfather says.

I grab my phone off the nightstand. "You looked at my phone?"

"No, no, slow down, buddy. I sent you a text message, but I saw that you hadn't read it, so I came in to deliver the message personally. That's what I meant." My grandfather's eyes are wandering around my room.

I read the message aloud: "Frode, your father is having a very hard time right now. He wasn't able to get ahold of your mother last night, and he really wanted to tell her about how he had a nice talk with you and Caleb. He's devastated, he thinks she's ignoring him on purpose."

I rub the inner corners of my eyes with my thumb and pointer finger. "Why did you text me like a story and why are you feeling bad for him all the time?" I ask.

"He is my son and he's hurting. He's not the one to be blamed for what happened, you know? Anyway, I was hoping that you could try and reach out to your mother for him. You know, put in a good word, and tell her that he talked to you and Caleb last night."

I shake my head and put my phone down. I stand up from my bed and my grandfather looks me up and down. "You're in good shape, Frode. You been hitting the gym? Or are these soccer muscles?" he asks me.

"Both, probably. I don't know. Listen, Grandpa, I have to get ready for school. I can't be late. I, um, I don't know when I'll talk to my mom next, but when I do, I will tell her that you are concerned about my dad. I'm not gonna say all that other stuff. He didn't help us, that's the truth. Whether you think anything is his fault or not, is your opinion, but I know that there are things that are his fault. And forget about the stuff with Caleb, my dad hasn't been willing to listen to me for a long time. He is the biggest baby I've ever seen, Grandpa. I won't tell my mother that he helped me."

I pull open my drawers and pull my uniform pants out along with my socks and underwear. My grandfather stands from my bed. "Well, if you don't feel bad for him, I can't make you. But about last night, let's just leave whatever happened between us. I don't want to upset your father any more than he already is."

"Yeah, okay," I say as my grandfather leaves my room.

The question is, what the hell is he talking about? Did he hear Caleb and I or is he talking about the fact that he walked in on me? Either way, he isn't going to tell my dad, but it still makes me feel a bit nervous. I don't know how long I'll be able to hide what happened with my mom from him, either.

We don't have school tomorrow because of a vampire holiday. Which, as a student. I'm grateful for, but I also just don't understand. Why give us a day off in the middle of the week? Shouldn't we just celebrate on a different day, like a Friday? Being off on a Wednesday is stupid, but at least that means more time with Caleb. Hopefully, we can talk to our moms by then. I don't even truly understand this holiday, it's like the anniversary of when my great-great-grandfather had his first bite while on spring break. I don't know, it's a weird story and even though we celebrate it, it's not in any history books. Some vamps say it was really based of two white-haired vampires. Who freaking knows?

I'm really anxious to find out what happened with Caleb's dad and to see what his mom said. My mom's phone is still off or dead, since I have no missed calls or texts from her. Funny thing, too, is that Wolfman hasn't texted or called me back. He definitely knows where she is, she wouldn't do anything without telling him. I need to try and get to Wolfie this morning, he can help me. His dad is a sucker for him. Yeah, Wolfie can definitely help me.

I'm staring at my reflection in the mirror, trying to decide if I should do my classic high bun or put my hair into my housewife bun. Well, with my grandfather here, I guess I'm not going to use the ribbon. I really liked the way it looked, though. You know what? Fang it. I grab my black bristle brush and flip my head upside down, gathering all my hair tightly on top. I wrap the black elastic around it and pull the ponytail forward. I grab a piece of the ribbon from the mystery drawer and tie it around the base of my ponytail. My ponytail reaches just above the small of my back and the two strands of the bright red ribbon are hanging on both sides.

I walk inside my closet and begin flipping through my capes. I'll have to wear a cape with a plain clasp today, since I wore the other one two days in a row. This one is nicer, though; the inside is blood red with a thinly stenciled floral print inside. I got it as a present from my aunt one year. I always thought it was very pretty, but I was never brave enough to wear it. Especially in front of my dad, who mocked it relentlessly when I opened it. It was so mean; my poor aunt was so proud of it and my father just made fun of it. Well, with my grandfather here, he isn't going to say anything to me about wearing it. I do a final check in the mirror and leave my room.

Walking downstairs I can hear my grandfather talking. Damn it, I forgot briefly about his stench. I really hope it doesn't get on me. I'll need to try and dodge him once I grab breakfast. I'm surely not resorting to bite spray, but shit, he literally smells like shit.

I open the refrigerator and smile quickly at my grandfather. My father's back is to me as he reads his morning paper.

I quickly grab a smoothie out and close the fridge. I head for the door and say, "See you later, Grandpa and I'll see you after school, Dad."

"Stop," my father says. I can hear the newspaper being placed down as I turn around.

"Yeah?" I ask with one hand on the doorknob,

My father is looking me up and down. "You are not going to school in that hideous flowery cape. Go back upstairs and take it off, and what the hell is in your hair?" he asks.

"Now, Drac, son, you can't tell the boy what to wear, or what to do with his hair. Remember what we talked about. Besides, Mel made him that cape. Your sister will be so happy knowing that he's wearing it," my grandfather says.

"I'm leaving," I say and walk outside.

Chapter 13
Your Mouth is Mine

I take only a few steps off the patio and Caleb quickly wraps his arms around me from behind. "Your hair looks really cute like that, and I love this cape," he says.

"Thanks, let's go. I don't want to stay on the ground any longer than we have to," I say.

Caleb's magnificent scent overwhelms me as I fly beside him. I'm a little worried about my own scent, though, with all of the time I spent around my grandpa this morning.

"Do I smell bad, Caleb?"

Caleb turns to look at me. "Of course not. Why would you ask that? Are you asking because I didn't kiss you? Because, if so, you didn't give me a chance to, since we were in front of your house. It's too noisy in your head right now for me to hear what you're freaking out about."

"No, I was just worried because I was around my grandfather for a while this morning. He was sitting on my bed waiting for me to wake up. It was terrible, I was having a really good dream at the time, too. But, wait, we need to talk about your mom, or your dad, well, both. Did you find anything out?"

Caleb is shaking his head. "Well, my dad was yelling about

someone, I think it was your mom, honestly, but I don't know who he was talking to. I can only guess that it was your mom he was yelling about, though. It was something about her being gone for a long time and then just pretending everything is fine, like she always did before. He also said a few things that sounded like he could have been talking about your dad, but I don't know. I'm sure my dad knows a lot of idiot vampires. Nothing concrete was said. I didn't hear anything useful."

"Well, that sucks. And, obviously, your mom didn't come home last night, right?" I ask.

"Nope and my dad was gone this morning when I left. Either way, I think you should come home with me today. You could stay the night since we're off tomorrow."

Whaaat?! Spend the night? With my boyfriend? At his house? How could I do that? I can't do that.

"That would be cool," I say calmly, pretending to be unafraid.

"What are you afraid of? I'd be more afraid of free period if I were you. I'm not holding back anymore, not after your little incident last night," he says.

We land in front of the school and Caleb quickly pulls me against his body. His left arm is wrapped around my waist and his right hand is cradling the back of my head. "I am taking it today," he whispers. "You can spend the night, or not, but we will not separate tonight until we're both satisfied."

My eyes may fall out of my head, or I may just fall over dead. How the hell am I supposed to deal with this? That was too fucking hot.

Caleb tilts his head, and our lips meet softly. "Mmm. You taste so good. I never tire of it," he says when I pull back from the kiss.

We're holding hands walking toward the school entrance and I see Wolfie. Yes! That is exactly who I need right now.

"Wolfie!" I yell while cupping my hands around my mouth.

Wolfie gives me a nod and jogs toward us.

"What's up, guys?" Wolfie asks.

I lightly smack him with the backside of my hand on his shoulder a few times. "I need a favor, a big one," I say.

"Of course, what do you need?" he asks.

"Let's start walking so we aren't late, and I'll explain."

As we reach our first class, I finish telling Wolfie everything that has happened.

"Alright, well, I'll call my dad at lunch from the office. So, if you stay in the cafeteria, or meet me in the library during free period, I can tell you what he says. This would be so much easier if we were allowed to have cell phones. Such a stupid rule your dad put into place," Wolfie says.

"Yeah, that's cool. Caleb and I will just hang out in the cafeteria until you're done talking to him. I don't want to go to the library, though, it's a long story."

Caleb is shaking his head no at me.

I shrug at him as the bell rings. "What? You want the library?" I ask.

I can read his mind, though…shit. I forgot that ten minutes ago he said free period was going to basically be the time that we released together. Now, I just told Wolfie we'd meet him in the cafeteria. I am such an idiot.

Wolfie is looking at the two of us confused. "This is wild that you guys can hear each other's thoughts. I actually wanted to go to the library during free period anyway, so let's meet there. I don't think Kat will be there. She hasn't texted me back this morning. I'm not sure what's going on, it's kind of frustrating me."

"Alright," I say as Wolfie and I bump fists. Caleb gives him a nod, but his face is more than annoyed. He's not a fan of me giving away our free period time in exchange for possible information on our mothers.

Caleb and I sit together at the back corner desk of the classroom. Mr. Prinaldi's sweat is already on full display and the class has just started.

"Good morning," Mr. Prinaldi says. "Now, everyone was split into pairs yesterday and, unless something cataclysmic happens, you will remain in those pairs for the remainder of the year. Our first assignment will be for all partners to do a report on the science of vampirism in fiction. Every year, you all have to do a boring report, but this year I thought we'd do something fun and add a fictional aspect to the assignment. Does anyone have any questions?"

Caleb raises his hand.

"What is your question, Caleb?" Mr. Prinaldi asks.

"Well," Caleb says. "That was a bit confusing, are you saying we are writing a fictional report on vampirism or are you saying we write a report on how fictional books explain the science of vampirism?"

"The latter," Mr. Prinaldi confirms.

Caleb nods in understanding. He rolls his eyes and looks at me. "Could this be any dumber? Who cares about how vampire science is explained in fiction? What does that have to do with anything? Seems like a dumb assignment for a biology class."

While I agree with Caleb, I'm really just freaking out about way too many things right now. I was really looking forward to free period, too, not to mention if we go to the library, Ms. Beagle will be there and we're gonna have to deal with her. I also want to sleep over at Caleb's. Falling asleep next to him would be amazing. I bet he's a really good vampire to sleep with.

Caleb lightly laughs; I assume he heard what I was thinking.

He whispers in my ear, "I may be biased, but I think I am a very good vampire to sleep with. I should warn you, though; I usually start off with sweatpants on, and often wake naked. I get very hot when I sleep, so if you sleep next to me, I imagine you are going to get very hot, too."

I lightly shove his face back with my hand. Unbelievable that he would say those things to me, so early in the morning. Damn it, how am I going to last all day like this? Now I don't even have the promise of free period.

I lean my head back and slouch in my chair. The girls at the desk next to us are staring over. I can't even remember their names. I'm lucky I remember my own name at this point. One of the girls stands, she's walking in front of Caleb and me.

"We want to ask you both something," she says, glancing at her friend then back to Caleb and me.

"I'd rather you didn't," Caleb says.

"Oh, okay. Never mind then," she says, walking away. Her mouth is wide as she walks back to her friend. She definitely wasn't expecting him to say that.

"Caleb, you're going to make everyone hate you. She may have just needed help with something," I say.

Caleb is shaking his head, no, resolutely. "Ask her what she wanted. I guarantee you it was something about whether we liked girls, or would date girls, or do something with girls. Guarantee it. If I'm wrong, I'll do whatever you want."

"And what if you're right?" I ask. "What will I have to do?"

"Hmm…this is intriguing. Let's do the same for both outcomes. Whoever is wrong has to do whatever the other wants," Caleb says.

Caleb turns toward the girls on the right. "Excuse me. Would you mind telling me what it was that you needed? My boyfriend's curiosity has gotten the best of him. As you know, curiosity killed the bat, but he can't help himself and I'm a sucker for him, so please, state your case."

The girl, who approached us a few moments ago, speaks, "Well, we were just wondering if you guys didn't have anything to do after school, if maybe we could hang out together."

"To what end?" Caleb asks her, then smirks at me.

"Well, we are both birgins, so if you wanted to, we would let you guys bite us. We could do whatever you guys wanted us to."

"What the fuck?" I ask, then quickly cover my mouth.

"Never. We will never bite you. You should be embarrassed to even have said that to us. Aren't you vampires taught any type of respect for hierarchy here? How can you even speak to us like that? Please don't talk to either of us again." Caleb makes a shooing motion toward her, then turns back toward me.

"Frode, you will do things," he says. "Great things because you are sleeping over tonight. That is what I want, since I won the bet."

I can't believe he was right. I can't believe that those girls would even say that. Okay, well, I can definitely believe it because it's not the first time someone has said that to me. But, damn, they know we're together, so what the hell would possess them to even say that? Is this a thing that I'm unaware of? Do single vampires go around throwing themselves at vampires in relationships? I mean if I were dating a girl, no girl would just throw an offer to bite them on the table…actually, they would, they definitely would. I've had way more vampires ask me to bite them than I can count. Still, though, taking the fact that we're royalty aside, I would never just ask someone to bite me that I wasn't in a relationship with. I want my boyfriend to bite me and I'm definitely going to bite him, but having girls, who I don't even know, throw their necks around just makes me feel cheap or something. I really don't like that anyone thinks of Caleb biting them either. Caleb's mouth is mine. I'm the only one that he's going to bite. Why would they even offer that to us?

"You're hot, Frode. You know that, right? I know that you do. Of course, they throw themselves at you. I threw myself at you, don't you remember? You think the silliest things sometimes. Don't waste so much brain space on nonsense. But I will warn you, if you keep thinking about me biting you, it's going to happen sooner than you think. If you want me to wait until after school, then put it out of your mind. I'm not afraid to get in trouble for cutting class if it means I get to bite you. So don't tempt me further."

I nod and straighten my posture as the bell rings. I must have been in my head for a long time because it feels like we just got here and class is already over. Caleb stands and holds my hand. The two girls that were sitting next to us leave before anyone else. I'm sure they're pretty embarrassed. I actually feel bad for anyone that hits on Caleb, or me when I'm with Caleb. Caleb is not afraid to put vampires in their place. It's pretty funny to me, but still, he's new, so vamps haven't probably spread the word about his cocky attitude yet. I was never mean to anyone, I just kind of turned them down nicely, or ignored them, but Caleb's way is probably better, honestly. This way, there's no chance of anyone mistaking kindness for a mutual interest. There is no fluff in his rejections, he just puts vampires right in their place and flicks his wrist afterward. It's pretty funny, really. Well, except for the part where there are girls thinking about my boyfriend, that just pisses me off.

Oh shit…Caleb has me pinned against the wall while other vampires pass by us in the crowded hallway. "Hey, my cape is gonna get all scratched up if you push me against the bricks," I say.

Caleb is nodding at me. His body is pressed against mine and he's whispering in my ear. I actually love that he isn't at all fazed by anyone seeing us. I'm not either. I'd actually like a picture of this, I could definitely use it. If it looks half as hot as it feels, it would be more than enough for nights like last night.

"What will it take to get you out of your own head? You're

thinking the inanest things. I hate everyone else; this is not news to you. I will never bite anyone besides you, and you will never bite anyone besides me. I am going to take you right here if you don't knock it off. We have to go to class, so come on." He quickly kisses me and pulls my hand behind him, dragging me like a child.

"Oooh! Nice hair, Frode!" a high-pitched voice says from the left side.

I turn to see who said that to me, and bump into Caleb's back. I guess he stopped walking. There are no vampires besides the two of us stopped, though, so I have no idea who said it. It's rather nice that someone complimented it. My hair does look great today. I'm happy that someone said that, but I would have liked to thank them, whoever it was.

Caleb tilts his head at me, and I stand beside him. "I said your hair looked really cute as soon as I saw you this morning. Do you need someone else to say it?" he asks.

"Well, no, but it still feels nice that someone else noticed that I did something with it. I'm only interested in impressing you. It's not the same. But I like when vamps notice things that I put an effort into."

"Okay, because I think it looks very, very cute. And if you need me to tell you that every few minutes, I will do that. But who said that just now? Did you recognize the voice?" he asks me.

"No, I didn't recognize the voice and, really, everyone in the school knows who I am, so there's a chance I don't even know who the vampire was. Come on, Ms. Phlip said we could sit beside one another if there were no open seats, but she's not going to let you just move desks around if we're late." I pull Caleb toward the classroom door.

We walk inside and there are two seats in the back open. Yes, thank fangs. Kressa and Kat are in the back row, but they are both one seat further over than yesterday. Caleb and I claim the back two seats for ourselves and sit down.

Ms. Phlip enters and goes straight into the lesson plan. Caleb looks so studious when he's paying attention. My dad mentioned his test scores, and he does speak much more eloquently than I do. Maybe he is really smart, like book smart. He's Frode smart, that much I know. Shit, I gotta pay attention. It's hard, though, with him sitting there actually paying attention to something other than me.

"Ouch!" I yell as a folded pointy triangle hits me in the face.

"Sorry," Kat whispers.

Oh, it's a note from Kat, I guess she learned a new way to fold notes. The paper is all tucked inside itself into a tight triangle. I will never understand the way she wastes her time on things. How long could such a stupidly useless skill have taken her to learn?

I open the note from Kat and read it:

Hey, I hung out with Kressa last night after school. I think I kind of like her. She's cool, Frody.

I shrug at her and give a false good-for-you, I guess, sort of clap. Kat is tilting her head at me. What kind of a reaction does she want from me? She has no idea what I've been going through, so I can't blame her, but why would she need to tell me that she thinks Kressa is cool? I think she's cool, too, so what? She knows I'm dating Caleb, so what would she be feeling around for? Fangs, girls make no sense.

I put the note in my pocket and turn back toward Ms. Phlip in the front of the classroom.

Another triangle note just hit me directly next to my eye. "Damn it! Kat!" I shout, drawing the attention of the whole class, as well as Ms. Phlip. She could've poked my eye out with that damn thing.

Ms. Phlip says, "Frode, what have you got there? Is that a note? You know that you're not allowed to pass notes in class. Bring it up here."

Kat's face is terrified. Ms. Phlip reads all notes aloud that are caught being passed around in class. She even reads the ones that say bad things about her. She does not care. I stand with the note in my hand. What do I do? I can't give her Kat's note. Kat looks like she's going to cry, but what do I do?

"Please don't give it to her," Kat whispers while looking at me with desperate eyes.

"Froderick! Now, bring it up here. I'm sure the whole class wants to know what you and Mr. Cheval are discussing. Let's have a read together." She is holding her palm open toward me from the front of the class.

Caleb stands and says, "Mr. Cheval and Mr. Dracula were not passing notes, so you can all keep dreaming." He gives the class a false smile, then sits back down.

I take a step toward Ms. Phlip, maybe I'll just beg her not to read it when I get up there.

"Frode, please? No!" Kat screams.

Instinctively I place the folded triangle in my mouth and look at Ms. Phlip with a shoulder shrug. "Can't read it now, it's all wet," I say as I pull the note out of my mouth and drop it in the trash bin beside the desks.

"Why did you do that?!" Caleb shouts.

Ms. Phlip is shaking her head as the rest of the class laughs. Kat looks more than relieved. Her face is red and she's covering her mouth, but she looks grateful and she damn well better be. That was disgusting.

"Sit down, Froderick," Ms. Phlip says. "Kat do not pass notes in my class again. Next time, I will take the note out of his mouth with gloves on and read it aloud. You have been warned."

Caleb is so mad right now looking at me. He scoots his desk closer to mine as Ms. Phlip writes on the dry erase board. "I have to kiss you; you shouldn't put things like that in your mouth. That was disgusting," he says.

"You don't *have* to do anything," I say and fold my arms.

"Well, yes, I do, and besides just last class you had the thought that my mouth was yours. Is the same not true of yours? If mine is yours, then yours is mine, and I don't want ink-covered paper in your mouth."

"Okay, Caleb. I get it," I say through clenched teeth.

Fangfully, the bell is ringing and it's time to switch classes. I walk over to Kat, and Caleb stands beside me. "What the hell, Kat? You were willing to get in trouble just so you could tell me that you made a friend? By the way, my mouth tastes disgusting now."

Kat rolls her eyes at me. "You are so dense! That's not what I was saying. I'll just call you later, or maybe I'll see you at lunch or before free period."

Caleb holds my hand, and we leave the class together.

"What was so important that you needed to stick that note in your mouth?" he asks.

"I don't really know because I didn't read it, but the note before that is in my pocket. I'll show it to you in the next class."

Chapter 14
Accidental Ally

As we reach the next class, luckily, the back double desk is open. We sit down beside one another under the cool air vent. Caleb wraps his arm around me, and I pass him the note from inside my pocket.

"Ohhhh, that's what I thought," he says.

I look at Caleb with my mouth pulled to the side. I have no effing clue what he's figured out. It was just a pointless note.

His eyebrow drops and he asks, "Are you seriously telling me you don't understand why she gave you this?"

I shrug and say, "You can hear my thoughts. Does it sound like I know why she did?"

"She's telling you that she *likes* Kressa. She *likes* her. Get it?" Caleb asks.

I nod. "Okay, I get it now. I didn't read it that way. No wonder she wanted me to hide the second note. It was probably a full-on confession. Oh man, I'm glad I shoved that note in my mouth. I do need water, though."

"Well, you can get some, I'll save your seat. Or I can go grab you a bottle, just tell me where the closest machine is," Caleb says.

"No, it's fine. It's lunch time after this. I'll have a drink then. Besides, I know you didn't forget that Leslie and Robert are in this class. I can't imagine you'd want to leave me here in this classroom with them."

"Nope. I would not like that," Caleb says. He pulls me in tight with his left arm around my waist, and I lay my head on his shoulder. I hope the teacher shows up today. It was so crazy that yesterday the teacher never showed up. I probably should have told my dad about that. Nah, I shouldn't have. I wonder if anyone else told their parents, though? Caleb is softly kissing the top of my head. Man, the sound of his kisses is just so stimulating. They're just soft kisses, but the sound is, like, very pleasing to hear.

"Ouch! Why is everyone hurting me today?" I ask, as Caleb squeezes my arm a little too tightly.

"Sorry, I didn't mean to hurt you," he says as he rubs my arm.

I see what happened. He noticed Leslie and Robert walking in. This is annoying that they're in the same class, so I can't blame him. Especially because Leslie is so over exaggerative in everything she does, and Robert just has a stupid look on his face, like he has no idea what's happening. What a pair they are.

Anyway, I really wonder if my mom is home. If not, then, hopefully, Wolfie can get some answers for me from his dad. I still can't believe my grandpa this morning. Actually, asking me to lie to my mother for my dad.

The teacher still isn't here. What the hell is the deal with this teacher? I don't even remember which teacher should be in this class. Maybe it's Ms. Dirfus?

Oh my fangs… No. I lean my head back and separate my body from Caleb's grip as my father walks into the classroom.

His eyes immediately lock on Caleb and me in the back row. He stands in front of the class and says, "Velcome, good morning. We are having some trouble finding your teacher. I am sure everything is fine, but we don't have a substitute at this time because we weren't given any notice that the teacher would be out. I am here for just a few minutes, until the bell rings, just to be sure you don't get into any trouble. So, I will take any random questions that you have, and try to answer them, the best way that a school ruler can."

I swallow hard. This is too close, I'm too close to Caleb with my dad here. He didn't see us cuddled up, but we *are* in the back seats, which traditionally are for couples who want to feel each other up, since the teacher can't see what's happening behind the desks. My dad is not a fan of whatever he thinks the two of us have going on, that much is for certain. His eyes continue to linger on us, as other vampires ask him questions.

Leslie is raising her hand.

Oh shit, she isn't going to do what I think she's going to do, is she?

My father acknowledges her. "Yes, Leslie, how are you, dear? Do you have a question or just saying hello to your favorite grown-up?"

Leslie stands, I avert my eyes, so I don't see her full ass, which is definitely sticking out of her skirt as she stands. Ridiculous that we don't have any sort of skirt length requirement and, yet, we can't have cell phones. Seems like eliminating short skirts should be a priority, too.

Leslie flips her hair to the back. She smiles at my father and says, "Hello, Mr. Dracula. I'm so happy you're here because I've been wanting to ask how you feel about Caleb and Frody?"

Caleb stands quickly and approaches my father. My father is nodding as Caleb is whispering and pointing toward Leslie and Robert with his hands. My father's face is shocked at whatever it is that Caleb is telling him. I have no idea what that is, though, but my father doesn't look angry at me. If anything, he looks disgusted looking at Robert and Leslie.

Oh wait, if I'd just shut up, I could hear his thoughts. Oh…that's the angle he used. That's pretty funny. Caleb is explaining that Leslie is not in love with me, but that she is obsessed with me just because of our family ranking. Now, he's telling him that Robert is upset that I haven't been hanging out with him, so he's dating Leslie just to try and get a reaction out of me. My dad is buying all of it. He's eating it up with a spoon. It's really not that far off from the truth anyway.

Caleb pats my father on the back while my father uncomfortably straightens his own standing collar. Caleb is walking back toward me with a big smile on his face. He's really happy with what he just did and, honestly, I am, too. Saved our asses big time.

"Well," my father says loudly. "You learn something new every day. Now, Leslie, I think that Frode and Caleb make a great pair and I'm thrilled about it. Two of a kind. Nobles belong together." My father appears quite proud of himself for saying that. The gigantic grin he's giving me is too much for me to handle.

I laugh loudly while the rest of the class is in shock at my father's proclamation. See, the funny thing is, that everyone else is assuming that he means he accepts that we are gay and in a relationship, but that's not the case. He's saying he approves of Caleb and I being friends, and he approves of Caleb keeping Leslie away from me. But the rest of the class doesn't know that. They think my extremely unbending father has just proudly announced that he supports us dating.

Leslie, who is still standing for some reason, says, "Um, okay, I wasn't expecting that. But, Mr. Dracula, they are kind of mean to other vampires sometimes. They've been making like a bunch of girls cry."

Caleb stands back up and slams his hand on the desk. I jolt backward at the sound. "See, Mr. Dracula?" Caleb asks. "She is impertinent, she smells terrible, and she dares to speak about us this way. I won't tolerate this."

Caleb is even hotter when he's angry.

My father places a hand on his forehead. "Leslie, dear. You can't speak about them this way. Surely, you understand that vampires of higher nobility are to be respected."

Leslie is pretending to cry; she's holding her face in her hands, as she stands beside Robert.

My father hates when girls cry. I hate it when anyone cries, too, but I don't give a shit when anyone fake cries, and Leslie is definitely faking right now. Caleb is still standing with his arms crossed. Man, he's just gorgeous. I'm trying very hard to control my face. I am so attracted to him that I'm almost afraid to look at him with my father so close.

"Oh, now, don't cry, Leslie," my father says. "Frode and Caleb are two of a kind, it is only natural that since they've found one another, that other vampires will begin to feel threatened or uncomfortable with their way of speaking. Frode has been the only noble for a long time, now that he has Caleb, his personality is bound to change a bit."

I really need to stop this conversation because if Leslie or anyone else points out that we are dating, my dad is going to flip out in front of the whole class. Right now, he's very proud that we are "together" as a pair of nobles, but he will not be proud if he finds out that we are an actual couple.

"But, Mr. Dracula," she says.

Robert suddenly stands up.

Oh no. Please don't do it, please.

Caleb is also standing. His posture has changed, though. He's kind of standing in more of an offensive pose, than a defensive one like he was just a minute ago. Again, it's very hot.

Leslie puts her hand on Robert's shoulder and looks at him.

There are no tears on her face. I knew she was faking. Robert shakes his shoulder from her grip and walks toward the door.

"Did you need something?" my father asks Robert as he reaches the door.

Robert turns his head toward us as he holds the doorknob. "Frode's personality has changed more than just a bit," he says then walks out of the room.

"Ridiculous!" Caleb says while throwing a hand up.

"Well, he's frustrated, it's understandable, given his situation," my father says.

What? What the actual hell? My father is being understanding of someone else's feelings? I mean, he's standing there and acting supportive of Robert's outburst? How is this possible? If I was to tell him I had feelings about anything, he'd freak out, and yet he just told Caleb that Robert's behavior is understandable.

"Ridiculous!" I echo Caleb and slam my hand on the desk while standing up.

My father tilts his head at me and raises his eyebrows. The bell sounds loudly before any more words are exchanged between us. Leslie is quickly surrounded by two other girls, who are consoling her, as she leaves the classroom.

Caleb instinctively grabs my hand and I quickly pull it back. My father didn't see it, though, because there are other vampires shuffling past us. We have to get out of here quick. I really don't want my father to try and eat lunch with us again.

Caleb and I try to blend in with the group that's leaving, before my father stops us.

"Wait," my father's voice calls out.

I whisper to Caleb, "Just keep walking."

Caleb nods and we continue toward the door.

"Froderick, Caleb, wait. Come back here," my father says.

We both stop walking and turn around to face him. The rest of the class has left, and we are all alone with my dad now.

My father walks past us and closes the classroom door.

"I'm sure you both want to get to lunch, but we could leave school and go get something if you want to," he says.

I'm confused by this, honestly. He seems like he genuinely wants to go out to eat with us. I don't trust it; he's got an angle. He is my father after all.

"No, thanks, Dad. We have plans already. We have to go," I say.

"Frode. Have you spoken to your mother? I have been trying to call her, but she hasn't returned my calls. She didn't even read the texts I sent either. She must be really upset after you told her that I didn't listen to you yesterday. Now she isn't talking to me at all."

I sigh loudly. What do I do? Should I tell him the truth? I feel like he doesn't deserve the truth, honestly, but maybe I should just tell him. Wait, I just had a great idea!

"No, I had a great idea!" Caleb says loudly.

I stomp my foot. "Damn it, no, Caleb! I had an idea and you just heard it."

Caleb is tilting his head at me, and his right eyebrow is lowered. He whispers in my ear, "Just say it. We can argue about whose idea it was after it works."

My father has been staring at his phone this whole time. He can have his phone, but no one else can. I think most teachers have them, though, just not students.

"Dad, let's make a deal," I say.

My father doesn't look up from his phone. "It better be something about you helping me fix things with your mother, or I'm not interested."

See? And I should feel bad for lying to him? No effing way.

"It does. How about I agree to call mom right now and leave her a voicemail, saying that you were very helpful, but in exchange, I want to sleep over at Caleb's tonight."

Before my father can answer, Caleb adds, "We have a rather strange Biology assignment, and we'd like the extra time to work on it. We need to try and find material that no one else is going to use so we get a good grade. There is a bookstore in my old town that is open late and that's when they put the new books out. I'd like to take Frode there as soon as the new releases hit tonight then we can also work on our project."

"You are going to call your mother and tell her I helped?" my father asks while finally looking up from his phone.

"Yes, I will call her and tell her that, if I can sleep over at Caleb's."

"Okay, but I want you to call her now; right in front of me, and if she doesn't answer I want you to leave a voicemail."

My father passes me his phone. This is actually perfect because when she does hear the message, she'll know my father forced me to say it since the voicemail will come from his phone number.

My mom's phone is ringing…wait it's ringing? What the hell? My eyes are wide as I look at Caleb. Caleb's eyes widen hearing my thoughts. Please don't answer, please don't answer. Phew, it's her voicemail.

"Hi, Mom, I wanted to talk to you about some things, but I also really want to tell you that dad talked to me last night and was very…helpful. Please call me back when you get this. Bye."

"Why did you pause before you said helpful?" my father asks while taking his phone. Is he for real? He really thinks he was helpful last night. That's the sad part. He is completely unaware that he was acting like a gigantic baby, like always.

"Oh, well, I didn't expect that her phone was going to ring," I say.

Caleb covers my mouth and gives a nervous laugh. "Yeah, I'm

sure you thought she would just send your dad straight to voicemail, right?"

"Yes, exactly." I say.

What the hell would I do without Caleb? I almost just screwed up and he covered for me.

"Yes, well, she has been sending me to voicemail all morning, but now I'm sure she'll at least call you back. Make sure you don't forget your phone before you go to Caleb's later. And, Frode, you will call me the second your mother calls you and tell me everything that she said."

"Got it, Pops," I say as Caleb and I leave the classroom before he can say anything else.

Lunch is already almost over thanks to my dad, and I can't make out with Caleb in the hallway like we've been doing since the old sack of blood is nearby. This sucks, oh, but wait, I got permission to sleep over at Caleb's house.

Caleb holds his hand up to me and we high five each other. We're both chuckling as we walk toward the cafeteria. This is the funniest thing ever. The idiot just gave me permission to get laid. He has no effing clue either. The question is, do I have sex, or let Caleb bite me first? Or maybe I bite Caleb first? Hmm…there is a lot to consider. Oh, I hadn't even thought about protection either. I wonder if Caleb has thought about that.

"I have and it's already taken care of. Seriously though, why are you asking yourself all of these questions when I'm standing right here? I don't understand. You know I can hear your thoughts and yet you choose to have full conversations by yourself instead of just talking to me about all these things," Caleb says.

We reach the cafeteria and Caleb holds the door open for me. We walk inside and all eyes are on us. Caleb grabs my hand tightly, I'm not sure why he just did that, but I like it.

"Caleb, about what you said before. Not about the protection, but the talking to myself part; I actually forget that you can hear inside my head most of the time. I'm just used to over-thinking I guess."

"But you can hear my thoughts, too, so how can you forget that I can hear yours?" Caleb asks.

We walk toward the lunch cashier, and she passes us each a tray with a chicken sandwich, a banana and yogurt. We both thank her and walk toward the private lunch table that we sat at the other day. I really don't normally eat over here, but I guess that it's going to be my new thing for this year. Caleb wouldn't like sitting with everyone else anyway, and I don't really want other vampires watching him eat yogurt. The sight of that the other day, was too hot.

"Caleb, I can hear your thoughts, but I have to really focus, well not really focus, but I have to tell myself to shut up and then I can hear what you're thinking. It's much quieter in your head than it is in mine. Speaking of that, you're the only vampire that's ever been inside my head, do you think my thoughts are normal? Because it really is very quiet inside your head most of the time, do you have to meditate to keep your mind that still?"

Caleb picks his sandwich up and takes a bite while raising his eyebrows at me. I can hear his thoughts pretty clearly. He thinks I'm very cute, but he also thinks my thoughts are far from normal. I'm fine with that, though, honestly.

"Are you not nervous at all about me sleeping over?" I ask.

Caleb shrugs and picks his banana up. "What would I be nervous about, Frode?"

Caleb is peeling the banana, and I'm really focusing on not thinking about anything while he does that. I know, I'll peel my banana, too.

I grab the banana off my tray and begin peeling it back. Caleb tilts his head at me inquisitively. He looks side to side. "How far did you get it in the other day?" he asks.

My eyes widen and I look at the banana then back to Caleb. "I don't know what you're talking about," I say.

Caleb brings his banana to his mouth while looking at me. "You know what I'm talking about. You're thinking about it right now. I'll show you how far I can do it, if you show me first."

I'm shaking my head, no. There is no way I can show him, it's too embarrassing. I know it wasn't far at all, what if he doesn't want to do anything with me after he sees how pitiful my attempt is?

"Watch," Caleb says. His tongue is barely out as he brings the banana slowly toward his mouth.

I feel a certain part begin to tingle and I shake my head profusely. "Stop, vampires are looking at you. I try to grab the banana from his hand, and he puts his hands on mine and brings the banana to his mouth taking a huge bite off, nearly swallowing the whole damn thing. "Holy shit! You're gonna choke!" I scream.

Caleb is fine, he isn't choking, he chewed the whole thing up and swallowed it. He's proudly showing me his exposed tongue and empty mouth.

"I'm really mad at you, Caleb. I told you that vampires were looking over. Now, everyone saw you do that. You already had them staring, now they know how far you can take a freaking banana down your throat."

Caleb is looking around. He pinches my chin. "No one saw what I did. Your hands were blocking everyone else's view. Come on, don't be mad."

"I am mad," I say turning my head slightly.

"Yeah, but you're mad because you can't get as much of the banana in as I can," he says with a smile.

The bell rings, it's time for free period. I stand and shake my head. I'm quite annoyed now because I really want to just leave school for the day and not deal with this mom stuff. But, Wolfie is going out of his way, so we need to head over to the library and wait for him. Caleb stands and takes my hand as we dump our remaining food in the garbage, and place our trays on the stack with the other dirty ones. We can technically leave them on the table because of our status, but how fanging gross is that? Like we shouldn't have to throw our own garbage out just because we're noble? Give me a break. I can throw my damn food out and stack my tray like everyone else. Oh, now that I think about it, I think the other day I didn't. I'm pretty sure we left our trays on the table. Oops. Well, who could blame me? I had like fifty crazy things happen to me just at lunch time alone.

Caleb takes my hand and kisses it softly. I really can't be mad at him. He was right and I really was just embarrassed over how terrible my gag reflex is.

We walk toward the library, and I hear Kat laughing loudly behind us. I turn to face her; she's walking with someone I don't recognize.

"Hey, Frody! Where are you guys going? You hitting the locker room?" she asks.

"No," I say. "We're meeting Wolfie in the library. Have you talked to him today, by the way? He said he couldn't get ahold of you yesterday, seemed like he was maybe worried."

The vampire beside her hasn't spoken and they are avoiding eye contact with Caleb and me. Caleb doesn't look like he likes this vampire, but that's nothing new.

"Oh," Kat says. "No, I haven't, but we all have gym together after free period, so I'll talk to him then. Thanks for chewing the note up in front of Ms. Phlip, I owe you," she says, lightly punching me in the stomach.

Caleb's head turns toward Kat quickly and he places his hand on my stomach. "You really shouldn't touch other vampire's boyfriends and he didn't chew the note up, he just placed it in his mouth. Don't make it sound so revolting," he says to Kat.

Kat pulls her head back. "Woah, I thought he chewed it. My bad. Also, I've touched way more than his stomach, we've been friends for a long time, so chill. I'm not interested in him," Kat says.

The vampire next to her is making an even more disagreeable face than Caleb. They are whispering in Kat's ear.

Kat shakes her head and giggles. "This is my friend Tahni, they think you guys don't know them, but I'm sure at least you do, right, Frode?"

I have no idea who they are, but I don't want to be rude or hurt any vampire's feelings.

"Oh, um, well, Tahni, this is my boyfriend, Caleb Cheval. I don't think you know each other."

Tahni is wearing the uniform skirt as well as black leggings under it. Their long black curly hair covers half of their face, but their bright smile can be seen smiling at Caleb and me now.

They haven't spoken yet, though, but at least they are smiling. It's not really uncommon for vampires to get starstruck around me, though. I don't remember them, but they definitely haven't met Caleb until now, and Caleb is just hot. Anyone would sweat looking at him.

Caleb is smiling, but he's starting to pull me away. "We'll be late for meeting Wolfie, come on," he says.

"Bye, Kat. Bye, Tahni," I say as I'm pulled away.

Caleb kisses my cheek quickly and hangs his arm around my neck. We enter the library and, fangfully, Ms. Beagle isn't around. I didn't tell Wolfie where we would meet, though, so I'm not sure where he is. We're walking around the lower level and I don't see him anywhere.

"Upstairs?" Caleb whispers.

I nod and we walk up the staircase. Sure enough, there he is. Wolfie is sitting at a table near the back wall. We sit down across from him. He looks upset for some reason.

I ask him, "Hey, what's going on? Did you talk to your dad?"

"Yeah, I did," Wolfie says. "He said that he isn't supposed to say anything, but to tell you that your moms don't want to be bothered right now. He wouldn't say anything else."

"Okay, well, at least we know they're together and nothing is wrong," Caleb says.

Wolfie looks really upset, though. I doubt it's because of my mom. I mean why would he really care about that? He couldn't have gotten in trouble; his dad is like the nicest guy on the planet.

"What's wrong then? Why do you look upset?" I ask Wolfie.

Wolfie rubs his thumbs together, looking down at the table. "It's just Kat, I thought we had a good thing going on and now she's just ghosting me. I was kind of feeling things for her that I didn't think I would feel for a girl, you know?"

"I had no idea you were actually feeling things like that for her. You said it was just a cover. What changed? I mean, I'm just confused."

"Yeah, well, I wouldn't expect that you would realize. Since you met Caleb, you've been totally distant, too. I haven't even gone to your house after school for the past two days," he says. He looks up at Caleb. "No offense, Caleb, by the way. I like you and I'm happy for you both, I'm just upset about Kat. It's really not you guys."

I kick Wolfie under the table lightly. "Hey, be happy you didn't come over yesterday. You know who was there? The smelliest member of my family. So be grateful," I say with a smile.

Wolfie's mouth is wide. "No! Grandpa Lugo?! Ah, he smells like effing calabash. Disgusting. Just like toilet water, but I love that guy. He's so funny."

"Calabash! That's it! That's the smell! Caleb had no idea what that was, when I was thinking it yesterday."

Caleb shakes his head at me. "No, I absolutely know what calabash is. *You* said bottle gourd or something… Of course, I know what calabash is. Smells terrible, but I've heard it tastes great in soup."

"Okay, but, Caleb, they are the same thing, so now do you agree that he smells like calabash?" I ask.

Caleb nods. "Yeah, I definitely do. He smelled very bad, and I still don't know how he snuck up on us the way he did. He basically shook the floor when he walked away."

Wolfie pulls his head back and looks at the two of us and asks, "What do you mean he snuck up on you two? What were you doing?"

"Just making out, getting interrupted like every other damn time something almost happens. He came and knocked on the door. Still don't know if he knows what we were doing, but that wasn't the worst part. Actually, forget I said that."

"No, no, best friends tell each other everything. Come on," Wolfie says.

I tilt my head back and look up at the ceiling. Caleb can't believe that I'm about to tell Wolfie this, but, believe it or not, his thoughts are stuck on Wolfie calling himself my best friend. Which is hilarious. His face is kind of pouting a bit. It's cute.

"Grandpa Lugo walked in on me with my dick in my hand last night, after Caleb left."

Wolfie covers his mouth. "No! Your grandpa caught you—you know, doing that? That is so embarrassing. Oh, and if he came in right after Caleb left and you were doing it, I'm sure he knows about you guys. Otherwise, why would you need to do that like the second Caleb left? We all do it, but not the second our friends leave. Your grandpa isn't an idiot like your old man. I'm sure he figured it out. Still though, so embarrassing. Were your pants at your ankles, too?"

"What are you trying to get a visual, you damn pervert?" I ask.

"No, but it's even funnier if your pants were at your ankles," Wolfie says while laughing.

I sigh and shake my head. "Well, sorry to disappoint you buddy, but no, they weren't."

"I think we've talked enough about this," Caleb says while standing.

Chapter 15
Keep It Cool at School

The bell rings and it's time for gym. Last class of the day. Then I get to go home, grab my stuff and go to Caleb's. Wow. I'm really gonna get bitten tonight…or laid, or both. I'm pretty excited about all of those possibilities. I stand and Caleb holds my hand. Wolfie walks beside us while we walk downstairs. Ms. Beagle still isn't here. Maybe she's off today? I am going to ask my dad about her when I get back home tomorrow. I wonder if he ended up meeting with her.

Caleb whispers in my ear, "Good boy, don't think about the dirty stuff. Not when we still have another class. Keep thinking about Ms. Beagle." He kisses my cheek.

I stop walking and look at him confused. "Did you just say 'good boy' to me?"

Caleb raises his eyebrows and asks, "Did you like it? Because if you did, then yes, but if you didn't, then no, I didn't."

I playfully shove him and his body bumps lightly into Wolfie.

Wolfie inhales and says, "You guys both smell like cherry bubble gum. You know that? It's like you both have the same scent. That's weird. How can you two smell the same?"

Caleb brings my hand to his mouth and kisses it as we approach the locker room door.

I lead Caleb to where my locker is, I know that his will be right beside mine because mine is in a special place away from the other lockers. Caleb hasn't seen this side of the locker room yet. There are only two other lockers next to mine and they've always remained empty, but since Caleb is noble, his will be beside mine.

Wolfie turns toward the opposite direction and says, "Alright, well the common vampire lockers are this way, so I'll see you guys after you get dressed. Hey, by the way Frode, your hair looks good like that. You better take that ribbon out, though. Who knows what sport we're playing today." He gives a playful salute and heads to the other side of the locker room.

Caleb walks beside me toward the other section of lockers. We stand in front of the row and just as I thought, the first and second lockers are ours. The name plates on the tall black lockers show: *Dracula* and *Cheval*.

Caleb slides the locker button upward while I do the same on mine. "How are there clothes and shoes in here? I didn't bring these things," Caleb says with a look of confusion.

I lift my black gym shorts and red gym shirt out along with the socks and sneakers inside. "Your mom had to pay for all that stuff when she signed you up. We all have to wear exactly the same thing so no one feels bad about what clothes they can or can't afford. Just put the clothes and shoes on. I'm gonna change in this room over here. You can use the one next to me," I say while turning the handle on the small private dressing room.

"Why can't we change together? We'll be doing more than changing together later," Caleb says with a wink.

I walk inside the room and start to close the door, just peeking my head out. "Because you won't be able to control yourself and neither will I, then we'll be late or get caught. Either would be bad."

"Real question, I will respect your answer. I promise. Do you actually want me to come in and you're just playfully teasing me, or do you want me to use the other room? I don't want to misread the situation, but your words are saying one thing, and your thoughts are saying the opposite."

I open the door and allow Caleb to join me, then close it as he enters. "Of course I wanted you to come in here, but you have to keep your hands to yourself. We have probably two minutes to get dressed and inside the gym. Dahvi is nice, but they will be pissed if we are late. Don't mistake their kindness yesterday for them being a pushover. Dahvi does not play."

I quickly pull my shirt off and replace it with the T-shirt from my locker. Caleb's head was inside his own shirt, so he didn't see anything. Which is good because I don't want to tempt him. At this point, having any amount of clothing off near him feels dangerous. But I'm seeing all of Caleb's chest right now. He looks delicious and I really want to touch him. No, no. I have to hurry. I remove my belt and unbutton my pants, quickly pulling them down. I grab the shorts off the tiny bench inside the room. Caleb is moving much slower as he removes his pants. Holy shit! Caleb is in his underwear. Caleb is in his underwear… I shake my head and turn away. I can't look. I have to hurry up and get out of here. I remove my dress socks and replace them with low-cut, black athletic socks. As I bend down to put a sock on, I feel Caleb's strong hands gripping me tightly, on the sides of my waist. I drop my head and exhale. I'm not going to be able to hold back.

"Yo, you guys better hurry up!" Wolfie yells. "You know Dahvi isn't above making you do shuttle runs!"

I put my socks on, slip into my shoes and pull the ribbon from my hair. I lay the ribbon atop my pile of neatly folded clothes and look at Caleb, who is hurrying to get dressed now.

"That was close, you almost did something that I wasn't going to be able to say no to," I say.

"I don't want to talk about what just almost happened. I can't believe he just yelled like that. Ugh. I was so close to pulling your shorts down. Speaking of that, do vampires pants each other here? These shorts are really loose, and the drawstring doesn't really help at all," Caleb says while tugging his shorts outward.

I open the door and step outside of the dressing room. "What the hell does 'pants each other' mean?" I ask. "You're wearing shorts, what the hell are you talking about? Also, you just showed me your underwear when you did that. Please don't do that when we're in the gym."

Caleb follows behind me. "Pantsing is when your buddies pull at your pants or shorts, like, they pull them down and everyone sees your ass or underwear, sometimes more. Do vampires not do that here?"

"Oh, they do that here, but there isn't, like, a name for it. Sometimes, vampires, usually Martin, pull other guys shorts down, there are a few other vamps that do it, but no one would do that to me, so no one is going to do it to you," I say.

Caleb looks left to right and kisses my lips quickly then opens the door to the gym.

The rest of the class is already standing in front of Dahvi, who is holding two white volleyballs, one under each arm.

Shit, we're gonna get lit up. This is going to be awful. I hate getting yelled at, but I hate shuttle runs even more.

"Dahvi," Caleb says then jogs ahead of me. I walk quickly to catch up to him.

Dahvi looks at their watch, then at Caleb. With sass, they say, "Yes, hello. Nice of you two noble purebloods to decide to join us.

What happened in there? I told you two yesterday to keep it cool at school."

"No, Dahvi, nothing happened. I just wasn't familiar with the protocol for clothes and lockers here. I was a bit thrown off by the terrible clothes that Frode said we have to wear. It's my fault entirely."

Dahvi gives the both of us an eyeroll, and we walk around to the back of the group. Leslie and Robert aren't standing near one another, but Kat is standing in front of me with Kressa and Tahni beside her. Wolfie stands next to me and gives me a nod.

Dahvi holds the volleyballs up high and says, "Volleyball today. We're splitting into two teams. Froderick is a captain, and Martin is a captain. Froderick, we all know you're going to pick Caleb, and Martin, Caleb wouldn't join your team even if you asked him, so go ahead and pick next, Martin."

After many rounds of drafting, we split into two teams and line up on opposite sides of the net.

Caleb is pretty good at volleyball; this is the first time I'm seeing him play any sport. I like it, he's getting kind of sweaty, which is really getting me a little heated. I actually feel hot just looking at him. Caleb is watching me as we wait for the serve from the other team. Martin is explaining to Tahni how they should hit the ball over the net. I yell over that they can have a few practice serves. I always feel bad when vampires who are unfamiliar with a sport are put on the spot in these competitive situations. It's just unnecessary and it makes them feel uncomfortable, well, it makes non-competitive vampires uncomfortable. Vampires like me love it. I'll compete with anyone for anything and I'll win, too. Okay, well, maybe not at whatever that one sport is, that Dahvi makes us play sometimes, with the shuttlecock, haha. I have no idea what the sport is, but I always remember the name of the thing that we hit around. It's hilarious. Anyway, I suck at that, whatever that is.

Caleb's eyes are stuck to me like glue. He's thinking about tonight, I can tell. I lift my shirt on purpose and rub my fingers near the top of my waistband. He is shaking his head at me. He walks over near Dahvi, who grabs him a bottle of water out of the soft sided cooler. Dahvi is just the best, they always have several bottled waters in case anyone needs one. I guess Caleb is really thirsty. I'm thirsty, too, in more ways than one right now. Caleb lifts his chin at me like he wants me to see something. I look left to right and shrug, I have no idea what he wants me to look at. Caleb untwists the bottle cap and lifts the bottom of his shirt like I just did. He takes a long drink, and I swear he just licked that damn bottle opening. There's a little bit of water dripping down his neck. Oh, okay, I see what he's doing. He's just teasing me. Nice. Well, it's working because I—.

"Son of a witch!" I scream as the ball pelts me in the side of my face. Damn, that really hurt. I stayed on my feet, but, fangs, that was not pleasant. The entire side of my face is stinging while Martin is laughing along with Leslie and a few others. I squint on the right side and rub my face.

Caleb rushes over, he places his hand on my shoulder. "Are you okay? How did that not knock you down? I thought you were looking at me, how did you even brace for that?" Caleb asks me.

"I have no idea; I was looking at you. It took me a minute to realize that you were teasing me on purpose, but by the time I realized it, the ball pelted me in the face. It effing hurt." I rub my cheek a little more. I'm probably going to have a big bruise now.

Dahvi is walking over with a disposable ice pack. "You alright or do you need the nurse?" they ask me while handing me the ice pack.

"I'm fine, I think. I feel a little dizzy, but I think I'm good."

"Well, hold that on your face for a few minutes," Dahvi says. "You and Caleb take a break over there."

Caleb and I walk toward the wall of the gym where there are

five chairs lined up. I honestly do feel pretty dizzy, so I think I'm just gonna sit here until Dahvi forces us to get up.

"Here, let me hold that for you," Caleb says.

"Thanks," I say while giving him a little smile. The side of my face where the ball hit feels really hot. It's a weird feeling having the ice pack on it, but I think it's sweet that Caleb is holding it for me.

Robert is staring over from the other side of the court. I don't know what his problem is. His damn remark really pissed me off earlier and I'd completely forgotten about it until now. So rude and, really, my dad just totally accepting that Robert said that about me, and validating his frustration—just wow. I'm tempted to flip Robert the bat right now, but it probably won't look nice raising my middle finger from this distance.

"Why is he staring at you like that when I'm sitting right here?" Caleb asks me.

"How the hell should I know? I'm sitting next to you. I can't even think straight right now, and my face actually hurts. Here, you can take the ice off. How does it look?" I ask Caleb while tilting my cheek upward.

"Mmm," he says while rubbing my cheek with a frown. He kisses the sore spot. "It looks red and it's probably going to bruise. You really should keep the ice on."

I shake my head. "Nah, it's alright. My cheek is too cold with it on there, but thanks."

Caleb looks at me softly then turns back toward the game. "Okay, well, this is enough," Caleb says as he stands.

Caleb is really angry. He yells over with his arms wide, "Watermelon vamp! You and your boyfriend keep looking over here. Did you need something? Is there something over here that interests either of you so much that you can't keep your eyes on the game?"

Dahvi blows their whistle and is walking quickly over toward Caleb.

Dahvi places a hand on Caleb's shoulder. "What are you yelling about over here? You can't let vampires staring over here bother you. They're probably just trying to make sure that Frode is okay. Everyone loves Frode, that, or they're checking you out. I have no idea, but let's take it down a couple notches, okay? And don't try to pull the noble card on me either," they say as they turn to walk away. "Oh wait," Dahvi says then turns back around. Dahvi looks at the two of us with one hand on their hip. Their nails are painted with red glitter today, it looks really good, and the gym lights really show off the sparkles. "Frode, I heard that your father told everyone that he is in full support of your relationship. How in the world did that happen? I heard students gossiping about it, but I don't believe it," Dahvi says.

I let out a laugh. "Well, don't believe it. Vampires took it out of context. He's a moron, he was saying that he supports us being a pair, like, as in friends. He definitely wasn't saying he supports us as a couple, but the way that it sounded made it seem like he did. I didn't correct him because I thought it was funny. If I had my phone, I would've recorded it. It was priceless, Dahvi."

Dahvi smiles at us. "Well, I'm glad you're laughing about it. I knew there was no way it was true." Dahvi lets out a sigh, gives us a smile and shakes their head. "Just be yourselves and don't worry about what he accepts," they say.

Robert is still staring over, it's almost like he's thinking about saying something, but he's not quite brave enough to do it. He better knock it off, Caleb is really angry. Man, his temper is way hotter than I imagined. Leslie has at least stopped staring over for the time being. Wolfie is talking to Robert now, through the net, while pointing over.

I bounce out of my chair at the sound of the dismissal bell. Caleb raises his eyebrows at me and takes my hand, leading me toward the locker room. "Time to go," he says.

Vamps are flooding inside the locker room to grab their clothes and change. Most vampires just leave school in their gym clothes, sometimes I do, sometimes I don't, but today I'm definitely changing back into my clothes. I need to take a shower before I head to Caleb's anyway, but I don't want to leave these hideous gym clothes on any longer than I have to. I toss the disposable ice pack in the garbage while Caleb stares at me strangely.

"You didn't even sweat, what is this shower nonsense you're thinking of?" Caleb asks.

My mouth is turned down at his suggestion. "Uh, well, I may not have sweat, but I still need to take a shower. I was gonna just go home, shower and meet you at your place. I'm not gonna sleep in a bed with you and feel dirty and gross." I playfully shove him toward the lockers.

I can hear Caleb's thoughts. Wow, he is thinking very dirty things. I am actually very interested in what he's thinking about. My eyes widen looking at him.

"What, why are you looking at me like that?" Caleb asks. "You just pushed me into the lockers, now what, you're thinking about dirty things?"

I point at him and open the dressing room where our clothes are. "You were thinking about dirty things. I was thinking of taking a shower. Don't try to flip this on me," I say while I take my shirt off.

The locker room was basically empty earlier, but now it's full of vampires and it's not free period so everyone is being extremely loud. I can see Caleb's eyes looking at me like he wants me, but I'm gonna cut that thought off right now.

"Don't even think about it," I say. "Let's just hurry and get changed, then I'll go shower and head to your house after."

"I don't want you to have to separate from me. I'll just go to your house with you. I can talk to your grandpa if he's there, or I can hang out with your dad, since he loves me, again," Caleb says.

His shirt is off and so are his pants. Sweet hell, he is fine. There is nothing about him that is unappealing. I don't know what he even just asked or said at this point. I'm completely entranced by his body.

"Can we do that?" he asks me.

"Uh, yeah, yeah, whatever you want, Caleb. Just put your pants on, please. Pants first, then shirt," I finish getting dressed and toss my dirty gym clothes inside the hamper of my changing room. I'm holding my gym shoes, and my cape is hanging over the inside of my arm. We're leaving so I don't need to put it back on. Caleb is nearly finished getting dressed now. I can barely hear a conversation between Wolfie and someone else. I think it's Robert, but I'm not sure.

Caleb slips his shoes back on and takes my cape from me. He's holding both capes over his arm. "We just leave our dirty clothes in this dirty bin? Who washes them?" he asks.

I open the door to our changing room and say, "The janitorial staff washes them. Toss the stuff in and leave it. Grab your shoes, though, we need to put those back in our lockers."

We walk over toward our lockers and place the shoes inside. As we shut the lockers, Caleb gives me a big smile. "I'm so excited about this. I've never had anyone sleep over before."

I nod nervously at him. I don't know why, but I kind of hate that he said that. I know he meant it like I was special, but for some reason it made me think about the other times that he did things with other vampires. There was never anyone serious, but still, things happened. The same can be said for me, though, so I can't get upset about it. It's just different, though, because Caleb is the only guy that I've ever kissed or let touch me. Fangs, I think I'm gonna throw up. Why am I thinking about this?

Caleb pulls my hand bringing me out of my head. "Hey, what's going on? Your thoughts are all over the place. What did I do? Why are you thinking about this stuff right now?"

"No, it's nothing, don't worry about it. Let's just go. I'm really excited, too," I say with a half-smile.

Chapter 16
Don't Try to Kiss Me

We leave school and reach my house faster than ever. As we land in front of my house, I see a very unwelcome visitor standing in front of my door, talking to my grandfather. It's Robert.

"What the hell is he doing here?" Caleb asks.

Robert looks really upset as he notices the two of us walking over together. I pull Caleb's shirt back a bit and say, "Listen, just let me talk to him. I have no idea why he's here, but if he's here, it must be something important. He knows we're together so it's not like he's going to try anything. Besides my grandfather is standing right there, we can't go over there holding hands. Just be cool."

"I will *not* be cool," Caleb says.

I stop my approach and turn my body toward Caleb. My eyebrows are raised. "You *will* be cool or I'm not going to sleep over."

I don't mean that, I definitely don't mean that. There is no way in hell that I'm not sleeping over, but I really do need Caleb to chill, so we can see what Robert wants.

Caleb nods with a devilish grin. I can see his fangs. "I know you don't mean that, but I'll behave."

I exhale and we start walking toward my grandfather and Robert again.

"Ah, Froderick, look who stopped by, it's your good buddy. And hello, Caleb, good to see you again," my grandfather says.

My grandfather's scent is so bad, I don't know how Robert is standing so close to him. Funny thing is that my grandfather has no idea who Robert is, though—he says good buddy, but that must just be what Robert told him. My grandfather has never met him before now.

Caleb smiles wide, but he's not happy at all. "It's great to see you, too, Mr. Lugo, I'm terribly sorry that I stayed over so late with Frode last night. He's spending the night at my house this evening, though, so you won't have to chase me out again tonight," Caleb says.

Okay, well, I think everyone standing here knows exactly whose benefit that was said for, and it wasn't my grandfather's.

Robert leans his head back and closes his eyes. His hands are on his hips.

"Grandpa, let us have some time to talk, okay? This is just vampire gossip, you don't need to hear it," I say.

"You got it," my grandpa says. "What time does your dad usually get home by the way? I've been waiting here all day for him. I thought he would be back early, but he hasn't texted me all day. I tried to call your mother a few times, too, she didn't answer my calls either. I do hope you'll change your mind and help your father out. Maybe you could just call her when you guys are done out here."

"I already did call her. If you go inside and let me finish up out here, I can see if she called me back. I don't have my phone, it's upstairs. For all I know, she could have called me already." I gesture toward the door.

"Oh, that is fangtastic, Froderick. I'm real proud of you. That was a stand-up thing to do for your dad. Poor guy, he loves her so much, it's been long enough now. She needs to just come back to him," my grandpa says.

"Right," I say as I open the door for my grandfather. He obviously wasn't going to do it himself.

"Oh, okay, yeah, I'm going, I'm going," my grandpa says as I guide him inside and close the door.

"What the hell are you doing here?" Caleb asks Robert.

Robert inhales, then calmly replies. "Caleb, I am here to talk to Frode. I would really appreciate it if I could just talk to him alone for a few minutes, please."

I'm shaking my head no, and Caleb's mouth is wide open.

"Not a chance in hell," Caleb says with a smile.

I place a hand softly on Caleb's chest, standing in between the two. "Robert, there is nothing that you need to say to me that Caleb can't hear. He's my boyfriend, we've been over this. I'm going to tell him whatever you say anyway, so, no, he's not going to leave us alone. You heard him say I was sleeping over at his house. I need to get my stuff and leave. Also, there's a bunch of stuff going on with my mom and my dad and Caleb's—"

"Get back on track," Caleb says with a smile.

"Right," I say. "So go ahead, what do you need to say Robert?"

"Fine," Robert says. "I think I'm in love with you."

I couldn't have heard that right. I'm sure I didn't. I mean, not only is it ridiculous, but also, he knows that I'm with Caleb, who is literally four feet away from him.

Caleb lets out a quiet laugh, tilting his head back. Ahhh, that sexy deviant laugh, it gets me every time. Oh wait, I can't get distracted by my hot boyfriend right now. I can't believe that Robert just said that and by the look on Robert's face, he can't believe he just said it either.

"Ohhhkay," I say. "Well, thank you for the update on your feelings." I shrug and suck my lips in.

"I know that you have feelings for me," Robert says. "Well, at least you did, until Caleb came into the picture. I know you did…and all summer, the only thing I thought about was you. Everything was going to be perfect, then Caleb rolls in and now you won't even talk to me. What did I do? How did I lose this?"

Caleb exhales and takes a step closer toward Robert. I place my body squarely in between Caleb and Robert with my back facing Caleb. "Just wait," I say over my shoulder to Caleb.

I have a hand on my forehead and now I'm feeling very uncomfortable. This whole thing is stupid. Who cares how I felt before? Who cares who I liked or didn't like. Right now, I only care about Caleb. I mean, I love Caleb. I really do. I'd do anything for Caleb. Robert, I feel nothing for in that way. Shit. I just said something in my head that I had not even thought about before and I know Caleb heard that. I'm not even going to turn around. Just gonna blow past it.

"Me too," Caleb whispers, behind me.

"Really?" I ask as I turn to face Caleb.

"Definitely," Caleb says.

Alright, I kind of want to cry, or have sex, or bite the shit out of him right now, but I really should wrap this business with Robert up. This is hard. I'm trying to be a nice guy here, but damn, my boyfriend just told me he loves me, and I have some other guy standing here interrupting the moment.

"Robert. You didn't do anything," I say. "There was a time when I was maybe physically attracted to you, but I don't feel that way anymore. Besides, I never felt anything beyond an attraction, that was it. I never acted on it, and I didn't see it going anywhere, besides—"

"Nope," Caleb says loudly.

I start again, "So, anyway, I'm sorry that you feel wronged or hurt or whatever, but I didn't do anything to you, and I don't feel anything for you. I can't say anything else."

Robert's arms are crossed. "Well, then why did you look like you were about to cry a minute ago?" he asks me. "You looked like you were really thinking about it."

"Well, Caleb and I just told each other that we love each other like thirty seconds ago, so maybe that's what you saw. Otherwise, I have no idea what you're talking about."

Robert is shaking his head at me. "I've been standing here the whole time," he says. "You literally had tears in your eyes and said 'really,' Caleb said 'definitely' and that's it. Who said they loved each other?"

Caleb has had enough of this, and he takes a step beside me. "Listen, we can hear each other's thoughts, that's how strong our bond is. We don't need to talk aloud for anyone else to hear. Unlike you, who seems to need, I don't know, a third form of communication, maybe? Frode has given you his answer... My boyfriend, that I love, has given you, his answer. It is time for you to go away now. I'm being nice here. Please, just go," Caleb says.

Robert nods and takes a step toward me. It seems like he's going to try and, I don't know, kiss me or something. I back up instinctively and Caleb places his arm across my chest.

"Fine, forget it," Robert says as he turns to leave.

"WHAAAT?!" I screech as Robert flies away.

"That guy was actually going to try to kiss you just then. Wow. That's the craziest thing ever," Caleb says.

"I don't know what the eff just happened, Caleb." Using my chin, I point upward, so Caleb can see what I just noticed. "I want to kiss you right now, but my grandfather is watching from the upstairs window, so I can't. Let's go upstairs."

Caleb follows me inside; we're walking fast, so that hopefully we can reach my room without running into my grandfather. We walk inside my bedroom and close the door. Caleb places our capes on my dresser and smiles at me.

I hold my pointer finger up to him, as I pull my hair tie out. My hair falls down and I shake it out. I grab my phone and Caleb is already behind me wrapping his arms around my waist. He's kissing the outside of my shoulder softly through my shirt while I look at my phone. His kisses are slowly making their way toward my neck. Instinctively I tilt my head to the side. His open mouth softly kisses the first piece of exposed skin. I jump forward. "Don't bite me, Caleb!" I shout.

Caleb is holding in a laugh. "What? You tilted your neck toward me. I wasn't going to take a full bite. You didn't need to shout. You're so crazy sometimes."

I hold my phone toward Caleb. "Look, my mom still hasn't called, and she didn't reply to my texts either. I guess it doesn't matter, but I still want to know why we have the connection that we do. I mean, it can't just be because we love each other. I just figured that out a few minutes ago, so it can't be that."

Caleb sits down on my bed. "Don't worry about it. We'll talk to them eventually. Ooh my book! Did you read any of it last night?" he asks while picking it up.

"You know that I didn't. I would have told you. I'll read it soon, though. I need to take a shower and, no, you absolutely cannot come in with me in case my grandfather or father comes in. So don't even ask. Really, are you sure you wouldn't rather just go home and wait until I get there? You're going to be bored just sitting out here."

He holds the brightly colored book up. "Nope, I'm flipping to page 245, one of my favorite parts." He lays down on my bed, kicking his shoes off like he owns the place. "I'm good. Take your time." His eyes are already locked on the book and the page he turned to.

"Alright," I say. I open my dresser and pull out a pair of jeans, and underwear. I walk over beside Caleb; he lays the book open on his chest and holds my face. He kisses me deeper than I planned for when I first bent down. I just wanted to give him a quick kiss, but now he's fully inside my mouth.

"Mmm," I moan while trying to pull my face back.

Caleb moves his hands to the sides of my waist and gives me a little pull toward his body. I don't know what the hell I'm thinking, but I allow him to move my body atop his. Our mouths have yet to fully separate since that first soft kiss. Caleb's hands are on my back, he pulls my shirt up from the back and I help him remove it. He pulls my body close, and I press our mouths together again. I want to take Caleb's shirt off, too. I want to feel the warmth of his skin.

I stop moving at the sound of my grandfather and father's voices outside of my door.

"Frode, Caleb," my father says. I quickly jump off Caleb, as my father enters the room.

"Yeah, what's up, Dad? I was just getting in the shower before I head to Caleb's." I grab the clothes off the ground that I dropped when Caleb pulled me on top of him.

My dad gives the two of us a sort of discerning look. Probably because I have my shirt off and seem slightly out of breath. "Well, Caleb, you don't have to stay in here while he showers. You can come downstairs and hang out with us if you want."

Caleb might actually agree to that. I'm not gonna let that happen. "No, Dad. Caleb is gonna read his book. He's fine. Did you need something?"

Grandpa Lugo enters with a big smile on his face.

My father walks beside my dresser and leans against it. "Well, your grandfather told me I missed quite a scene earlier. Who was it that came here to talk to you?"

"Oh, it was just Robert. No big deal. It's over. I really need to get in the shower, Dad." I walk to my bathroom door and open it.

"It is a very big deal. Your grandfather could tell things were awkward out there. Now that I know it was Robert, that makes more sense. What did he want? Your grandfather said he looked like he was broken hearted, did Leslie dump him?"

I shrug my shoulders. No matter how much I don't like Robert right now, I'm not going to out him to my father. "I have no idea, Dad. He was just whining about not spending time with me and saying that I've changed. I don't know. It's not important to me. I told him that Caleb is my boy—I mean, best friend, and I, um, don't need any other friends."

"Yeah, that's what it looked like," my grandfather interjects. "Then that kid looked like maybe he was gonna hug Frode, but Caleb put his arm in between the two of them."

My father looks at me seriously. "Well, why wouldn't you hug him? You three sat here last night lecturing me on how boys hug other boys. What makes Robert different?"

Caleb sits up. "I don't think that a pureblood vampire from a non-noble house should be touching a noble. He shouldn't have even been on the property uninvited, much less been trying to touch Frode. Of course, I put my arm in between them."

Man, Caleb knows exactly how to swing my dad. My dad eats that noble crap up.

"Yes, well. I do agree with that. You two shouldn't be hugging one another, either. I mean, that's what you have mothers for. Go hug your mothers if you need a hug. Boys really don't belong—"

My grandfather cuts in, "Drac, remember, Alessandra would not approve of where this sentence is going. Think carefully about what you say to her most precious child, and his special friend." My grandfather gives my dad a big smile.

"Oh, come on. Alessandra isn't here. Why should I have to lie about how I feel if she isn't even here? She's not even calling me back or answering my calls." My father walks toward my bed and sits on the edge near Caleb's feet. His hands are in his lap and he's shaking his head while spinning his wedding band. "I shouldn't even be wearing this ring. She doesn't care about me. It's not fair. I didn't do anything wrong. All I did was tell these two that maybe they were imagining their connection. How does that make me wrong? Oh, forget it," he says as he slouches with a pout.

My grandfather rubs my father's back and consoles him, "I'm here, I'm here, it's okay. Now, let's go downstairs, we'll watch your favorite show, maybe we can order a pizza. You just need some food, that's all, you're hungry from working so hard. You go find Alexandra, and I'll order the pizza. Sit downstairs on the couch, hold your beautiful cat, and I'll be right there."

My father leaves my room with a silent nod at my grandfather.

My grandfather waits until my father is gone. He's standing half-in and half-out of my room. He points at us and says, "You two. I'm not gonna say anything, but there is one adult here, who knows what's going on, and he didn't just leave the room pouting. You understand me? Your father gave his permission for this sleeping arrangement because he trusts you, you would do well to remember that, Frode. Also, did you check your phone to see if your mother called?"

Unbelievable. Absolutely unbelievable. I come from the nerviest vampires around, really. So, he knows about Caleb and me, or at least he thinks he does. I still don't know exactly *what* he knows but it doesn't really matter. It's just funny to me that my grandfather can threaten me and then ask me to help my father all in one breath.

"My mom didn't call me or text me. I'm getting in the shower now, Grandpa." I walk inside the bathroom and watch as my grandfather leaves, closing the door behind himself.

Caleb stands up from the bed. He's walking toward my bedroom door. "What are you doing?" I ask.

"I am trying to see if this lock on your door works." He twists the lock, then turns the doorknob. "It works. So, why? Why don't you ever lock your door?" he asks me.

I shrug my shoulders. "It's normally just me and my dad here, so I don't have a reason to. Whenever you come over, I just don't even think about it. But I'll lock it from now on."

Caleb smiles and walks toward me. He cups my face in his hands. "Can you please hurry up? We've already been here for so long. I'm getting a little impatient."

My mouth drops open. "Not my fault, but yes, I'll hurry."

Caleb squeezes my face gently and kisses me quickly. I turn and close the bathroom door.

I turn the shower on hot and get inside after removing my clothes. Rinsing off in the shower, I can't help but realize that I am completely naked, and Caleb is right on the other side of the wall in my bed. I've never let anyone see me full-on naked before. I mean even with—ugh, I can't even think about it, but during anything else I've done, some part of me was always clothed. Being naked just feels so, I don't know, vulnerable, I guess. I mean, I do look good, that's for sure, but I saw Caleb in his underwear, and I think he looks way better. I'm still not too sure what's going to happen tonight at Caleb's, but I do want everything to happen. I want to do anything that I possibly can with him. I just hope I'm good at it. I still need to let him bite me, though. I wonder how bad that will hurt? Hmm…what will hurt more? Oh, forget it, I can't think about these things. Everything that I want to do is meant for fun, it's not meant to hurt.

It's not like I have anything to be afraid of. But for some reason, I am kind of afraid.

I finish my shower quickly and put the pair of jeans that I brought in with me on. I didn't grab a shirt, so I'll need to get one out of my closet. I put my deodorant on and squeeze my hair inside a thick white towel. I hang the towel around my shoulders and bring my hair up front, so it lays on both sides of the towel.

I open the bathroom door and Caleb looks at me from my bed. He closes the book and places it back on my nightstand. I give him a smile and walk toward my closet.

"Your body looks extra hot right now. But I think you know that—which is why you came out without a shirt on. Am I right?" Caleb asks.

I open my closet and grab a burgundy long sleeve shirt and put it on. It fits me nice and snug; it's one of my favorites. I grab a long-sleeved, navy-blue, lightweight shirt for tomorrow and close the closet door. I didn't answer Caleb on purpose, by the way. I mean, what could I really say to what he asked me anyway? He can hear my thoughts, there's no point in lying. I open my dresser and pull out a pair of gray pants, along with socks and underwear. I grab an empty backpack from beside my dresser and put my clothes inside of it. I clap my hands together once. "Alright, that's everything I need. Let's go."

Caleb stands up from my bed. He grabs his cape and takes my backpack from my hands. "I'll wear this," he says, placing a strap over each shoulder. "By the way, your face looks good after the shower. The spot where the volleyball hit you earlier isn't even red or swollen. Pretty unbelievable. I thought for sure it was going to bruise."

I give him a smile and we head downstairs. "Walk really fast, okay? They're probably in the living room watching TV, so we need to just go straight out of the kitchen door," I say.

We make it out of the house without being stopped. Caleb looks really cute flying with my backpack on. I never use my backpack since we don't need it for school. Not that many vampires use them anymore. I really only bring any type of bag with me if I have soccer practice or I'm going somewhere right after school. Soccer season doesn't start for another few months, and I'm not sure if I'll join this year or not. Kind of depends on what Caleb does, honestly. There's really nothing that sounds better to me than being with Caleb, so if he doesn't want to play soccer, I probably won't either. It's not that important to me.

Caleb smiles and says, "You can play whatever you want. I don't know if I'll join the soccer team, but I would if you wanted me to. Since you don't care either way, I suppose I don't really, either. But we can definitely do it together, if you want to."

"Yeah, I don't know, Caleb. I like soccer and I have fun when I'm playing, but I'm not sure if I want to join again. Plus, with our band, I don't know what's going to happen. I need to make some time to practice with Wolfie after school this week, or on the weekend. You could hang out and watch band practice if you want to."

"Of course, and I can't wait to see it," Caleb says.

Chapter 17
The Brains and the Beef

We land in the backyard of Caleb's home. The air smells fresher here for some reason. Like clean laundry or something. It's a really nice scent.

Caleb is sniffing while he holds my hand. "Okay, I think my dad is here. Just ignore him. He probably won't even say anything to us, so if he happens to be in our path on the way to my room, just pretend you don't see him."

"I can't do that! If I see your dad, I at least have to introduce myself. I can't be rude. I'm a Dracula—do you know how much trouble I would be in if my parents ever found out that I didn't introduce myself properly to another noble?"

"Alright, I understand. Just keep your voice down when we walk inside. Hopefully, he's on the other side of the house," Caleb says as he opens the door slowly.

Walking inside Caleb's house, the scent of clean laundry is even stronger. I don't remember smelling this yesterday.

Caleb looks side-to-side before we enter the large foyer with the staircase. He pulls my hand and leads me upstairs. As my foot passes the last step, Caleb's head drops. "Hello, son," his father says, rubbing his shoulders from behind.

I turn and smile at Caleb's father, who somehow looks exactly like Caleb—a grown-up Caleb. Oh my fangs. Well, they say you'll grow up to look like one of your parents if you're a noble vampire, and I am not mad at what I see standing beside Caleb right now. I thought he looked like his mom, but he actually looks like a younger version of his father.

Caleb's mouth is open a bit and he looks like he's in shock. Oh, right, my thoughts. He heard what I was thinking. Whoops. I give Caleb an apologetic smile.

Before I can introduce myself, Caleb's father reaches his hand toward me and says, "Oh, you are most definitely the son of Alessandra and the idiot. You look just like your mother. You must be thrilled about that. Greetings, I am Andrew Cheval, Caleb's father. No doubt your mother and father have told you all about me," he says.

What the fangs am I supposed to say here? I don't want to upset nobility, or insult him, but my parents have told me nothing about him. In fact, until last night, I had no idea that my family even knew Caleb's father. I mean, he called my dad an idiot, though, so he definitely knows my parents.

"It's nice to meet you. I am Froderick Cheval," I say while shaking Caleb's father's hand.

Caleb lets out a light chuckle and holds my other hand.

Caleb's father says, "Oh, I had no idea you were a Cheval, how exactly are we related?" he asks then laughs.

"Did I say Cheval?" I ask.

Caleb and his father nod at me.

"Oh, wow. I did? I'm Froderick Dracula. I have Caleb on the brain right now and I wasn't expecting to meet you, so I think I was just nervous. Sorry," I say.

"No apology necessary. It was funny. How is your father? I'm curious to hear what he's told you about me. Let's talk for a bit inside my office."

"No, Dad, we need to go to the bookstore, then we have to study for this report that we have to write." Caleb pulls my hand in the opposite direction.

"This will only take a few minutes," his father says.

Who am I supposed to follow? I feel like it's Caleb's father since he's an adult, but Caleb doesn't really like him, so I'm not sure if that's actually the right choice.

"Frode, do you want to talk to my dad or do you want to head to the bookstore?"

"Either one," I say with a nervous smile.

"Settled," Caleb's father says, walking in front of the two of us.

We follow behind him holding hands. Caleb looks all kinds of annoyed right now, but I'm not really bothered by it. I want to know what his dad's relationship with my parents is. Maybe Caleb's dad might even be able to help us figure out the reason for the connection. Or maybe he knows where our moms are. He was so confident that my dad had talked about him before, which is pretty funny, too.

Caleb whispers in my ear, "Sorry about this."

I squeeze his hand three times and smile. I want to convey that I love him, but I still feel kind of funny saying it out loud. Especially with his dad here, since I don't know him, or the type of relationship he has with my parents.

Caleb smiles, he squeezes my hand twice. He can hear my thoughts. "Me too," he says aloud.

We reach Caleb's father's office and sit inside the dimly lit room. Caleb places my backpack on the floor beside his chair. The walls are lined with bookcases and certificates of accomplishment. Wow, it looks like he even has a few different degrees. I have no idea what he does for a living, though, just based on what I'm seeing.

There is one picture that catches my eye on a shelf. It's an older picture, I can see Caleb's mom and father smiling, it looks like it's maybe a college graduation photo. The picture is folded inside the frame, though, as if the other vampires in the photo were too important to be ripped out, but not important enough to be seen. Hmm. I wonder if my parents are in that photo. Nah, that's stupid. It was probably just some photobomber that popped in the shot or something.

I can't imagine what taking pictures must have been like in the 90s or early 2000s. They had no filters or re-dos, nothing could be cropped or edited. I mean, they didn't even know what the pictures looked like until someone at a photo shop printed them out. My mother has told me of this many times. Her original author picture is one that Wolfman took, and she explained that they used three rolls of film just to be sure they would get one good picture. That must have been annoying.

Caleb's father is smiling at me as Caleb pulls his chair close to mine.

"So, you two are a couple?" his father asks us.

Caleb holds my hand and nods. "Yes, we're going out," he says.

I love that Caleb said that, but I'm also nervous that he said that. But really, I shouldn't be nervous, although he does know my father, he can't know him that well. Besides, when my dad said his name the other night, I don't think it sounded like he liked him.

"Oh, well, that is very interesting to me personally, for many reasons. How does your father feel about this?" Caleb's father asks me.

Caleb squeezes my hand and shakes his head at me not to answer. I can hear what he's thinking and he's gonna try and get some answers for me. "Dad, what is your relationship with Frode's parents? I didn't know that you knew them. I only found out yesterday that our moms knew each other. I always knew that you both didn't like Dracula, but were you actually friends?"

Oh, okay, this is something I was not prepared for. Caleb's dad is doing a version of the deviant laugh. It's not as intriguing as Caleb's, but still, I could see other vampires being into that. Caleb is shaking his head at me after hearing my thoughts. I don't know when I'll learn to not think about these things—and really, how can I control it? I give Caleb a smile and squeeze his hand.

Caleb's father is sitting tall in his chair. His face is somewhat arrogant as he speaks to Caleb. "You're asking several questions, Caleb. First of all, sit up straight, your posture is terrible."

I can't believe his dad even said that. Caleb is sitting up straighter than I ever could. His posture is always perfect, unless he's pouting, of course.

Caleb is doing the opposite right now, though; he's slinking down into his chair. Definitely doing it out of spite.

"How's this?" Caleb asks his father with a false smile.

Caleb's father is shaking his head at him. "Well, our relationship, that is to say, mine and your father's, Frode, is different from that of the relationship I had with your mother. As far as your father goes, he *was* my rival in all things when we were very young. Growing up in a small town and both being the only sons of nobles, we were often pitted against one another. I was better at everything naturally, well, because your father, he's always been very stupid— that's the nicest way I can say that—I mean no offense."

I hold my hands palms-out and say, "None taken."

Caleb's father smiles and continues, "So, we had all the same classes, same teachers, we liked the same foods, and eventually we realized we had more in common than just being from noble houses.

We started hanging out with each other after our middle school teacher assigned us a project that we had to work on together. I hung out at your dad's parents' house, with your grandfather—who smelled just awful, by the way, but he was very nice. Your dad hung out at my house, which my parents loved, because, let's face it, although the house of Cheval is noble and ranked alongside the house of Dracula, your father's family are still the head of the vampire world. Of course, the house of Serafino hadn't immigrated yet at the time, so our two houses were the highest. Anyway, after the project, we took on everything together. Your father was not better looking than me by any stretch of the imagination, but still there were more girls flocking to him than one could count. So, I was the brains, and your dad was considered to be the beef in our friendship."

"Disgusting," Caleb says.

I chuckle lightly. I thought the brains and beef thing was pretty funny.

"Oh, Caleb you really need to lighten up. You're so serious all the time. I'm saying that vampires were only interested in his father's looks. Which didn't make sense because I *was and still am better looking*. It was more that your father was just so dumb, that vampires referred to us as the smart one and the…hot one. Ugh, I can barely say it. So, we took the vampire world on and ran through all the girls in town, we both had our first bites when we were fifteen, on opposite sides of a wall with a couple of vamps we met at a bowling alley. They were cute, but we really just wanted to see what would happen if we bit them, since we'd heard so much about what happens when a noble bites someone. It was pretty incredible, really, not the biting part, but the rush of emotions that we felt when we bit them. It was probably not as fun for the girls since we both hurried out of the rooms to tell each other what happened, as soon as we'd done it."

Caleb's father is kind of laughing and also sort of scoffing at the memory. He spins in his chair and stands up. He grabs the silver picture frame that holds the picture I noticed of his parents earlier. He places it on his desk without saying anything and sits back down.

"What was that like?" I ask.

"The bite was pretty bland, I mean, you've both tasted blood before, so it's no different than if you're biting someone you don't care about. The feeling of seeing someone's memories and living their life in an instant was quite exhilarating, though. We were young, as were the girls, so there wasn't much to be seen aside from childhood memories, school memories, bouts of insecurities, oh, and the girl I'd bitten, Violeta, had a crush on your father, so that was an added treat. I was able to see everything that she was thinking about him, which was rather humiliating for me, but I didn't think that immediately. At the time, I just thought it was cool because your father and I had just bitten girls for the first time. The connection wasn't strong and as I tried to see any deeper I couldn't, your father couldn't either with the girl he'd bitten. We weren't in a relationship with the girls so, after we bit them, we left the girls' house and didn't ask to see them again.

"As soon as we left the house we were in, the connection was broken. Both your father and I couldn't believe it. We weren't prepared to lose what we'd just gained. Your father was not smart, but he was cool, and he said, 'Drew, let's go bite some more girls and see how long we can make the connection last.' I remember that I just wanted to do whatever he did because he was my best—well, we were close. Anyway, for the rest of the year, we basically bit any pair of girls that we came across. If there was one for your dad and one for me, then we bit them. Same thing happened every time, as soon as we left, the connection was lost. When we started high school, two new vampires had transferred in, both beautiful, one blonde and one brunette. Any guesses as to who they were?"

Caleb is annoyed, he really wants to leave and have sex. He's usually not thinking about sex as often as I am, but right now, he's not interested in anything his dad is saying. He rolls his eyes at his father. "Obviously it was mom and Frode's mom," Caleb says.

"Yes, that is correct. Miranda and Alessandra came in and took the whole high school by storm. Both purebloods, both noble, it was incredible. Drac and I, well, we felt like we'd been gifted something by the two of them falling into our hands like this. We were wrong, though, because the only one who was interested in us at all was Miranda. She talked a bit to us here and there after classes and cheerleading practice, but not Alessandra. Alessandra wanted nothing to do with either of us. She was snobby, but in a way that made you want her more. She was born from the highest vampires, and she looked more perfect than any vampire either of us had ever seen. Unfortunately for Drac and I, Alessandra knew how pretty she was, and she knew that she was sought after. She was in no way giving off any type of sign that she would have anything to do with either of us. So, since it was a new school year, that meant it was time for the homecoming football game and dance. Well, Drac and I decided that we'd take our chances with the girls. Now, I thought that your father knew that I liked Alessandra and your father thought that I knew that he did. In reality, we both pictured the other one with Miranda and ourselves with Alessandra."

Caleb sits up straight and shakes his head. He interrupts his father, "This is terrible, Dad. Really mean, and I don't even know why you're telling us this. That's my mom and your wife you're talking about."

I rub Caleb on the shoulder and smile at him. "Hey, just let him finish. I want to hear," I say.

"Caleb, if this makes you uncomfortable, you can leave, and I can just chat with Froderick here. Would you feel better if we did that?" his father asks.

Caleb's dad is kind of a jerk. Like the stuff he says to Caleb may not sound mean, but it's all in the tone. Like he says stuff in a very demeaning way, almost. We're almost eighteen, but he talks to Caleb like he's five or something.

Caleb huffs and says, "No, Frode is interested. Please continue. But, really, we need to head to the bookstore and do some other stuff, so can you like speed it up?"

His father rolls his eyes. "Yes, fine. Anyway, we both ask Alessandra to homecoming without the other knowing because we both think the other is asking Miranda. Alessandra says yes to Drac and then says she would have said yes to me if I'd asked her first. So, I told your father what she said, but your father didn't believe me. So, being the idiot that he is, he went and asked her if it was true. Well, Alessandra did not like that. So, she rescinded her agreement to go to homecoming with him. She walked right over to me and said, 'Ask me again, and I will say yes.' So, I did, because, you see, Alessandra had this sort of power over me and whatever she said, I just listened to. So, your father was really mad, he asked Miranda, who happily agreed because she didn't know that she was his second choice."

I'm really interested in this story, but Caleb is having a hard time listening. I squeeze his hand and smile, while his father continues talking. I don't think he would stop talking even if we asked him to at this point.

"Then, leading up to homecoming, the four of us started eating lunch together. Not as two couples, just as four vampires in the same grade. Of course, vampires whispered and imagined which of us should be paired up. One day, in the middle of the cafeteria, hearing vampires gossiping, your mother wrapped her arm around Miranda and kissed her right on the cheek. Your father and I were speechless, and Miranda was embarrassed, but Alessandra never wanted anyone to tell her what to do. So, because vampires were saying she should be with me, or Drac, she was determined to make those whispers go away. Anyway, they weren't a real couple, but Alessandra and your mother would flutter about the school holding hands, whispering and inspiring all kinds of rumors. Everyone was terrified of your mother's status, of course, and no one dared say anything. Well, the night for homecoming arrived and we all went together. Alessandra wanted nothing to do with me, but she was very interested in Drac. Talk about whiplash for me, right? So, I'm sitting off to the side in the decorated gym, which is where our school dances were held, and I'm not wearing shoes because for whatever reason we weren't allowed to wear shoes on the gym floor, and I'm stuck just watching your dad and Alessandra hit it off. Miranda asked me to dance, and so we did. I think that for Miranda, she was instantly into me, at least she says she was, but, for me, it took longer because I was still stuck on Alessandra and the fact that I, the smartest vampire in school, had lost the most beautiful girl in the school to my idiot best friend."

"So, you weren't even focused on mom?" Caleb asks. "You were just pouting about Frode's mother?"

Caleb's father sighs and rolls his eyes. "Anyway, they began dating right away, and I began dating your mother about six months after that, when I'd finally given up. Anyway, Drac and Alessandra fought all the time, just constant power struggles, all kinds of things. Mostly, to put it in a blood capsule, your father and your mother fought because your father was just not very smart and your mother was extremely intelligent. Well, I grew tired of it as we reached our senior year and your father and I just stopped speaking to one another. Having to hear him whine all the time was just exhausting.

"Your mother was no better, she constantly complained to Miranda, but of course Miranda didn't mind, because she truly loved

Alessandra as her best friend. Miranda and I went to college, and we got married. I went to a different college than Miranda and Alessandra, though. During that time, I'm not sure what happened between them, but their bond grew even stronger. There were times that Miranda threatened that both she and Alessandra were going to leave Drac and I, and just go live comfortably on a beach somewhere together. Their friendship was so strong that I truly believed they might do it. So, I focused on being a better husband and listened while your mother talked about Alessandra and Drac endlessly. It was the same as high school—always fighting.

"After college, you two were born and your mothers were overjoyed at the two of you being born around the same time. You were two very adorable children and you both loved to play with one another. Your father and I were not on speaking terms, though, so I was less than thrilled that my son was playing with his. Then all of that stuff happened with Wolf—who I will not talk about because I don't want to pick a side there, and your mother wrote her book. She killed off the character that Miranda loved and they ended their friendship on the spot. I still don't really understand it. There must have been more to that story, as far as Miranda was concerned, but I've never been able to figure it out. If the story had to do with anyone, it was… Anyway, as a result of their friendship ending, you two were never able to play together again. So, imagine my surprise when I come home and see you two holding hands… Wow. I am exhausted. Now, if you would be so kind as to tell me how your parents explained their relationship with me, I'd love to hear it."

"They didn't…uh, tell me anything," I say.

Caleb's father is opening the back of the silver picture frame, while shaking his head in disbelief. He pulls the picture out and I can see my mother and father off to the side. It looks like they were maybe arguing, or maybe it was just a bad angle.

Caleb's father passes me the picture and says, "This was from your mother and Miranda's college graduation. You can see back here that your parents are fighting. I wasn't speaking to Drac at the time, because our friendship had ended years prior, but your mother was trying to get him to take a picture with the four of us together and your father couldn't even bring himself to do that much."

Caleb's dad's facial expression is really weird right now. I can't quite describe it. It's like he appears to be fully annoyed and extremely hurt at the same time. He straightens his already perfect posture and shakes his head slowly. "I really don't understand how I never came up in conversation. I was not expecting you to say that."

Caleb puts my backpack on, stands and holds his hand out to me. I stand and pass the picture back to Caleb's father.

"Dad, you and Mom never talked about Mr. Dracula or Frode's mother either. The only thing I knew was that you and mom didn't like him, but I never knew why. So, I don't think it's so strange that his parents never talked about you." Caleb takes my hand in his and turns toward the office door to leave.

I turn back and look at his father. I feel bad after everything that he just told me. Well, I feel confused more than bad, I guess, but I do hate seeing vampires upset, and right now Caleb's father looks upset. "I've never really talked to my parents about their past either, so really don't take offense. My dad is usually whining about life being unfair or yelling at me. There aren't many father/son conversations."

"Well, he sounds exactly the same then. I guess some things never change. I can't imagine he likes the fact that you two are dating, though. Even when Alessandra and Miranda were fooling around, he was very put off by it. He couldn't understand it, but I guess if he can accept you two being together, maybe he *has* changed."

"Oh, no, he has no idea we are together," I say.

Caleb's father leans back in his chair and puts his hands behind his head. "Really…" he says with a devilish grin.

Caleb pulls me out of the room, while I wave goodbye over my shoulder.

Chapter 18
Claim Your Neck

Once we reach Caleb's room, he puts my backpack on his dresser, then lays flat on his bed and I lay beside him. His room really is so big, and his bed is huge. I wonder if we'll end up sleeping close together tonight. Man, I can't think about this right now. I really feel like my brain may explode from the influx of information that Caleb's father just poured into us. So many things were said, that I don't even know which one to focus on. I pull my phone out of my pocket and check to see if my mother has called me, which she hasn't.

"They're probably at the beach," Caleb says.

"Who is at the beach?" I ask, while looking over at him.

Caleb turns on his side and props his head on his hand. "Our moms. My dad said they always threatened to just go live on a beach somewhere, maybe they just decided to do it."

"Nah, I'm not trying to pretend I know everything, but honestly, they could be at the beach, but my mom wouldn't run away with your mom for many reasons. First and foremost, my mom loves men. She could not live without men in her life, so even if they fixed their friendship, it would only be a friendship—they definitely won't be, like, *together*. My mother has told me in excruciating detail of her love for the male body. Trust me when I say she absolutely does not feel the same about the female body. In fact, there was one time that she mentioned a friend in college that she experimented with and said they both realized they weren't into each other that way. I am just now realizing that was probably your mother, as unsettling as that is, but, yeah, she said it wasn't for her. My mom is always honest when it comes to desire. She loves talking about it. It's gross, but she does it."

"Wait, are you saying our moms, like, did *stuff* together?" Caleb asks.

"Maybe? She could have just meant kissing or maybe it wasn't your mom. How the hell should I know? I mean, my head is still spinning from everything that your dad just told me, Caleb. I can't think clearly."

Caleb stands from his bed. He's walking over toward his dresser while shaking his head. "I need to take a shower and get out of this uniform before we go to the bookstore. Wait, did you actually want to go to the bookstore? Or were you just playing along because I said it to your dad earlier?"

I'm still lying flat on Caleb's bed. My arms are spread wide and I'm staring at the light fixture above. "We can go to the bookstore," I say. "Honestly, I want to do, you know, other stuff, but I'm kind of uncomfortable now that I know your dad is in the house. I felt a little weird about the way he reacted when I told him that my dad didn't know about us yet. Is your dad actually a jerk? Like would he tell my dad about us, just because he knows it will piss him off?"

"Well, he is a jerk, as I'm sure you could tell just from speaking with him. I don't know if he would tell him or not. I don't want you to do this, and if you say yes, I'm going to go with you, but do you want to go home? I can feel how worried you are, and I don't want you to feel that way. I want you to be able to relax and if you won't be able to relax, we can just go hang out at your house. Wait, you know, now that I think about it—I don't know if I've ever heard you relax, except for when we're making out. No, even then, I think you're still freaking out."

I sigh and place a hand on my forehead. "I am always freaking out. I'm definitely freaking out now, but, no, I don't want to go home. If your dad told him about us, it would probably be better for us anyway. But we completely forgot to ask him if he knew where our moms were. Now that we know a little more, it's kind of a crazy story, right? I feel bad for your mom, kind of, I'm not sure why."

"Don't worry about it. I told you, my parents are together, but not together. I'm sure my mom already knows all of this. It's old news. Nothing for you to worry about. So, bookstore or just"—he pumps his eyebrows at me—"shower and *study*?"

"Let's hit the bookstore. I don't think I'm ready to *study* just yet. Strange as that is. But, yeah, with your dad here, I'm just a little nervous," I say, standing up from the bed.

Caleb wraps his arms around me, he's squeezing me tight. I tuck my face next to his neck. His neck is perfect, and I feel the urge to bite him, wrapped up like this.

"He won't stay the night," Caleb says. "He never does. I'm sure after the bookstore, he'll be gone." He's lifting my chin with just his thumb. He presses his lips gently against mine. His pale blue eyes are searching my face softly. It's like his eyes are saying so many things right now, well, I mean, I can hear his thoughts, but his eyes are really doing the talking. He kisses my forehead and pulls back from the embrace.

Caleb smiles at me and says, "I want to give you something before we leave, okay? Come over here. I have to find it."

I follow Caleb into his large walk-in closet. There is a gorgeous, tall, black armoire pushed against the inside of the closet, and Caleb quickly opens the left side of it. It's full of jewelry. Wow, what a collection he has. Tons of rings, and necklaces, bracelets…wow. I don't have this much stuff. Caleb is really searching now; he's pulling open different drawers and boxes.

I feel bad because he looks like he's really worried that he's lost something. "What are you looking for? Can I help?" I ask while placing a hand on his shoulder.

Caleb opens the opposite side of the armoire and says, "I'm looking for a black box, it has a red "C" on it. If you want to help, that will speed things up, look in the other side of the cabinet, I'll keep searching through these drawers. Start with the bottom, though, and work your way up. It will be in one of the larger drawers. The top drawers on that side just have rings in them."

I kneel down and open the bottom drawer. There are all kinds of boxes in here and, of course, most are black. I don't see one with a "C" on it, though. Oh, oh, oh bats…I don't see a box, but Caleb's package is right next to my face. His uniform pants fit him so nicely. Shit, I can't think about this. He'll hear my thoughts. I'm looking back inside the bottom drawer again, trying to ignore the curiosity and the extremely strong urge I'm feeling. Didn't work, Caleb must have either noticed it at the same time, or he heard my thoughts. His hand is on my head and he's kind of lightly patting it. Shit, what do I do? No. I'm not going to look up at him, if I look up at him, I'll do something that I really shouldn't. I continue looking through the drawer and Caleb rubs my head a few more times then goes back to looking inside the drawers on his side. We were thinking about the same thing. Oh fangs…I hope one of us finds this box soon. I pull the next drawer open and see a black box with a red "C" on it.

I pull the box out and hold it up, again, avoiding eye contact. "Is this it?" I ask.

Caleb takes the box from my hand and opens it. "Yes! You did it! This is it. Thank you. Come on, I'm gonna get dressed and then we'll head to the bookstore."

I stand up while keeping my eyes locked on the jewelry cabinet. There is no way I'm looking over at Caleb's D while I'm standing up. Too many urges right now.

Caleb lets out a light chuckle and taps my mouth with his pointer finger. "Later," he says softly.

I'm not even going to play dumb here, since I already know that we are thinking about the same thing. "Maybe," I say with a smile. I walk over and sit on the edge of Caleb's bed. I want to ask him what's in the box, but I'm sure he'll tell me soon, since he can hear what I'm thinking anyway. I definitely can't watch him getting dressed right now. I pull my phone out and scroll through my text messages. It's amazing how fewer messages I'm getting, now that Caleb and I are together. I did get one from Wolfie, though. Hmm, it seems that Robert told him what happened. That's weird. They weren't ever close, kind of feels strange that he would go to my best friend and tell him what happened. Wolfie doesn't seem to mind, though, not based on the text he sent me. I still can't believe that happened.

"Hmmph," Caleb says while buttoning his shirt. "That guy, honestly, Frode, that was the craziest thing to ever happen to me. I really think he was going to try and kiss you or, at least, hug you. He should be more afraid of me than he is."

"Yeah, I think so, too. Your face gets all scary when you're looking at him. Sorry that he did that. I obviously wasn't expecting that to happen."

Caleb is finished getting dressed. Damn, he looks good. He's walking over toward me while holding the box.

"Listen, I want you to wear this, even though I know what it means. I already intend to do this with you so, it shouldn't matter if we have, or we haven't yet."

I have no idea what he's talking about as he sits beside me. Caleb opens the box and inside there is a thin gold necklace with a ruby encrusted "C" charm on it.

It's a really nice necklace, I'm not sure what the significance is, though, I mean, I assume the "C" is for Caleb, but why is he acting so serious about it?

Caleb is smiling brightly while taking the necklace out. "Again, you have a conversation all by yourself without asking me. I forgot that some things are specific to a vampire's territory, maybe this is one of those things. I should tell you what it means then, before you put it on."

The necklace business sounds serious, but, I mean, it's just a necklace. I tilt my head at him and say, "Yes, it is a nice necklace, but I do want to know why it matters."

"So, the "C," is for Cheval. This was given to me by my grandparents on my sixteenth birthday. Nobles where I'm from usually get one from their grandparents, or sometimes their parents. Normally, you then give this necklace to the vampire who will be your forever bite, after you've bitten them. It's sort of like a claim on your neck that tells other vampires that you're taken by a noble house. So, for me, I haven't bitten you yet, but I will, and I know it's kind of bold for me, but I want you to wear this. If you don't want to, I can kind of understand, but I would love it if you did."

I lift my hair and turn my body to the side without saying anything. I can't really think of anything to say. I've never heard of such a romantic tradition, and I think anything I say will just ruin the mood.

Caleb gently kisses the nape of my neck once. His hands are shaking as he reaches around and secures the necklace on me.

I lift the charm with my fingers and admire it. It's beautiful and I love it. Caleb wraps his arms around my waist and rests his chin on my shoulder. "Thank you," he says.

"What are you thanking me for? I should be thanking you. I feel like I should give you something, too. We don't have this necklace tradition, though, so I have no idea what I could give you."

Caleb rubs my shoulders and stands. He pumps his eyebrows at me, "Tonight," he says with a smirk.

I grab one of the square black pillows from his bed and toss it at him. He laughs as it hits the floor. I stand and look in the mirror at the necklace. It looks really good against my skin and it feels good, too. "Thank you, Caleb. I love it. I really do."

"I'm glad. I love that you're wearing it. Now, let's go. I can feel my own thoughts beginning to stray from the bookstore, and if I'm thinking those things, I know that you are too."

Caleb extends his hand toward me; we hold hands and leave his room. Heading downstairs, I can hear his brothers arguing with his father. Caleb quickens our pace, and we leave before anyone hears us.

"So annoying when he's home," Caleb says of his father, as we fly into the cloudy sky. The sun has set and it's not dark out yet, which is nice because it makes the air a bit cooler than in the daytime.

"How far away is this bookstore?" I ask. It feels strange with this necklace hanging from my neck. It's very light and I'm kind of afraid it's going to break or fall off. I'm holding the small "C" tightly in between my thumb and pointer finger.

Caleb gently elbows me against my arm. "I forgot to tell you that the only one that can take that necklace off is me. It will never fall off, and the bookstore is probably only another few minutes away."

My mouth is open, and I screech, "Whaaat?! You put like a crazy magic necklace on me? I thought this was like a sweet love thing you did. This is like a collar or something. What the hell?"

I'm only half-serious, okay, less than half, really, I'm not serious at all. I don't mind being marked as Caleb's, but I would have liked to know that I wouldn't be able to ever take it off by myself. I'm kind of claustrophobic, and now that I know I can't take it off, I feel almost like I'm choking.

"Woah…your thoughts and your words, Frode. I'm sorry, I didn't keep that from you on purpose, I just forgot to say it. I can always take it off whenever you want me to, but, no, you are supposed to keep it on, always. And you're not choking, you're fine."

I sigh loudly. "Well, at least it won't fall off. I'm happy about that, but before you give me something that I can't remove, let me know first next time."

Caleb is thinking about something very dirty right now. I can't even say it. Wow, he's already decided what my role in all this will be. Honestly, I have, too, so I'm okay with it, but, damn, that was really dirty.

Caleb is smirking at me. "Frode, if you want to talk about it, we can talk about it, but the bookstore is right down there, so maybe we'll save that conversation for later. Or we turn around and I can show you what I think your role is right now."

I'm shaking my head no at him while we land in front of the bookstore. Wow, this place is smaller than I thought it would be. Seems like it will be kind of cramped inside, but maybe it's like a clown car and even though it looks small on the outside, it's actually big inside.

Caleb pulls me in for a hug as his feet hit the ground. It's kind of romantic being out with him and being away from home in a different town. Feels nice. He lifts my chin and stares deep into my eyes, our lips are pressed together now. I don't even know which one of us started it, but the kiss is slow, and it feels really soft and intimate. Mmm, I love kissing Caleb, especially these soft teasing sort of kisses. I can't wait to do other things with Caleb tonight. I really hope his father is gone when we get back. Ugh, I'm gonna smell like outside now, though. I took a shower so this wouldn't happen, too. Whenever I am outside for too long, my hair smells like outside air. I hate the way it smells. I don't want Caleb to think my hair smells bad.

Caleb pulls back from the kiss with a slight giggle. "You think too much," he says and kisses me quickly once more.

I smile at him as he holds my hand, and we walk toward the store entrance. *Fran's Fangtastic Books* the sign on the door says. Oh no, there is a picture of my mother on the window advertising a book signing for her latest novel, *Boys Kiss Boys or We Riot*. Stupidest title ever, and she's had more than a few stupid ones. The premise is about a group of high schoolers who are fighting to have LGBTQ+ books put into their school library. Anyway, it looks like she's scheduled to be here on the weekend, so hopefully she'll be back from whatever she's doing.

Caleb holds the door open for me and as I step inside the smell of old books overwhelms my senses. It does not smell good. Caleb is pressing his cheek next to mine. I'm not sure why—oh, okay, he wants me to smell him. That's cute. He gives me a smile and leads me down the left aisle of books. The store is a bit bigger than it seemed outside, but the aisles are almost set up like a maze. It's very bright and warm inside, the lights feel like heat lamps shining down from the high ceilings.

"We're going toward the back, that's where the fiction section is. We should be able to find something for our report over there, hopefully something new that no one else is using," Caleb says.

I smile and say, "Well, both our families have huge libraries, so if we can't find something here, I'm sure we can just use something from one of our houses."

Caleb stops briefly and looks to the right side. His eyes are wide and he looks super excited standing in front of the Erotic Fiction section. I completely forgot about this. It's fine, though, whatever is in those books we'll probably be doing tonight anyway, so I'm not too worried about it. Wait, unless I should be worried about it. Judging by Caleb's thoughts when I just relaxed, maybe I should be nervous. Oh fangs. I tilt my head back as Caleb smiles at me. Caleb pinches my necklace charm in between his fingers and says, "It will be fine, and I don't see anything new here. I have all of these books anyway. Well, except for the ones that aren't any good. Come on, the section we want is right over there."

Caleb leads me down a twisty section of books leading to a large open area. There are a few tables inside, with vampires sitting at them. There's even a little mini café.

I point at the counter and say, "This is nice and cozy, Caleb. Did you used to come here and read a lot? Does the café have anything good?"

"Yeah, I used to come here a lot, but I would just sit over there in that corner by myself. I don't really like it when vampires bother me when I'm reading. Normally, I just read at home, though, but when I wasn't sure if I wanted a book, I would sit over there," he says, pointing toward a small one-vampire table in the corner.

Standing in front of the new release sections, Caleb is quickly scanning for a book that we may be able to use. I am kind of hungry and thirsty, though, so I think I want to see what the café has.

"I'm gonna grab a drink and maybe something to eat. Are you hungry or thirsty?" I ask.

"They have a really good caramel cappuccino, so please order me that and, here, use this card," he says, pulling his wallet out.

I pull my head back and turn away, not taking the card from him. "You are not paying for this. No way."

I stop in my tracks hearing Caleb's thoughts, well really it was more like a silent threat.

I walk back toward him in absolute disbelief. He's holding the card toward me with a cocky grin on his face.

"I can't believe you would threaten me with not doing it tonight, just because I was going to pay for your stupid drink," I say while snatching the card from him.

"You believed me, so that's on you. Just use the card. I don't want you paying for things. That's dumb," Caleb says.

I shake my head and walk toward the café counter. I don't know why it matters, we're both rich, it's not like it's either of our money that's being spent. So, what does it really matter whose card pays for it? Anyway, I guess it's sweet that he wanted to pay for me, but, still, he shouldn't have threatened me with *that*. He knows me too well after being inside my head. He knew exactly what to think to get his way.

A bright-eyed employee wearing all black greets me. Her name tag says *Olivia, she/her*. "Hello, Can I have a name for your order?" she asks.

"Oh, my name is Froderick."

"Froderick…like Froderick Dracula?" she asks.

The few vampires within earshot all turn to look at me. This is exactly why I don't use my full name. I can't believe this girl just said my name aloud.

I sigh loudly and give her a smile. "Yes, thank you."

"Oh wow, I'm, like, so excited to meet you. You're, like, really cute. How old are you?" she asks.

My necklace has kind of tucked itself under my collar. I pull it out and move the charm around, purposely drawing her attention to it. Caleb said this is a well-known thing here, so let's see how well-known it is.

She notices the necklace immediately and her eyes widen. "Oh, I'm sorry. I didn't know you were already taken. Is that "C" for Cheval? As in Caleb Cheval?"

How could she even know that just from the "C"? I'm so confused, but I also don't really feel like talking to this vampire anymore. I'm pretty hungry. "Yes, Caleb Cheval. Can I please place my order? We're here looking for a book, but I'm starving."

"Oh, wow. Oh wow…uh…yeah, of course. Sorry. Go ahead, what can I get for you?" she asks.

I see her eyes looking behind me and she looks like she wants to say something. I turn before placing my order and notice another guy talking to Caleb by the back wall… What the fuck?

"Forget the order," I say and turn away.

Chapter 19
Bow, Knave

Caleb is looking over at me confused. He looks really uncomfortable and annoyed. I'm trying to hear his thoughts, but I can't keep my own damn mind quiet. I'm so frustrated at the sight of this guy standing near Caleb. His body language is pissing me off already. He's just a little too close to what's mine and he keeps rubbing his own neck. Fangs it's so slutty to rub your neck like that by another vampire's boyfriend. He might as well be asking him to bite him. I approach and stand beside Caleb, again making sure my necklace is on full display.

Caleb kisses my cheek and asks, "Did you order the stuff?"

I know he can read my damn mind, but I am thinking so many crazy things right now, that he probably just can't even make sense of what's going on in there.

"No, I didn't order anything. I saw this vampire over here talking to you and you looked uncomfortable, so I came over."

"Caleb, uncomfortable? Around me? Ha! You obviously have no idea who I am," the vampire says in the cockiest of tones.

"Come on, Frode, let's go. He's not worthy of a conversation with you," Caleb says, pulling my hand.

I'm very interested in who this vampire is, and his cocky attitude just made things worse. Worse for him, not me.

"Who even are you?" I ask.

"Oh, me? I think Caleb could probably answer that better, but I'm Tobias, my name tag says so right here," he says, pointing to his nametag.

"Tobias, give it a rest. You mean nothing to me, and you never have. Don't try to make my actual boyfriend feel like you ever mattered."

Tobias cocks his head to the side. "Oh, I never mattered? That's funny. Let me ask you, boyfriend, are you a bleegan, too? Because I bet you didn't know this, but Caleb here is such a bleegan, never bit anyone and hates blood."

Caleb is really trying to pull me away from this guy, but I'm not one to back down from a fight and right now, I'm going to push back against this jerk, who is acting like my boyfriend belongs to him or something.

"Hmm, well, Caleb gave me this necklace, so are you confused, or do you not understand what this means?" I ask, showing him my necklace.

Tobias covers his mouth and points at my necklace. "What the hell is that, Caleb? You bit him? You, you…I got this job after you left school because I knew you would eventually come back here, and now you're back after only a few days and you've already… I… This is a joke, right?" Tobias asks.

"Enough of this," Caleb says and turns toward me. He takes both my hands in his and says, "Frode, we talked about everything I have ever done, remember?"

I nod at him uncomfortably. I can hear his thoughts. He's telling me that this is the vampire that he had sex with, just once. He didn't have feelings for him, and it was just a one-time thing. I know that to be true because Caleb told me so. Also, I can hear his thoughts and feel what he's feeling. He feels nothing but annoyance with this vampire and the feeling he has is more of a disgust with himself and a hurt that I'm standing here listening to all of this right now.

Tobias's body language has changed a bit as he watches us. "Oh, okay, so you did bite him, because you're obviously communicating right now. What, are you a noble, too?" Tobias asks me with a scoff.

"I am Froderick Dracula, does that answer your question?"

Tobias holds his hands out in shock. He lowers his head slightly and says, "Dracula? I-I had no idea. I had no right."

Yes, bow, knave. Of course, you had no idea. I want to punch this guy. His hair is terrible and he smells awful. Ugh, he uses the worst kind of bite spray, it's disgusting.

Tobias lifts his head and continues apologizing. "Oh, okay. Yeah, well, never mind about all that stuff I said earlier. Listen, I got this job to try and pick up guys. Caleb never really felt anything for me. I wish he did, but he didn't. I do have a flair for the dramatic, though, and thought it would be funny to mess with you a bit."

I rub Caleb's back and reply, "That's not funny at all. And you kind of pissed me off. I'm not really sure what you thought either of us would find funny about what you just did. I feel a lot of things right now, but I definitely don't feel like laughing," I say.

I can hear Caleb's thoughts. Turns out I'm not the only one who gets turned on by jealousy or possessiveness…whatever you want to call what I'm feeling right now. Either way, Caleb is really into it, I can feel it.

Caleb takes my hand and kisses it. "Tobias, you are a ridiculous vampire. You always have been. I can't believe they even let you work here. Please just go away. We really need to find a book for our report."

Now that I look at this vampire, he has bite marks all over his neck and his arms. Ugh gross. He's been bitten so many times. I hope those were all after Caleb. Thank fangs, Caleb never bit this guy.

"Never even considered it and, yes, that was a very long time ago," Caleb whispers and kisses me on the cheek.

"I really did think you were a bleegan, though, Caleb. I wasn't trying to be a jerk when I said that. If you're actually not, let me buy you guys a drink from the café. We just got this new energy drink in, it's called Bluhdy Amped. Have you guys had it? It's amazing, they only use the purest blood in it, it's so refreshing. Come on, let me buy you both one and we can sit down and talk for a while. I'm a big fan of your father, Froderick. It would be an honor to sit with you."

Okay, here's the thing, there are vampires who absolutely love the taste of blood, hence all the marketing and products that pair vampires up with blood. But the thing with blood is, the more you have it, the more you crave it. It's kind of like a caffeine addiction, but stronger. For me, I've had blood forced into my food since I was a baby, I don't hate it, but I also don't love or crave it. This guy seems like he's just dying to taste me and my boyfriend, which I am not a fan of. Suddenly I'm feeling very possessive. Hearing him talk about Caleb is really pissing me off and I don't really lose my temper often. I don't know what to—

My thoughts are interrupted as Caleb takes my face in his hands; his tongue is invading my mouth. He's kissing me with so much force and passion, right in front of this guy. Damn, this is hot.

Caleb pulls back softly and says, "Mmm, I love only you, Frode. My blood is yours; we are already one, no other shall ever taste me."

I kiss him softly and smile. "Me too."

Tobias looks a bit in shock. "So, no drinks then?" he asks with a laugh.

"No drinks," I say, while Caleb takes my hand and pulls me away.

"Tobias," Caleb says over his shoulder. "If you see us in here again, don't talk to us. I know that you are aware of how many things you just did wrong. Pretend you don't know us and neither of us will mention this to our fathers."

"I am sorry, Caleb and Froderick. I really shouldn't have," Tobias says.

I feel a little bad for him, but not really. I still want to punch him a little bit, but when Caleb puts someone in their place it's very intimidating. So, I can understand that this Tobias guy is afraid right now.

Tobias calls out as we've left the section that he's standing in, "Of course, if the two of you ever want maybe a third to take part in your—"

Okay, I'm gonna punch him. I drop Caleb's hand and turn to walk back toward Tobias, Caleb pulls my shoulder back.

"I was kidding, I was kidding. I just wanted to end things with a joke, so you weren't upset. I'm truly sorry," Tobias says, with his arms extended palms facing out.

Caleb wraps his arm around my waist and pulls me toward the back wall display. He's shaking his head. He's really embarrassed right now and he feels really bad. He also doesn't find that vampire attractive and is questioning how he ever did that with him. I have to stop listening, though, or I'm gonna maybe hear something I don't want to. It seems like his thoughts are leading him toward how he ended up in that situation to begin with. I don't want to hear it all again.

"Okay, what should we look for?" I ask and kiss him on the cheek.

He smiles at me lightly and rubs his temple staring at the display. "Do you want to just leave? I'm so pissed off and upset that I can't focus. I never wanted you to come in contact with him. I'm more than embarrassed, I'm mortified right now. Why don't we just use a book from my parents' library?" he asks.

I take both his hands in mine and shake my head. "Caleb, it's okay. Don't forget that I can hear everything you're thinking, but I can also feel everything, too. I'm not really upset about it. I don't want your thoughts to linger on what happened in the past. If you want to look for a book then let's do it, if not, then let's leave."

Caleb kisses my mouth quickly and looks back at the shelf. He's moving a few books around. He really is so cute no matter what he's doing. I mean how can someone look cute just by moving books around on a shelf? I have no idea, but it's happening right in front of me.

Another vampire with very big blonde hair and glasses approaches from the right side. Oh, her nametag says *Fran, she/her*. She must be the owner of the bookstore; she looks much older than us. She smells kind of like apple pie. Which I don't hate, but it reminds me of a farm or something. Not that I've ever been on a farm, but that's what I imagine, apples and apple pie.

"Caleb, my dear! I haven't seen you in a week! You promised you would keep coming in after you moved!" she says with a smile.

Caleb smiles brightly at her. He really likes this vampire. I don't see him smile at many vampires aside from me. He has such a gorgeous smile. It seems like a waste for him to hide it all the time, but I do like that it is generally reserved for me.

"Hi, Ms. Fran, I came in before I left last week, it hasn't even been a full week yet. You exaggerate," Caleb says.

"Oh, yes, I know dear, I just miss seeing my favorite face." Her head peeks around behind Caleb at me. "Oh, my pearly fangs! You, you are Froderick Dracula! I have been dying to meet you! I'm Fran, this is my store. Oh, welcome!"

She grabs my right hand in both of hers and shakes it.

"Hello, yes, I am. It's nice to meet you," I say. "I really like your store. I especially like the way it's set up. The way the aisles twist, makes it like a fun game when walking around."

Fran's face is overjoyed. "I'm so glad you like it! Your mother loves it, too! She's coming this weekend for a signing, which I'm sure you already know. Oh, I know how close you and your mother are."

Her eyes pause on my neck as she notices my necklace. Her gaze shifts to Caleb, then back toward my neck. She's looking for bite marks, but trying to pretend she isn't.

"Caleb, dear, I noticed you two holding hands, but I had no idea that you had already claimed him. When did this happen?"

Caleb lowers his eyebrows at her. "Now, Ms. Fran, that is a bit too personal. He's wearing the necklace, there's nothing else to be said."

She removes her glasses and wipes them with her shirt. "Yes, well, what did your mom say about this, Froderick?" she asks. "I'm very close with her and I know how she feels about Caleb's mother. I can't believe she didn't tell me this. Probably waiting to make it into a story and didn't want to spoil it for me. I need to call her."

Well, sure, my mom was happy I came out to her and that I had a boyfriend. She seemed to like Caleb, but how she really felt about the two of us being together, I can't really say, because I have no idea.

I answer her as truthfully as I can, "Oh, well, she was happy, but…it's hard to say exactly what happened. I haven't been able to get in touch with her."

"You should call her. I talked to her just a few minutes ago. She's out with a friend, she wouldn't say whom, but said they were grabbing drinks and looking for men," she says with a cackle.

"You talked to my mother today?" I ask.

"Yes, of course it was just a few minutes ago. I wish I had known you were here. That would have been a hoot!" Fran says.

I pull my phone from my pocket and try to call my mother. The phone rings only once and she sends it to voicemail. That's great. So, this bookstore owner is more important than her own son? Wow. I feel wonderful about that.

Caleb pulls his phone out and I can see he's calling his mother. He squeezes his eyes shut and places the phone back in his pocket. "Voicemail," he says.

I shrug my shoulders and say, "Oh well. I guess they just don't want to talk to us."

Fran is a bit confused judging by her facial expression, but that doesn't really matter to me right now. I'm really just ready to leave, so hopefully this conversation can end.

Fran is looking around the room. She says, "Oh, Caleb, dear, did you see that we hired that boy from your old school, Tobias? He said you two were good friends, or else I probably wouldn't have hired him. Seems like a bit of trouble if you ask me, but since he was your friend, I gave him the job."

Caleb scoffs with his mouth open. "Tobias is not my friend. Are you saying he used me as a reference?"

"Wait, are you saying he's not your friend? Well, that is not what he said. He said that I could trust him since he was friends with you. What in the world? Who would claim to know someone they don't know?" she asks with her hands on her hips.

Caleb knows that I want to leave. I'm really not interested in him explaining whatever relationship they had, well, didn't have, to her. I'm literally thinking of nothing else but leaving. I'm so over this conversation.

Caleb nods at me in understanding and takes my hand in his. "Alright, well, Ms. Fran, we have to go. We have a report that's due at the end of the week. Since we're off tomorrow we thought we'd try and find a book to use here that no one else had seen yet. But we've already been here for a while and we should get going."

"Oh no, wait, dear," she says. "What is the report on? I can't have you leave empty handed. Also, please let me take a picture with you two before you go. It will be great for my website and my social posts. Besides, I want to send it to your mother. She'll be so jealous that I'm with you, Froderick. That woman, you're all she ever talks about."

It's funny to think that my mom talks about me so much that this woman would say that. I mean it seems unlikely, honestly, because when she's with me she just talks about her books, or ideas for books, or herself. Well, that and she complains about my dad.

Caleb is looking at me to see whether I want to take the picture or not. I honestly don't mind. I don't have any pictures of Caleb and me, so I'd quite like one right now. I'll ask her after we take one with the three of us together, to use my phone and take one of just Caleb and me.

"Sure, I say. No problem."

Caleb wraps his arms around my waist and rests his chin on my shoulder. Ms. Fran stands beside me and holds her phone up in selfie mode. "Aww, look at you two. So adorable with your face on his shoulder like that, Caleb. Ugh, I gotta get a partner soon. I'll die alone in this bookstore with all of the many loves of my life in these books, if I'm not taken soon. Alright, one, two and three, smile!" All three of us smile and she brings her phone down to check the picture. "Lovely, just lovely," she says.

Caleb is pulling his phone out of his pocket. He hands it to her and asks, "Can you please take one of the two of us?"

"One for me, too, please." I add, handing her my phone.

Caleb wraps his arms back around me and kisses my cheek. Keeping his mouth in place for the picture. "There we go," Ms. Fran says. I turn my mouth toward him and kiss him quickly. I hear the camera button click on my phone. Ms. Fran giggles. "Okay, well I got both pictures with this phone. Do it again for this one," she says.

Caleb stands in front of me and makes sure my necklace is on full display for the next picture. It was already out, though, so he didn't need to do that. It was cute, though. He walks behind me and places his head back in the same position, but this time he lightly kisses the side of my neck as Ms. Fran takes the picture. I turn toward him with a smile and playfully kiss his nose, which Ms. Fran takes a picture of.

"Oh, you two! You're not yet eighteen, it's not fair for you to look at one another so. Truly at fifty-six years old, I've never had anyone look at me that way." She sighs and passes our phones back to us. "Now, Froderick, what about your band? Your mom said that sometimes you use different locations for your shows. Would you like to do a show here? I could move the shelves back and we could use the area beside the café? Would you like that? She said you are also into fashion, like Wolf, maybe we could get creative and do a joint show with fashion and music." Her eyes widen in excitement at her own suggestion.

Everything she said about me is true, and her idea sounds really fun, but the store is not that big and I'm not sure how many vampires could really fit in here, but I don't need to worry about that.

"That all sounds great!" I say. "I'll need to talk to my bandmates and see about the show, but I can say for certain that the fashion aspect is definitely a yes, I'm sure of that much. Thank you, it's very nice of you to offer."

"Wonderful, well you just let me know when you decide and I'm going to go post this photo online. I'm going to get so many views, and I can't wait to make your mother jealous that we were hanging out," she says and laughs.

Caleb has realized that she didn't give us a book yet and I can feel him struggling with whether he should ask her again. Caleb is also thinking about…*other* things right now and he's very anxious to leave and go do them with me…or *to* me would probably be more accurate to say. I know he wants the book, though, so I don't want him to regret not getting one later.

I ask, "Ms. Fran before we leave, we have to do a report on Vampire Biology as portrayed in fiction. Do you have anything new that might be able to be used for that?"

Caleb is smiling at me. I love that smile. Oh, wait he's not smiling about the book. He's still thinking of other stuff.

He drops his right eyebrow and says, "The smile is for asking about the book and the *other stuff*."

"Yes, well why don't you use your mother's book?" Fran asks. "It's wonderful and the boys are in high school just like you two. I think it would fit great, there is a part in the book where she talks about vampire biology— of course, it's fictional, but she does a rather splendid job with her own hilarious ideals. Other than that, there aren't many new books that could work."

I am absolutely not using my mother's book. I have zero desire to do that.

"Sure, we'll try it out," Caleb says.

Whaaat?! Is he serious? I'm not using that garbage! How embarrassing would it be to use my mother's book? Ugh, I don't want to. I give him a pout and a bit of an angry look, but Caleb is just smirking at me, while he grabs the book off the display.

"I'll pay for this and then we'll be on our way," he says to Fran, while holding the book in his hand.

Fran is walking with us toward the front of the store where the registers are. She steps behind the counter and scans the book, then passes it back to Caleb without any exchange of money.

"I have an account, she doesn't need my card," he whispers.

Fran smiles and waves. "Thank you, boys, and it was just lovely meeting you, Froderick. Don't forget to let me know about the concert and show."

"I'll let you know, and thank you," I say. Caleb smiles and thanks her, too.

As we step outside and start to fly, the air is much cooler than when we arrived. There's not a cloud in the sky, as Caleb and I fly side by side. The stars are shining so brightly that it seems like we could just reach up and touch them. I feel so at peace right now. I've had so many of these moments where everything just feels utterly perfect over the past few days with Caleb.

Chapter 20
Get Out of Your Head

As we land in Caleb's back yard, I don't smell the same scent from earlier. It just smells like flowers now. That's strange. Well, it's not strange that it smells like flowers, because we are surrounded by flowers. But scents don't usually change so fast for me. Normally, I smell what I smell and it stays that way.

Caleb opens the door and smiles at me. "My dad is gone. The laundry scent from earlier was him. I think he'd walked in right before us this afternoon, which is why you smelled that."

Walking behind Caleb inside his house, he places my mother's book down on the kitchen counter and walks toward the refrigerator. He opens the doors to the fridge and looks at me, but says nothing.

I shrug at him and look around. I don't know what he was gonna say, but he didn't say anything and now he's just head deep inside the fridge.

Caleb peeks his head back out and says, "I was trying to figure out what you want to eat. You said you were hungry and then we didn't eat anything."

I know what I want to eat right now and it's not in that damn fridge. My phone is dinging like crazy all of a sudden. I pull it out and look at the notifications. I guess a lot of vampires saw the picture that Fran posted and they're commenting on it. Pfft…wow, the stuff vampires say is crazy.

Caleb has somehow made his way in front of me without me even noticing. I must have been too focused on my phone. "Hello," I say as he brings his face directly in front of mine. The tips of our noses touch and my desire for Caleb overwhelms me. I place my hands in his hair and lightly grip it. I wonder if he likes this as much as I do. I love it when he grabs my hair, maybe he does, too. Oh shit, my hair. No, no, my hair must smell disgusting. I can't do this. I quickly separate from Caleb and take a few steps back.

Caleb sighs loudly, but he's smiling. "How are we going to do anything if you can't stay out of your own head?" he asks me.

"Caleb, listen, you've already figured out that I can't stay out of my own head, that's not news to you. But I truly cannot have any physical contact with you now that we're in your house and my hair smells like this. It's out of the question. I have to wash my hair."

Caleb takes a step toward me, and I take another step backward. He thinks I'm kidding. He really does.

Caleb tilts his head to the side with a hand on his hip. "Just put it up, like in your housewife bun. Or wrap it up in that tight knot that you usually put it in. I don't care what your hair smells like. You have to know that the way your hair smells is the last thing on my mind right now."

I cock my head to the side and say, "Uh, no, I don't, because right now all you're thinking about is my hair. I can hear your thoughts, too."

Caleb places both hands on the sides of his face and shakes his head at me seriously. "Frode, you don't understand. The only reason I'm thinking about this is because of you. You're thinking about it, so I'm thinking about how to get you to stop thinking about it. That's it. I honestly do not care how your hair smells."

"Let me help you understand," I say. I take two steps toward him then look side-to-side to be sure there is no one else in earshot. "If I don't wash my hair, I'm not sleeping in the same bed as you. You can forget about anything else."

I'm not kidding either. I'll sleep on a couch or the floor, but he is definitely not gonna smell this all—

Caleb is pulling me upstairs; he left the book on the counter, but I don't really feel like reminding him about it.

He flings the door to his bedroom open and pulls me toward the bathroom inside his room. Oh, wow, this is really nice. I think it's nicer than mine. The floor is super shiny black tile with a bit of a sparkle to it. Caleb hasn't said a word to me since I threatened him. He's just dragging me around the bathroom as he grabs three towels out of the closet. Why did he grab three towels, though? He's shaking his head at me and I kind of want to laugh, but I won't, because, believe it or not, he really does seem mad. He releases my hand and opens the door to the large glass shower. He turns the water on and closes the door to the shower again.

Caleb is fully dressed and his hands are on his hips. "Strip," he says.

"Whaaat?! With you just standing in here watching me like some kind of a pervert? No, no, thank you. That would be uncomfortable," I say.

Caleb is removing his shirt and now he's taking his pants off. He's standing in front of me in only his tight black underwear. He's gesturing for me to hurry up and take my clothes off. I guess this is okay, I mean he's gonna see everything anyway, so maybe it doesn't matter if we take a shower together. I feel really nervous, though. But why should I? I'm hot, too. I have nothing to be nervous about.

"You don't have anything to be nervous about, well, you rarely do when you're with me and, yet, you still are," Caleb says.

I pull my shirt off and the necklace gets caught on the fabric a bit. I forgot that I'm wearing this necklace. The necklace that Caleb gave to me… Oh wow, the meaning behind the necklace just hit me again. I really don't have anything to be nervous about.

I unbuckle my belt and take my pants off. As I step out of my pants, Caleb smiles and pulls me toward him. My body is really interested now and there is no hiding that fact. Caleb has both of my hands in his and he places them on his sides. My thumbs reach into the sides of his underwear and I freeze for a moment. I'm not sure what to do, I know what I want to do, but is this okay? Fangs…this shouldn't be so complicated.

Caleb kisses my cheek and pulls me into an embrace. He says softly, "You are making this so much harder than it needs to be. I love you, Frode, and I mean that. If you want to shower alone, I'll just wait until you're done. Or, if you don't want to do anything, that's okay, too. But you have to get out of your head for this, or it's not gonna work. Also, the third towel is for your hair."

Oh fangs, I'm gonna do it. I pull Caleb's underwear down in one quick motion, drawing a laugh from Caleb's delicious mouth. Caleb's hands are on my waist and he slides my underwear down much gentler than I did to him. Steam is beginning to fill the room; the shower must be really hot.

Caleb takes my hand and steps inside the shower with me. I'm only going to think about Caleb right now and honestly that's all that I want to think about. Caleb stands under the water, and I'm completely entranced watching the water drip down his face and chest. I'm trying hard not to stare at Caleb's very impressive body. I quickly avert my eyes and watch as he grabs a white bottle of shampoo from the shelf inside of the shower. He squeezes some inside his hand and he passes the bottle to me. Oh right, I'm supposed to be showering, too. I squeeze the shampoo in my hand, it smells like coconut, it's a very nice scent. I never smell it on Caleb, though, I think his natural scent is just so damn intoxicating that it's impossible for my brain to register anything else. I work the shampoo into a lather, while Caleb rinses his hair out. I turn facing away from him, so that I can flip my hair upside down without hitting him with it. There's no other way for me to clean all of it, if I don't flip it. As I flip my head over, I feel Caleb's hands on my waist, he's gripping me tightly. I let out a little chuckle because I'm actually very ticklish and his fingers are kind of hitting a spot that forces a giggle out of me every time. His hands are moving down now, he's squeezing both sides of my ass.

"That's better," I say. "I'm really ticklish, Caleb. I should have mentioned that to you. If you hover around by my sides, I won't be able to concentrate on anything. The ass is fine, though."

"How about this? Is this fine?" Caleb asks.

I feel Caleb's teeth and the tips of his fangs lightly bite into the left side of my ass.

"Um…yeah…that's uh, fine, but I'd rather you fully bite my neck, before my ass," I say nervously. Holy shit…Caleb's damn delicious mouth was just on my ass. Wow.

Caleb is already standing again and he's smiling at me. My hair is all sudsy and I can feel some of the shampoo beginning to drip down the sides of my face. We swap places and I stand under the shower and rinse the shampoo from my hair. Caleb passes me a bottle of conditioner as I open my eyes.

"Thank you," I say.

Caleb is holding his hand out for the bottle. "I can do it for you, it must be hard to get the conditioner all the way through the ends."

"Well, I'm used to it, but I hate doing it, so if you want to, I'm certainly not going to stop you." I say, while I pass the bottle back to him.

"Swap spots with me and I'll do it," Caleb says.

I move in front of Caleb and the back of my body glides against the front of Caleb's. I want to touch him, all of him, but I need to finish washing my hair. If I don't condition it, it will be all frizzy and unmanageable. It will just look and feel awful. I couldn't let Caleb see it like that.

"This is why I'm doing this," Caleb says as he squeezes the conditioner in his hand. "You know, Frode, I feel like I should get extra points for being a good boyfriend right now. You're in my shower, naked, standing in front of me and I'm just putting conditioner in your hair. Resisting all temptation." Caleb's fingers are rubbing the conditioner all the way through to my ends.

"Well, what else would you be doing when I've made it clear that we won't do anything else until my hair is properly cleaned?"

He's actually really taking the time to massage the conditioner all the way in. He's probably doing a better job than I normally do.

Caleb sighs and says, "Nothing, because if you're uncomfortable, then I'm not interested in anything else. But once this is done, I have some definite ideas of what we will be doing. Oh, and don't even try and say that you need to dry it because you didn't dry it earlier and it was fine."

"Why would I say that? Do you think it's easier for me right now with your hands running through my hair like this? I can barely hold back. Actually, did you already get it all the way to the ends? It feels like you did."

"I did. Just finished, but your hair is so nice that I just want to run my fingers through it. Plus, the view from back here is rather amazing, so I'm in no rush for you to move."

Caleb's body is pressed against the back of mine now. His arms are wrapped around me. This feels so good with him squeezing me tightly against himself. I really want to get out of this shower and do it. I turn my body around to face him and hang my arms loosely around his neck while the water runs over his shoulders and down the front of him.

I whisper in his ear, "Get out of the way, so I can rinse this…go wait for me in your bed." I kiss him on the mouth quickly and pull back, then run my fingers through my hair.

Caleb's eyes widen in excitement. He sticks his face under the running water one more time, then steps outside of the shower. I begin to rinse the conditioner from my hair and I'm seriously considering what's about to go down, once I leave this shower. Okay, so do I want him to bite me first? Or do I want to have sex? I really don't know at this point, and I don't know if it's something that I can actually decide… Do I just let things happen or should I have some kind of a plan?

Caleb's bottom half is wrapped in a white towel and his skin looks especially good under the lights in his bathroom. He smiles at me before he leaves the room and says, "I'm going to leave you and your thoughts in here for a bit while I go wait in my bed. Try not to take too long, okay?"

"Very funny," I say.

Watching Caleb leave, I feel the urge to chase after him, but I have to make sure I get all this conditioner out of my hair. Not only that, but everything that has happened to me lately is kind of hitting me all at once. I really don't understand what's going on with my mom and I still don't understand this connection that Caleb and I have. There has to be some kind of a reason for it. Sure, I could come up with some romantic notion that it's because we're meant to be together or whatever, but it seems like there has to be another reason for it. I shake the water from my ears and the red "C" around my neck is sparkling as the water runs down my chest. Looking down at it, I feel instantly comforted. I really need to hurry up and get out of this shower.

I open the shower door and wrap my bottom half in the towel that Caleb left for me. I flip my hair upside down and wrap it in the other towel that he laid out.

As I open the door to Caleb's room, I smile at him, he's lying in his bed. He has a white T-shirt on and a pair of gray gym shorts. He's reading a book and gives me a smile. "Aww, look at your hair all wrapped up. I knew you would look adorable coming out of the shower. Are you done with your overthinking?" he asks.

"You know, for someone who wants to sleep with me, you're really pushing it with the teasing. I'm just grabbing my stuff out of my backpack and then I'll be done." I grab my backpack off Caleb's dresser and bring it back inside his bathroom.

"Hey, wait," Caleb says. "I'm just messing around. Take all the time that you need. I don't mind you overthinking, you know that, right?"

I give him a false smile and close the bathroom door. He's too cute and if he's gonna tease me, I'm gonna tease him back. I pull the towel from my hair and brush through it. It's still damp, but it's okay. I grab a spare hair tie out of my bag and tie it into my housewife bun. It's gonna end up putting a crease in my hair, but it's okay. If I lay down with it all wet like this, it'll make me feel cold and uncomfortable, and I won't feel like having sex at all. I pull my clothes out of my backpack that I brought for nighttime and slip into a pair of black gym shorts and a gray T-shirt. I pick my other clothes up from the floor where I left them earlier and shove them inside my bag. Caleb's clothes are still on the floor. I want to pick them up for him, but I don't know where his dirty clothes go. I give myself another check in the mirror and stare at my neck for a moment. I wonder what my neck is going to look like after this. I also wonder if it will hurt. I just have no idea what to expect. I'm not sure which is going to hurt worse. Well, I'm ready to find out.

I leave the bathroom and walk inside Caleb's room again. Caleb stands and pulls me into an embrace. "Your hair looks really cute," he says. "I like seeing you in comfortable clothes like this, too." Caleb sniffs my hair and whispers in my ear, "You smell like cotton candy. I can't smell the shampoo; you just smell very hot." He kisses the side of my neck softly.

Okay, I'm literally going to do anything that he wants me to do. I can't resist him. I press my lips to his and put my arms around his neck. Caleb kisses me softly, his tongue is barely moving inside of my mouth; he's being so gentle with me. It's like he's afraid he's going to break me. I love every way that Caleb kisses me, and this kind of soft sweet kiss is just so perfect. Caleb pulls back from my mouth and he's kissing my face, just gentle little kisses while he holds both sides of my neck in his hands.

But I want more, and I need more, I grab his face and press our lips together again, our tongues meet and I thirstily kiss him, like the last drop of blood in the world is inside of his mouth. I want Caleb to take me, right now. While keeping pace with my mouth, he grabs my waist and turns my body forcefully toward the bed. He lifts my shirt while in between kissing me and pushes me onto the bed. He pulls his own shirt off and stares down at me. Caleb lays atop me and our bodies are hot and pressed against one another. He holds my right hand tight in his above my head, while rubbing my neck with his other hand. He's kissing my shoulder, slowly making his way to my neck. I turn my head to the side and let out a moan. I want him so badly; I feel like I'm in actual pain waiting for this. My toes are gripping at Caleb's comforter and I'm squirming a bit underneath him.

"Shhh, you're okay. I have you. I'm not gonna hurt you," Caleb whispers.

Oh damn…this guy. I didn't think I could get any more turned on. Caleb is kissing my neck, teasing it with his tongue. I want to bite him, too, and I kind of *need* to do it right now. I can't explain it, but I need to bite, this urge is too strong. I'm trying to be patient, but his neck is right in front of my mouth, with my head tilted to the side like this.

I open my mouth and press my tongue against his neck. I can feel the blood coursing through his veins, it's so erotic. I move my tongue over his soft skin, and I can feel Caleb doing the same thing to me. Fuck. I can't take it. I open my mouth and suck as Caleb does the same on the opposite side of my neck. Our bodies are pressed so tightly together, and our mouths are desperately sucking at the same almost frantic pace. I pull my tongue back in and pause and Caleb does the same. He lifts his head from my neck and looks down at me. He's almost asking me for permission, but he knows I want it. I grab the back of his head and press his mouth back against my neck. I feel his mouth open on the softest part of my neck and I take the softest part of his in mine. I can't wait any more. I bite down softly and as my fangs hit his skin, I bite down harder, piercing through his neck. Caleb bites me at the same time. Oh shit, ouch! This hurts, but it feels so good, too. Caleb's blood is in my mouth, and it tastes better than anything I've ever tasted. I bite down harder as Caleb does the same to my neck. I can feel the blood leaving me, but it's being replaced with Caleb's blood. We're both sucking so hard right now, and I feel like I can't breathe. The immense pain I feel on the left side of my neck is being masked by the overwhelming pleasure I feel as I drink Caleb's blood.

Caleb's body is moving slightly atop mine and he releases my hand. I don't know which of us will stop sucking first, but neither of us have pulled back from the initial bite; our fangs are still deep inside one another's necks.

My head is hurting a bit, though, and my mind is getting a little fuzzy. What is this feeling? What am I seeing? My eyes are closed, but I can see something. Oh, oh, wow! It's Caleb. I can see Caleb, he's really small and he's playing with someone else. I think that's me…yeah, that's me…we're playing together just rolling a ball around. I see our moms sitting beside us. Aww, little Caleb is grabbing me…he's kind of hugging me as my small body falls over at his feet. Oh, how cute, I'm holding his foot and he's resting his head on my back. Wait…what? What the hell just happened? Little Caleb just bit my back and I just bit his ankle. We're both not crying, we're just staring at one another while our moms check the marks on our bodies. Our moms are laughing, but the two of us…we're so small and yet…we're just staring at one another. What a weird…I gasp for air and my eyes open. Caleb's head is on my chest and he's panting.

I rub Caleb's shoulders. "Hey, are you okay? Ouch, shit, my neck hurts. What's wrong?" I ask him frantically.

Caleb lifts his head. "I can't talk right now. No, I'm not hurt. I just I saw something…I think I saw the reason for our connection. I can't… Just let me lie here for a minute, okay? I love you. I just need a minute."

I rub his head softly and I want to rub the side of my neck, but I'm kind of afraid to. I'm afraid there's blood everywhere and I'm also really confused by what I saw. What was that? Wait, is that what Caleb is talking about? We bit each other when we were little, is that what caused this? Whaaat?! This can't be. We'd already bitten each other?!

I close my eyes again and try to tap back into the connection. I see the memory. I see it clearly. Oh, this is really cool. It's almost like

I'm watching a movie that I can just view any part of. Oh…oh, no…I don't like this…I can see Caleb, but now he's a teenager…no, I don't want to see this. My eyes open suddenly, and Caleb is kissing me. Oh, thank fangs, I'm back in bed with my Caleb.

"Frode, are you okay? What did you see?" Caleb asks me while gently kissing the side of my neck where he bit me.

I place my lips on the spot where I bit him. I taste his blood on my lips. Mmm, it's so good. I've never tasted anything so delectable. I've never wanted anything more. I really need to talk to Caleb, but I can't help myself right now. I'm too thirsty. I sink my fangs back in and suck again. Oh, bats, this is effing amazing. Caleb is sucking more of my blood out, too, but it doesn't hurt anymore. It feels like so much pressure is being released from my body and, at the same time, it's like a really strong force is circulating through my veins.

Caleb removes his mouth from my neck and gives me another soft kiss where he's bitten me. He's pulling his neck back from me a bit, but I'm not ready to stop yet. Caleb's right hand is rubbing down my chest and his knee is moving around in between my legs. I suck deeply once more and remove my fangs from his neck. I exhale and Caleb kisses my mouth softly.

I close my eyes and hold the back of his head with both hands. Caleb is kissing my naked chest now, as his hands pull down my shorts.

"I want all of you," Caleb says.

"I am yours, Caleb."

I close my eyes and my mind is flooded with Caleb. I'm torn in between images of Caleb's past, as well as the sensations and emotions that I'm feeling right now while Caleb rubs me. I don't want to see everything in his past. I already know what happened, because he already told me, but there must be something in this memory that is important because it keeps coming back to me.

My body is shaking, and I want to concentrate on the pleasure I feel as Caleb's mouth makes its way further down. I open my eyes and grip the top of Caleb's hair lightly and he lets out a light moan of approval, which can barely be heard above my own broken breathy and heavy moans. Caleb lifts his face and changes positions. His face is next to mine now, on the opposite side of where he'd bitten me. I reach my hand down and feel Caleb…oh wow. This is—this feels so good. I place both my hands on Caleb's chest pushing him, urging him to lay down. I lay atop him and kiss him softly while my hand makes its way back down. Following Caleb's lead, I'm pushed back around and I'm flat on my back again. He literally just flipped me right onto my back faster than I could realize. Caleb's hands are reaching down and I close my eyes again. He's—he's—oh.

Caleb's breaths are heavy. "Do you want me to stop?"

I swallow hard and shake my head.

Caleb is moving again and it's starting to feel better. The overwhelming force that is welling up inside is about to—

Caleb moans as his body slackens and he holds me breathless.

The feeling of our rapidly beating hearts pressed together is all encompassing in this moment. I never want to leave Caleb's arms.

"I love you, Froderick, and it seems that I always have."

"I love you, too, Caleb."

We're both still locked in a loose embrace, trying to slowly catch our breath. Caleb rolls to the side and stands beside the bed. He's walking around to my side of the bed. His hair is a mess, which I've only seen a few times, and the fang marks I left look very deep. Kind of hot, though, knowing that they're mine and they'll be there forever. I can't believe we just did that…well, I can believe it because my body—all of my body—can still feel it and some parts are more grateful than others in this moment. But my heart is so full and that is what I feel the most.

"Here take my hands and sit up," Caleb says, standing next to the bed.

"Oh, no, thank you. I don't want to. I'm gonna stay in this position forever. I can already tell it's going to hurt if I stand. I'm good like this for a bit."

Caleb is sucking his lips in with one hand on his hip, completely naked. He's touching the bite mark I left on him. "Damn, that feels deep," he says. He gives me a smile then says, "I'll be honest with you, if you don't get up and rinse off, I'm gonna want to do it again. I'm having way too many feelings in between the things I'm seeing in your past, the way that just felt, and remembering how good your blood tasted."

I shake my head at him and cover my face with both hands. "Definitely not doing it again right now," I say with a small laugh. "I don't want to move, though, but it feels like I should."

"You should," Caleb says. He extends his hands toward me and I allow him to lazily pull me up.

Ugh, fangs…this…this hurts. My neck feels fine, but the rest of me doesn't.

Caleb holds my hand and we walk into the shower to rinse off. I hadn't thought about the fact that I'd need a shower after, but the warm water hitting my body feels really good. Ouch, shit…except for my neck. That doesn't feel good.

Caleb sees me wincing and he places his hand over the bite while I rinse under the water.

"The water pressure is probably too strong since the bite is so deep. I'll cover it for you," he says.

Caleb is so considerate. I hadn't even thought about whether I hurt him when I bit him and here he is covering my bite mark. I place my hand over the mark I left on him. "Did it hurt when I did this to you?" I ask.

Caleb shakes his head no, with a smirk. "It was very hot. I enjoyed it. I was also biting you at the time, which was way more delicious than I thought it would be. I had no idea that blood could taste so sweet. Your blood tastes the same as your scent. It's just like cotton candy with a bit of freshly baked Italian bread. Exactly the same as when I first smelled you. I fear for your safety at this point, because your blood—I'm going to need a lot of it." He winks at me and kisses my cheek.

We finish rinsing off and step outside of the shower. I feel a little embarrassed and I'm not really sure why. Caleb walks past me and heads outside the bathroom. I lean over his sink and stare at the bite on my neck in the mirror. Damn, this looks as deep as it feels. I see Caleb coming back in from behind me. He's wearing his gym shorts and he has mine in his hand, too.

"Thank you," I say as he passes the shorts to me and I quickly put them on. I wince a little at the small amount of pain I just felt when I bent over.

I stand and Caleb has me wrapped tightly in a hug; he's looking at the bite mark on my neck. "Did the bite hurt really bad? I can feel that you're in pain, but there's so much going on inside my mind that I can't tell what's hurting you."

I push him backward lightly while we walk out of the bathroom. "Are you serious? You can't tell what's hurting me? You're not serious. I know you're not. You know damn well what's hurting me and it's not my neck. Don't make me say it."

Caleb is sticking his bottom lip out as he pinches my chin. "I'm sorry, was it that bad? I don't like thinking that I hurt you. Especially not when I really want to do it again." He pumps his eyebrows at me and gives me a naughty smile.

Okay, now I really smack him on the shoulder. "What is wrong with you? We just did it and, yes, it hurt that bad. Everything else was fine, but *that* took a bit of getting used to. It was good, though, really good… Like, really, really, good."

"Then let's do it again," Caleb says as he playfully pushes me back onto the bed.

My body falls into the wrinkled sheets, and I can't help but laugh.

Caleb lays on his side, next to me, with his head propped on his hand. "Hey, this necklace looks really good against your skin," he says as he rubs the charm in between his fingers.

"Thanks, my boyfriend gave it to me," I say with a smile.

Caleb sits up. "Boyfriend? Ugh. Boyfriend sounds so common. I thought the same thing earlier when I said it. There has to be a better term for it." Caleb stands and playfully shakes my foot at the bottom of the bed. "I'm gonna go get some water. You need some, too. You just lost a lot of blood."

"Yeah, true, but I drank a lot of blood, too," I say. I sit up straight and point to my phone on Caleb's dresser. "Can you pass me that, please, *partner?*"

Caleb's mouth turns down. "Oh, no I don't like partner. Boyfriend is better than partner, don't ever call me partner, again. Reminds me of that disgusting watermelon vamp—I don't want to think about that now that I can see it." Caleb grabs my phone and looks down at it. "Whoa, you missed a lot of calls and texts and there are like notifications all over this thing. I'm glad it was on silent."

I take the phone from him and shake my head. "Thank you, Caleb. I won't call you partner if you don't like it, but while you're getting the water, try and see if you can think of something that you'd like to be called instead of boyfriend. I want to post the picture of us on my socials and I need to call you something."

"Deal. I'll be right back," Caleb says with a smile.

You know it's strange to think that he can see everything in my past now. I mean it's the same for me, but still, it's just weird that he can see everything. It's different than I thought it would be. The images are only there if I choose to view them, otherwise it's just the same. Well, kind of, I can definitely feel Caleb's thoughts and feelings much stronger than before.

Oh, look at that, my mom tried to call me, sent me a text, too. Oh, that's great… Wait till I tell Caleb about this. I have a text from my dad, too, priceless. Oh, now this is very interesting. Caleb is going to laugh so hard when he gets back here and I show him all of this.

Caleb is back, with two bottles of water. Man, he looks good walking around without a shirt on. I wish I could stay here with him forever. Adults are so lucky that they can sleep wherever they want and do whatever they want. I'll be an adult soon, though, then maybe Caleb and I will get our own place. I'm definitely not staying with my dad after I turn eighteen.

"Forever," Caleb says as he sits in bed next to me and passes me a water bottle.

"Thanks," I say as I take the water. "Forever, what?"

"That's what I want you to call me," he says.

I'm sipping from the bottle and my eyebrows are squished together. I have no idea how he expects me to call him that. How would that fit in place of boyfriend?

"Easily," Caleb says aloud after hearing my thoughts. "Like this: Hello, I'm Caleb Cheval and this is my forever, Froderick Dracula. Or I'm Caleb and this is my forever, Frode. See? Easy and it fits."

I nod in agreement while still drinking the water. Damn, I really was thirsty. I knew this would happen, though, the water is almost gone and my brain instinctively paired my thirst up with the need for Caleb's blood. It was like my brain just said, you're thirsty, time for Caleb's blood. I have to try and resist for now, though.

"Caleb, my mom called and texted me. She said she and your

mother will meet us at my house tomorrow around noon. She said they need to talk to the both of us, I guess she wants my dad to be there. Then my dad texted me and he wants to be sure we're going to only say things that make him look good in front of my mother. He was shocked that my mom wasn't upset about us being *friends*. I don't think he knows your mom is going to be there. I'm also not sure if my mom knows that my grandfather will be there, so that will be fun, too. Oh, and to top it off, aside from all the dirty comments that vampires are leaving about the picture of us, look who went to the movies together." I lean my head against Caleb's shoulder and pass him my phone so he can see.

"What? Are you kidding? Robert and Wolfie? That's crazy. Well, I'm sure it's just a friend thing. I mean, Wolfie was just almost in tears over Kat and we both know what Robert was doing a few hours ago outside the front of your house. That guy is strange…or maybe he's just lonely. I really don't care as long as he stays away from you."

Caleb passes my phone back to me and picks his phone up from his nightstand. He's shaking his head while looking at the screen. "My mom texted me, but she didn't call me," he says. "She said the same thing as your mom, that they'll meet us at your house tomorrow. This should be interesting, especially now that we know so much about their history. Hey, I want another picture of us, okay? I want to remember this night with you. I know how serious you are about your hair, though, so check it in the camera really quick before I take a picture."

I take Caleb's phone from his hand and turn the camera on. My hair is pretty messy because it's still in my housewife bun that I've just been tightening every once in a while. I don't feel like brushing it, though, and putting it up properly. "Do you think my hair is okay like this?" I ask.

Caleb kisses me and holds his phone up to the side, while our mouths are pressed together, and he takes a picture.

"Perfect," he says. "Now watch, I'm posting it and the caption says: *Me and my forever*. See, it fits!"

Caleb is so proud of himself and he's so cute that how could I argue with him? "My forever, it is," I say and kiss him on the cheek. "Here, I'm reposting it on my profile."

I let out a big yawn, I really am quite tired. I slip my legs under Caleb's sheets and lie flat on the fluffy pillow. Caleb lays beside me on his side. He's rubbing my face softly with the back of his hand. It feels so nice and relaxing.

Chapter 21
The Taste of My Forever

The sound of arguing wakes me. Oh, wow, it's already morning? Caleb's arms are wrapped around me and he's holding me tight in a spooning position on my side. I whisper, "Caleb, are you awake?" Caleb isn't moving, his breathing is pretty heavy. I guess he's one of those vampires that can sleep through anything, because the arguing outside his door is really loud. Should I wake him? I don't know what to do. I'll just lay here, I'm sure it's just his brothers fighting. I can't reach my phone and I don't really want to wake Caleb when he's sleeping so soundly. This connection that allows me to see Caleb's life is pretty fascinating, though. I want to see more, but I also don't, which must seem stupid. I wonder if I can see what happened yesterday. Can I watch us doing *it* over again? I close my eyes and try to see if I can find the memory. My eyes shoot open as something loud hits Caleb's door.

Caleb's body jolts at the sound and his arms squeeze me tight. He kisses the spot where he bit my neck last night. "Mmm…good morning," he says.

I turn my head slightly to kiss his cheek. "Good morning. Something is going on outside your door," I say.

"My stupid brothers, just ignore them," Caleb says.

Another loud bang hits the door. Caleb jumps out of bed and he's walking toward the door. I sit up and try to fix my hair, which is in a very big knot, thanks to sleeping with it in my housewife bun.

Caleb flings the door open. Two vampires fall inside the room and onto the floor, wrestling with one another, right at Caleb's feet. Caleb pushes the two vampires, who I assume are his brothers, with his foot. "Hey, get up and get out. I have company," Caleb says.

The two boys both look up and see me sitting on the bed. They release one another and stand. They look just like Caleb, I'm not sure why he said earlier that they didn't. Really, the whole family looks alike.

"Frode, these are my brothers."

I smile at the two.

Caleb pats the smaller brother on the head and says, "This one is Cassius, he's thirteen." Caleb elbows his other brother. "This is Michael, he is older than me, but only by a year."

"Yeah, but I'm already in college, because I'm so much smarter than you," Michael says to Caleb.

"You're taking two college classes from home, in your bedroom, and they aren't even impressive classes. You are definitely not smarter than me," Caleb says with an eyeroll.

I wave and smile from the bed. "Hi, I'm Froderick Dracula."

Both brothers smile and give me a nod.

Caleb pushes his little brother on the shoulder. "Did Dad say if he was coming back today?" Caleb asks.

"Dad never says if he's coming back, but Mom said she was doing something with a friend and she'd be back tonight," Cassius says.

"Holy fangs! Is that your forever necklace that he's wearing?" Michael asks while pointing at me.

Caleb turns his head to the side showing his brother where I bit him. I am so embarrassed right now. I don't have brothers, so I have no idea if this is just what brothers do or if this is just really weird that Caleb is kind of showing off.

Caleb smiles at me and says, "It's not weird that I'm showing off. Every time Michael hooks up with a girl, I have to see pictures of her and hear stories about everything they did together. Of course, I'm gonna show off my forever."

"I can't believe you found your forever bite, you're younger than me," Michael says to Caleb. That's crazy. I know how picky you are, though, so I don't doubt that he's the one. I've never even seen you let anyone in your bedroom."

Cassius has just been listening to the whole conversation pretty quietly. His expression has remained pretty neutral and he doesn't seem like he's really interested in anything since Caleb asked him about their dad. He looks like he has something to say right now, though.

Caleb is sort of bragging about last night, but he's not going into great detail, which I'm grateful for. I want to ask his little brother why he's looking at me the way he is, but I just met him and he's younger than me. I don't want to come off like a jerk in front of my boyfr—I mean, my forever's brothers. Not calling Caleb my boyfriend is gonna take some getting used to. I like calling him both. Saying Caleb is my forever definitely tells others something much different than boyfriend. It sounds permanent, which I'm perfectly happy with. Alright, this kid just won't stop staring at me. I have to ask him if he has something to say.

Caleb ruffles Cassius' hair and asks, "Hey, what are you staring at him for? He's already mine; don't get any ideas."

Cassius pushes Caleb playfully and looks at me. "Froderick, how long is your hair?" Cassius asks. "Your bun is falling out and it looks really long."

"Oh, you're staring at my hair? It's probably a mess because I didn't dry it last night." I want to stand and shake my hair out so he can see how long it is, but, well, it's morning and I am a guy. Regardless of how awkward it is to be woken up in the way I just was, my guy downstairs doesn't care. Ugh, so embarrassing that this happens. I pull the covers up a bit higher; then I raise my knees. Hopefully, they didn't notice my guy poking against the sheet a minute ago. "Here, I'll show you," I say while I pull my hair tie out. I shake my hair out and run my fingers through it. "The creases probably make it look shorter."

Cassius' eyes are wide and he's walking toward me. Shit, I don't want him to sit next to me. Aaaand he's sitting next to me. His hand is touching the bottom pieces of my hair that are laying on the pillow.

"Wow! You don't have any split ends or damage. It's so shiny, too," Cassius says.

Caleb obviously finds his little brother adorable; he's beaming brightly at him. "Cassius wants to open his own hair salon someday. He loves all things hair," Caleb says.

Michael laughs and says to me, "Yep, that's Cass, as soon as he saw you, I knew what he was thinking about. Cass is all about hair. He's always doing our mom's hair for her. He does it badly, but he does it."

Cassius is still holding the bottom of my hair in his hand and he's kind of rubbing it. "Your hair is an interesting color, too, it's black, but it's also too shiny to just be called black, you have like all kinds of undertones in it. I wonder if this is because you're a noble. I've never seen black hair with this much depth."

I pull my head back and look at him confused. "How old are you? I thought Caleb said you were thirteen. You don't sound thirteen."

Michael laughs. "What should he be talking about instead of

hair? The fact that you're trying to hide your little morning problem while he's sitting next to you?"

My mouth falls open and I cover my face. "Shut up," I say. I have never been more embarrassed. Who would even point something like that out?

Caleb wraps his arm around Michael's neck, he has him in a headlock. "Leave him alone, we're all guys here. You're such an ass," Caleb says as he releases Michael and pushes him outside of the door.

Cassius releases my hair and pulls his mouth to the side while staring at my face. He says, "I should tell you something, I think…"

My hands are still covering my face, I spread my fingers apart to fully see him. "What?" I ask.

"Well, my dad was really mad and I heard him talking about your dad," Cassius says. "Normally, if he's talking about him, it's pretty normal stuff—calls him an idiot, says he hates him, just regular stuff. But last night he sounded different. I guess I can't explain it. Just sounded like he was planning something. I don't know. Just sounded weird."

"Oh, yeah, that did happen, right after he yelled at us," Michael says, standing outside the door.

Caleb holds his arms open at his sides in frustration. "What are you guys talking about? You have no idea what you've just done inside Frode's head. Tell me what happened," he says, looking at his brothers.

They definitely have no idea what they've done inside my head. Caleb's dad seemed like a serious jerk and when we left, I could've sworn it was almost as if he was just trying to find out the best way to tell my dad about Caleb and me. Now, listening to this, I'm pretty sure that's what he's gonna do or at least what he wanted to do. He couldn't have done it last night because my dad would have called me. I really don't want to have this conversation with my dad yet. I'm completely fine with just going on with things the way they are. He's never gonna understand…but if it has to happen and it happens today, I mean, my mom, Caleb's mom and my grandpa will be there, so I don't know how bad it could really be if he finds out today. OH MY FANGS! I'm worried about Caleb's father going rogue, but what about our mothers?! They're probably the real threat to our secret.

Caleb exhales loudly, he's walking around to the opposite side of the bed, as his brother's watch him. He sits on the bed beside me and holds my hand. "Sshhh. You need to calm down. Please, I can't concentrate on anything with you freaking out like this."

Cassius and Michael are looking at Caleb confused, and why wouldn't they be. I haven't said a word about anything aloud.

Cassius stands from the bed and asks, "Caleb, why are you saying he's freaking out? He's not even doing anything."

Michael steps back inside of the bedroom to hear Caleb's answer.

"You guys know how it works. Mom and Dad have told you about this. We can hear each other's thoughts, along with feeling the other's emotions. Well, we actually started off being able to do that before we bit one another, but since the bite last night, it's even stronger. Don't worry about it. I asked you both to tell me what happened with Dad. So, come on, let's have it. What did Dad say that was so strange?"

Michael is shaking his head no at Caleb. "I don't understand, so you can always hear what the other is thinking? That's effing crazy. Oh, man, I'm never biting a noble. Some of the girls I've gone out with…ugh, I definitely wouldn't want them to hear all my thoughts. When I bit them, I could see their past and stuff, but I couldn't share feelings or thoughts. Who would want that? That sounds awful. Especially with you, Caleb; you're such a cocky little shit. You're so judgmental all the time."

Caleb squeezes my hand and rolls his eyes at his brother. "Fine, Michael, shut up and leave my room. Cass, what did Dad say?" Caleb asks.

Cassius takes a few steps toward the door then answers, "Well, he said that Dracula deserved to know something, even though he was a…I forget what he called him, it was some weird word. He kept going on, saying he wanted to see the look on his face when he found something out. It was like an hour he was talking about it. Michael heard him, too."

Michael nods in agreement. "Yeah, that was about it, but probably fifteen minutes, it wasn't an hour-long conversation. Maybe it wasn't about you, though. I mean does your dad not know that you're going out with Caleb?"

"Nope. My dad does not know that, because my dad is a moron who is stuck on his own very dated ideas around relationships."

Michael raises his eyebrows and says, "Ohhhh, then, yeah, my dad was definitely talking about you, Froderick. For sure. No doubt. What's wrong with your dad, though? Damn, where we were raised it was way more normal to be anything, but straight. I'm not even straight. I mean, I prefer girls, but I've done it with a few guys, too. I can't imagine what our lives would be like if we were raised here."

"What would your dad do if you told him the truth?" Cassius asks me.

Caleb wraps his arm around me and I lay my head against his shoulder. "I don't know. Caleb and I have talked to him a few times, but he's really dense. He didn't pick up on anything that Caleb said, and he dropped more than a few hints."

"That's funny," Michael says. "Because Caleb is definitely not subtle when he speaks. If he weren't a noble, he would've gotten his ass kicked a ton of times for it."

Caleb kisses the top of my head. "Yeah, his dad is an idiot, though. He won't accept it, which is funny because Frode's mom only writes boy love stories, well, stories of guys in love. It's so strange, seems like they have nothing in common."

"Neither do our parents," Michael says. "Either way, Caleb, if Froderick is your forever bite, his dad is gonna find out someday, unless you guys hide it forever, which I don't know how you would."

"I know," Caleb says as he points at the door.

"It was nice meeting you both," I say as the two wave and leave the room.

"Shut the door!" Caleb yells.

Cassius reaches back in and closes the door. He gives me one more small smile, then leaves.

"OH MY FANGS! CALEB! What the hell are we gonna do? Why? What? I don't even know where to start."

Caleb is leaning toward me; he gently pushes my body down and I lay my head on his pillow. Oh, okay, I guess…Caleb is not interested in talking right now. He's moving my hair from my shoulder. His mouth is on my neck and he's thirsty. Caleb's fangs are deep and he's drinking so intensely, it's a feeling that's hard to explain, but there is no more pain, only a strong pleasurable sensation.

"Mmmm, Caleb, wait…I'm thirsty, too," I say.

Caleb moves his head slightly and I sink my fangs into his neck. Delicious… My forever tastes absolutely delicious.

Caleb seems to have reached his limit being so close to my body like this. His arms are wrapped underneath me and he's flipping me over. I quickly pull my fangs from his neck.

"Caleb what are you—" My face is in Caleb's pillow and his hands are on my waist.

"I want to do it again, can I?" he asks.

I nod with my face in the pillow. It's cute that he asked me so sweetly after he just flipped me over like an animal.

Caleb stands from the bed and I turn to look at him, propping myself on my elbows. "What are you doing? I nodded; did you not see me? It's fine, I want to do it, too."

Caleb smiles and locks the door to his bedroom.

Caleb's skin is so soft as he lays beside me. He's kissing my back gently and I can feel how much he's holding back while he rubs me. He's trying to be considerate, but I really don't need that right now. We have to go to my house soon, so he really needs to just do what we both want.

"Careful, your thoughts will drive me to do things much rougher than last night. I don't want to hurt you," Caleb says softly beside my ear. His hands are all over me and I'm just trapped underneath his hot body.

"Do it, come on. You keep saying things like that…just do it," I say.

It's been about twenty minutes since Caleb and I finished, and my body has never felt lighter, while my thoughts have never been heavier. Caleb's head is resting on my chest and he kisses my "C" charm. When all this started with him, I had no idea that I would ever feel this way. I thought that this kind of connection was something they only wrote about in books. Seeing my parents' relationship, and other vampires' relationships growing up, I didn't think I'd find someone who truly wanted to be with me for anything other than my status. Sure, there are lots of girl vampires that want to be with me, and if I want to take my place as the highest in vampire royalty one day, I'd need to choose one. But if the choice is between that stupid crown and Caleb, I couldn't care less about that fanging crown or my status. This must be how Wolfie's mom felt when she met his dad. She just threw it all away for him. I understand that now.

Caleb lets out a light chuckle and rubs my charm in between his fingers. "Not sure how I feel about being compared to a werewolf. I mean, I am a noble, too. So, I don't think it's the same thing. Also, you're talking about your dad's crown? Does he even wear it? If you want a crown, I have some in my closet. You can have all of them."

I ruffle his hair softly. "You know what I mean. No, I have plenty of my own crowns, I just—I don't know what's going to happen to us, in the eyes of the vampire world. Like you said, being gay is normal where you come from, and it's normal to me, but I don't know what will happen to our status—either of us. I never want to do anything that could hurt you. But selfishly, I hope that—"

Caleb kisses me softly, then pulls back and lightly rubs our noses together. "Shh, there is no crown, nor vampire in the world, that could sway me from you. You know that. I know you do."

"I do know that. Especially now that I can see everything so clearly. You know, it feels like I'm gonna pass out when I'm looking at your memories. Do you feel the same?"

Caleb lays flat on his back with his arms behind his head. "Hmm…yeah, I think so. I'm trying to avoid it. There's something about it that feels wrong. I feel almost like I should ask permission or something."

I laugh loudly. "Are you serious? You're in my head all the time, how is this different?"

Caleb's smile is so perfect. I could stare at it all day.

"The difference is that hearing your thoughts is something I can't really control, but I can control going through your memories."

"Caleb, hearing my thoughts is way worse than going through my memories."

"No, it most certainly is not. You can tell me that you felt something, or I can hear it or feel it, but seeing it, and being a bystander is not pleasant, and definitely not the same."

"Well, you are right about that. I don't even want to think about some of the stuff I've seen. Ugh…we have to get up and I don't want to. I want to stay in this bed with you all day—not go deal with my parents."

"I don't want to do it either, but I'm with you. It will be fine. Come on, let's get up," he says, squeezing my hand.

Caleb and I are standing in our towels inside of his closet. We're looking for shirts with high-collars that cover our bite marks. It's just easier if our parents don't see them right now, well, it's easier if my dad doesn't see it, my mom wouldn't care.

"We could just wear capes," Caleb says.

I shake my head at him and continue flipping through the shirts in his closet. "If I show up at my house wearing one of your capes, what will that look like? It's a day off from school, what reason would I have to be wearing not only a cape, but one of your capes?"

"Yeah, that's true. What about these?" Caleb asks, pulling out two thin turtleneck shirts. One black, one gray. "These will cover everything. Do you want to wear one of these? It will look good on you."

I take the black one from his hands and smile. "This is fine. I'm sure no one is going to notice that we're wearing the same kind of shirt and besides it's not like any of them know what's in style anyway. We can just say everyone is wearing turtlenecks now." I slip the shirt on over my head as Caleb stares at me. "Don't look at me like that. You look like you're gonna eat me!" I say as I give him a light push and leave the closet.

Caleb is staring at my bottom half. "I'm going to, if you don't put your pants on. Your neck is covered, but I may bite your ass if you don't hurry up."

"What is this? You're like a super pervert now!" I say as I grab my underwear and jeans from my backpack. I slide my underwear on beneath my towel and quickly put my jeans on.

Caleb walks over toward his dresser and takes the things he needs out of his drawer. He's looking at me in a very sexual way as he answers, "I have no idea, but doing all of this with you definitely changed something in me. My mind is racing constantly with visions of things that we've done. The need to have you close to me is even stronger than before."

I'm standing beside Caleb's door and holding my phone in my hand. I yell, "Put your jeans on! Are you crazy? Saying all this stuff in a sexual way while you're just walking around in your towel. Unbelievable. Is this what my life is going to be like?"

Of course, I wouldn't mind that, but right now I'm kind of sore and I'm actually a little embarrassed that Caleb could do it again, because I definitely couldn't. Also, we do need to leave, well, we should've left like fifteen minutes ago, so I definitely have to stop whatever he's thinking about.

Caleb gets dressed and gives me a taste of that open-mouth deviant laugh. He's too sexy to look at, I have to look away. I look down at my phone and see a text from Kat. It looks like she, Kressa, and Tahni are hanging out at the beach. They all look very close in this picture she sent me. I thought Kat liked Kressa, but Tahni is in between them and all three of their faces are squished together.

Caleb grabs my backpack from his bed and puts it on his back. He's holding his hand toward me. Unfortunately for Caleb, I can read his mind, so I'm not gonna hold his hand right now.

"Caleb, I know you're gonna try and pin me on the bed again, and you can just forget it. Come on, we can't leave our moms alone with my dad. If they get there before us, who knows what we'll be walking into."

Caleb gives an exaggerated sigh. "Alright, fine. Let's go."

Caleb's brothers aren't around as we head down the stairs toward the back door. I haven't seen the full house yet and I'm very interested in what the rest of it looks like. I can't ask about that right now because we definitely need to fly fast to beat our moms. My mom is rarely late, and she'll be there before us if we don't hurry.

Chapter 22
I Hate Tea!

Flying toward my house, I feel kind of sad. I liked sleeping next to Caleb and waking up with him. It sucks that I won't be able to do that tonight. I really can't wait until I'm eighteen. Ugh, and I'm also just really worried about what's gonna happen when I get home, and this collar is really uncomfortable. I know Caleb said it looks nice, but it is summer and there is really no logical reason for us to both be wearing turtlenecks. I mean, my dad is stupid, though, so he probably won't say anything. I can already see Caleb convincing him as to why we're wearing them. As for my mom, I'm sure she's literally written something like this in one of her books. Oh, shit, we left the book at Caleb's house and we didn't even look at it. Ah, it's fine. I really didn't want to use her book anyway.

Landing in front of my house, I don't see my mom's carriage, so they probably aren't here. Yes, my mother uses a flying carriage. She's such a diva, rarely anyone uses them because they're so expensive, but she has her own personal chauffeur, and he takes her everywhere. He literally has nothing else to do all day, except drive her around. I have no idea what his life is like, just bending at her every whim.

Caleb holds my hand and I quickly release it, remembering that I have to pretend that we aren't together. This is gonna be hard.

Caleb smiles at me, knowing that I feel bad. "I love you," he says softly as I grab the door handle.

I smile and whisper, "I love you, too, Caleb."

I turn the doorknob and the smell of my grandfather smacks me in the face. It almost knocks me off my feet. It's exceptionally strong today. From outside, I hear my mother's carriage arrive. I close the door quickly behind us. Why did I do that? I should have asked her what the reason for this meeting was. I panicked, though, and now I'm too committed, because my grandfather is standing directly in front of us with a smile on his face.

"Frode and Caleb! Hello, fellas! Did you two get your project done that you were working on?" my grandfather asks as he hugs me.

Ugh, Calabash…bottle gourd…toilet…awful. I'm holding my breath until he releases me.

Caleb answers my grandfather for me, "We didn't get much work done, Frode was pretty tired last night. We had a lot of fun, but he was worn out from the day pretty quickly."

My grandfather releases me, and I hear my mother's and Caleb's mother's voices approaching the outside of the door.

My grandfather's eyes widen and he whispers, "Oh, your mom is here. I have to go tell your father. He's waiting to make an entrance. He's been practicing all morning. I'll be right back."

My grandfather leaves and my mother and Caleb's mother enter from behind us. They are both smiling broadly at the two of us and they're wearing the most fangtastic dresses! My mother has definitely been to the beach, she looks tanner than when I saw her two days ago. I only saw Caleb's mother briefly, so I have no idea if this is what she normally looks like.

My mother extends her arms to me and says, "Frody, my darling, come hug mommy!" My mother smells like wine, which, of course, she does because my mother loves to drink. She wraps me in a tight hug, and I see Caleb's mother do the same to him.

"I'm mad at you," I say to my mother.

She pulls back from the hug and looks at me in shock as if she has no idea what I could possibly be mad about. "What would you be upset with mommy about? No, you can't be upset, please, you'll rub your little bad mood all over your father and we don't want that"—she looks at Caleb's mother—"do we Miranda?"

"No, we certainly don't!" Caleb's mother says. She lets out a hearty cackle and my mother joins her in laughter.

Oh, here we go…I hear my father taking the most dramatic footsteps ever down the stairs.

My father is wearing his favorite cape. You could call it his classic cape, it's black, with red trim and the collar is extremely high. He extends his arms toward Caleb and I and says, "Oh Froderick, my boy, and Caleb, I'm so happy you two are back. We had such a fun time the other night. Dinner wasn't the same without my two favorite guys yesterday. Next time, Caleb, you sleep here," my father says.

He's pretending he doesn't see my mother; does he think she's stupid? She's literally standing right next to me.

"Hello, dear," my mother says to my father.

My father lifts his head and looks at her, feigning surprise. "Alessandra! You look ravishing darling. I didn't see you there. I'd missed Frode so much that he was the first thing I noticed when I entered the room. We've just gotten so close lately. I love your dress, is that new?"

Ah, now he's actually surprised, he just noticed Caleb's mother. His facial expression is priceless.

"What the hell?" my father asks. "Miranda? What are you—? Ahem. I mean, hello, Miranda, how wonderful and not awkward at all to see you here in my home. You look gorg—normal, you look very normal. What are you doing here with Alessandra? Or did you just happen by to pick Caleb up or something?" my father asks.

My mother rolls her eyes and Caleb's mother does the same.

"Yes, I just happened by to pick up my seventeen-year-old son, from your kitchen, at the exact time as your wife appeared. You're just as stupid as ever," Caleb's mother says.

My grandfather enters the kitchen with the happiest of smiles on his face. "Alessandra! My beauty! How are you, doll face?" My grandfather kisses my mother's hand in lieu of a hug.

"Hello, dear, I am well. Miranda is here also, it's been some time since you've seen her, hasn't it?" my mother asks my grandfather.

"Yes, of course, I haven't seen her since Frode was in diapers! Beautiful as ever, you are, Miranda. And your son is a really good boy. I'm so happy that he and our Frode are getting along so well. Two good boys, we have here," My grandfather says with a smile.

My father looks aggravated. Seeing Caleb's mother really threw him off. He straightens his collar and walks toward the refrigerator. If he was smart, he wouldn't even think of pulling a drink out right now. Especially not that smelly beer. But my father is not smart and he's pulling that disgusting Bluhdy Goode beer out. He sticks his head out of the refrigerator while holding a single beer in his hand and asks, "Does anyone want anything to drink?"

A knock at the door draws everyone's attention. My father raises his chin at me to answer the door. I roll my eyes and walk to the back of the kitchen.

Opening the door, I hear a carriage leaving. Who besides my mother would be so ridiculous as to use a carriage?

"Ah, hello, Froderick, do tell me, is your father home?"

It's Caleb's father…it's Caleb's father…I shut the door quickly and turn around. Everyone is staring at me while Caleb's father knocks on the door again. No one besides me saw who it was and the only other vampire who knows is Caleb, because he can hear my thoughts. Caleb's eyes are wide and he looks around, he's the same level of panicked as me. He's silently mouthing "Dad" to his mother.

My father asks, "Who did you just slam the door on? That was very rude behavior, Frode. I know your mother and I raised you better than that."

My father places his beer on the counter while walking toward the door.

"Dad, it was just, uh, some bite spray sales pitch. They'll go away. Just leave it," I say.

"I wouldn't answer that," Caleb's mother warns.

My mother is giving her a confused look, because she has no idea who is on the other side of the door.

"Don't be ridiculous, Miranda, the house of Dracula is welcoming to all vampires regardless of their station in life," my father says, looking at her, as he opens the door.

Pfffttt…yeah, right. My dad is so full of it.

"Hello, Drac, it's been a while. I have some tea for you," Caleb's father says.

My father slams the door in Caleb's father's face and turns around quickly.

"Was that Andrew?" my mother asks, pushing past my father.

"Oh, Alessandra, leave him out there. What could he want if not trouble? Please, you and I have only just made up," Caleb's mother says.

"Why the hell is Andrew Cheval outside my door?" my father yells to no one in particular. "And what the hell is he bringing me tea for? I hate tea!"

Caleb's father's voice can be heard through the door, "It's not actual tea, you moron! It's an expression!"

My mother opens the door and Caleb's father's face is more than pleased at the sight of her. His eyes look like they may fall out of his head as he looks at her and says, "Alessandra…I…you look…"

Caleb's mother stands beside my mother and Caleb's father shakes his head. He starts over and says, "Yes, hello, Alessandra, you look normal, very normal." He turns his face toward Caleb's mother. "Miranda, my love, what the hell are you doing here?"

"What the hell are *any of you* doing here?!" my father screams while throwing his hands up.

My grandfather rubs my father's back. He whispers, "Calm down. It's okay, Alessandra is here to see you and, remember, Frode and Caleb are here, too. I have no idea why Caleb's parents are here, but let's keep calm, alright? Alessandra does not like it when you are unreasonable. Be a good host." My grandfather gives him a sort of gentle, supportive push toward the door.

My father is shaking his head in disagreement.

"Well, Andrew, this is a surprise," my mother says. She turns toward Caleb's mother. "Miranda, did you know this flea was coming here?"

Caleb's father's face is red in embarrassment, I think from the initial shock of seeing my mother. But maybe also because of what she just said. "Flea? Did you just call me a flea? What did I do to deserve that?" Caleb's father asks.

Caleb's mother answers my mother, "Of course I had no idea that he would be here." She turns toward Caleb's father and says, "I don't feel like reading your thoughts right now, so just get on with it. Why are you here? Did Caleb tell you to come here?"

All eyes move to Caleb, as he shakes his head no while rolling his eyes. I want to hold his hand so badly, and I want to say so many things, but I can't. I have to just stand here and pretend that Caleb is just my friend. It's harder than I thought it would be, especially because I can hear his thoughts. Luckily, it goes both ways, so he knows I want to comfort him and I know he feels the same.

"Of course, Caleb didn't invite him!" my father interjects. "I bet your son doesn't even like you! Not like my son, who is my best friend."

There is not a vampire in the room that believes what he just said, except maybe my grandfather.

Caleb's father is looking at Caleb and I, almost like he's threatening to tell our secret.

My grandfather is making his way toward the door. "Well, hello, Andrew, it has been quite some time since I've seen you! What a treat! I get to see both you and Miranda after all these years at the same time. Why don't you come in and we can all sit and reminisce, that sounds like a good idea. Don't you think so, Drac?" My grandfather is looking at my father. He's raising his chin at him trying to get him to agree with his very stupid idea.

"That's a terrible idea," my father says with a pout.

Caleb's father is giving a fake pout, as he mocks my father. "Oh, look at the big bad king of all the vampires…pouting! You're exactly the same as you used to be! Can't even force yourself to have a simple conversation with someone that you were once friends with. Hopeless."

"I agree," my mother says.

"Of course, you would agree with him!" my father shouts.

Caleb's father is smirking as he steps inside and stands beside Caleb's mother.

My mother yells at my father, "No, you dolt! I'm agreeing with *you!*"

My father is somewhat in shock, since my mother never agrees with him. He grabs his beer off the counter and takes a long sip while staring blankly at her.

My grandfather, ever the peacekeeper, is clapping his hands and smiling. "There we go!" he says. "Andrew, have a seat, everyone just…let's just sit down, there's plenty of room. We can all sit around and just talk. Talking is easy, there's nothing hard about talking." My grandfather is ushering my father toward his seat at the head of the table. He literally looks like he's forcing a pouting child into a classroom. My father is not even moving his feet as my grandfather pushes him.

"I don't want to talk to Andrew!" my father says as my grandfather pulls my father's chair out for him.

Caleb's father is pulling a chair out for his mother while she looks less than thrilled at his presence.

My father hasn't sat down yet and he's not going to right now. He notices Caleb's father pulling out the chair for Caleb's mother, so he quickly pulls a chair out beside him for my mother. "Alessandra, *my wife*, allow me to pull your chair out for you," he says while turning his gaze toward Caleb's father. My mother sits down looking very annoyed. My father moves my mother's long hair and admires it from behind as he slides her chair in. Again, he's looking at Caleb's father, but speaking to my mother, he says, "I'm so grateful to be the one to walk this life beside you, my love."

Walk beside her? What the hell is he talking about? She doesn't even live here. I don't know who he thinks he's fooling, but he definitely thinks he's fooling someone.

My father straightens his collar and takes a seat at the head of the table. Caleb and I are still standing off to the side. I really don't want to sit down, honestly. I'd much rather they talk about whatever it is they need to talk about without us here. The vibe is really strange and it doesn't feel like anyone is going to say or do anything that would out me in front of my father, but I can't be sure. I mean, why would Caleb's dad be here if not for that? Caleb is thinking the same thing and he's warning me to be cautious. He thinks we can steer this conversation away from us, but I'm not very confident that we can do that.

Our mothers are staring at one another, seemingly waiting for the other to say something. Caleb's mother is shrugging and tilting her head toward Caleb's father.

"Alright, well, I'll start," my mother says. "Miranda and I are best friends again."

Umm…okay…that's fine. Doesn't seem like we needed a family meeting to say that, but that's cool.

"Yes, best, best friends," Caleb's mother adds with a smile toward my father.

"Well, why were you ever not friends to begin with? All because of a character dying in a story? You've wasted so many years over something so ridiculous," Caleb's father says.

"For once, I agree with you," my father says to Caleb's dad. "It was such a ridiculous fight."

"It was not! Caleb's mother argues. "I wouldn't expect you two obtuse creatures to understand!"

My mother reaches across the table and holds Caleb's mother's hand. "Now, Miranda, don't get upset, it's in the past. Of course, they don't understand. We've not yet explained it."

"Explained what?" my father asks as he finishes his beer.

"You see, Miranda felt like the story of Vincent and Mario was more or less a retelling of our own relationship. Now, of course, I didn't write it that way, but after she explained it to me, I could completely understand what she felt. And I was devastated to hear that all these years she thought that by me killing Mario off, I was killing her off and thus throwing our relationship in the garbage. My sweet, dear friend." Our mothers are still holding hands across the table.

"That is the stupidest thing I've ever heard," my father says.

"What?" Caleb's mother asks.

"I agree with the idiot," Caleb's father says. "Dumbest thing I've ever heard. I had no idea you felt that way Miranda. How could they have been you two? If anything, I was Mario and Alessandra was Vincent."

"What?" my mother asks, looking at Caleb's father.

My father crosses his arms across his chest and shakes his head at Caleb's father.

Caleb nudges me toward the stairs, I think we may be able to just disappear into my bedroom and Caleb agrees. We're slowly making our way over, just a few footsteps at a time. I have no idea what the hell is happening between our parents, but as long as we don't come up in conversation, I don't really care.

My mother notices us. She's snapping her fingers above her head and pointing toward the two empty chairs at the foot of the table. Damn it. We almost made it, too. I drop my head and Caleb and I walk back toward the table and begrudgingly sit down.

"Yes, of course," Caleb's father says. "Alessandra liked me first, so the characters were a retelling of what our lives could have been, but she ended up having to kill me off to leave the feelings she had for me behind. That's what I read. Had nothing to do with you, Miranda."

"Well, now, that is the dumbest one that I've heard so far," my grandfather says.

The adults are all arguing now, each talking over the other. It's impossible to decipher who is arguing what idiotic point. Complete nonsense.

My mother stands and smacks the table. "Enough! I wrote a story about two fictional characters that I created in my head. I did not write them as any sort of retelling or parallel or whatever anyone thinks it was. Andrew, I am terribly sorry, but I have never been interested in you. I did love to toy with boys when I was younger, so I vaguely remember using you to make Drac jealous, but that was it. Fangs, have you really thought this whole time that I harbored feelings for you?"

Caleb's mother is giggling while looking at her husband. What a weird relationship they have for his mother to be so unaffected by what his father just said.

Caleb's father tilts his head at my mother and holds his hand up. "Of course, I have always thought that! Isn't that why you've always argued with Drac? He's an idiot and you've always wished you'd chosen me, instead of letting Miranda have me. That's the truth, right?"

The arguing in the room between our parents is almost indiscernible now. They're all talking over one another again; each one thinks the other is ridiculous.

"Can we leave, please? This has nothing to do with us," Caleb says.

All eyes turn to Caleb and me. The arguing stops momentarily while our parents look at the two of us. My grandfather is shaking his head, standing beside my father.

"Well, I have no problem with you and Frode leaving. Same goes for the other two Chevals," my father says as he points at Caleb's parents.

Caleb and I stand, and my mother quickly snaps her fingers and points at our seats. "Absolutely not," she says. You two are the reason that Miranda and I are here, we owe the two of you for bringing us back together."

"Well, if anyone should be thanked it should be me," my father says.

"And how did you come to that conclusion?" Caleb's mother asks my father while propping her chin on her hand.

"Who else should be responsible for bringing those two together? I accepted Caleb as a transfer when you approached Ms. Tansy; that was my decision, behind the scenes. I also arranged for Froderick to not only show Caleb around on his first day, but I put them in all the same classes. Had it not been for me, they may not have even met one another again," my father says proudly.

My mother and Caleb's mother share a secret kind of smirk across the table.

"We would have met each other, even if you hadn't done any of that," Caleb says.

I'm cringing because I can feel how close Caleb is to saying that we're together and I really don't want him to. Fangs, I really don't want him to say it because I'm scared, but there's a part of me that also wants to say it myself.

Caleb's father leans back in his chair and looks across the table at the two of us. He seems to be warning us not to say anything with his eyes, which is very confusing, isn't that why he's effing here?!

My grandfather pats my father on the shoulder. "Caleb is right," he says. "They're both nobles, both purebloods, of course they would have met one another again. No need for you to take credit, son. Everyone knows how important being a school ruler is. Alessandra knows everything that you do for our little Frode."

My mother is giving my grandfather a discerning look, she's trying to figure out if he already knows about us. Well, that's what it looks like anyway.

Caleb's mother points at my father with attitude. "Say, Drac, what part are you most proud of?" she asks. "The part where they came to you, and you told them their connection was all in their heads, or the part where you said it would be absolutely impossible for two boys to ever share a connection?"

"I am proud of both of those things. I had a good talk with them," my father says.

My mother covers her face with both hands in frustration. "How can you be proud of that? I am so mad at you over what happened. Why do you think I'm here?"

"Well, I thought you were coming here because you were going to tell me you were moving back in," my father says. "I thought you were happy when you said you were coming over and you even made it a point to say that Frode would be here, too. What else would I have thought? Why are you still mad at me?"

"I have a better question," Caleb's father says. "Why isn't anyone interested in the fact that both of these boys are wearing turtleneck shirts, that are both Caleb's by the way, in the middle of August?"

"Oh, no one cares what they're wearing, shut up, Andrew. I'm arguing with my husband," my mother says.

My mother's eyes widen, as soon as she finishes her sentence, and she turns to look at me. She pulls her phone out and is texting someone. My phone chimes with a notification.

Looking at my phone I see that it was me that my mom texted:
Mom: Andrew knows, too?

I put my phone in my pocket and nod at her.

She shakes her head at me. "That was stupid," she says under her breath.

"I am interested. Our son is a noble; he should not be wearing someone else's clothes," my father says. "Andrew was right to bring it up. Thank you, Andrew." Holding his arms out wide he asks, "Well, Frode, why are you wearing Caleb's shirt? Did you forget to bring an extra one last night? You should go change right away."

I stand and Caleb stands alongside me. "Yeah, I forgot to bring an extra one. I'll go and change, Dad."

"Next question," Caleb's father says. "Do you really not use social media, Drac? Have you not seen anything posted recently that you would find especially upsetting or interesting, maybe?"

My mother stands and says, "Andrew Cheval, I am warning you right now that if you continue this line of questioning with my husband, I will do something to you that I have only done to one other vampire. I have the power to do it," she warns.

"Are you threatening to bite him, Alessandra?! He would love that! Why would you threaten him with that?" my idiot father asks.

"Oh…how I *would* love that," Caleb's father says. "But, no, I think she means she will use her status to exile me."

"That *is* what she means," Caleb's mother says. "And I'll help her. Just drop it. What are you even here for? You're the only vampire whose presence is unexplained, Andrew."

Caleb and I start walking toward the stairs. I think we may actually be able to duck out of this situation thanks to my mother.

"Wait," my father says. "When Andrew and I were younger and we were mouthed by a couple of real trashy low-level vamps, we wore shirts like that to hide the marks on our necks. You remember, right, Dad?" my father says as he looks to my grandfather.

My grandfather smiles and says, "Oh, yes, I remember. You two thought you would be in trouble because they bit you and they weren't nobles, but really, they were just love bites or hickeys, they didn't even get the fangs in, but you two were all marked up. Yes, I definitely remember. You two were pretty young then."

Caleb's father is obviously taking my mother's threat seriously because he isn't reacting at all to what my father or grandfather said.

"So?" my father asks, looking at Caleb and me. "Is that what happened? You two went out last night and got marked up by a couple of vamps?"

I turn to Caleb and whisper, "I don't want to hide this anymore."

Caleb can feel how nervous and unsure I am. He turns to my father and says, "Can we please just have a minute to talk about something. Frode and I want to tell you something, but I need to talk about it with him first. We're going to go get him changed and then we'll be back down." Caleb gives his mother a desperate sort of silent plea for help with his eyes.

"Well, why do you need to go with him when he's changing clothes, Caleb?" my father asks.

"Alessandra and I have been at the beach for the past two days!" Caleb's mother announces loudly.

"Excuse me?" My father says with attitude as he folds his arms.

My mother nods toward the stairs, telling me that we're in the clear.

Chapter 23
I'm Not Afraid

Caleb and I are rushing up the stairs before my father's attention turns back to us.

I can hear my grandfather trying to soothe my father as we open my bedroom door.

I lie flat on my back on my bed and Caleb sits beside me. He takes my hand in his and asks, "Are you sure you want to tell him? We can just leave if you're uncomfortable. We'll just go to my house or go away for a few days. We could leave a note or something. You don't have to tell him just because you are uncomfortable."

I sit up and pull Caleb into an embrace. I'm suddenly overcome with emotion. I'm scared and I'm sad…I don't know what my father will do when I tell him. Tears begin to fall, despite every effort to hold them back. Fangs, I never cry.

Caleb wipes my tears and asks me softly, "Why are you crying? Don't cry. Nothing has happened. Nothing has changed. I have you, I'll take care of you. You have to know that's true." He kisses my cheek and presses our foreheads together.

"What if…what if he hates me, Caleb? What if he never wants to talk to me again? What if he exiles me? What will I do? I don't want him to hate me." More tears fall and I try desperately to stop them.

"Shh…no. That's not going to happen. Your dad will accept it, eventually. I've learned a lot about him over the past few days and it seems like he's not all that bad. I think if he's given time, he will come to understand and accept our love. But listen to me, no one is forcing you to do anything. You don't have to tell him. Do you understand? I will go down there right now and pull my dad out of the house with me. I'll make up something ridiculous if you want me to. I'll do whatever you want, but don't make a decision like this based on fear. You love me and I love you, the decision to share that needs to be based on love and confidence, not in fear. Don't be afraid that someone else will tell him… Well, I did not think about the social media thing, though, does your dad really not use social media at all?"

I shake my head. "No, he really doesn't, but I did forget about that, too. It's only a matter of time until someone tells him or he sees something. It's better if I just do it and get it over with." I wipe my eyes and force a smile.

"No," Caleb says. "I won't allow it if this is why you're doing it. You do this when *you* want to, and how *you* want to. This is about you and me, not about him or what he wants."

I pull Caleb's face into mine and press our lips together. This is better. This is all I want right now, to be held and kissed by Caleb. We're kissing so softly and I couldn't feel any more secure than I do in this moment with Caleb's arms around me. I pull back from him gently and say, "I'm ready. I want to do it. I want to do it for me and for us. I'm not afraid…okay, well, I am afraid, but I'm not doing it *because* I'm afraid. I'm just a little afraid of what may happen, but as long as I have you, I know it's going to be okay."

Caleb kisses my forehead and nods in approval. He places his hands on the sides of my shirt and pulls it over my head. He lifts his arms and I pull his shirt off, too.

"Oh, are we doing this bare chested or are we putting regular T-shirts on when we tell him?" Caleb asks.

"Why are you asking me that? You can hear my thoughts. You already know I was thinking we would both wear my shirts, but ones that show off our bites and my necklace." I push Caleb playfully on the chest. Oh, damn, I shouldn't have touched his chest like that. It was so warm and hard and now I feel thirsty. No, no. I have to focus.

"Come on take a little sip, it will help you relax," Caleb says, tilting his neck to the side.

Oh fuck. I pull Caleb in by the back of his head and sink my fangs into his neck, greedily drinking as fast as I can. Caleb wraps his hand round my waist and buries his face in my neck, piercing my skin with his fangs and sucking at the same desperate pace.

Several minutes have passed and we're still taking in one another's blood, though our pace has slowed. I pull my fangs out and wipe my mouth. "Thank you, that does feel much better," I say.

"Mmm, I love you, Frode. Let's get changed and go downstairs."

"Yes, lets, and while we're at it, we'll show off our freshly made bite marks," I say with a grin.

We walk into my closet and pull out two identical V-neck shirts, both black. Caleb quickly puts the shirt on. He looks so good wearing my clothes. I pull my shirt over my head, and I make sure that my chain from Caleb is on the outside of my shirt. These shirts definitely do not hide our bites. Not at all. They are on full display, as is the necklace.

"I'm with you," Caleb says as he takes my hand in his and squeezes it three times.

"I love you. Time to tell my idiot father that we're in love."

To be continued...

About the Author

Cali Kitsu lives in a very sunny state with her amazing husband and daughters, and she enjoys making people smile. She tries to bring a little bit of her Cali sunshine and energy wherever she goes. Cali believes that love is for everyone, and she's found the perfect way to express that in her writing. Cali absolutely loves writing—she's having so much fun telling steamy boy love stories, with a bit of her Cali sense of humor!

Aside from co-hosting the *Cali & Craig Talk...* podcast with her bestie Craig Gibb, Cali is also the Executive Assistant at the publishing house.

Cali's other hobbies include watching Anime, reading Manga, baking, going to the beach, and she's an avid gamer in all forms: console, tabletop, strategy card games... *Magic the Gathering* is probably her favorite strategy card game.

Books by Cali Kitsu
You Can Call Me Cooper
Froderick, Gay Son of Dracula

Also from Deep Hearts YA

You Can Call Me Cooper
Cali Kitsu

Eighteen and newly single, baseball all-star Coop Morgan should feel devastated, but instead he feels… ambivalent. That is, until Ethan Prescott, his coach's gorgeous son, joins the team. Coop and Ethan feel an immediate connection, one that Coop has never felt before.

Just when Coop is about to make a move on Ethan, he stumbles on his late mother's journal and learns old secrets—about his family, about the people around him, about his past, and about his present. Secrets that had forever altered the course of his life to bring him to where he is now.

Between these long-buried secrets, forbidden romances, baseball shenanigans, and more, Coop is driven to embrace what he truly wants—Ethan. It takes everything Coop has to free himself from the shackles of the past, but in doing so, he might just be the key to everyone getting their happy-ever-afters.

Available now in ebook and paperback

Also from Deep Hearts YA

Drag Queens, Emo Teens & Big Dreams
Dylan James

Corbin has two secrets.

The first secret is that he's gay. He's known it for a while now and six months ago he met a cute guy and they've been dating ever since. But he can't tell anyone. His father is like a one-man Marine recruitment poster and has made every effort to raise Corbin to be an alpha male. If he finds out Corbin is gay, he'll forbid Corbin from seeing his boyfriend, dooming the relationship to an unhappy end.

The second secret is that he's a drag queen. On Sundays he heads to the queer café and dons his best dress, wig, and heels, and becomes Misty Rain, putting on a captivating show to an adoring crowd. While coming out as gay would lead to a crack-down from his Dad, the punishment for putting on a dress and heels would be ten times worse—he'd be shipped off to military school and there'd be absolutely no hope for Corbin and his love.

So far, Corbin has managed to keep his secrets.

But when his older brother comes home while on leave from the Marines, he happens to catch the drag show featuring Corbin—and he spots his brother right away.

Corbin's perfectly structured life and his big dreams are all about to come crashing down.

Available now in ebook and paperback

Also from Deep Hearts YA

The Reign of Ruth
Jazel L. Faith

In the Forest of Dahlia's depths, witches have long hidden from the clutches of malicious hunters. But as their numbers dwindle and hope fades, they turn to a sacrifice to create the most formidable witch to ever exist: Ruby, known only as the Red Demon.

Bound by fate, Ruby is thrust into a treacherous quest for freedom, her only ally being Lilith, a witch with the power to glimpse into the future. Together, they venture beyond their sanctuary, stepping into a world of hunters, life-changing discoveries, secrets, royalties, and magic to seek peace for their kind at last.

The girls will soon learn that no battle comes without sacrifice, and their choices hold the power to shape the destinies of all witches.

Available now in ebook and paperback

9 781998 055555